SANCTUM

GUARDS OF THE SHADOWLANDS

Book 1

SANC

TUM

SARAH FINE

Amazon Publishing
Attn: Amazon Children's Publishing
P.O. Box 400818
Las Vegas, NV 89140
www.amazon.com/amazonchildrenspublishing

ISBN: 978-1-4778-1033-0
Book design by The Black Rabbit
Map design by Luka Rejec
Editor: Courtney Miller

For Jennifer,

who was there from the beginning.

The "Dark City" as depicted by Malachi on a wall at the Guard Station.

Some notes appended to aid the reader.

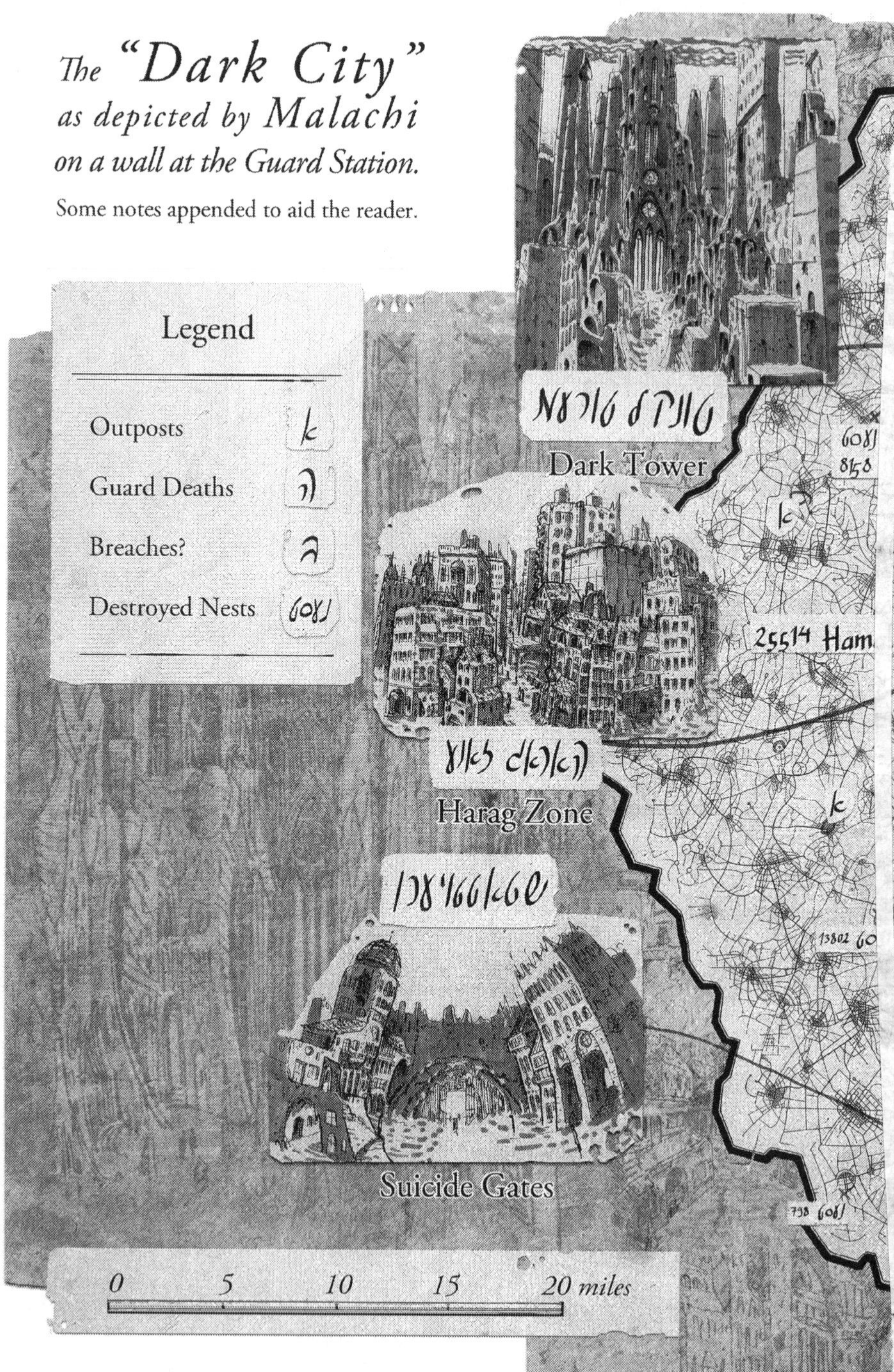

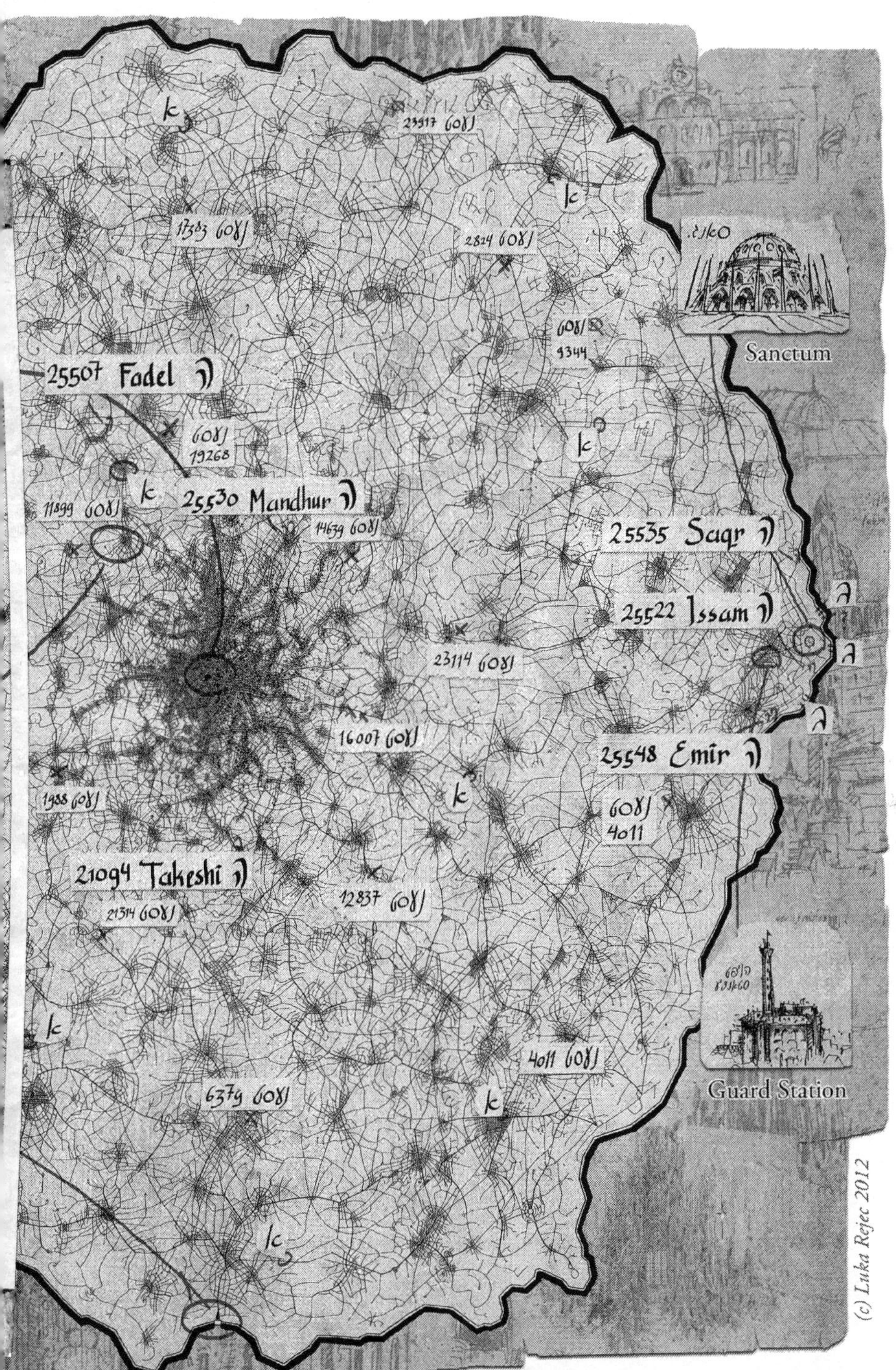
25507 Fadel
25530 Mandhur
25535 Saqr
25522 Issam
25548 Emir
21094 Takeshi
Sanctum
Guard Station
(c) Luka Rejec 2012

PROLOGUE

ON MY FIRST DAY at Warwick High School, if you'd told me I would choose to go to hell for *any* of the students, let alone Warwick's queen bee, I would have laughed. Or maybe I would have stabbed you with a ballpoint pen (it was kind of a rough day).

I was out behind the school, lighting up a badly needed lunchtime cigarette, when I first saw her. She was pretty, blonde, and wearing something more expensive than a year's worth of foster care checks. Her pale blue eyes darted across the fence and landed on this tall, skinny kid in dirty jeans who was standing next to me. She walked up to him, her voice shaking as she asked, "Angela told me you have OC?"

Dirty Jeans peeled himself off the fence. "Angela might be right, depending on what you have for *me*."

The girl reached into her purse, pulled out several bills, and held them up. I felt like slapping her in the back of the head. Nobody ever taught her not to wave money around in public?

Dirty Jeans smiled as he pivoted around and backed her against the fence. "I think you might have more than that for me. Is this your first time?"

Now, what do they call that? Something French. Double fucking entendre. I should have jammed my cigarette in his eye right then. I can't be the only girl who fantasizes about these things.

The blonde's face crumpled. "My first . . . oh, coming back here . . . yes?"

Couldn't she tell this punk wanted to take advantage of her? He was obviously going to take her money, but she'd asked for it. And by the way he was looking at her, I was betting he would try to double-charge for her fix. She had *not* asked for that.

I shouldn't have cared. I'd been listening to girls like her make bitchy comments about my wild hair and cheap-ass Kmart-special outfit ever since I showed up this morning for my first day of school, escorted to the office by my new foster mom and my probation officer. I'd watched those girls shrink back as I walked down the hall. I'd heard them whispering about how I'd killed someone, which was totally untrue. I'd *almost* killed someone. And I'd expected all those rumors, all those pinch-faced expressions, and already decided I didn't care what they thought, didn't care about *them*. So what did it matter that *this* preppy girl was about to get some involuntary up-close with a wannabe drug dealer?

But . . . the moment I saw the blood drain from her already-pale face, I knew I wasn't going to be able to watch this go down.

I crushed out my cigarette and took a few steps closer to them. I'm not huge, but I'm not one of those anorexic walking stalks of celery, either. I could do man push-ups. I'd had some time on my hands while I was at the RITS: Rhode Island's teen jail. I also knew the value of being able to protect myself. Just one of the many side effects of having been Rick Jenson's foster kid. After months spent under his "care," I'd tried to kill myself. And when that didn't turn out to be the escape I'd hoped for, I'd escaped in a different way. By beating the crap out of him and getting myself sent to juvie. Where I learned not to be afraid of kids like Dirty Jeans.

"Come on now," I snapped, taking another step closer. "Let her buy her pills and run back to her friends."

"Shut up," replied Dirty Jeans as he leaned closer to the girl, towering over her. He didn't even look at me. He didn't think I was a threat. Awesome.

The bell signaled the end of lunch. I was one fuckup away from getting sent right back to the RITS and should have been scurrying to class, but I couldn't force myself to leave her. I knew what it felt like to be helpless and pinned, no matter how hard I tried to forget.

"Take the cash," she whimpered, "and let me go to class."

"Oh, you can't leave now. We have to discuss payment," Dirty Jeans crooned as he spared me a sidelong glance. I could almost see the gears turning in his tiny brain, like he thought he could get a twofer, like he thought I'd go along. And sure enough, he started to snake his arm around my neck as he spoke to the girl. "I want to feel your pretty mouth on my—"

I punched him in the stomach and he doubled over. I turned to the girl, who looked like she was about to hurl. "What are you waiting for? Get out of he—"

Dirty Jeans grabbed my hair, then jerked me backward. I smashed my heel down on his foot and elbowed him in the stomach. He gasped and let go of my hair. I darted behind him, pulling the only weapon I had out of my pocket: a ball-point pen.

I aimed a sharp kick at the back of his knee and got a fistful of his hair as he staggered. He fell to his knees, and I kept hold of his hair as I snapped his head back. I held the point of the pen to his neck. "Ready to go back to class?" I allowed myself the luxury of pressing the pen into his neck, just a little. It left a satisfyingly deep indentation ringed with blue ink.

His hands rose from his sides but dropped quickly as the pen sank farther into his skin. He winced and rasped, "Yeah, but I'm gonna find you after school—"

I rocked his head back and forth. "Your rich-kid-wannabe-gangsta act doesn't impress me at all. Believe me when I say I will fuck you up if you so much as twitch in my direction. I even have some friends in Providence who would love to help me. Would you like to meet them?"

I didn't really. But if you had my rep and told *this* type of kid you had "friends in Providence," they thought one thing: Latin Kings, baby. If I had to deal with the stereotype, why not make it work in my favor sometimes?

Dirty Jeans shook his head. He didn't look me in the eye, which meant he wouldn't give up . . . and would attack from behind next time. Suddenly tired, I let go of his hair.

"I heard about you. You're that girl who just got out of the RITS, right? That means you're on probation." Little flecks of spit flew from his mouth as he got to his feet. "So guess what? You're going back there—"

"No, she isn't," snapped the girl. I had almost forgotten she was there. "If you tell anyone what just happened, I'll take my *pretty mouth* straight to the principal's office, crying that you sexually assaulted me. Then we'll see who ends up in the RITS."

I was starting to like this girl.

Dirty Jeans fell silent. Although anyone would believe him if he accused *me* of attacking him, no one would buy the story if *she* backed me up.

"You better watch your back, bitch." He spun around and jogged toward the school.

The girl turned to me. She looked so relieved that I thought she might fall to the ground. "Thank you so much," she said, holding out a trembling hand. "I'm Nadia Vetter."

It was such a formal gesture that I almost laughed out loud and ruined everything. Instead, I shook her hand. "Lela Santos," I replied. "You're welcome. And thank you, too."

The bell rang again and I groaned. Nadia tilted her head. "What's your next?"

"English. With—" I pulled my crumpled schedule out of my pocket. "Hoffstedler?"

She leaned over and checked the room number. "I've got History one hall over. Come on. I'll walk you to class." She started toward the entrance to the school, then paused and looked over her shoulder. "You coming? It'll be better if I take you there. Then we can blame your tardiness on me." Her smile was bright. "They *always* forgive me."

I opened and closed my mouth a few times, trying to wrap my mind around the idea that this preppy girl was actually being nice, when I'd expected her to give me a quick thank-you and then start pretending I didn't exist. Finally, I stopped trying to find the right words to say and simply followed her into the school.

By my second day at Warwick High School, if you'd told me I would choose to go to hell for its queen bee, I might have believed you.

ONE

A year later

MY MUSCLES CONTRACTED, POWERFUL and controlled, pushing me up from the ground and lowering me to the floor again. Over and over, until my arms trembled and my breath exploded from my throat in sharp bursts. And then a few more times after that, just to be sure I could. I finished my push-ups and moved on to sit-ups.

The knock at my door pulled me from my mindless reps. "Baby? You're awful quiet in there."

I sank back and tilted my head to the door, brushing away my curly hair, now damp with sweat. Diane, my foster mother, opened the door a crack and peeked in.

I sat up and wiped my face with my sleeve. "I'm just finishing. You can come in."

She opened the door all the way. "You work yourself hard."

I grabbed the glass of water from my bedside table. "I thought that's what I was supposed to be doing."

She nodded at the books and papers scattered across my desk. "I don't see how you have so much energy. You stay up so late." A frown creased her deep brown skin. "I *know* you don't get enough sleep."

Sleep hadn't actually been *restful* for the past few years, but I didn't talk about that. "I've had a lot of catching up to do." In the year I'd lived with Diane, I had managed to pull my GPA out of the two-point-argh range, but just barely.

"You've done a lot more than that. Have you checked the mail today?"

"Yup. Nothing."

She shrugged. "It's coming, baby. I can feel it." Sometimes I got the sense that the one college application I'd sent in meant more to Diane than it did to me. As much as I hated to admit it, though, I'd started to let myself hope for a future I'd never thought was possible.

"You have plans with Nadia tonight?" Diane asked.

"I'm going to stay over at her house. Her mom's in the Seychelles with her new boyfriend."

"Don't get up to any trouble."

We never got up to any trouble. That was why Diane liked Nadia so much. Aside from anxiety about always having to be perfect, Nadia was, well, perfect. I frowned. Or maybe not. She seemed really stressed lately.

After a quick shower, I shoved my stuff into my backpack and headed out the door. The drive to Nadia's was short, but turning onto her street was like entering a different world. I wondered if her neighbors locked their doors and pulled their blinds when they saw me coming. Or maybe they paid someone else to do it for them.

The old, beat-up Corolla that Diane's uncle had lent me felt small and shabby as I rolled to a stop in front of the row of garage doors at the head of Nadia's driveway. I parked next to Tegan's BMW. Usually Nadia's other friends cleared out when they knew I was going to be around. Even though we'd been hanging out for almost a year, her friends—especially Tegan—remained pissed and baffled that she was spending time with someone like me. About a week ago, though, Nadia got sick of it and told Tegan I wasn't going anywhere and that she had to at least talk to me.

I wished Nadia had consulted me first.

Nadia pulled open the front door before I reached it. "I was going to let you two take it slow, but apparently Tegan's therapist told her she needed to *bond* with you."

"That sounds . . . really unpleasant."

She bit her lip, half laughing, half cringing. "Don't be mad."

I shouldered my pack and walked cautiously up the front steps. I'd long since gotten over my urge to kick Tegan's ass. "It's fine. Unless she starts talking extreme makeover, and then the gloves come off."

Tegan peeked over Nadia's shoulder. Her short brown hair was stylishly jagged around her face. "Hi, Lela. Glad your probation officer let you come over," she said as she handed Nadia a bottle of soda.

Tegan sucked at bonding.

Nadia took the bottle and gently bonked Tegan on the head with it. "Cut it out. I want to relax tonight."

Tegan stuck out her tongue at Nadia, then turned to me. "Hey, I read about some Dominican festival this weekend. Maybe we could go and celebrate your roots."

I closed my eyes and shook my head, deeply regretting this new, talking-to-me Tegan. "Lela's not from the Dominican Republic," Nadia answered for me.

"Close enough, right?" Tegan looked sincerely confused, probably because I was the only person of color she'd ever spoken to. "Where are you from, then?"

"Um, here?"

She rolled her eyes. "No, I mean originally."

My hand closed over the strap of my backpack, turning my knuckles pale. *"Here."*

"Oh, come on, Lela, give us the specifics. Maybe your peeps have a festival, too."

I sighed. "I think I'm Puerto Rican."

"You *think*? Don't people know that kind of thing for sure?"

Nadia skipped forward and offered me the soda. "You can have it if you don't kill her," she sang.

"Well, Tegan," I explained in my painful-death-is-too-good-for-you voice, "I haven't seen my mother since I was four years old, and I didn't think to ask her then."

Tegan nodded like I'd just told her I enjoyed watching *The Bachelor* or something. "That's too bad. I was hoping you were Cuban. I really like those sandwiches."

Nadia closed her eyes and shook her head. "Um, how about you go order the pizza?" She handed Tegan a menu.

Tegan shot us a prettily manicured finger and skipped into the kitchen.

As I set my backpack down on the living-room table, I saw the large, thick envelope from the University of Rhode Island. "Oh my God, is that what I think it is?"

Nadia nodded. "Just arrived today. Did you get one?"

"No. I mean, not yet." I picked up the envelope and stared at it. "Congratulations, Nadia," I said, grinning. "Looks like we have something to celebrate tonight."

She gave me a small smile that didn't quite reach her eyes. "Thanks."

She turned and walked toward the kitchen, obviously expecting me to follow. But I just stood there, that envelope in my hands, wondering what had changed. Six months ago, she'd practically forced me to fill out an application. Until then I'd never really thought about the future. I was too busy trying to survive each moment. But meeting Nadia had changed all that. So I'd filled out the application and sent it off. At first Nadia had been absolutely stoked. She'd taken me down to tour the campus with her, talked nonstop about how great it was going to be if we both got in. Lately, though, she'd stopped talking about it so much. I set the envelope back down and headed for the kitchen.

A few hours later, we were lounging in front of the giant flat-screen in the entertainment room. Tegan was pretty much passed out, done in by her third glass of Merlot.

Nadia cradled her own wineglass against her chest like she didn't trust herself not to drop it. "You're the first person who's congratulated me about getting into URI. Tegan wasn't impressed because she's headed to Wellesley, and Mom . . ."

I set my soda on a coaster and muted the volume. "I take it she wasn't happy?"

Mrs. Vetter wasn't happy about much—especially that I had become friends with Nadia. I hadn't known her before Nadia's dad died, so I'd tried to give her the benefit of the doubt.

Nadia shook her head and took a sip of wine. "She wants me to go to Wellesley with Teg." She smiled sadly. "I'd rather stay here. URI was good enough for my dad . . . "

I got up and went to the window, parting the heavy curtains and staring out at the Narragansett Bay. She'd been the one to bring up college, and I'd been picturing going through all of that *with* her.

When I turned back around, she gave me the I-can-see-straight-through-you look. "I'd miss you, too, Lela. But don't worry about it. We're going to go to college together—here. I need you to keep me sane."

She'd said that to me more than once. That I kept her from going off the deep end. "You have way too much faith in me," I mumbled.

"You have way too little faith in yourself. Come on. I need you. You can use your fab butt-kicking skills to get me out of bed in time for class every morning." She folded her hands beneath her chin and batted her eyelashes. "Roomies?"

"Roomies? Have you seen my room?" I laughed, refusing to get my hopes up. I hadn't even gotten an acceptance.

She shrugged. "It's a bit cluttered, and you've developed a weird obsession with photography. But I can live with that."

"Hey, you're the one who gave me the camera."

She laughed. "I have never regretted anything more. I've created a monster."

I'd spent most of my life trying to forget what had happened to me. Since meeting Nadia, I had moments I wanted to relive, to hold close. When she'd given me that camera for my seventeenth birthday, it was like she'd given me permission to capture it all, like she was saying our friendship was real.

"You weren't complaining when *your* birthday came around."

"No. The photograph you gave me was beautiful." I'd worked really hard to get the perfect shot of her favorite spot on the Newport shoreline and had sat on those rocks for hours, waiting for the sun to drop into place.

Nadia grinned like she knew what I was thinking. "I just got a new frame—we can hang it in our dorm room!" She threw her arm around me, and I flinched, a reflex I could not control. A year of friendship and a touch still freaked me out—too many people had put their hands on me without permission, and now that instinctive recoil was a part of me, no matter how badly I wanted to get over it. Her arm fell away from me, and she gave me an apologetic smile, which made me feel even worse. She hadn't really done anything wrong. It wasn't her fault I was broken.

A faint rattling pulled me from sleep, which was a relief because I'd been caught in yet another nightmare. After what Rick, my now-former foster father, had done to me, one would think *he'd* be the one haunting my dreams. And he had something to do with it—he'd revived me the night I'd tried to kill myself. In the moments before he had, I was certain I'd been standing at the gates of hell, about to be sucked in. Unfortunately, when Rick revived me, I'd brought a piece of hell back with me. *That* was what I dreamed about. Every night. A dark, walled city. Wandering, lost, trapped. A voice whispering to me, *You're perfect. Come back.*

Stay.

I shuddered and sat up, shaking off the dream, listening hard. Tegan's soft snores came from the couch across the room. And Nadia wasn't in her bed.

With a sick feeling in my stomach,I got up and padded over to the bathroom, staring at the strip of yellow light coming from beneath the closed door. A quiet whimper made me grit my teeth and knock. "Nadia?"

"I'll be right out."

My hand was already on the doorknob. "Coming in."

She was sitting on the bathroom floor, and she swiped a tear from her face with the backs of her fingers as I walked in and shut the door behind me. The bottle of pills was still clutched in her hand.

I sank to the tiles in front of her. "What's up?"

She closed her eyes. "Couldn't sleep."

I tugged the little brown pill bottle from her limp fingers. The label had been peeled off. I pressed the lid and twisted, then peeked inside. Little green pills, OC stamped into their round faces. *Goddammit.* "You told me you were done with this stuff." She'd told me that a few times, actually. And each time, I'd hoped it was true.

Her smile was ghostly. "I was. And I will be. It's just been so stressful lately."

"I get that. But all these do is make you stupid and sleepy." She was never herself when she was on it, and it pissed me off. Without it, she was my best friend, the girl who had poked her way through my defenses, who had made me trust her, who had made me believe things would get better. On it, she was . . . gone.

She sniffled. "It's just an escape, Lela. Don't you ever need to escape?"

I let out a humorless snort. "Yeah. I tried that once. It's highly overrated."

"Sometimes I'm so tired. I just want to sleep." She pulled her knees to her chest and gave me a cautious look. "And sometimes I don't want to wake up."

A cold sweat prickled on my palms and the back of my neck as I drew in a sharp breath, willing my voice to stay quiet and calm. "You don't know what you're saying. Seriously."

She frowned. I squeezed my eyes shut, forcing the words from my mouth. "Did you know I tried to kill myself a few years ago?"

"What?"

"Yeah. It was . . . a really rough time. And I wanted to escape. So I wrapped a belt around my neck and pulled it tight."

I heard her shift, and her hand closed over my wrist. "God, Lela. What happened?"

I opened my eyes and stared at her pale fingers wrapped over my skin, warm and clammy. Her hand fell away. "At first I really thought I'd done it. It felt amazing. Like flying." I looked up at her. "That was the lack of oxygen in my brain."

She flinched.

"But then I was falling. And I hit the ground. Hard." I pressed my lips together as the sensations tumbled through my head, dragging me back there, to the moment I died. *My scrabbling fingers curled around cobblestone, the grit digging up under my fingernails. I raised my head, and I saw the Gates. They swung wide, like the pincers of a giant insect, their spires rising into a black-and-purple sky, their hinges shrieking, shrieking, shrieking.*

Beyond them lay a city bathed in darkness.

My new home.

Like a hook buried in my stomach, it reached for me. My bare feet moved automatically, slapping against rough stone. Shoulders jostled me.

Someone stumbled against me and grabbed a fistful of my nightgown, and I ripped myself away. I was in the middle of an endless, faceless crowd, all of us lurching like zombies toward the Gates.

I blinked. Nadia's eyes were wide as she watched me. "You hit . . . what do you mean?" she whispered.

"I don't know. Maybe that's just what dying feels like. Hitting bottom." I spoke slowly, choosing each word. I wanted to tell her so badly. *If you kill yourself, you go where the monsters are.* But I had enough experience to know that people who talked about stuff like this honestly usually ended up in psych wards. Sometimes I wondered if that was where I belonged. I shuddered.

In front of the Gates stood massive creatures, like men but not men. They wore armor, like medieval knights, and curved swords hung from their belts. They shoved people through the open Gates, jeering and laughing, their eyes glowing like lanterns.

"Welcome to the Suicide Gates!" one of them bellowed over and over again until his chant echoed in my head like a pulse.

I shot to my feet and grabbed a cup from the side of the sink. With trembling hands, I turned on the faucet, still trapped in my memories.

No matter which way I twisted, the Gates were in front of me, sucking me in, hungry for me.

Rick's voice closed around me like a net. "Wake up, you little bitch."

My head jerked to the side with his slap. Beneath my cheek I felt the grubby nubs of my yellow bedroom rug. The belt was no longer around my neck. It hung from the broad hand of my foster father, who was waving it in front of my face as he crouched over me.

"What the fuck were you trying to do? Get a little attention? Don't I give you enough?" He pinched my hip and lowered himself on top of me, crushing my body with his, huffing his beer-soaked breath into my face. I was too stunned and disoriented to even try to get away this time.

I reached for my throat and winced as my fingers hit raw, swollen welts. My eyes darted to Rick's face. It was twisted with rage and fear—but also lit up with a glint of excitement that turned my stomach and told me exactly what was coming next.

The voices of those monster Guards still rang in the buzzing space between my ears as Rick tossed me onto my bed. His thick fingers closed around the back of my neck, pulling at my sweaty, tangled hair, pressing my face into the sheets. "I won't let anything happen to you, baby." His voice was gentler now, which filled me with dread.

As his throaty words hit my ears, telling me how lucky I was that he'd found me in time, that he wouldn't let me end up in the psych ward or on the streets, that he wouldn't tell if I wouldn't, that no one would believe me anyway, that I'd never had it so good . . . I stared at the wall. But all I saw was the Suicide Gates opening for me, calling me back. It hurt more than he did. Because now I knew death was no escape.

I blinked as my mind finally brought me back to the now. The faucet was still running, the cup in my hands overflowing. "Trust me," I said to Nadia as I turned off the water. "There's no better, happy place you go to. Running away from it doesn't fix anything. Turning yourself into a zombie doesn't either. Deal with your shit here, Nadia. And do it sober."

"It's easy for you to say, since you never drink or take anything. You're strong. And I can't even stand up to my own mother." Her voice was raspy, like she was trying not to cry.

I looked down at her. I wasn't strong. The only reason I didn't take drugs was because I was scared of losing control, of not being able to protect myself. And my mind was a scary enough place as it was. If I were strong, I would have been able to get over all of it and move on. It had been two years since I tried to die. My life had gotten so much better. But every night that dark city sucked me in, like it hadn't quite let me go when I'd returned to the land of the living. Other times, too, that horrible place appeared around me, like it was waiting for me to come back. That dark, deep voice whispered to me, urging me to stay there. *Perfect*, the unseen monster always said, his rank breath hot on the back of my neck. *You're perfect*. Each time, I gasped myself awake or rubbed my eyes until the real world appeared again, and wondered why it wouldn't leave me alone. I had things to live for now. I was never going back.

I put the cup back and leaned against the sink. "You're stronger than you think. If you weren't, you wouldn't have been able to tolerate being my friend." I was reaching for humor, anything to chase away the memories clamoring in my skull.

She smiled and rolled her eyes. "You don't make it easy." Her playful tone lowered my heart rate. She almost sounded like herself.

It made me brave. I scooped the pill bottle from the floor and handed it to her. "And I never will. Flush them."

She took the bottle from me and examined it. I could tell she wanted to argue, but then she looked up at me and nodded. With slow, heavy movements that told me she'd already taken enough to make her dizzy and loose, Nadia dumped the pills into the toilet and flushed, blinking as the green tablets swirled and disappeared. I sighed with relief. "If you feel like this again, will you talk to me? *Before* you talk to a dealer?"

Her cheeks got pink. "Sure. I'm fine, though. Really." Her pale blue eyes met mine. "Don't tell anyone, okay? It's just stress." Seeing my uncertain look, she laughed. "Come on, Lela. A cheesy old movie is all the escape I need. Van Wilder is calling our names."

I shook my head and chuckled, my mood rising quickly as a heavy weight lifted from my shoulders. "The things I do for friendship."

TWO

FOR A FEW WEEKS after our sleepover, Nadia stayed unusually busy. She seemed better, though, mostly back to her old self. But I started to wonder if she was avoiding me. I finally caught up with her after school and asked her if she wanted to hang out, but she said she had some stuff to do and needed to get home. Again.

When I pulled into my own driveway, Diane was standing on the front porch, jiggling with excitement. "Baby, it's here," she hollered as soon as I opened the car door. She hurried down the cement steps, waving a thick envelope. "I've been waiting. Don't make me wait any longer."

Diane thrust the envelope at me and bounced up and down while I ripped it open with shaking hands. I'd started to wonder if they'd just laughed and chucked my application as soon as they received it.

A huge smile stretched my face as I read the acceptance letter. The delinquent girl had turned it around. I was university-bound.

I read the letter quickly and then flipped to the next page, expecting an enrollment form or something. "Oh my God," I whispered as I read a second letter tucked behind the acceptance. "They're giving me a scholarsh—"

Diane crushed me to her before I had a chance to duck away. My head was pressed to her breast as she jumped up and down, whooping and crying. I was suffocating and wanted to pull away, but this was her moment, too. She'd taken me in when no other foster parent was willing risk it. And her gamble had paid off.

I let her squeeze me for a few seconds and then held up the letter to distract her. She released me and grabbed it. I stepped back, took my cell from my pocket, and hit SEND on Nadia's number. She didn't pick up.

"I'll make anything you want for dinner tonight, baby," Diane said, wiping her eyes. "Anything."

"Can I take a rain check on that? I want to show this to Nadia." Whatever she had going on, I knew she'd be excited.

Diane nodded and handed me the letter. "Go ahead. Tell her thank you for me." She wagged her finger at me. "And be nice when she says 'I told you so'."

I laid the letter flat on my passenger seat and reread it at every stoplight until I turned onto Nadia's waterfront street. I knocked at her front door a few times, but no one answered. Letter in hand, I jogged along the side of the house toward the back terrace. The cool, humid wind off the bay lifted my hair, bringing my curls to life. I pushed the strands back impatiently. "Nadia? Are you here?"

She was in her usual spot on the rear patio, looking out at the water from her chaise lounge, knees pulled to her chest. I skipped onto the elaborate brickwork, waiting for her to turn her head. I touched her shoulder. "Hey, you didn't answer your phone."

She looked up at me. Her eyes were so pale, her pupils tiny pinpoints. I muscled past a twist of anxiety and squinted, hoping it was a trick of the early-evening light. Nope.

"I couldn't . . . find it," she said.

She was numbed up and high once again.

I drew a long breath through my nose. I didn't want to get into another argument with her tonight. Not when we had so much to be happy about. "I got the letter today. It's official. And guess what?"

I waved the paper in front of her, wanting her to perk up and reach for it. She didn't, so I laid it on the chaise next to her pedicured toes. She was still looking up at me, a vague smile on her face. "You're happy. It's good to see you happy."

"We did it!" I laughed. "We're going! We can fill out that housing form now."

Her smile guttered and faded. "*You* did it," she whispered. She took a deep breath and sat up straighter. "I'm so proud of you. You're going to have such a good time."

"What?" I asked as the door to the breakfast room slid open.

"Nadia," sighed Mrs. Vetter, a wineglass in her heavily jeweled hand. As usual, she didn't even acknowledge me. "John is picking me up in a few minutes."

For a moment I was struck by the resemblance between mother and daughter, which had grown more apparent over the last few months as we neared the finish line for graduation. Both of them were rail thin, well dressed, pale and beautiful . . . and had tiny pupils.

Nadia waved her hand absently.

"Good," Mrs. Vetter said. "I'll see you in the morning." The door slid shut, and her presence was forgotten, like a raindrop hitting the surface of the ocean.

"So," I prompted, pushing my scholarship letter toward Nadia again. "Read it! See what your hard work and constant nagging accomplished."

Nadia's eyes had returned to the choppy gray waters of the Narragansett Bay. Deep in my belly, anger coiled. This was the shining moment, the one where I proved I was worth the time she'd spent on me. I needed her to see it. I needed her to say it.

I needed her to be all right.

I stood up and waved my hand in front of her face. "How much did you take this time?"

She leaned back and grinned. Her arms splayed out, open and helpless. "No idea."

"Do you know how fucking pathetic that sounds?" I blurted, unable to hold back my frustration any longer. I snatched the now-creased letter from the lounge, crushing it in my fist.

She closed her eyes. "It feels fucking *good*, though."

I had to step back to keep from kicking her chair over in a desperate attempt to snap her out of her trance, to bring back the Nadia who gave a shit. "Maybe I *don't* want to room with you. I'll actually be at URI to accomplish something, not just to hang out between fixes."

I wanted her to wince. To tell me what a bitch I was. To show me I meant enough to her to be able to reach her.

Instead, she smiled again, a special smile, a devastating smile. The ultimate brush-off smile. In the time we'd been friends, I'd seen her do it to other people, this slow, fake-indulgent quirk of the lips that killed conversations, withering girls and boys alike with its confident chill. It was a smile that said *No matter what you say, you can't make me care.* I'd seen her give it to her worthless ex-boyfriend Greg a thousand times. Her mom, too. I'd even seen her give it to Tegan once. And now she was aiming it at me for the first time. "Go home, Lela. You're kind of a buzz kill."

"Okay," I said, voice shaking. "You've turned into a real bitch, you know that?"

Her hand rose slowly, trembling slightly as she raised her middle finger.

In my head, the world was caving in. This was the thing I'd feared ever since I'd let myself get close to her—that like everyone else, she would turn her back on me. I felt like such an idiot having all these dreams of being away at college with my best friend. I had started to trust it. And I should have known better. No one could possibly feel that way about me.

That cold smile hadn't left her face, and I wanted to smack her. I wanted to shake her. Anything to get a reaction, to get some response that showed I mattered to her, that she was as afraid of losing me as I was of losing her. I stood there, waiting for the slightest change in her expression, the slightest twitch of her fingers.

Nothing.

Tears stung my eyes, but the heat of my anger burned them away. "You're gonna be just like your mom, Nadia. Congratulations. Thanks for saving me from having to watch."

I crammed the letter into my pocket and stomped across the manicured lawn, wishing I had something heavy to throw at the wide, crystal clear bay windows. My panic had short-circuited me—the *one* thing I'd had to hang on to was falling apart. I sucked in a few breaths as I reached my car, trying to calm down enough to drive. She would be better tomorrow. I'd show her the letter then.

I never got the chance, though. Tegan called the next morning. I barely made out the words through her hysterical sobbing, but after a few repetitions, they finally sank in.

Mrs. Vetter had discovered her daughter on the floor of the bathroom, an empty pill bottle next to her.

Nadia was dead.

THREE

MY GAZE TRACED THE zombie's oozing features as the sharp whine of the tattoo gun burrowed into my ears. The undead creature was forceful and intimidating, saturated with color and menace. I watched Dunn, the zombie's owner, wondering what it said about him, that he had decided to carry this monster on his flesh. As I eyed his wiry little body, I decided he'd probably been bullied as a child. He was certainly compensating for *something*. I kept searching for more clues, grateful for distraction from the throb and sting radiating across my skin. And from the guilt eating away at my heart.

Dunn's face twisted in concentration as he deftly maneuvered the needles. I bit back a shiver at the pain, forcing myself into stillness, afraid the tiniest move would ruin the portrait taking shape on my arm.

"Halfway there," Dunn commented. "You need a break?"

I shook my head. "Keep going."

"You look pale."

"I'm fine," I replied through gritted teeth.

Dunn grunted and bent to his task again. He had some mad skills. Even through the blood and the swelling, Nadia's delicate face was instantly recognizable. It had only taken him a few days from the first time he saw the photograph to sketch her face and map where it would lie on my forearm. It was sort of hilarious that, for all my bad-girl rep, the only thing I'd ever used my fake ID for was to get this tattoo. Dunn had even given me a discount. It still ate a chunk out of my pathetic college fund, but that wasn't a problem now. I'd gotten a scholarship, after all.

I looked out the window of the shop, watching cars thread their way along Wickenden Street's narrow lanes. Maybe this tattoo would do it. The school memorial hadn't—I'd stared at Nadia's glossy, poster-size photo from the back row of the bleachers, watching all her other friends cry and hug each other in the front row, and it still hadn't chased her ghost out of my head. The wake hadn't done it either—after seeing her lying there, pale and perfect, the dreams still haunted me. The funeral had failed me, too—even after gutting my way through the priest's promises that she was in a better place, the nightly visions of her trapped in that dark city, the very same place I'd carried in my head for the past two years, remained. Now she was there. And it was my fault.

Diane said I needed to find my own way to say goodbye. She promised it would make me feel better. So here it was, my personal memorial to Nadia. I'd wear her solemn, haunted expression on my skin forever: a reminder of what I'd had, what I'd missed, what I'd lost.

Someone came out from the back of the shop, and the door's hinges creaked in protest. I gasped as the Suicide Gates appeared in front of me, reaching for me, trying to swallow me. I'd walked through them with Nadia that night just a week ago, over ground I knew well, screaming at her to get back, to turn around. Begging her not to go through. But she'd just looked up at the city beyond the Gates, crying and terrified. She was all alone, even though she was surrounded by hundreds of people mumbling in a bunch of different languages. Those enormous, armored Guards stood on either side of the Gates, wielding their curved swords as they herded the crowd into a vast, dark city. One of the monsters had laughed at Nadia when she'd begged for his help. *Welcome to the Suicide Gates,* he'd shouted.

I'd jerked awake, so relieved it was just a dream, unaware that she was already dead.

"You okay?" Dunn pulled his tattoo gun back, and by his expression, I knew I'd just done something spastic.

I cleared my throat. "Fine. Why?"

"You were, uh . . . moaning? Not that I minded . . . " The twist of his lips made me seriously consider taking to my former ways and stabbing him with his tattoo gun.

"Sorry. It hurts. Go ahead." I stared out the window, trying desperately not to think of what I'd seen in those dreams.

The needles fell silent again. "Finished," announced Dunn, squeezing my hand. "What do you think?"

I looked down at the inside of my right forearm. Nadia's face looked back at me. "She's perfect," I murmured. "Thank you."

He bandaged me up and I headed home, hoping this would put an end to the nightmares of Nadia. Every night since she died, I'd walked with her deeper into that infinite, dark city. She was surrounded by strangers wandering the streets, all wearing glassy-eyed looks of sorrow and torment. Except for the enormous Guards who patrolled the streets, nearly everyone in the city looked completely miserable. Nadia wanted to ask for help, but no one would look at her. She couldn't hear me calling her name. I was just a ghost hovering by her side. I woke up every morning, my grief fresh, my heart aching. Maybe now she would rest in peace and let me get back to my regularly scheduled nightmares. Anything was better than seeing her suffer.

Diane's car was in the driveway when I pulled in. I tugged at my sleeve as I walked through the door. Diane would be curious if she saw the bandage, not to mention pissed if she saw the tattoo.

"What happened to you, baby?" She trundled out of the kitchen, serving spoon in hand.

"Nothing. Hanging out with, um, Tegan."

Diane's eyebrows shot up. "Tegan just called to see if you were going to the vigil tomorrow night."

Great. Tegan had decided to be a decent human being at exactly the wrong moment. I sank into a chair at the kitchen table. "I needed some time to myself. I went for a drive."

Her brow furrowed. "Is more alone time really what you need?"

I closed my eyes so she couldn't see me rolling them. "I don't know what I need, Diane. I'm not sure it matters, either."

"It would matter to Nadia."

I winced. When I had dreamed of Nadia, the only thing that had mattered to her was escaping from her pain. Just as I'd warned her, it hadn't ended when she killed herself. "You don't know that."

Diane's arms rose from her sides. She wanted to hug me, but she knew better than to try. She crossed her arms over her chest instead. "You were important to her, and don't pretend you don't know that." Her eyes narrowed. "You've been having nightmares again, haven't you? They're just dreams, baby. Bad dreams, I know, but still just dreams."

I turned my back to her, opening the cabinet and staring sightlessly at the plates and glasses. They didn't feel like dreams. In last night's nightmare, a cackling old lady had tried to drag Nadia away—like some type of animal. *Perfect,* she'd said to Nadia. *You're perfect.* It was a different voice than the one that had whispered to me in so many of my own nightmares, but she'd said the same ominous words. When Nadia had run, the evil animal granny chased her—*on all fours*, palms and feet slapping the cobblestone street. I'd lurched awake before I got to see what happened to her.

"You think you could have saved her. You feel guilty," Diane commented as she reached around me and grabbed two plates.

"Of course I do," I snapped hoarsely, swiping a sleeve across my leaking eyes. "You should have heard the stuff I said to her that night. What if I drove her to it?"

She shook her head and made this disapproving *mm-mm-mm* sound in her throat. "Do you think Nadia would want you to feel this way? That girl was pure good. I wish she'd loved herself as much as she loved everyone else. She left a lasting mark on this world, and on you. When you came to me a year ago, I was afraid you'd end up right back in the RITS, but instead, here you are—going to college!"

Yeah, Nadia was the reason I had that kind of future. And what had I done for her? She'd said I was the one who kept her grounded, the one who saw past the trivial stuff.

She said she needed me because I was real. Strong. Funny. *Good.* I'd actually started to believe that stuff about myself, to believe I had something to give her in return for everything she'd given me. Then I'd walked away from her right when she needed me most.

I pressed my hand over the bandage and let the pain bleed through my whole body. I *deserved* this hurt. A flash of panic rushed through me as the dark city flashed in front of my eyes. I yanked my hand away from the tattoo like it had burned me, and the real world returned.

Diane offered me a plate. "You want to talk about it while we eat?"

God, no. "I'm sorry, Diane. Dinner looks great, but I'm going to go do some homework and then go to bed."

She gave me a sad smile. "I'm here if you need me, baby."

I went back to my room and scattered my pictures of Nadia across the floor. In almost all of them, Nadia wore that I-rule-the-world smile. I flipped through the snapshots, wondering how someone so confident, so *alive*, could ever want to hurt herself. Then I got to one of the photos I'd taken of her as we sat in the bleachers watching the boys' baseball practice.

In that picture she stared into space, eyes dull and haunted. That was the face of a person who could down enough pills to kill herself many times over. That was the face on my arm. That was how she looked when she thought no one else was watching. At first I'd thought it was a fluke. None of my other prints held any hint of this sad, desperate Nadia. But then I'd remembered all the other photos on my camera, the ones I hadn't thought worthy of printing out. Sure enough—there weren't many, but they were there, stretching as far back as last summer. Pictures of Nadia caught in honest moments, too distracted or exhausted to ratchet that breathtaking smile onto her face.

My vision blurred beneath the weight of my tears. How could I have let her slip away? I gathered all the photos, the best moments of my life with the only friend I'd ever had. I carried them to the backyard and fired up Diane's little charcoal grill.

FOUR

THE FLAMES LICKED AT the edges of the pictures and then hungrily gobbled Nadia's fake smiles. I inhaled the bitter smoke. My eyes watered as I watched the last image of her face catch fire. "Are you really there, Nadia? Or am I just crazy?"

As soon as her image disappeared, I was already missing her. I peeled the bandage off and looked down at her face on my still-aching arm. Her eyes caught me, made me feel like I was falling. Heavy, tingling prickles raced up my legs, and my breath quickened. The bricks on the patio rounded, transforming into cobblestones. Diane's hanging plants drew their tendrils up and became gas lamps hanging from thick posts, giving off a greenish glow in the darkness.

Nadia's arms pumped in front of me as she ran along the uneven street, high-rises hemming her in on either side.

I was with Nadia. I *was* Nadia. Somehow, I was in her head, seeing things through her eyes as she fled through the dark city. My stomach heaved with her fear. Her heart—*my* heart—was beating so hard, and I realized I was no longer in Diane's backyard. Was something chasing us—her—again? That evil animal granny who'd tried to take her away?

I felt a dull pain in my shoulder as we dove behind a Dumpster. We whipped around to see if the danger was near, just in time to see a man's body land in a heap a few feet away. She craned her neck and immediately shrank behind the metal wall again, but not before we caught a glimpse.

The guy's neck was laid open to the spine.

My mind lit up, trying to process what I was seeing. I thought this was the afterlife, that these people were already dead. But this guy had just been killed, and he didn't look like he was going to rise any time soon.

My horrified thoughts fell silent at the sharp crash of metal on metal. Nadia peeked out from behind the Dumpster, wondering frantically how to escape. She knew enough from her encounter with the animal old lady to realize folks here were dangerous. She didn't want to step into plain sight or make enough noise to draw attention to herself, so she was stuck until these people went away. I would have told her that was a good plan, but I knew she was deaf to me, even though I could hear her thoughts like they were my own.

In front of us, two men and one woman advanced on their prey, wielding curved swords that looked exactly like the ones carried by the Guards who patrolled the city. The man in the center was tan with raven hair and wore dingy white robes, like some sheik from the Middle East. The man to his left was tall and blond, like a modern Viking. On the right stood a middle-aged woman wearing a tracksuit and running shoes. Suburban housewife. The group looked exactly like all the other poor, oblivious suicides who roamed the streets of the city, except these folks were the opposite of aimless. They had a purpose: kill somebody.

As the sheik took a single step forward, the others took two, creating a V formation around their adversary. Their faces carried identical expressions of hatred mixed with anticipation. I recognized the look. I'd seen it on the detention officers in the RITS—they thought they were going to win, but they didn't expect it to be easy.

Nadia shifted, finally giving me a view of the opposing side. Which consisted of . . . one guy. He was sort of dressed like one of those giant Guards but didn't look anything like them. He was fairly tall, but not bulky and huge like the others. His chest was covered not with metal armor but with molded leather, buckled together at the shoulders and sides like a medieval bulletproof vest, with a ridged collar that was higher at the back. The same kind of leather covered his forearms and surrounded his legs below the knees. He didn't wear a helmet or visor like the other Guards did, so I could see that he was young, not much older than I was. He had olive skin and closely cut black hair, and the hint of a killer smile played at the corners of his lips while his dark eyes swept back and forth, assessing.

"You Mazikin have been busy lately, Ibram. I just wanted to ask you some questions about it," said the Guard in a clipped, hard sort of accent. He sounded so calm for a guy who wasn't even holding a weapon. The sheath at his hip was empty, and his sword lay several feet away. Then my gaze drifted down to the twin circles of leather surrounding his thighs—each one held two double-edged knives, and he had a police baton clipped to his belt. Didn't seem like much against three people armed with swords, though.

The sheik, Ibram, laughed. "If all you wanted to do was talk, you wouldn't have killed Frank." He glanced over at the dead man. "Good thing I brought plenty of backup."

"And more stolen scimitars." The Guard took a few more steps back, moving with complete precision and control. There was no hesitation in his movements, but no rush, either.

Ibram eyed the elegant curve of the blade in his hand, then gave the Guard a meaningful once-over. A grin lit his golden face. "Yes, the only things worth keeping in this city.

Beautiful and effective." His teeth flashed sharp and white under the light of a streetlamp. "A nice extension of our natural weaponry, don't you think?"

The Guard didn't answer. A muscle in his jaw jumped rhythmically. His backtracking had brought him into a pool of lamplight, and with a shock I noticed he was bleeding; the fabric of his fitted shirt gaped at the shoulder, showing just how effective the scimitar was. The gash was so deep I swear I saw muscle and bone. Blood fell in steady drops from the fingertips of his left hand. I suddenly felt sympathy for the guy. As much as I despised those enormous Guards at the Gates, I didn't want to watch this one die.

I got totally distracted looking at him, but then I heard Nadia wondering hysterically if she was about to watch this outnumbered, injured guy get slaughtered right in front of her. At first glance he *did* seem trapped and hopelessly overmatched. But as he shifted his weight to his rear leg and drew the police baton from his hip in a smooth, unhurried motion, I knew he wasn't. I could *see* how dangerous he was.

The housewife and the Viking lunged forward, attacking from both sides. The Guard was in motion instantly. His baton extended, tripling in length to become a long, narrow staff. Before it reached its full length, it arced in a blurring motion. The Guard was the axis, the eye of the storm, as the staff rocketed around and struck the blade from the housewife's hands, then reversed its motion and crunched into the

Viking's face. The Guard pulled the staff back and jabbed it into the neck of the Viking, who crumpled to the ground. A millisecond later, the housewife was on the ground, too, clutching at her throat.

The Guard's dark gaze returned to Ibram, who smiled and shrugged. "They were new" was all Ibram said before he attacked. He was forced to a halt as he blocked two throwing knives with the whirling motion of his sword. I hadn't even seen the Guard throw them. Ibram blocked the other two just as easily. The Guard was out of throwing knives.

"Damn," the Guard said as he shifted the staff to his right hand. "You've been practicing."

Ibram darted forward, taking full advantage of his opponent's wound, which obviously slowed him down. The Guard looked like he was fighting purely in self-defense, using the staff to create a circle of protection to prevent the wicked blade from finding its mark. Twice Ibram almost got him, striping the Guard's breastplate with deep gashes. But the Guard wasted no opportunity, and the first time Ibram left himself open, the staff smashed into the side of the sheik's face. Ibram slashed his sword down sharply, splintering the staff. Both men stumbled back.

The Guard's eyes scanned the street, mapping the distance to every weapon in the area. Then he was running, but not toward any of the blades I could see. He ran straight toward Ibram, hurling the remnant of his broken staff at the sheik's blade arm and forcing him to raise his weapon to block it. Ibram recovered instantly and swung the blade back toward his attacker, but the Guard was too close and too fast. He jabbed the edge of his hand against Ibram's wrist, sending the weapon clattering to the ground, then shot a vicious punch to Ibram's groin before nailing him with a final elbow strike. Ibram fell to the ground like a sack of cement. I was glad Nadia couldn't hear my thoughts at that moment . . . because I couldn't help but admire the Guard's style.

He looked down at Ibram for a moment, then, apparently satisfied with the sheik's comatose state, walked quickly to the Viking, who had begun to reach for his sword. The Guard knelt next to him and pulled a knife from his ankle sheath.

"Don't take me to that awful place," the Viking begged.

"You don't have to worry. I have no intention of doing that," the Guard said as he stroked a long hand over the Viking's head. At first I thought he might be comforting the guy. But when he rose and walked away, I saw he'd cut the man's throat, ear to ear.

Holy crap.

The Guard approached the trembling housewife. "My name is Lucy Stein," the woman said in a high-pitched, childlike voice as she tried to scoot away.

The Guard dropped to his knees beside her, a mixture of sadness and determination on his face. "Your name *was* Lucy Stein."

He cut her throat before she had a chance to reply.

Oh, shit, Nadia, stay where you are. Don't move.

The Guard got up slowly and swayed in place. He bowed his head as he bent over, bracing his hands against his thighs. I wondered if he was about to collapse from his injuries. I hoped he would, so Nadia could get the hell out of there. He was breathing hard, but I wasn't sure it was from the fight. His eyes were on the dead housewife as her blood haloed around her face. The Guard winced and closed his eyes, his lips moving in a silent chant. Was he praying? Blood from his shoulder joined the puddle on the concrete, mingling with his victim's.

Nadia shifted, ready to bolt. My thoughts went into overdrive. *Don't move don't breathe don't scream don't run.* Her heartbeat roared in my ears—she was convinced this man would cut her throat, too, if he knew she'd witnessed his crimes. She stumbled back and collided with a bunch of overflowing garbage cans. They hit the ground with a deafening clang. When Nadia raised her head from the pile of trash she'd tumbled into, both of us gasped. The Guard's leather-armored shins were right in front of her face.

A squeak of terror burst from Nadia as the Guard tugged her to her feet and pushed her against a wall. His right hand wrapped firmly around her neck. I found myself looking straight into his black-brown eyes. I felt the heat of his breath on Nadia's face, smelled the scent of leather on his skin. He tilted his head and inhaled deeply, his nose grazing Nadia's cheek, before stepping back and releasing her.

"*Deutsch*?" he asked. Nadia stared at him helplessly. He sighed. "English?"

Nadia nodded.

"You need to find shelter," he advised in a tired voice. "The Mazikin are out recruiting tonight, so you shouldn't be on the street." There was a noise behind him, and he turned abruptly. Nadia looked in time to see Ibram disappearing around a corner. The Guard cursed loudly. Well, it was in a foreign language, but I could guess at the translation from the sheer aggravation in his voice. He sheathed his knife and took two steps toward the mouth of the alley before turning back to Nadia. He pointed in the direction she had tried to run. "Don't go that way. It's not safe." He pointed across the road to a high-rise. "There are empty apartments in that building. You'll know which ones are available. The doors are open. You can make your bed in any of them. Do you understand me?"

When Nadia nodded again, he sprinted after Ibram. We sank to the ground, sobbing.

"Lela! Snap out of it!"

I jerked my head up to see the gas lamps sprouting leafy tendrils that unfurled toward the ground. The cobblestones beneath my feet flattened into bricks again. Fingers curled around my shoulders and shook me.

Diane's face swam in front of mine, her eyes bright with panic. "I'm calling an ambulance!"

I shook my head, half surprised to be in control of my own body again. "Don't." My voice was hoarse. I squirmed away from Diane's grasping hands and struggled to my feet. I had been sitting on the ground, crouched against the side of the house. The overturned grill lay in front of me, dull, papery ashes strewn across the brick patio.

"You were screaming Nadia's name. You were telling her not to move, not to run. I couldn't get you to talk to me. You could have burned yourself," Diane panted, pulling her phone from her pocket and waving it in the air. "I know you're grieving, baby, but that's not normal."

I almost laughed at her understatement. "I just got a little . . . overwhelmed. It won't happen again." My hands trembled as I dusted off my pants, so I grabbed a broom leaning against a bench near the sliding glass door and gripped the handle. "See? I'm fine. I'll clean this up and come inside."

Diane eyed me as she fingered the buttons on the phone.

"Diane, if you call now, they're going to come, see that I'm totally fine, and be kinda irritated with you for the false alarm."

She put her hands on her hips, and I almost took a step back. Diane worked down at the medium-security lockup, and she had a better game face than any thug I'd ever met.

"We're going to the doctor tomorrow, and that's the end of this," she snapped.

"Fine," I muttered as I swept. "Whatever."

As soon as she disappeared into the house, I let myself collapse back onto the ground. I stared at the little pile of ashes in the dustpan, at the gray smears across the patio. Two possibilities. One: I was going utterly insane. My best friend's death had driven me over the edge, and if this continued, I'd be headed for the psych ward sometime very soon. Two: I was actually connecting with Nadia, and I knew where she was. But it was so much worse than the place that had haunted me over the last two years. It was dangerous. People bled there. They *died* there, even though they were already dead. For all I knew, one of those sword-wielding freaks might be attacking her right now.

I finished sweeping up as quickly as I could and waved cheerfully as Diane gave me a concerned look. I headed back to my room, the smile sliding off my face as soon as I turned away. I lay on my bed and held my hands up in front of me, trying to recall the exact sensation of being in Nadia's head. Of *being* Nadia. Nothing. I closed my eyes and tried to sleep. Maybe I could dream about her. Maybe I could see if she'd gotten into one of those apartments. Maybe she would hear me this time. Maybe I could talk to her. Maybe I could be with her again.

Of course, the only time I'd ever *wished* for one of those nightmares, I couldn't even get myself to sleep. My tattoo itched and ached, sending spikes of pain up and down my arm, but it didn't draw me into her head again. I stared at it, the dark ink on my reddened, raw skin. It had been meant as a good-bye—but what if it had drilled her deeper into my heart? Before, I'd wanted the dreams to stop. Now, I wanted more. That vision had felt so real. Not like a shadow over the real world; it *had* been the real world. Like what I'd seen was really happening. And if it was, Nadia was in deep trouble. I lay there for hours, trying to coax a vision into my brain. My heart ticked in time with the blinking light on my alarm clock, each second winding me tighter. What if she didn't make it into one of those apartments?

What if you really do belong in the psych ward?

I threw the covers back, unwilling to think about that possibility, too focused on Nadia to worry about it anyway.

If I couldn't get a vision of Nadia to come to me, maybe I could go find one.

FIVE

IT WAS AROUND FIVE in the morning when I finally gave in, pulled on some flip-flops, grabbed my keys and a jacket, and tiptoed out of the house. Once on the highway, I steered the car toward Newport. I spent my last two bucks on the tolls and drove over the bridges, straight to the southern tip of Aquidneck Island. There, the narrow Cliff Walk began its winding, three-mile path between mansions and ocean.

Nadia once said that when she was on that rocky trail—luxury on one side, crashing waves on the other—the two halves of her came together. She'd brought me here a bunch of times. This was where I'd taken that picture of the shoreline she liked so much. Maybe this was the place I would find her again.

I parked at the side of the road, right by the entrance to the Cliff Walk. The wind gusted around me, tangling my hair around my neck and face. The chill of it sliced right through my thin jacket as I stepped onto the stony trail, making the tattoo on my arm flash with bright, sharp pain.

As soon as it did, a hallway appeared in front of me. My mouth filled with a sour tang. I looked down at my hand. On my palm . . . *Nadia's palm* . . . sat a few pills. I was in her head again. She wanted to numb herself up, too tired and terrified to care about anything but nothing. Deep inside her chest, I felt it: a gnawing, festering emptiness, a yawning chasm. She was going to try to fill it with those pills. *Don't,* I whispered, but just like always, she didn't hear me. She put one foot in front of the other, making her way down the dimly lit corridor to an open doorway at the end of the hall. With a flash of relief, I realized she had taken the Guard's advice. She was headed for an apartment.

As her head buzzed with need, my own vision sharpened. Wherever her gaze landed, I soaked it in. Lanterns hung from sconces along the hallway, casting sickly greenish light across the closed doors, which were covered in peeling, dark pink paint. The pale orange walls were streaked black, and the floor was kind of furry. *What the* . . . ? It was mold, growing like moss, all over the carpet. She left footprints in the damp, squishy clumps as she plodded toward her destination. Her fingers closed over the pills. Her mouth watered.

Something shifted behind her. She didn't notice. All she could think about was getting into that apartment and lying on the floor, letting the pills shut her down for a while. She didn't hear the faint brush of steps along the moldy carpet, the quiet hiss of breath coming closer with each second. *Look behind you, Nadia.*

She didn't. She just shuffled toward that open door, oblivious to the soft, hooting laughter now coming from whoever or whatever was in that hallway with her. *Run,* I shouted. *Please, run,* I whispered.

She didn't hear me.

Her heartbeat was slow and steady in my chest, but my thoughts were my own, and they were on fire. I had no trouble hearing the reedy voice cackle, "She's perfect." My muscles ached with tension, trying to make her sprint, but it was like running in water. She had all the control and we moved at her speed. *Faster. You're almost there. Lock yourself in that apartment.*

The footsteps quickened. They were just behind her now. I felt a warm breath against my neck and smelled something rotten, but she did not turn, did not feel, did not smell it. She leaned on the doorjamb and stumbled into the apartment, forgetting to close the door behind her. . . .

My entire body shuddered as I was hit with a gust of chilly wind. I opened my eyes. I was now standing at the summit of a hill high above the ocean surrounded by low, bristling scrub. A thin band of orange rimmed the water as the sun emerged from the sea. The waves slapped in echoing rhythm against the rocks below. I had no time to think about how the hell I'd gotten there. All I could think was *Did she make it? Did they get her?*

In my helpless frustration, I shouted at the sky. "This isn't fair! First I'm punished with these visions, and now I can't have one when I need it most? What kind of bullshit divine justice is this? I need to know if she's okay!" I took another step forward, trying to get closer to whoever might be listening up there. "I have to know if she made it. Please—Oh, shit!"

A sharp gust of wind hit me, and I slipped and tumbled over the scrub. My arms pinwheeled as I tried to grab at the scraggly, brittle shrubs, but they snapped off in my hands. My hips and legs bounced off the side of the boulder as I fell, but then I was plummeting through open air, plunging toward the jagged rocks and ocean below. My scream unfurled from my throat, high and clear. *Oh God oh no oh no no no no—*

As soon as I became aware of myself, I knew I was dead. I recognized the soaring feeling of freedom from the night I'd tried to kill myself, and I waited for the crash.

It didn't come. Instead a bubble of contentment inflated inside my chest, bright and shining, somehow reassuring me that the fight was over, that everything would be all right.

A fleeting worry crossed my mind: *please don't let Diane think I jumped.* . . . But I couldn't hold onto it, because the feeling of safety and happiness crowded it out, leaving no room for longing or fear or regret.

I lay on my back and stared at the piercing blue, cloudless sky. I was lying in a field, and the grass cradled me, silken and fragrant, soft as any bed. I sat up slowly, trying to recall exactly what had happened. I only remembered falling, then nothing else. I had a faint memory of being upset but couldn't remember why. Nothing seemed worth worrying about at the moment.

I got to my feet, smiling.

And realized I wasn't alone.

People appeared around me every few seconds, materializing out of nowhere, lying in the grass and then rising, grins lighting their faces. Each of them looked around, some slightly puzzled, none afraid. They turned their faces to the sun and walked away across the flowered meadow, backs straight, strides relaxed and smooth. Old, young, of every color. All happy. I understood their expressions. I felt the same way. I'd never really had a home, but this sure felt like one. I raised my arms to the sky in silent gratitude, soaking in the warmth of the sun above.

Then I saw her face on my arm.

She'd come with me, haunting and hunted. The sorrow in her eyes hit me like a solid punch to the gut, deflating my bubble of contentment instantly. My arms fell to my sides, and that's when I heard it: the unmistakable shriek from my nightmares. The Suicide Gates swinging open. I spun around, trying to locate the source of the sound, amazed I hadn't noticed it before.

There, in the distance, a city sprawled, ringed by a high wall. A dome of darkness arced over it, veiling the skyline in constant midnight. As soon as I saw the Gates, as soon as I heard them, I recognized the place. And I knew Nadia was in there. All I'd dreamed, all I'd seen was real.

The people around me didn't seem to hear the metallic screams of those Gates. None of them turned their heads. None of them were aware of the city that loomed on the hill behind them. But once I saw it, I couldn't look away.

I hiked through the grass toward the dome, flowers tickling my ankles, my joy just another distant memory. When I reached the boundary between light and darkness, indecision kicked my feet out from under me, and I sank to the ground.

What if . . .

What if she'd made it safely into that apartment? What if I could find her? What if I could get her out? What if I could bring her into the sunlight? What if I could do in death what I hadn't done in life?

What if I could save her?

But saving her would mean I'd have to go in there. The place I'd been trying to escape for years. Did I really want to put myself through that? What if I couldn't help her at all?

I have no idea how long I sat there staring into the darkness, listening to the Gates swinging open and slamming shut. I have no idea how long it took me to decide. It was harder than I would have expected. All the times I'd dreamed of the city, I'd never had any idea of what lay outside its walls. It was heaven out here in the Countryside, and I didn't want to leave. Everything I'd ever needed was here. I was sure of it.

But how could I walk away from Nadia? How could I enjoy my afterlife if I never found out what happened to her? After everything she'd done for me—all those nights of studying with me, sticking up for me to her friends, even writing a letter to my probation officer . . . after she'd showed me I was worth something, after she'd told me she had faith in me . . . how could I turn my back on her when I *knew* what she was going through? Would I fail her *again*?

No. I couldn't. I had to go after her. I could only hope I wasn't too late.

My plan: Get into the city. Get Nadia. Keep us safe. Find a way out. Simple.

I got up, took a breath, and stepped through the veil of darkness before I could change my mind. It rested heavy against my skin, clammy and chilling, weighing me down. I fell forward, hit by a barrage of despair. I lay, forehead against the ground, palms against the stones, any remaining hope and happiness leaching away.

I was back.

The road leading to the city was paved with rough slabs of stone and teemed with hunched, moaning people. A wet, scrunching noise made me jump. A young man with dark skin and hair appeared in a heap just to my left. Slack jawed and blinking, he raised his head to the Gates and let out a cry in a foreign language, then staggered to his feet and joined the crowd.

Dazed, limp souls materialized in pathetic piles behind me and on both sides, a grisly parody of what was happening just on the other side of the veil. These poor folks rose automatically and stumbled toward the mouth of the city. The Suicide Gates sucked them all in. No one tried to escape or resist. They looked neither left nor right. Like most of the people in my nightmares, including Nadia, they seemed concerned only with themselves and whatever they were going through. I waited for that feeling, that urge to walk toward the Gates. But it wasn't there. I could go in, but I didn't have to. I still had a choice.

Behind the Gates, the city clung to the slopes of its hill, a cement fungus. The tallest buildings clustered at its massive center, rising so high I couldn't tell where they ended and the sky began. The only disruption to the pattern of the city, in which low buildings lay at the outskirts and grew in circular patterns toward the center, was on its farthest wall, where an enormous, shining white building rose. In a place that ate light, absorbed it like a sponge, this building glowed. I suddenly felt total sympathy for those insects that get drawn into bug zappers. I didn't know what that building was, but it called to me.

I tore my eyes from the building. I only had a few more minutes before I walked through the Suicide Gates and let the city swallow me, so I allowed myself one final look at all I had left behind. The lush, rolling Countryside was still visible though the sooty veil of night. Beyond the far edge of the city, a wild forest stretched for miles. Behind me, shimmering rivers meandered through golden wheat fields. And the sun shone above it all.

Nadia needed that. She needed to be out there.

I turned back to the Gates, clenched my teeth, and marched forward. Others pressed in behind me, trapping me against layers of bodies, filling me with nausea as they pushed against my back, reminding me of things I'd worked really hard to forget. I wriggled myself along, carefully nudging past arms and shoulders, chests and heads, toward the outer edge of the crowd. Time for a close encounter with the Guards. I wailed and cried, uniting my voice with others' despairing sobs.

"Please," I cried, reaching out toward the Guard and drawing his attention with my waving arms, "please, help me."

When the gloved hand reached for my hair, I ducked quickly. Fingers closed around my forearm. The Guard jerked me off my feet and onto the back of the man in front of me. The poor guy fell to the ground in a crumple of arms and legs. I used the Guard's grip as leverage to pull myself toward his armored chest. As soon as I was close enough, I twisted my arm from his grasp and used both feet to push against his metal breastplate, sending myself to the ground. I reached up quickly and yanked an elderly Asian woman down on top of me. I'd created a human pileup. Now there was a small mass of people at the Guard's feet, and I was on my hands and knees at the bottom of the heap, right next to his boots.

Above me, the hapless victims of my plan whined and groaned. The Guard snarled angrily. He teetered against the writhing bodies shoving against him as they tried to right themselves. I lunged against the Guard's shins, hoping *all* the Guards carried the same kind of hunting knife the deadly young Guard had, smiling when I found the sheath at this one's ankle. As he took a few steps back, I unfastened the leather strap and pulled the knife free. I stuffed one hand up my shirt, holding the knife against my body, and inched forward on my knees. With my other arm, I held the Asian woman against my back like a shield, praying the Guard wouldn't notice me creeping away with his knife.

My knees were torn and bruised by the time I made it over the threshold of the city. I collapsed to the ground, trying to catch my breath. Released from my grip, the old woman rolled to the dirt, got up, and shuffled away.

The razor-sharp blade bit my skin. I needed to be careful—the knife would do me no good if I stabbed myself with it.

One glance back at the Guard told me he hadn't noticed my theft. He had returned to his task of herding people through the Suicide Gates. I scanned the wide plaza in which I lay. No one was paying attention to me. I got to my feet.

New arrivals dotted the open square, taking a few moments to recover before wandering off. Freed or imprisoned—I didn't know which. I watched the Gates slam shut one more time and then turned toward the interior of the city, taking in all the details I'd never really noticed before. Old-fashioned gaslights lined the cobblestone streets, giving off a sickish pale glow. None of the light extended more than a few feet beyond each lamp, leaving broad patches of darkness along the road. Unlike the streets, which were uniform in style, the buildings in front of me were an odd assortment. The one on my left was modern, like an office building, all right angles, reflective gray glass, and metal. To my right, a crumbling adobe house squatted stolidly at the edge of the square. East meets Southwest. The city planners in hell either had very bad taste or a strange sense of humor.

I trudged forward slowly, like the people around me, even though I wanted to sprint for cover. I bent over, one arm curled around my middle, hoping any Guard who saw me would assume I was nursing an injury rather than concealing a weapon. My pants were splotched with blood from my knees, so I certainly looked the part. I felt nothing but relief as I finally reached an alley off the main road.

I crouched at the mouth of the alley for several seconds, listening for the presence of things I might not be able to see under the blanket of darkness. Hearing nothing, I sank into the murk and started to watch.

SIX

I HAD SPENT YEARS living in and around Providence. I had been to Boston many times. Once, in middle school, I even got to go on a field trip to New York City. The dark city was nothing like those cities.

In cities, the smells assaulted me. Diesel, dust, spice, salt, aggressive and sharp, rubbing against my skin, embedding themselves in my nose. In the dark city, scents were faint and thin—nothing to hold on to, nothing that repelled me, nothing that drew me in.

In cities, even at night, light pierced through the spaces in beams and columns, glowing from neon tubes and giant television screens and flashing fluorescents. In the dark city, something sucked the life out of the color. Something vital had bled from it, leaving it easily defeated by darkness.

In cities, sounds were deep. All pitches and rhythms, layered and clashing. I loved to feel them vibrating in my gut like a pulse. In the dark city, sounds were shallow. Nothing startled or sang. No cars or buses. No bicycles, either. No wheels, no motors. Everyone was on foot, plodding along the roads. I was struck by the silence. No conversations. Many of those who passed my hiding place muttered softly, in all languages. But they were talking to themselves. I wondered if that was what I had looked like, wandering along in my dreams, drowning in myself. The only sound that reverberated with any power was the screech and clang of the Gates as they swung wide, welcoming the suicides.

People trudged by, watching the road in front of them. Some of them carried bags of groceries. Even though everyone here was dead, it was clear they still lived in apartments and ate food . . . and there must be a market nearby, which was good. *I* wasn't hungry, but I was betting I would need to feed Nadia as soon as I found her—she was in no shape to find herself something to eat. As soon as I found her. . . . The hugeness of this task overwhelmed me, and I pressed my back to the wall and tucked my head against my knees. "Breathe." *It might be a Rhode Island–size city, but you can do this. She got into that apartment, and now you just need to find her. Stand up and get a fucking move on, Lela Santos. Now.*

I shot to my feet and examined the stolen knife. It was a wicked-looking thing. The blade was about six inches long, curved at the tip, and serrated along the bottom edge. The molded grip was made for a hand much larger than mine. I wrapped my fingers around it and turned it in my palm—made for me or not, I could do some damage if I had to. It didn't seem like a good idea to go traipsing down the street with a knife hanging casually from one of my fists, though.

Backing farther into the alley, I stripped off my T-shirt and used the knife to cut about three inches off the bottom. I pulled and double-looped the resulting band and squeezed it back around my hips, below the waistline of my pants, and slid the knife between the strips of fabric. The makeshift sheath wouldn't last long—the blade would eventually wear through the cloth—but I was pretty sure it would survive a trip to the market. I put my shirt back on and was happy my jacket was long enough to cover the handle of the knife at my hip.

I exited the alley and proceeded in the direction from which the grocery-toting folks had come. Sure enough, a block away, a shabby brick building bore a sign: FOOD.

The advertisements in this city left something to be desired.

I peeked through the windows. I had no money and wondered if I was going to have to add petty theft to my list of sins. But there was no cashier at the front of the store, which housed just a few aisles of produce and packaged foods. People were gathering various items, placing them in bags, and walking out without paying. Maybe there was some sort of credit system?

Shuffling footsteps and the muted crinkling of paper bags were the only sounds I heard as I entered the store. Still puzzled by the lack of any monetary exchange, I decided to ask someone rather than zip straight into an afterlife of crime. A sallow-skinned woman stood in the produce aisle wearing a smock over her abundant folds of flesh. The skin under her arms wobbled as she loaded limp celery stalks, one by one, into a bag.

"Excuse me," I said as I approached her. "I'm . . . new in town. How do you pay for groceries?"

The woman stopped mid-wobble. "I've paid enough," she said in a flat monotone, her eyes filling with tears.

"Thanks, sorry to bother you," I said brightly, backtracking. I thought I'd seen a horror movie like this once and didn't want to wait for the sadistic guy in the clown mask to arrive.

I took one more look around the store, trying to figure out if anyone was in charge, and saw nothing but miserable, lost-looking people loading unappetizing food into paper bags. *If that's how they do it here* . . . I pulled a paper bag, which was ripped on one side and covered in grease spots, from a nearby stack and walked the aisles in search of rations.

Nothing looked edible.

The apples were spotted and soft. The potatoes had sprouted. The rolls were hard as rocks. Bags of crackers and chips were stacked on a little cart, but when I tried to grab one, it turned out to be connected to the bag next to it with threads of stretchy brown goo. I yanked my hand back and wiped it on my pants. Apparently, the food here was free, and I could have as much as I wanted. The problem? I didn't want any of it. I tossed the paper sack, grabbed a few rolls and the least spotty apple I could find, and left as quickly as my scraped-up legs could carry me.

I shoved the rolls in my jacket pocket and chucked the apple into an alley after my thumb sank into one of its mushy spots. I began to explore the city, counting blocks and identifying landmarks, trying not to lose my way completely.

The streets were clogged with people, but each one seemed alone, locked in a private world, oblivious to everyone else. Well, the woman in the food store had spoken to me—sort of—so maybe some of these folks would, too. Time to deploy my secret weapon. I rolled up my right jacket sleeve and approached a woman wearing a sari. "Hi," I said cheerfully. "Have you seen this girl around?"

The woman blinked up at me, then looked at my outstretched arm. She mumbled something unintelligible. Duh. She probably spoke Hindi. Or Farsi. Or Chinese. It didn't matter because whatever she spoke wasn't English, and I was a monolingual girl. She trudged away without looking at me again. I took a deep breath and managed not to scream.

Over the next several hours I showed Nadia's face to hundreds of people and searched for some hint of recognition in their eyes. Less than twenty of them spoke English. Not that it helped when they did. I couldn't get anyone to focus on the tattoo for more than a second. All of them walked away pretty much right after that. Some were too absorbed to even respond to my questioning. One guy was sitting on a bench, staring at his outstretched hand. As I tried to get his attention, a small lump of brown ooze grew on his upturned palm, almost like it had slithered from his skin. It twisted and stretched, all on its own, like a living thing, until it finally took shape. A cigar. The guy pulled a few strings of slime from its tip, stuck it in his mouth, and stared straight ahead as he chomped on it.

I backed away slowly, sank down on a stoop, and examined one of the stale rolls, thinking about how stupid and naive I'd been. Nadia could be anywhere within this maze of misery, and all I knew right now was the last place I'd seen her: a hallway with orange walls and dark pink doors. I peeked into the next dozen apartment buildings I came to, but all of them had grayish-purple walls with maroon doors.

I walked out of an apartment building, hitching a smile onto my face to combat the helpless tears threatening to break free. *Stay calm. You have the rest of your afterlife to find her.* I was 156 blocks in. Ahead of me, the pebbled surface of the road stretched into the darkness.

Stuttering steps interrupted my thoughts, and I looked up to see an elderly man approaching me. Unlike everyone else I had encountered, he seemed to be looking at me, seeing me. His face cradled a gummy smile.

"*¿Habla Española?*" he asked.

"Nope. English," I answered, thinking this was going to be a very short interaction.

"Oh, good. I thought you were one of those spics," he lisped.

I know I should have been really insulted, but there's something incredibly funny about a toothless person trying to say "spics."

Thpickth.

"Ooh, hey," I replied, "thank God I'm not one of those. I do happen to be a *spic*, though. Sorry about that." I almost walked away—it seemed wiser than punching him—but this guy was the most coherent person I'd spoken to since I'd gotten here. So I forced myself to stand there and roll up my sleeve for the hundredth time.

"No matter, no matter." He licked his lips and cheerfully waved away my undesirable ethnic origins. "Have somewhere to stay?"

"Not yet. I'm looking for someone. Have you seen this girl?" I leaned closer and showed him my arm, noticing in that moment how bad the old guy smelled. *Epic* old-man stink: rot and sick, sweet incense. I scooted back and wrestled with my gag reflex.

The old man's gnarled fingers encircled my wrist. "Perfect," he said, squeezing my arm in a shockingly strong grip. "You're perfect. Come along."

The horror of hearing those words sent a violent shudder through my body. I clenched my fist and was about to introduce him to my *perfect* uppercut when something grabbed my hair and yanked me off balance. The old man let go of me and sprinted away, eerily spry . . . *on all fours*, like the animal granny. I didn't have time to contemplate that, however, because a steel-covered arm was folding itself over my neck.

I bit back a panicked scream and tucked my chin to my chest, slipping free before my new attacker got a good grip on me. I ducked between his tree-trunk legs and was turning to scramble away when he grabbed my left ankle and, with one arm, hoisted me up in the air.

"Your friend got away," he grunted in heavily accented English as he held me up like a prize, "but you're not going to find a victim tonight, Mazikin. Tonight, all you're going to get is me."

It was, of course, one of the bull-like Guards. Brilliant. Like all the others I'd seen, my current companion wore a heavy helmet and a visor. The only part of his face I could see was his eyes, startling sea-green orbs that glowed like tiny lanterns.

Judging by how far I was from the ground, the Guard was definitely more than seven feet tall and possibly almost as wide. From our first few dance steps, I could tell I was faster than he was, but that didn't mean he was slow—I *was* the one hanging upside down, after all. My only advantage was that he obviously didn't think I was a threat. He hadn't drawn a weapon yet and was enjoying his strength advantage so much that he'd left his body and legs unshielded. Most of it was covered by armor, but there were open joints . . . and I had a knife.

Locking my arm against my body to hold the blade in place, I wriggled and squirmed, testing his strength and grip. He was straining, more interested in intimidating me than in conserving his energy. He didn't anticipate needing it. Thank God for the male ego.

His arm started to shake, sending tremors skittering along my leg. Just as it seemed he would have to put me down or use both arms to hold me, I stomped my right foot against his forearm and raised my arms to catch myself as he dropped me. I hit the ground and jumped to the side when he grabbed at me. Again he tried to get a grip on my hair. But before he could yank me up, I twisted quickly, drew the knife from its sheath, and rammed it into the opening in his armor just behind his knee. He roared and let me go.

I shed my flip-flops and took off running, exalting in my freedom. It lasted about nine seconds. I whirled around a corner and ran smack into another Guard. "I'm not as stupid as he is," the guttural voice commented just before something hit me hard on the head and everything went dark.

SEVEN

THE FLOOR BENEATH ME was cold. I tensed against the shivers, trying to remain still while I figured out where the hell I was.

Oh yeah. Hell.

I kept my eyes closed and listened. Nearby, deep voices conversed in accented English. The scuffs of their boots against stone, the clank and creak of their armor, the huffs and grunts of their breaths and laughter . . . there were at least two of them. This was very bad.

I cracked open an eye—a cell. Stone on all sides except the front, which was barred. The Guards were just on the other side. Slowly, carefully, I turned my head. It was more difficult than I expected. First, because my skull felt like it had been turned inside out. The knot on my temple ached fiercely. Second, because something was wrapped around the lower half of my face.

Oh. God. I was wearing a freaking *muzzle*.

I tried to lift my shaking hands to tug at it. But my hands . . . they were covered with leather mittens strapped tightly to my arms. Panic snaked straight up my back and into my brain. I sat up quickly.

I regretted it an instant later. My vision blurred and my head throbbed. I leaned over and dry heaved. Fortunately for my muzzled self, my stomach was empty. I curled into a ball on my side and pretended to sink back into unconsciousness, shielding my face with mittened hands but leaving a sliver of space through which I could observe the Guards. They sat at a rough wooden table in the middle of a large room, surrounded on three sides by cells like mine. Some were empty, others occupied; shadows slithered behind the bars. Gas lanterns hung from the walls and ceiling, weakly lighting the windowless space. Three wooden doors marked the rear wall.

One of the Guards noticed my movements. He shot a meaty elbow at his pal and turned to me.

The two of them approached my cage. They looked like twins. Their features were thick and bulbous, with jutting square jaws, bald scalps, and prominent foreheads that hung over glowing, jewel-colored eyes. And they both looked very interested in me.

"I think it's quite cute, Bilal. Are we sure it's a Mazikin?" said the one with sapphire-blue eyes. "It doesn't smell like one."

"Well, Hani," answered Bilal, "this one stuck Amid pretty good, which in my estimation makes it less cute and more likely to be a Mazikin."

"We'll certainly know once Malachi's done with it," Hani mused.

Bilal looked concerned. "Does Amid know it's awake?"

Hani looked back over his shoulder. "Not yet. I was hoping it would stay down until Malachi got here so he could deal with it."

All three of us jumped as one of the doors at the back of the room crashed open. Another Guard—the one I'd stabbed. "I was told Malachi has been summoned," he boomed.

"Amid, it's procedure to summon the Captain when we capture a live Mazikin," Bilal said apologetically.

"I will question it myself," snarled Amid. He pulled a set of skeleton keys from a peg on the wall and fingered them. When he found the right one, he jammed it into the keyhole at the door of my cell.

Bilal laid a hand on Amid's arm. "Remain in control of yourself."

Amid jerked his arm away. "I will question it. I bet I can get it to spill its secrets before Malachi steps over our humble threshold. Then he will see who's in control."

Hani looked at Bilal and shook his head. "Let's go get something to eat."

Bilal looked disgusted, but all he said was "Malachi will not be happy."

My heart sank as I watched them disappear through the door on the far left side of the room.

Amid wrenched open the door of my cell and took a few cautious steps inside. I lay still but could not completely conceal my helpless, terrified tremors.

"Oh good," Amid chortled evilly, "you're awake." He nearly took one of my arms out of its socket as he dragged me to my feet. "Let's go someplace where we can talk, just you and me."

Amid yanked me out of the cell and shoved me in front of him. It was all I could do to put one foot in front of the other. My head was killing me.

He clamped his enormous hands around my arms from behind. The hot tar of memory started to bubble up from the caverns of my mind. I shook my head to try to stay in the moment, knowing I'd need every bit of wit and cunning I had to make it out of this situation alive. I immediately found out shaking your head after you've just gotten a concussion is a really stupid idea, though, and was almost carried away by the waves of nausea that crashed over me.

Amid guided me roughly toward the door on our left and locked an arm around my neck as he tugged it open. Some of those thick, sticky memory bubbles popped, and I thrashed as he edged up hard behind me. Then he kicked me right at the base of my spine. I landed on my side on the rough cement floor and scrambled to my feet, but it felt like my vertebrae were in pieces, and I couldn't quite stand up straight. The floor suddenly looked very inviting.

I backed against the rear wall as Amid advanced. "I said I just wanted to talk," he explained as he reached out. "I'm going to take off your muzzle and mitts, and you're going to be a nice little monster, all right? Relax, Mazikin—I'm going to give you something you want."

I stood still as he unbuckled my restraints. As soon as they were loose, I scooted away. "Thanks," I said as I put as much distance between us as possible. The room was large, but not nearly large enough for my liking.

"How's your leg?" I asked as my gaze streaked along the walls. The only way out was the door we'd just come through. Amid grunted by way of an answer and watched me with an expression that was a nauseating combination of amusement and hatred. "By the way," I added as I edged a few inches closer to the door, "just to clear things up, my name's not Mazikin. It's Lela."

His sea-green eyes narrowed, and he knelt to pull his hunting knife from its sheath. "You can call yourself whatever you want." His gaze bored into mine as he sent the knife sliding across the floor toward me. "Now—try to cut me again."

Well, shit.

Because I had no choice, I scooped the knife from the floor. I wondered whether it was going to be plunged into my flesh sometime in the next few minutes. It seemed highly likely.

"I thought we were going to talk," I said in what I hoped was a friendly voice. "I really *am* sorry about your leg. You kind of caught me by surprise. Survival instinct, you know. Nothing personal."

I shuffled sideways, trying to find a path to the door that kept me out of his reach. He grunted again and stalked toward me. Crap. This guy was going to slaughter me, and I had no idea why, apart from the fact that I'd escaped the first time he'd tried. It seemed like a case of mistaken identity—he kept calling me a Mazikin, and I had nothing to do with those sword-wielding folks the other Guard had killed. I crouched low (in part because I couldn't actually stand up straight) and realized I had nowhere to go. He was now between me and the door.

For a crazy moment I pondered whether there might be an afterlife after my afterlife. When he killed me, where would I go? I was already dead. Wasn't dying once enough? For me, it definitely was. Desperate to postpone my seemingly inevitable second death just a few moments longer, I cocked my arm and threw the knife with all the strength I had.

Amid had obviously not expected me to do something so ballsy. He looked down, stupidly surprised, at the knife sticking out of his gut.

It took me less than a second to see it wasn't deep enough to slow the freaking rhino down, and I was limping along the edge of the wall before he'd pulled the blade from his belly. Although I expected to feel it between my ribs any moment, I just couldn't kick the habit of survival.

He laughed. "That was a good trick, Mazikin. But I hope you have something better than that."

I scuttled like a pathetic crab around the edge of the room. "Nope. Any chance you'd believe me if I told you again that I'm not a Mazikin?"

"Nope," he mimicked. He blocked my path to the door with two long strides as he threw the knife into the farthest corner of the room. "Care to try again?"

"No." I shrank back, trapped.

"Too bad." He punched me sharply in the side, sending me straight to the floor. I collapsed in on myself, all my smart words gone, unable to breathe, wondering absently if the ribs he'd shattered had punctured a lung. Amid grabbed my ankle and jerked me toward him. "Stand up, Mazikin."

I actually tried to comply, anything to keep him from hitting me again. But I didn't move fast enough for him. He grabbed my hair and wrenched me to my feet, then pressed me back into the corner, bending over me. The fog of his breath coiled around me, dragging me back in time.

On my belly in the dark and the weight of his body presses me into pink sheets.

No. Not again. This will not happen again. My fist shot up and connected with Amid's nose as I reached for his baton with my other hand. I tore it free as he stumbled back, transferring it to my left hand because I couldn't raise my right arm above my shoulder. I took a desperate, running leap and smacked him across the face with the baton. The crunch of it vibrated up my arm. He bellowed in pain. I threw myself toward the door and reached it just as he charged.

I managed to bang and scream for help only once before he grabbed me again. He slammed my head into the door and whipped me back, sending me crashing into another wall. I tried to swing the baton at him, but I couldn't breathe. I couldn't see. I just flailed, helpless. I heard the snap of the bones in my wrist as he twisted my arm away from his weapon, but the pain did not hit me fully until he pinned me against the wall again, holding my arms above my head.

I screamed for help, for mercy, for vengeance, face and hips and knees pressed against the cinder blocks, drowning in panicked memories. I was there but not *there*. Despite my crazed struggling, my mind was unforgiving—it easily registered the sickening pressure of Amid's body as he crushed me against the wall. No. *No.*

I kicked but couldn't hit anything. Streaks of light and dark blazed across my vision. His thick fingers curled into the hair at my scalp as he lurched my head back and bounced it off the wall again. And then I couldn't see anything at all. Grunts and whimpers flew from my mouth until I ran out of air. Amid was too close behind me to allow me to draw a breath. *Facedown in the pink sheets, suffocating. No one will hear my screams.*

Then several things happened at once, and I was only able to sort it out later. The door of the room splintered and fell open. A voice shook the walls with fury as it roared, "*No.*" The weight at my back lifted. The cement of the floor greeted me like a long-lost friend. Metal hit flesh with smacking thuds punctuated by Amid's grunts of pain. Voices argued in an incomprehensible language. It might have been English, but I was past understanding.

I was too busy dying. Again.

EIGHT

SHEETS BENEATH ME. FINGERS touching my face.

No, shrieked a voice. My voice.

I pressed myself to the floor, heart pounding. My face was wet. I wiped at it impatiently and crouched low next to an empty cot. Its rumpled sheet tangled around my naked body.

From my position on the floor, I could see a table across from me, surrounded by two folding chairs. A gas lantern sitting on the table was the only source of light, battling futilely against the darkness that claimed most of the room. My eyes skimmed along the wall to my left until they found the door. Before I had time to seriously consider bolting, a voice interrupted my escape plans.

"It's locked. And you should know better." It was a male voice, accent clipped and precise, coming from my right, on the other side of the room. I pulled the sheet tighter around my body and raised my head over the edge of the cot.

He sat on a folding chair several feet away, leaning back so I couldn't see his features in the shadows. "I guess you're not thirsty after all," he commented. With a hollow clunk, he set what must have been a cup on the floor.

There was something familiar about him.

"It's okay with me if you want to stay where you are," he continued, "but you might be more comfortable if you got back in bed. You've been through a lot."

"What happened?" I assumed he would know what I meant. Before I'd lost consciousness, I'd been sure I was dying of internal injuries. And my wrist had been shattered. Now—I felt fine. Absolutely fine.

"Your physical injuries were healed."

"You must have a hell of a medical facility here then," I snapped. "Why did I have any injuries at all? I'm dead, right?"

He chuckled drily. "We're all dead. But we breathe. We bleed, too. The body you have here can be hurt just like the one you had before. It can be killed as well. And you never know where you'll end up if that happens."

I nodded cautiously.

"There's a clean shirt and pants here for you." He tossed the garments onto the cot between us, along with a flimsy pair of slippers.

I reached for them. "Turn your back."

He laughed. "You're joking, right? If you want to put the clothes on, put them on. Or feel free to crouch on the floor, wrapped in a sheet. Either way, we're going to talk."

This time I was the one who laughed, but even to me, it sounded just this side of hysterical. "The last time one of you said that to me, it didn't go so well."

"Ah. I'm sorry about that. Amid has been short-tempered and restless lately. And you humiliated him—*several* times. But what he did was unacceptable. We don't work like that."

"Glad to hear it." I glared at him as I sat down on the floor and tied the sheet around the back of my neck so it covered the front of my body. I pulled the pants on under it and wrenched the shirt over the top. Unfortunately, the shirt was more like a tent, and the pants hung loosely from my hips, threatening a humiliating slide at the worst moment. "Would a belt be too much to ask?"

"It would," he said as he stood up and leaned forward into the weak pool of lamplight, giving me the first real glimpse of his face. "I'm Malachi, by the way." He held out his hand.

Crap. It was him—the Guard from the street fight. The guy the rhino Guards had said would wring the truth out of me. The one they seemed to fear and hate. The one who murdered two people right in front of Nadia.

His features were smooth and unlined, and yet somehow still carried that air of ferocity and defiance I'd observed before. The deep voids of his eyes were surrounded by thick, black lashes and full of confidence and threat. It was as if he'd already assessed my weaknesses and ticked off all the possible ways to kill me, so now he could relax and be friendly. His was not a soft face, but it held a harsh, dangerous sort of beauty. *Dangerous* being the operative word. I reached out carefully to shake his hand, like I might pet a viper or a shark.

"I'm Lela."

His hand was warm over mine. His grip was strong. I pulled back quickly. He let me, though his gaze lingered on mine. "A pleasure, Lela. Now, please tell me what you're doing in my city."

"Um . . . the same thing as everyone else. I killed myself," I explained dully, trying to droop my face into that look of sorrowful self-absorption I'd seen on all the residents in this city. I'd seen what he did to people who defied him, and I didn't feel like being introduced to the business end of his knife. I would play dumb until I figured out the magical combination of words that would spring the lock on this cage.

"Your behavior suggests you have another agenda." His voice was mild as he pulled out one of the folding chairs next to the table and sat down. He crossed his arms over his chest and leaned back. He wasn't wearing armor or any obvious weaponry and looked perfectly casual in a pair of fatigue pants and a snug, long-sleeved T-shirt. He looked like any ordinary high school senior. One who was in terrific shape. One who killed people in his spare time.

Satisfied that he was at a reasonably safe distance, I sank down on the cot, happy not to have to hold my pants up any longer. "I don't know what you're talking about," I replied, still attempting to sound mournful.

His eyebrows shot up, though he didn't really look surprised. "Is that so? Let me give *you* some information, then. Apart from the Guards, there are only two types of creatures in this city who pay any attention to others. Most of the souls within these walls are pretty busy dealing with themselves. But I think you know that."

"Who says I'm not busy dealing with myself?"

"You were seen trying to talk to several people last night."

I rolled my eyes, then caught myself and tried to look depressed again. "Is that against the law here?"

He smiled. "Not at all," he said evenly, "but it does draw our attention."

"I haven't been here long. I'm just trying to figure this place out."

"Again, that's not typical behavior for the residents of this city. Which makes you one of two things. Either you're a Mazikin, and I will destroy you, or you are ready to go before the Judge and get out of this city."

I definitely did not want to be destroyed. I also didn't want to get out of the city. Well, I did, desperately—but not before I found Nadia. "I have no idea what a Mazikin is. I'd know if I was one, right? I'm not quite ready to leave, though. I have some issues to deal with . . . ." I tried to sound dazed.

God, I am such a pathetic actress.

The side of his mouth twitched, like he was trying not to laugh. "Lela, you have exhibited some very *aggressive* behavior. You assaulted a Guard when he tried to place you under arrest—"

That jerked my head up. "Hey now, he didn't say anything about arresting me. One minute I'm minding my own business, and the next he's assaulting *me*."

His eyes flashed. "He said you were consorting with a known Mazikin recruiter."

"What? I'd never seen that creepy little man until right before your friend jumped me."

"What did he say to you? What were you talking about?"

"He made some racist comment and then tried to get me to go with him."

"Did he say where?" He leaned forward, his elbows on his knees. He looked like he was ready to take action, which made me shrink back instinctively.

"He didn't have time. Your friend Amid rudely interrupted our conversation." My mouth didn't cower with the rest of me.

He sat back, as if I had disappointed him. "Ah, well, if he hadn't, you'd have found yourself in some very serious trouble."

I scoffed, the heat of frustration blasting along my skin. "Yeah, thanks. Glad I'm not in any 'serious trouble.' What the hell is wrong with you? I guess getting beaten to death by a huge, scary troll is just the funny, unserious kind of trouble around here . . . ."

"Again, I apologize for what Amid did. The Guards thought you were a Mazikin. I don't excuse their behavior, but they are on edge right now." The folding chair squeaked across the floor as he rose to pace. "In addition to their usual activities, Mazikin have killed five Guards in the last month, including Amid's closest friend."

Before I saw him move, he leaned over me, his face inches from mine, his arms braced on either side of the cot. He inhaled deeply, just like he'd done to Nadia. "You don't smell like them. But you don't smell like any of the others, either."

I managed to stay very still, terrified of what he would do next. His cheek brushed mine. All my muscles contracted at once, and my skin was suddenly too tight. I shook my head, trying to release some of the heat pooling in my cheeks. He pulled back abruptly. "If you're helping them, I'm going to find out. Tell me what I need to know now or—"

"Or what?" I challenged, refusing to back down from the threat in his eyes, glad for the reminder to stay focused. "You're going to pull an Amid and 'talk' to me?"

He made a frustrated sound and resumed his pacing. "It's my job to keep the residents of this city safe."

"Yeah," I muttered, "by cutting their throats."

"What did you say?"

"Nothing. I'm sure you're very good at your *job*."

He halted midpace and put his hands on his hips. "I need to know why you're in this city. You clearly don't belong here, but you don't seem to want to leave. Nearly everyone here wants to leave or at least find some kind of escape. So, since you don't, I need to know what you *do* want. Maybe I can help you."

I was so desperate to find Nadia that for a half second I wondered if maybe he could. He'd seen Nadia—maybe he knew where she was. Then the face of the frightened housewife shimmered in my head. He'd killed her in cold blood.

No, Malachi would not help me, and I couldn't trust him with Nadia. Or myself, for that matter.

"Help me? I'm surprised you haven't killed me yet."

"Do I look like someone who would want to kill you?" He smiled in a charming sort of way, obviously trying to look harmless. I almost laughed. He wasn't a very good actor either.

When I didn't answer, he sank back into the folding chair. "All right, you won't tell me why you're here. Let's try some simpler questions, then. Although it appears contrary to your very nature, could you *try* to give me some straightforward answers? Were you in the military?"

"Are you kidding me? I was in high school."

"High school," he said quietly. "You're American. And a civilian?"

"Uh, yes. An American civilian."

"Lovely. A straight answer. Keep it up. Did somebody train you?"

"No, nobody trained me. Unless you count the Rhode Island child welfare and juvenile justice systems. Why?"

Malachi held up his hand and ticked off the reasons with his fingers. "You stole a Guard's weapon. If I'm not mistaken, it belonged to a Gate Guard. Which means you managed to do it on your way into the city. You escaped Amid even after he had you in hand. You slashed his leg in just the right place, preventing him from chasing you.

Under extreme duress, injured and cornered, you threw a knife and hit a target—"

"It's not like I hit something vital."

"Under duress," he replied smoothly. "After he cracked several of your vertebrae and broke your ribs, you struck him with the force and angle necessary to break his nose—in very close quarters and despite his considerable size advantage. And then you stole one of his weapons and used it to shatter his cheekbone. That is my concrete, tangible evidence that you've been well trained. But how about the intangibles?"

He pointed a finger at me and continued. "You are crafty—I'm willing to bet you had a plan when you came into this city. You are observant—I can see it in every sweep of your eyes across this room. And you continued fighting in the face of insurmountable odds and what was, I do not doubt, excruciating pain. You were *still* trying to fight when I pulled Amid off you and picked you up off that floor, despite the fact that your injuries would likely have been fatal. So," he concluded, leaning forward with his elbows on his knees, "my theory is that you were trained and sent to infiltrate this city. I just want to know why."

Oh my God. No one in my whole life had ever given me that much credit. Too bad it was coming in exactly the wrong situation from exactly the wrong person. He made me sound like some assassin ninja spy. Watch out for evil Super Lela, here to bring your city down from the inside! I started to giggle. "For all your *evidence*, you have drawn some seriously demented conclusions."

In an instant he was out of his chair and behind me on the cot, pulling me against him, a long arm encircling me and pinning my arms in front of me.

I drew my feet up and stomped them on the mattress as I arched back. His head smacked against the wall, but he was much taller and stronger. He bent forward, folding me into a painful position that kept my legs straight and stole my leverage. Fighting my rising panic, I threw my head back in an effort to smash his face, but all it hit was the rock-hard ridge of his shoulder. He had positioned himself perfectly, preventing me from being able to strike at him in any way. Even through the inky wash of frantic thoughts and memories, I registered the snick of a blade being drawn.

I should have known he'd be armed.

He held the hunting knife in his right hand and used its razor-sharp tip to edge up the loose sleeve of my shirt, revealing my tattoo. I started to tremble. I hated feeling weak. I hated him even more for making me feel it.

"I've really enjoyed talking with you, but please don't mistake my amusement for patience," he said in a perfectly calm, completely deadly voice. His breath was warm as it skimmed across my cheek. "I take my job very seriously. Which means, unfortunately for you, that I will do whatever is necessary to discover your true purpose for being here." He positioned the blade of the knife against my arm, just above the tattoo. I bit back a whimper and tried to struggle, but he pressed the edge of the blade a little harder into my arm. I held still.

"That's better, thank you. Now, I believe this face is important to you. So if you don't tell me why you're here, right now, I will slice it off your arm and burn it in front of you. Do you believe me, Lela?"

I nodded. Furious tears streamed from the corners of my eyes, wetting his cheek. He smiled against my skin. "Speak, or I start cutting."

I knew he'd do it. I'd seen what he was capable of. He would steal Nadia from me forever if I didn't speak. "I'm here for her," I moaned. "I came here to get her out."

He pulled the blade away, letting it hover now, a threat, a promise. "Who is she?"

"Nadia. My best friend. She killed herself. I don't even know why. But she's here, and she's so scared." I cried helplessly, sagging forward. "I snuck into the city to get her." Malachi was motionless and silent. I took a chance. "Please," I begged, "after you kill me, don't go after her. She will never get out without help. Without me. She's no threat to you."

"I know that," he said dismissively. The stubble on his jaw scraped against my temple as he spoke. "You said you sneaked into the city. Didn't you arrive at the Suicide Gates?"

"No, not really. When I . . . died, I arrived outside, in a field. But I saw the city, and I knew that's where she was. I couldn't stay out there when I knew she was trapped in here."

"Are you telling me you arrived in the Countryside and *chose* to come into the city? To rescue your friend?" He sounded completely baffled.

"Yes. I didn't want to, but she needs me. I had to try." I stared at Nadia's face on my arm, knowing I would never see that face in person again. My tears hit the tattoo, became Nadia's tears.

"You didn't want to," he repeated, his voice harboring a million questions. But he didn't ask them. Instead, he straightened, giving me a little breathing room. His arm was wrapped across my chest, and his fingers curled over my shoulder, resting gently on me, almost tenderly, in sharp contrast to the blade he held in his other hand. I ventured a glance at his face.

"I think I believe you," he said quietly. His gaze dropped to my arm. "But how did you know what awaited you here?"

The bitter bark of laughter escaped before I could stop it. "I think it would be fair to say I grossly underestimated what awaited me here."

"You had a plan coming in. You have her face on your arm, you—"

"I had her face tattooed on my arm because I wanted her with me."

"But that's what you were doing, wasn't it? You were asking people if they'd seen her."

"Yes."

He shook his head. "So how did you know she was here? No one on Earth knows about this place. They only guess: Purgatory. Hell. Naraka. Hawiyah. Hades. Sheol. Gehenna. All religions attempt to explain what happens to people who kill themselves, but no one is certain. Many people who arrive here are in shock for a long time once they see where they are. How did *you* know what to expect?" His arms tightened around me as his thighs tensed on either side of mine.

The fluttering pace of my heart nearly choked me. There probably wouldn't be a second chance if he didn't like my answer, but I had no brain space for anything but the truth. "I . . . I tried to kill myself once. I showed up at the Gates and was about to go through when I was revived. But ever since then, this place has haunted me. I never really got away from it. I dreamed of it. Sometimes I even saw it—like a shadow over the real world. It was scary as hell, and I hated it, but it made me want to live."

"You wandered the city even when you were alive?"

Praying he would believe me, I nodded my head, and it bounced off his collarbone.

"I have heard of this," he said thoughtfully. "Ghosts who roam the city but are not really part of it. It makes sense that it would be people who had tried to kill themselves but did not succeed. But that doesn't explain how you know about your friend."

"When Nadia died, I started having nightmares and visions of her here. I was inside her head, seeing and feeling everything with her. I saw her come into the city. I've seen her wandering every day, starving and frightened. And I saw things I'd never noticed before in my own nightmares."

I saw you kill people.

"You saw the Guards. You noticed where we keep our weapons."

"Yes. When I decided to come get her, I thought I might need to defend myself. And her." *From you.*

"But these visions of your friend. Did you have *that* ability before?"

"You mean, was I, like, psychic or something? Uh, no."

A few minutes ticked by in silence. I tried not to squirm, but his breath was hot on my skin. His heart beat against my spine, making my insides vibrate in time with its rhythm. It was too much. Too much closeness. Too much heat. I couldn't translate the mixed signals inside my own body, let alone the warmth coming from his. Just when I was about to lose it, he said, "I'm going to let go of you slowly. I'm not going to hurt you, and I'd appreciate it if you wouldn't try to hurt me, though I guess I'd understand if you did."

He spread his arms. I darted forward and turned around, backing up against the wall with a folding chair between us.

Malachi sighed, eyeing my white-knuckled grip on the back of the chair. "Please don't try to hit me with that."

"So what happens now?" I asked, pleased that I sounded calm and controlled rather than like a seething mass of fury and despair and confusion.

He held my gaze for a moment, then looked away. "I'm sorry to tell you this, but you're on an impossible mission. Three thousand people arrive at the Suicide Gates every single day. Haven't you noticed the size of this city? You could wander for years and never find her. And if by some miracle you did, there is only one way out. You have to go before the Judge. If your friend is not ready to receive a positive verdict, she will not get out. End of story."

I clenched my teeth. "I have to find her. It's the only reason I'm here."

"I'm sorry, but I can't allow you to do that."

I pressed my back against the wall and looked to see if the knife was still in his hand. It wasn't. I'd been watching him for all but a few seconds, and he'd somehow concealed it again without my noticing.

As often as I'd assessed people for their soft spots, their vulnerabilities and weaknesses, I recognized a person without any. But then I saw an opening. I stared at him, taking in the glint of curiosity in his eyes as he returned my scrutiny, the subtle slide of his gaze along my body and over my face. Despite being on duty as my inquisitor and guard, he had just checked me out. As much as I hated to think about it, as much as I could barely stand any guy looking at me like that, a sneaky, sleazy thought occurred to me. *Maybe you could use this to get to his key . . . .*

I pushed the thought away and my gaze flicked back to the door, but his body blocked it from sight in the next second. "Don't, Lela." He pinned the folding chair to the ground with one of his knees. "You were in the Countryside—you know what it's like there. Don't you want to go back?"

What was I supposed to say to that? Of course I wanted to go back. I bowed my head. I couldn't look him in the eye.

"Most people here can't see it, even when they're right next to the wall. They're so absorbed in their own sadness that they can't see past the darkness. But you can. You belong out there." Something longing and broken in his voice brought my eyes to his. He moved a little closer. "I can take you to the Judge. I will take you myself."

Like a probation officer. Perfect. "I've been before judges in the past. Not pleasant experiences."

"This will be different, believe me. You'll get out."

I looked up at him and felt like I was drowning. Like I was sinking with weighted limbs into a bottomless sea, watching Nadia grow more distant and unreachable as I descended. Everyone has a limit, and I'm no different. I was tired and frightened and wanted to surrender to him. Certainly there seemed no way to defeat him. Then I looked down at my arm.

I shook my head. "You have no grounds to keep me here. I have to go find her."

He laughed bitterly and took a step back, moving his knee off the chair. "Where do you think you are?" He scoffed. "Americans. Your conceptions of civil rights have become truly comical. Look, I can keep you here for years if I want to. But that's not what I'm going to do. Instead, I will get you out of this city, whether you want to go or not."

I couldn't push my sneaky thought away any longer. Arguing wasn't working, so I had to go for pathetic and manipulative. And utterly terrifying. I took a deep breath. "All right," I said, stepping around the chair. "Fine. I'll go. Thank you for helping me."

He watched me with narrowed eyes as I approached him. I forced my feet forward, dread rising with each step. Did I really want to poke a sharp stick at this particular dragon?

I *had* to. If I could find and steal his key, I could figure out how to get out of there. He watched the motion of my hand as it rose slowly between us and came to rest on his chest. I hoped the way my hands shook would work in my favor. That he would interpret my unsteadiness as desire instead of fear. Encouraged by the hitch in his breath, by the way his eyes widened slightly as I touched him, I slid my other hand along his waist, searching for a key ring . . . and finding nothing but a *lot* of muscles.

His heart pounded beneath my palm, and I hoped his hormones might take over, that he might start acting like an actual teenage guy instead of a Guard. I leaned my forehead against his chest as spots floated across my vision. *Don't chicken out. This is for Nadia.*

His fingers closed around my chin and tipped it up until I was looking into his eyes. Every part of me tensed to keep from stumbling back. With agonizing slowness, he bent his head until his mouth was just a fraction of an inch from mine. My stomach lurched as I stared into his dangerous, dark gaze.

Stay still. You have to get that key.

My breath escaped my lungs in uneven little huffs. I wasn't sure I could endure this without screaming. It was too confusing and too intense. Too close, too real, too likely to get out of control. Too dangerous, too hot. Would he hurt me? Would he be rough? I almost pulled back at the raw images that plowed through my head.

But I had survived rough. I'd gotten pretty good at disconnecting my brain from my body when I absolutely had to.

I could get through it for her. Not wanting to think about it anymore, I tried to press my lips to his, but his fingers tightened on my chin and stopped me. For a moment he held me there. He closed his eyes and breathed me in. His fingers spread from my chin to stroke my cheek, a feather of a touch. I held my breath, waiting for his mouth to descend on mine, wondering what it would feel like, terrified to find out.

"I know what you're doing," he whispered against my mouth. I froze. He stepped away from me nimbly, wearing an amused smile. "I don't blame you for trying, but it's unnecessary. And I'm afraid you've just won yourself a stay in the holding cell. I'll come get you in the morning and take you to the Sanctum—where the Judge presides."

I stared at him, slack jawed, humiliated—and shamefully relieved. He hammered on the door twice with his closed fist, never taking his eyes off mine. Keys jangled as someone outside unlocked the door. He didn't have a key. He had locked himself in there with me. I felt very stupid.

Thus ended my initial foray as a sex kitten.

NINE

I PACED MY CELL, having fantasies about Malachi—specifically how I would like to kill him. It had been a while since I'd felt so out of control and off balance with another person. I liked being in control. It was why I hated pills. And alcohol. And most grown-ups. Staying one step ahead was the only way to keep myself from getting hurt again.

But Malachi seemed to know every move I would make *before* I made it. He seemed to know which buttons to push and had done so with a smile. The way he stared at me made me squirm. I only spent half a moment considering whether I'd be able to get away from him once he came to get me. He'd probably be ready for me to try.

My current babysitter, a Guard named Lutfi, had long since slumped over the Guards' table. His deep, rumbling snores scraped at my ears. As loud as they were, and with all my churning thoughts, I almost missed the urgent sound of a voice. My next-door neighbor—a fellow prisoner.

"Hey, girl. Can you hear me?" The sound came from the back of the cell.

I spun around. Near the bench that lined the back of the tiny space, just at the juncture of the two walls, a single brick had been chipped away, leaving a small hole. I pressed in and saw a pair of dark brown eyes looking back at me. "Are they going to execute you?"

I cringed. "I don't think so. Malachi said he was going to take me before the Judge."

"Malachi," the voice growled, drawing out each syllable with hatred. "Malachi is bad. He will kill you, girl."

"I think if he wanted to, he would have by now." I wasn't sure why I was defending him, except that, apart from being completely frustrating, he'd actually been pretty gentle and kind to me. He'd only seemed to want me to go back out into the Countryside. It wasn't his fault that I had no intention of doing that until I found Nadia.

"Malachi is ruthless. He will make you believe anything. He will kill you when he gets what he wants from you. He and his Guards have killed so many of my family," the voice whispered, then coughed out a sob.

"Oh my God. I'm so sorry."

"They're going to kill me, too, but Malachi will torture me first. That's what he always does, girl."

"Please call me Lela."

"Lela. I am Sil."

"Why are they keeping you here?" I stared into his eyes, wondering if he was just as innocent as I was.

"I am a Mazikin."

"That's what they thought I was, but nobody has told me what Mazikin are. Will you?"

Sil laughed, a rasping, high-pitched noise. "Come have a look, then." His eyes disappeared, leaving a peephole. I put my face to it. He stood back in his cell, looking exactly like . . . a Japanese businessman. Complete with suit and tie. And muzzle and mittens. I was reminded of the diverse group that had attacked Malachi in the street. He'd referred to them as Mazikin, too.

"Um, you look like everyone else here."

He stroked his mittens down his wiry physique, over his rumpled, dirty business attire. "Because we *are* like everyone else. But we are going to escape."

"Malachi said Mazikin have killed five Guards."

Sil nodded. "The Guards, they do not understand us. We come from a terrible place and we have ended up in a terrible place. It is hell, girl. All we want is to be free of it. But the Captain and his Guards do not think the Mazikin are worthy of happiness." He sniffled, and his face crumpled up, like he was trying not to cry again. "They do horrible things to us. They kill us for good. Forever." He raised his head and looked at me. His eyes were dark, peering at me from over the ridge of his muzzle. "We try to fight back. Sometimes we win. But they are merciless."

So "Mazikin" was like a resistance movement. That made sense as I remembered Malachi's fight with Ibram and the others. I looked Sil up and down. He seemed completely harmless. And the Guards, with their armor and weapons . . . it didn't seem fair. I glanced back at Lutfi, slumped on the table, scimitar at his side. I shivered. I think Sil noticed. "Girl. Lela. I have to get out of here. If you help me, I'll get you out, too."

Escape. That sounded good. I would disappear into the city. I would know how to avoid the Guards from now on. I would be much more careful. I would find Nadia and prove Malachi wrong.

"Count me in, but it has to be right now. He's coming back for me."

"Do you think you could unfasten my mitts?"

"Absolutely," I replied, heart speeding. I watched Lutfi closely, but he seemed unconscious and was still snoring loudly. My hand was narrow enough to fit through the hole, and Sil held up his arm. He whispered instructions as my fingers worked the buckles. After several minutes, Sil's hand was free, and he unfastened his other mitt. Hands unfettered, he unbuckled his muzzle, ripping it off his face in a near-frantic motion.

He threw his head back and took a deep, relieved breath. "Thank you."

He proceeded to dismantle the muzzle with amazing efficiency and soon had several pieces of metal in front of him. "I think I was an engineer, before," he commented as he worked, which struck me as a strange statement. Did people forget their lives if they were here long enough? His gaze flicked back to mine. "Do you think you could get the Guard out of the room?"

"Are you serious?"

Sil nodded emphatically. "Yes. You aren't muzzled. You aren't the same kind of prisoner I am. And you are attractive to them. They were talking about it earlier." *Ew, gross.* "And you are smaller than I am. He will not consider you a threat. Tell him you have to go to the bathroom. The Guards have one down the hall."

This already sounded like a very bad plan, but desperation drove me forward. "What are you going to do?"

He smiled as he examined the various parts of his disassembled muzzle. "You'll see. Don't worry. No one will get hurt, and we'll get out quickly. Give me a moment."

I watched as he repositioned the muzzle and mittens. He obviously wanted Lutfi to believe they were still fastened. Sil lay down on his bench. "Now."

I cleared my throat. *Here goes.* "Um, Lutfi?"

Lutfi jerked to attention with a grunt. "Eh?"

"I am so sorry to wake you," I said in my most helpless voice. "It's just . . . um, there's no toilet in this cell . . . and I need to go."

"Oh." The blush on his bulbous cheeks made him instantly less intimidating. "Certainly. Promise you won't try anything tricky? Don't break my nose or anything, little one." He laughed to himself, as if the prospect was ludicrous.

He took the ring of keys from its peg on the wall and unlocked my cell. He stepped back and pulled the door open, fastening the keys to his belt. I walked in front of him, his enormous, heavy palm resting on my shoulder. He was much gentler than Amid.

Through the middle door, to the right, then the left, down a stone hallway, the third door on the left. This place was a freaking maze, just like the rest of the city. The gray, musty bathroom contained a leaky sink and an extraordinarily large toilet. You had to pull some sort of chain to get it to flush.

I didn't need to go, though. Not hungry, not thirsty, so . . . I sat in the dingy chamber, staring at the strange assortment of porcelain figurines that lined the walls. Most of them were baby animals.

Lutfi courteously gave me privacy. I took my time, wanting to give Sil as much opportunity as possible to do whatever he was going to do. To occupy myself, I ripped my pants at the waist and tied the two frayed edges tightly together, making it far less likely that they would pool around my feet as I tried to flee. My heart pounded so frantically I was sure it was going to crack my newly healed ribs.

Finally, Lutfi knocked on the door. "Um, how are you doing in there?"

"I'm almost finished, thank you!" I dared to wait another minute and then emerged. His face was bright pink as he directed me back to the cell room. I walked as slowly as possible, praying he couldn't hear the blasts of my breath or the jackhammering of my heart.

"I hear you're going to the Sanctum to see the Judge in a few hours," he said. "The Captain says you'll get out. I'm glad for you, little one. You'll love it in the Countryside."

"Have you been there?" I hoped I sounded friendly rather than terrified.

"Ah, no." His guttural voice was wistful. "We're not allowed to go out there. We were created to guard the Shadowlands, and so we do until we die. But I can see it beyond the walls. Someday I will go. Not yet, though."

He winked as he pushed open the door of the cell room and put an arm out to guide me through. I caught a blur of movement out of the corner of my eye. Lutfi gasped and shoved me away from him.

"Run," he grunted as I hit the floor.

I rolled just in time to see Sil—who had pulled Lutfi's scimitar free while the Guard's hands were occupied—use the weapon with merciless efficiency. Lutfi fell to the floor without a sound. His head landed a few feet away, his amethyst eyes condemning me.

Sil turned to me and smiled. "Picked the lock," he said proudly, still holding the bloody sword. I tried to tamp down my certainty that I'd just made a terrible mistake while Sil removed Lutfi's sword belt and fastened it around his own waist, cinching it tight. He sheathed the scimitar and came toward me, his hand outstretched. His fingernails were disturbingly long and pointed. I wondered why I hadn't seen it before. "Let's go."

"Um . . . I think I'll just go on my own—"

"No, we can use you. You're perfect." His fingers curled around my upper arm, and he yanked me up. I was too shocked to fight back. I couldn't stop staring at Lutfi's slack face. I swear I could smell the rusty tang of his blood.

Sil tugged me roughly through the door. He stopped cold as a Guard entered the hallway from a room a few doors down.

It was Malachi.

He was wearing his leather armor and looked just as he had the first time I saw him through the eyes of my terrified friend. Only taller. More frightening. More beautiful. His eyes were on his shoulder as he fiddled with a buckle on his breastplate. His mouth twisted up at one corner in a secret smile. In the flash of a second before he saw us, I had time to wonder what thoughts could have put such a whimsical look on his serious face.

The smile disappeared, replaced by a grim line.

Sil and Malachi stared at each other, and then both moved simultaneously. Malachi reached for his knives, and Sil pulled me in front of him, shielding himself. Sil's hand went around my neck. His fingernails scraped against my skin. I smelled incense and something else, something rancid. His breath on my neck. His mouth was an inch away from my throat. That familiar panic struck me. I had to get away from him.

Stay here, stay now, I chanted to myself, chasing away the memories. *Stay focused. Get away.*

Just as my elbow arced forward, Malachi spoke very calmly. "Don't move, Lela. Don't fight him. Mazikin are venomous."

That froze me in place. It wasn't only what he had said. It was because, beneath the evenness of his voice, I heard it: fear. For me.

"Smart, Malachi." Sil's nose traced the junction of my shoulder and neck. I shuddered.

Malachi's jaw clenched. That muscle on the left side started to jump.

Sil chuckled. "My teeth will be deep in her neck if you don't get your hands away from those filthy knives of yours." He sounded like he was having fun.

I stared at Malachi, wishing I could explain, wondering why I wanted to try, knowing there was no adequate explanation. Yet again I'd been an idiot. Desperate to escape, I'd overlooked every danger sign, believed every word Sil had said, and ignored everything Malachi had told me. I had underestimated Sil's lethality and set up Lutfi, who'd spent the last second of his life trying to save mine, whose last word had been meant to ensure my survival.

"That's better," sneered Sil as Malachi raised his hands in the air. "Now, this girl and I are going to depart, and you are going to stay where you are. If I even think you are following, I will kill her, as slowly as possible." He giggled as his fingernails skimmed along my collarbone. "I won't extend her the same courtesy I did Lutfi, for instance."

Malachi's eyes narrowed in hatred as they shifted from me to Sil, but he didn't look surprised. No doubt he'd already noticed Lutfi's belt fastened at Sil's waist. "I won't follow," he said icily. "She obviously wants to go with you more than she wanted to go to the Sanctum, so she's all yours. I'd just kill her anyway for helping you escape."

My heart stuttered with fear at his words, but Sil's grip on me tightened. "Liar. You've already given yourself away,

Captain. If that were true, she'd already be dead. And so would I. Mazikin are not as stupid as you think."

I moaned quietly. Malachi probably *would* want to kill me as soon as he saw his beheaded friend, who had died with the bashful blush still on his cheeks.

"Come, girl. You'll feel like a brand-new person once you join my family. Don't worry. Let's get out of here." Sil walked backward, pulling me along. He seemed to know exactly where he was going and dragged me, stumbling, past several doors in the endless stone corridor. I half expected Malachi's knives to embed themselves in my chest at any moment, but he remained frozen in place, watching us go, his eyes alight with both fury and concern.

Sil stopped in front of a door, one that looked identical to every single door I'd seen in the building. He took the set of keys from Lutfi's belt and tried each one while managing to keep his eyes on Malachi. The seventh key turned easily. With a rush of stale air, the door opened onto an alley. Just as Sil tugged me through it, I leaned forward against his hand, which constricted painfully around my throat.

"I'm sorry," I tried to yell, but it came out as a strangled whisper. Malachi didn't move. The look in his eyes made me want to run. Away from him. Toward him. I was completely unsure of which.

Sil jerked me into the alley and sprinted away, towing me in his wake.

TEN

I TRIED TO COUNT blocks, but Sil took turn after turn and pulled me through several buildings to make it to our present position. I wasn't even sure how long we'd been running. "Please," I gasped, "can we rest for a while?"

"You're in luck," he cackled. "Some of my family will be waiting just up here. We'll get something to eat before we move on."

I wiped away a tear with my free hand. My other was clutched in his sweaty, clawed grasp. The back of my hand was bleeding and throbbing from the bite of his fingernails. I'd been trying to find a way to escape, but he hadn't let me go since we'd left the Guard Station. For a while I'd hoped Malachi would chase after us, would swoop down and rescue me. He certainly seemed capable of it. As the time passed, though, it seemed more and more probable that Malachi had simply let me go. It made my chest ache in an odd way, but I ignored that—this was no different from when I'd been alive. The only person I could depend on was me. And I needed to get myself out of here. I was certain I didn't want to go wherever Sil was taking me. His family didn't sound very hospitable.

An enormous, Samoan-looking man sat on a stoop outside a row of townhouses in the next block. "Chimola!" Sil called, a smile revealing his glistening teeth. "Where are the others?"

The man looked up and waved. He gave me a once-over that made me wish I was invisible. He pointed across the street as two women emerged from a high-rise apartment building hand in hand. One of them was young and frail looking. Most of her long, blonde hair cascaded in tiny braids around her face. It reminded me of those white girls who come back from their Jamaican spring breaks with cornrows, thinking they actually look good.

The other woman was older. Much older. Her iron-gray hair was in rollers; it looked as if the two women had been styling each other's hair. The older one stroked the young woman's shoulder and crooned to her as she helped the girl strap on a too-large sword belt. From a Guard, no doubt. The young woman was so petite that, from its sheath at her waist, the blade dragged against the ground. Interesting. I wondered if the girl's arm was even long enough to draw the scimitar. Maybe if I could get that girl alone . . .

A chuffing, pounding noise distracted me, and I looked away from the girl to see the old woman galloping toward me, on all fours.

Sil held my hand firmly, his fingernails burrowing.

"Girl watches Lacey," the old woman snarled.

"Be calm, Doris," Sil soothed, stroking her rollered hair with his free hand. "This girl will join our family soon. She's no threat. And look at her hair!"

Doris's watery blue eyes twitched up to my heavy mass of looping curls. "Perfect," she murmured, wet, raspy breaths punctuating the word. She had some sort of European accent. German maybe? She laid a thick, spotty hand on my head with surprising gentleness. "Good girl."

She huffed out a laugh that sounded more like a snore and loped back over to the young woman with the big sword, whose name was apparently Lacey. Doris took Lacey's face in her hands and kissed her sloppily on the lips, then led her across the street to where the giant, Chimola, sat. Excellent. The creepy frau wanted to do my hair. And possibly something else. I had to get out of there.

"Where's Juri?" Sil asked.

"Hunting," chimed Lacey in a recognizably southern accent. She fiddled with one of Doris's rollers. Doris sat down on the stoop and pulled Lacey onto her lap. I didn't know whether to laugh or scream. Doris's animal movements were nauseatingly strong and fast.

Sil made a whining sound in his throat. "We must leave soon. Do you think the Guard won't be looking for me? Malachi *knows* I escaped! You were all supposed to wait for me here. And where are your weapons? Only Lacey is prepared?"

Doris gave him a wolfish smile and reached behind Chimola's elephantine bulk, revealing two more scimitars. Great. All the crazy animal people were armed with swords.

I barely got to finish the thought when a hand snaked between me and Sil, closing around one of my breasts. I reacted instantly and intensely, whirling around and yanking Sil with me so he was between me and the groper. Sil blinked, mildly surprised, but didn't seem threatened or shocked.

"Juri!" he cheerfully greeted the groper, a hook-nosed man with a serious underbite and the build of a linebacker.

When Juri saw my face, his eyes widened for a moment, like he couldn't believe what he was seeing. He grinned. "It's *you*."

His voice sent a hard chill straight through me. It was the voice that had made me wake up screaming a hundred times before. He took a step toward me, his eyes glinting with an excitement I knew all too well.

"Stay the hell away from me," I snapped.

He chuckled, deep and raspy. "You always said that to me right before you disappeared. But now you are here. In the *flesh*." His hand shot out again and stroked my cheek.

I turned my face away. It was definitely him. The monster who whispered to me in my dreams, trying to keep me in the dark city forever.

"No longer a ghost," he whispered. Then his voice rose, echoing off the surrounding buildings. "This one is mine."

"No fucking way," I yelled, my panic rising.

All the Mazikin laughed, but Juri seemed to think it was particularly funny. He grinned at me and then licked his lips in a truly obscene way. "Mine," he repeated, opening and closing his hands in front of him. If my sense of self-preservation hadn't held me back, Sil would have. He had such a tight grip on my hand that it would have been impossible to get away unless I was willing to leave my arm behind.

"Do you have food?" Sil asked Juri.

"Ya." Juri opened a paper sack and removed various unappealing food items. The other Mazikin gathered around, pawing at the bag.

Sil let go of my hand to devote his attention to getting his fair share. "Girl, you go sit there. If you try anything, I'll send Doris after you."

Doris, who had a mouthful of something beige and juicy, winked at me and bared her teeth. It took everything I had not to run, but I managed to walk slowly across the street and sink down onto the curb.

Doris came over a few moments later and handed me a beer bottle, label peeled off. "Water," she said. "Good for you."

I took the bottle and sniffed at its contents. Something about it didn't smell right, and damned if I was going to drink anything these animal people gave me. But the bottle—*that* was worth having. "Thanks, Doris," I said with a grateful smile, tipping the neck toward her in salute. "Good for me."

Doris smiled, showing her teeth. I shuddered.

I leaned against a lamppost and looked the street up and down. I wondered if I'd missed my chance to escape when it was just me and Sil. I wondered how many more of these freaky people he considered a part of his family. And I wondered why he kept saying I was going to *join* their family. I would have to make my move soon, though. I didn't want to find out why they were trying, in their own bizarre way, to take such good care of me.

I tugged at my waistband, satisfied that my pants weren't going to fall down as I ran. Doris loped back over to Sil, who was in quiet conversation with the others. They were about ten yards away. All armed with scimitars, all toothed and clawed. I knew from experience that Sil was fast on his feet. Juri was packed with muscle, like a sprinter. Maybe he'd be slower over a long distance. Chimola, with his amazing girth, would not be able to keep up. Lacey looked nimble but maybe not so strong. And Doris—with her creepy four-legged run, Doris would probably catch me first. I pictured one of those slow-motion videos where a lion tackled a fleeing gazelle.

I looked around. Behind me was a line of brownstone-type houses, no alleys in sight, just a straight run up the street. Advantage, Mazikin. In front of us was an apartment building, smooth and modern, with alleys on either side. One was completely blocked with garbage cans piled high and overflowing. The other looked clear. If I could make it, maybe I could lose them in the alleys.

Or get cornered with no way out.

I banged my head softly against the lamppost in frustration.

I heard her before I saw her. She was speaking Spanish. I didn't speak it. I didn't understand it. I'd been told it was all I spoke until I was dumped into the system at age four, but all my foster parents spoke English, and I had lost that part of myself.

I looked in the direction of the sound. A dark-skinned teenager trudged up the street, mumbling to herself. She hunched within a bulky coat. As she walked into the green pool of light beneath one of the lampposts, her beautiful face echoed the same private agony I'd seen on so many faces since arriving here.

I closed my eyes, trying to absorb the language, trying to draw comfort from it, straining to understand. It was musical in its sound and rhythm, but her voice was mournful, pierced through with despair. I winced and opened my eyes. The girl, her long, black hair coiling down her back, had passed me now. And the five Mazikin were watching her. In fact, they seemed completely riveted. I heard Sil mutter something that sounded like "perfect." Chimola nodded and started to follow her.

I was totally stuck. The Mazikin were distracted. This was it. My opportunity to escape. But how could I let this poor girl get collared? What if it had been Nadia being stalked, being taken? *Run,* whispered my selfish sense of self-preservation. *Run.* They might not hurt her. She might not even flee if I pulled the Mazikin's attention away from her. People here didn't seem to notice much going on around them, so she might not take the opportunity my sacrifice would give her. Even knowing that, my fist clenched around the bottle and I stood up. I'd taken one step forward when Chimola reached the girl and laid a hand on her arm.

I blinked as everything switched into high-resolution fast-forward. Light from the windows of the surrounding buildings glinted off the steel of the girl's blade as she took Chimola's arm off and then finished him with another swing of her scimitar. Sil screamed with rage and drew Lutfi's sword as the girl turned to face him, her sorrowful face transformed, now alight with a sort of blazing glee.

She definitely did *not* need my help.

I took off, running in a diagonal pattern toward the garbage-filled alley to my right, planning to scramble over the bins and get out of view as quickly as possible. I smashed the bottle against a lamppost as I sprinted. It never hurt to have something sharp in your hand. Especially because I could already hear Doris behind me, closing fast.

I wasn't going to make it to the alley—she would catch me before I even made it across the street. Just as I was turning to face the maniacal granny armed only with a broken bottle, she snarled and shifted direction.

Malachi stepped from the mouth of the alley to my left, blade drawn. I almost wept with relief. His expression softened as soon as he saw me, but he could only spare me a glance before Doris got to him.

"Lela," he called, his voice controlled as he met Doris's initial scimitar blows with graceful blocks, "fold the handle down."

He tossed his baton, which landed at my feet. I looked at my broken bottle and looked back at the baton. And I looked at Lacey and Juri, now running toward us at full tilt.

"Right," I said, picking up the surprisingly heavy baton and holding it in front of me like it was a poisonous snake. *Watch me poke my eye out.*

"Just keep her off you," he said as he fought. He sounded so conversational, like he was having a cup of tea rather than engaging in mortal combat. "They won't want to kill you. I'll be there in a minute."

"Right."

Lacey was only a few yards away. Juri was behind her but took a detour toward Malachi and Doris. He obviously thought Lacey could subdue me without help.

I grasped the baton and folded the handle onto the grip, sending at least two feet of steel shooting out both ends. Then Lacey was on me, and despite what Malachi had said, the pixie-like Mazikin seemed to have completely deadly intentions. Out of pure reflex and instinct, I blocked Lacey's downward swing with the staff and kicked her in the stomach, then stepped to the side and thwacked her over the head. I jumped as Lacey shrieked and swung the scimitar back toward my legs. Steel grazed the bottoms of my slippers. I skipped back a few feet, taking clumsy, experimental swings with the staff.

I had time to see Malachi engaged in bone-jarring combat with Doris *and* Juri before I closed in on Lacey again, intent on doing my part and at least stripping her of the scimitar. But the tiny albino got to her feet with disappointing agility, braids swinging.

I moved my grip to one end of the staff and swung it, determined to keep Lacey at bay. She tried to block with the blade, but I was right—she wasn't that strong. The staff crashed into her arm and she yowled. My lack of skill became immediately apparent, though. I'd left my other side unprotected. Lacey lunged and I reared back, but not fast enough. Searing pain lanced through my hip. I smothered a scream and stumbled backward as she staggered past me. When I regained my balance, I arced the staff back like a baseball bat and smacked Lacey hard in the head. She crumpled to the ground.

I looked down—my shirt was torn and soaked through with crimson. I bent quickly and grabbed Lacey's blade, but tossed it away after I managed to slice my own pant leg with it. Out of sheer anger and pain, I kicked Lacey in the side. Doris roared with anger as Malachi shouted my name in warning.

I barely got the staff up and in front of me before Doris was on me, blade high, teeth bared.

Eyes widening.

Mouth slackening.

Doris fell to the ground, three knives embedded deep in her back.

Malachi's defense of me cost him. The scimitar flew from his grasp. He threw a hand up and caught Juri's sword arm, and then they were struggling for the weapon. They fell into the mouth of the alleyway just as a hand closed around my ankle. I raised the staff like a spear and jabbed downward—and kept jabbing—until Doris's hand fell away.

"Now I understand why he cuts your throats," I muttered.

The alley echoed with Malachi's and Juri's efforts to destroy each other, and Sil and the unknown girl were still at it, neither of them looking tired.

And then Malachi roared in pain.

I gripped the staff and scrambled toward the alley, my other hand pressed across my hip. Juri's back was to me. He had won the battle for the scimitar, but Malachi's last knife was sticking out of the back of his shoulder. Malachi was unarmed now, sheaths empty. And I held his staff in my hands. A chill raced through me as I read the pain in his eyes. Blood ringed his collar and covered his neck.

Then he saw me. His lips curled into a defiant smile. "Lela, hit him hard. Doesn't matter where."

Juri obviously thought Malachi was bluffing and didn't turn around. He laughed and said something to Malachi in a language that might have been Russian. Malachi's eyes flashed as he spat a retort in the same language. Juri growled and advanced on him. I guess Malachi was quite an effective trash talker.

I raised the staff. "This is for earlier, you pervert."

As soon as he heard my voice, Juri spun around with the scimitar leading the way. I cracked the staff down on his wrist. He dropped the blade but barreled into me, sending me crashing to the ground. My head hit the pavement, and when the stars cleared from my vision, Juri was lying next to me. Malachi was perched on his back, knees pinning the perv's muscular arms to the ground, calling my name. I squinted, trying to bring his face into focus.

"I'm all right," I mumbled, noticing the frantic edge in his voice. He stared at me for a few seconds, like he was deciding whether or not he believed me. Then he jerked the knife from Juri's back and grabbed a handful of the man's greasy hair, yanking his head up in this terrifying, I'm-going-to-destroy-you-now kind of way.

Juri didn't seem intimidated at all. He looked me right in the eye. "You. Are. *Mine*," he growled, then grunted with pain as Malachi slammed his forehead against the pavement.

I scooted back instinctively, needing to get as far as possible from both of them.

Malachi's eyes shifted back to mine, and indecision crossed his face. "Lela, would you please go see how Ana's doing?"

Something in his voice begged me not to argue, so I rolled painfully to my side and staggered toward the street. The girl, who I assumed was Ana, seemed to be holding her own. As I turned to tell Malachi so, he appeared behind me, blocking my view of Juri. He put his hands on my shoulders and steered me out of the alley. He turned toward the sword battle in the street and took a single step forward. As if he'd felt Malachi's eyes on him, Sil abruptly broke away from Ana and took off running.

Ana was after Sil like a shot, turning her head only to shout, "I've got this, Malachi!"

"Who's that?"

"A colleague," replied Malachi, watching her sprint around a corner. For a moment I thought he would go after them, but he turned back to me instead. His lips were pressed in a tight line. I couldn't read what lay in his eyes as he looked me over. Once again I was frozen in place, half of me wanting to run toward him, half wanting to run away. Saving me the trouble of making a decision, he closed the distance between us and knelt in front of me.

"How bad?" He gripped my waist and lifted my shirt, gently peeling back my pants from my hip. To my surprise, I didn't flinch away. I put my hands on his shoulders and looked up at the sky, wondering if he would catch me if I fell.

"I don't think it's bad," I tried to assure him at the same moment he saw the wound and cursed loudly.

"Did any of them bite you?" His hands roamed over my arms and legs, searching for other injuries.

"No." I looked down and noticed that Juri's blood was smeared across my shirt. And Malachi's hands were covered in it. "Shouldn't we be washing their blood off us? Won't it make us sick?"

He returned his attention to my hip. "Is a snake's blood venomous?"

"What?"

"Mazikin blood isn't the problem, Lela. It's harmless, like a snake's. But their mouths, their saliva . . ."

I glanced down at him and saw, for the first time, the source of the blood on his collar. He hadn't been as lucky as I had. The wound was ragged and deep. Blood oozed from it steadily, and a white crystalline substance crusted around the edges.

"Oh my God. He bit you," I whispered, reaching to turn his head so I could see it better.

He pulled my hand away and stood up quickly. "Sit down, unless it feels better to stand. I need to finish this, but then we've got to get going."

"But we're so far—Don't you have, like, walkie-talkies or something? Can't you call for someone to come get you?"

His brow crinkled. "A walkie . . . you mean a telephone?" He shrugged. "We don't have telephones here."

"Why—"

He winced and closed his eyes. "Maybe we can talk about this more later, but we have to go. Now."

I turned my head away as Malachi made sure Doris and Lacey would not get up. But as his whispered chant carried across the street, I turned to watch him, mesmerized, as he bent over their bodies, eyes closed, maybe apologizing, maybe praying. I'd never been so confused by anyone. One moment he was ruthless and merciless, and the next he was staring at his victims with sorrow in his eyes. One moment he was locking me up with an amused smile on his face, and a few hours later he was risking his life to save me. I knew how to read most people, what to expect from them. With Malachi . . . not so much.

When he was finished, he collected his weapons, wiping the blood on his pants before sheathing each knife. He collapsed his staff and snapped the baton to his waist. He walked into the alleyway and came back out with his scimitar and Juri's. With practiced movements he attached Juri's sheath to his own belt, and then approached me again.

"Can you walk?"

I pasted on a big, cheesy smile. "Of course. It's just a cut."

He laughed, his face transforming for a moment into that whimsical expression I'd seen earlier. "Can you run?"

"Probably," I said, eyeing him. "Can you?"

His face became serious as he met my eyes. "For now I can."

My heart clutched a little at his honesty. "Where are we going? How far?"

"We need to get back to the Station. I don't know how much time I have, and we both need to see Raphael."

Back to the Station. No freaking way. I shuffled backward. "I'm not sure I want to—"

He gave me a thoroughly exasperated look. "I swear I will carry you if I have to, and that would be unpleasant for both of us. Your hip is laid open to the bone, and I . . . I'll be dead in a few hours if we don't get back to the Station now. And I'm not going without you. So please cooperate, just this once."

Considering he'd rescued me from a chillingly unknown fate at the hands of the creepiest bunch of people I'd ever met, I decided not to argue. Especially because, despite my earlier vows to the contrary, I absolutely did not want him to die. Judging by what he'd said about his injury, I might be able to escape from him without actually having to go *into* the Station. But I wanted to help him get to safety first. "Lead the way."

"Thank you."

Malachi set a blistering, painful pace, and I forced myself to ignore the throbbing sting of my wound as I ran behind him through the alleys and streets of the city. Once again I tried to spot landmarks, identifying features . . . and once again I was totally lost. After what seemed like an hour, Malachi's long, steady strides faltered. He slumped down on a stoop in front of a dark building with shattered windows.

"I need to rest," he mumbled, "just for a minute."

"Sure," I huffed as I sat down next to him, "whatever you need."

I hadn't been sure I could keep up for much longer. He'd been running in front of me, so this was the first opportunity

I had to look at him since we'd started our return journey. I didn't like what I saw. His olive skin was sickly pale, stark against his black hair. He was shivering.

"How are you doing?" His teeth chattered as he spoke.

"Better than you are, I think." I raised a tentative hand to his face. He didn't react as my fingers brushed his cheek. It felt like I was afraid it would: clammy and cold. He was in bad shape, and I had no idea how far we were from the Station. I wouldn't be able to get him back there if he collapsed.

"Is Raphael a doctor?"

He nodded. "Sort of. He'll heal you. It won't be hard for him."

"And you?" He needed it more than I did.

"I don't know," he muttered. "At this point I don't know."

That was not what I wanted to hear. I stood up. "Let's go. Now."

He didn't move. "I need to rest. Just for a minute," he repeated.

"No way. You've rested enough. Up. Get up." I took his hand and pulled. He allowed me to guide him to his feet. I slipped beneath his arm and put mine around his waist. "You're going to have to help me or we won't get there. Come on. *Now.*" He leaned on me and let me lead him forward. "Tell me which way."

Much slower now, we trudged along a main road. Malachi mumbled a steady stream of instructions but got quieter as we proceeded. He started to have trouble lifting his feet.

"Numb," he whispered, closing his eyes and leaning his head on the top of my mine. We stood there for a second, and I realized this was as close as I'd ever willingly gotten to a guy. Malachi seemed perfectly content to stand there, half embracing, half leaning, but it was obvious to me he wouldn't be able to remain upright for long.

"How far are we from the Station?"

"Not far. But I don't think I can make it."

We were right in front of an apartment building, and it gave me an idea. I might be strong, but I wasn't strong enough to carry Malachi, who felt like two hundred pounds of solid muscle. "Listen to me. I'm going to leave you here, and you're going to tell me how to get to the Station. Can you do that?"

"No. You stay with me." He was obviously trying to sound commanding, but his voice was weak and filled with pain. It kind of ruined the effect.

"Sorry, but that's not going to happen. I'll be faster without you, so stop arguing. Are there empty units in this building?"

"In every building," he breathed, giving up.

"All right, let's go find one." I practically had to drag him through the doors. He tried to help, but his feet kept getting away from him. His arms were limp around me, as if they were now numb as well.

The hallway was dimly lit by those omnipresent gas lanterns, but there was enough light to allow me to step around the huge, furry spots of mold growing on the carpet. It was dead quiet, and if it hadn't been for the strips of greenish light shining from beneath the doors of every apartment, I'd have been sure the building was abandoned. It took forever, but I got him down the hallway and through the first open door we came to.

I was filled with relief to see that the apartment's threadbare carpet was free of mold, and the walls were just a dull tan—no streaks of mildew. Paired with the laminate wood furniture and cracked countertops, it felt a lot like some of the housing projects I'd lived in. But there was one major difference. "Hey, there's no lock on this door. Should I push some furniture in front of it or something?"

Malachi shook his head. "No one can come in now that we're here," he said hoarsely.

"Why, because you're a Guard?"

He shook his head again. Such a small movement, but it looked like it exhausted him. "Once an apartment is occupied, no one else can enter."

I nearly fell to the floor with relief. We were safe. But more importantly—Nadia was. She got into that apartment, and apparently whoever had been behind her couldn't follow her in. I hoped she'd stayed there.

I maneuvered Malachi through a door, into a bedroom that contained a single narrow cot. "Down, boy," I said as I lowered him carefully onto it. My hip was screaming, and the rest of me wasn't far behind. He was incredibly heavy. I couldn't rest, though. Not if I was going to help him survive.

His hand flopped onto his chest over one of the buckles. "I can't breathe."

"Right," I said, newly determined. "Let's get you comfortable, and then I'm going to go."

"No," he groaned, but I ignored him and went to work. I pushed his hands away and unfastened each buckle on his breastplate, awkwardly pulling it off him, trying not to brush his neck. When I failed, he made a sound so wrenching that I cried out with him.

I finished removing the breastplate and moved to his belt. "Don't," he begged as his arms twitched helplessly at his sides. Again I ignored him. I stayed focused on what I needed to do. If I hadn't, I think I might have collapsed on the grimy carpet in a useless puddle of panic and despair and guilt. He was hurt because of *me*. He might die because of *me*.

"You can't use your arms. These are not going to do you any good right now." I tugged his belt from his waist and set it next to the cot. I placed my palm on his chest and felt the shallowness of his breath. Blood saturated the front of his shirt. I had no idea he'd been bleeding so badly. "You have to tell me how to get to the Station."

"I thought I might not get to you in time," he said. "I'm so sorry you got hurt. I should have been faster."

I couldn't believe he was trying to apologize to me, especially because, by all rights, he should want to kill me. The gentleness and sorrow in his voice told me he thought these might be the last words he said to me. It got to me. "You are wasting breath and wasting my time," I said harshly. "Now give me directions or I will kill you myself."

He coughed out a laugh. "You are such an amazing creature."

Damn. "Come on. Snap out of it. Directions. Now."

"It was my mistake, putting you back in that cell. But if I hadn't, I would have—"

Desperate to jar some sense into him, I slapped him across the face. It wasn't the most therapeutic of moves, but he was really out of it, and I had no idea how to find the Station and get him help. He barely reacted, which made me nearly frantic. I leaned over and took his face in my hands, planning to shake him until he gave me the directions I needed.

He looked up at me, dark brown eyes shining. "You're so beautiful," he slurred, making me sure his lips were growing numb and his brain wasn't far behind.

Figures. The first time a guy tells me I'm beautiful, I'm in hell and he's delirious.

"*Please* give me directions. I'm going to feel pretty awful if you die."

"Say my name."

I rolled my eyes to fend off all the possible meanings in that simple request. "You're not making any sense."

He moaned as his chest shook with bemused laughter. "Have mercy and give me my dying wish. I want to hear you say it, just once. Please say my name, Lela." He was very still for a moment, like saying *my* name had sapped the last of his strength. I moved even closer. I truly thought he'd died, and it made my chest hurt in ways I didn't understand.

But then he opened his eyes again. They pulled me right in, and I didn't have any words left but one. I dipped my head until we were nose-to-nose, until my chest was pressed to his, until I could feel his heartbeat, unsteady and racing, through my shirt.

I took a deep breath. *"Malachi."*

His lips curled into a wistful smile. Then he started to whisper directions.

ELEVEN

I BURST INTO THE Guard Station like Lucifer himself was on my tail. The thick-walled building was low and square, like a fort, with a high, narrow tower jutting from its center. It looked deserted from the outside, but no fewer than four Guards met me in the entryway, barring my path.

I held up Malachi's scimitar and rattled it at them. "Malachi's been bitten by a Mazikin. He needs Raphael," I panted, grasping my hip, which had started bleeding again.

One of the Guards laughed. "It's obviously too late, love. If you've got his blade, it means he's dead. That's the only way you'd be able to get it from him."

I shook my head as I tried to catch my breath. "He's in an apartment building about twenty blocks from here, but he's in bad shape. I can take you to him. Is Raphael here?"

The Guard I recognized as Hani stepped forward, looking at me closely. "You left with a Mazikin. How do we know you're not one of them?"

Why hadn't I thought of that? It was probably why Malachi hadn't wanted me to come without him. But he wouldn't have given me directions if he'd thought it was a hopeless mission. I stood my ground and chose my words carefully, though I felt like running for my afterlife. "If you know Malachi, you know someone like me wouldn't have his sword unless he gave it to me," I ventured. "Please. He's weak. He needs help."

"Maybe you should come in," said Hani in a friendly voice, but I saw right through him. Bad acting was kind of an epidemic in hell.

"There's not much time. Malachi is going to *die*. He was barely conscious when I left him. If you just get Raphael, we can go now."

He advanced and curled his thick fingers around my arm. "I said, maybe you should *come in*."

I tried to wrench my arm free. "What is wrong with you people? Why aren't you mobilizing, or whatever you folks do around here?"

Some of the Guards had the grace to look a little ashamed, but a few laughed nastily. Why weren't they rushing to help him? Why weren't they calling Raphael? Hani started to drag me down the hall toward the holding cells as another Guard yanked Malachi's scimitar from my clenched fist. I remembered enough about my last visit to know I didn't want to go farther. But as I looked behind me, I could see that the Guards had the exit covered. No going back—which left only one option: causing a scene.

I kicked Hani in the shins, and as he flinched in surprise I shot a hard punch to his groin. I wouldn't have thought such a large man could make such a high-pitched noise, but it did the trick: he let me go.

I sprinted past him down the hall, shouting for Raphael and banging on every door I passed. Heavy huffs of breath and pounding footsteps filled my ears as at least one of the Guards pursued me. Ah, crap. This was going to hurt. In the next second, I ran into the barrier of my own enormous tent shirt as it pulled tight. A Guard had grabbed my collar. Then the asshole got a handful of my hair.

I struggled frantically as his meaty arms wrapped around me. One coiled across my body, one pressed over my face, blinding me, suffocating me. All I could see were the muddled images in my head. I tried to remember why I had come here and what I was supposed to be doing, but it just slipped through my fingers as I screamed.

A calm voice cut through the chaos. "Let her go."

The Guard obeyed immediately. I fell to the floor on my hands and knees. It felt like my right leg was about to fall off. My pants were soaked with blood. I couldn't stop shaking. I pressed my forehead to the stone floor, my thoughts churning.

"What have you done to her now?" chided the voice gently. "I just fixed her up last night."

I threw my head back and caught sight of . . . the most ordinary man I'd ever seen. Huh. For some reason, I'd expected someone a little more impressive looking. He appeared to be only a few inches taller than I was, with curly brown hair, gray eyes, and freckles. He had a blindingly beautiful smile, though my perception of it in that moment might have had something to do with the fact that I was sure this was Raphael.

It all rushed out of me in a breathless flow. "Malachi is sick. He's nearby in an apartment building, and he's been bitten. He was having trouble breathing. He said you could heal him. I can take you there."

One of the Guards grunted with contempt. "She brought his blade. The Captain would never give it up. How do we know she's not leading you into a trap, Raphael?"

Without looking in the Guard's direction, I shot him the finger. Why were we wasting so much freaking time?

Raphael looked down at me speculatively. "You're hurt." He held out his hand. "Why don't you come to my quarters so I can heal you?"

Shrieking rage boiled up inside me, and I gulped in one long breath to stop it, to try one more time. If I lost it and gave up now, Malachi would die for sure. I hadn't gotten to thank him for saving me. I hadn't gotten to apologize for making it necessary in the first place. I blew out the breath in a long stream.

"I. Am. Fine. This is *nothing*," I said very calmly and slowly, gesturing at my torn hip, "and I am going to say this one more time: Malachi is only a few blocks away, and he needs *help*. Do whatever you want to me. Put me in a cell, muzzle me, whatever. Go in force if you're afraid of an ambush, or sneak in the back for all I care. But for God's sake, *go*!" I roared the last word with all the air in my lungs.

Raphael took a step back.

He looked at the Guards. "She's not a Mazikin, and it's not a trap."

Whoa. I guess I'd said the magic words.

In unison, the Guards stepped back and cleared the way. Raphael reached down and pulled me to my feet, and I didn't fight him as he put his arm around me.

"He was right. You *are* tough," he murmured as he briskly led me back down the hall and out of the Station.

Within a few minutes we were outside the door to the apartment.

"How are we going to get in?" I asked as Raphael came up behind me. "Malachi said that once an apartment was occupied, no one else could enter."

Raphael reached around me and opened the door. "You originally entered under escort by a Guard member, so it won't be a problem for you." He stepped over the threshold. "And I have special privileges."

I flew past him, terrified we'd taken too long. Raphael followed as I scrambled through the living room and bolted through the bedroom door. Malachi was lying right where I'd left him. He was sickly pale, which made the awful wound on his neck stand out all the more. He wasn't moving. I couldn't tell if he was breathing.

Raphael sighed as he looked down at Malachi. "Well, Lela, you weren't kidding. Can you take off his bracers and greaves?"

"His what?"

"His armor. Can you take off the rest of his armor?"

"Oh, sure," I mumbled. I knelt beside Malachi's feet while Raphael leaned over to inspect the wound. For a few minutes I focused on unfastening the buckles that held the thick, molded leather to Malachi's shins. I took off his boots, placing them next to the foot of the cot. I moved up to his arms, trying to ignore the fact that I hadn't seen him take a breath since I'd returned.

Raphael hunched over Malachi's head and neck, chanting to himself. It occurred to me to ask why he didn't have any medical equipment with him, but at this point, the strangeness stretched to the horizon, and one more mile of random hellish weirdness wasn't going to make a difference. As long as Raphael made Malachi better, that worked for me. I slipped the leather sleeve from Malachi's arm and reached down impulsively to take his hand. It was calloused and rough. And cold. I squeezed it, and my chest ached when it did not squeeze back.

I reached over to Malachi's other arm, not wanting to disturb Raphael, who seemed deeply focused on his task. I pulled the final piece of armor free and lined it up neatly with the rest. I smoothed his shirt, dark and damp with blood and sweat, cool in the chilled air of the apartment. I limped into the bathroom and rooted through the linen closet, finding a prize in the very back: an old green blanket that looked and smelled like it had been there for half a century.

When I made it back to the room, Raphael was sitting on his heels, a freckled hand on Malachi's chest. "His heart still beats, but he's weak. Tell me, was he in pain when you left him?"

Something in the way he worded the question made me cringe. "Uh, not much . . . . Actually, I think he was pretty numb. And maybe delirious."

"Delirious?" he asked in this detached, clinical tone of voice. "Fascinating."

"Fascinating? You make him sound like a science project," I snapped. "Haven't you seen this sort of injury before?"

"Of course. Countless times. Delirium is not usually one of the symptoms. So it makes me wonder what he said to make you think he was."

My cheeks got very hot. He smiled and looked back at Malachi. "I'm glad he found you."

I crept forward and spread the blanket over Malachi's body, folding it across his chest. "I feel terrible. He got hurt because he tried to protect me," I whispered. Nadia and Diane were the only people who had ever tried to protect me. No one but Malachi had ever actually risked anything for me. And he had risked everything.

"Don't feel bad. I have no doubt he thought it was worth it. As young as he appears, Malachi knows how to make his own decisions."

"Was it just me, or did the Guards at the Station seem less than eager to help him?" I wondered if it was because he'd come to rescue me after what I'd done.

Raphael somehow read my mind. "Don't worry, it's not you. Malachi is a controversial character among the Guard.

He is their Captain, but he is not one of them. They were created to function as a unit, but he often operates alone or with Ana, who is human like him. He is the most merciless of them all but also the most principled. He has changed some policies for dealing with Mazikin in recent years, and the other Guards do not like it. He comes from a different place than they do, and his future is different from theirs. As it has been with all their human leaders, it is hard for the other Guards to understand him, and some of them don't try."

I took Malachi's hand again, feeling an odd sort of kinship with him. I folded his long fingers over mine. "Is he going to be okay?"

"I don't know yet. His wound is severe, and the venom has taken a firm grip on him."

I flinched and looked away, absently stroking the blanket over Malachi's chest. Raphael laid his warm hand over mine. "Let me heal you, Lela. If your clothes are anything to go by, whatever lies beneath has been torn pretty badly." Again, his word choice made me cringe.

"How long will it take?"

"An hour or two."

"Malachi needs you more. Make him better, and then you can work on me."

Raphael didn't argue. He bent over Malachi again. I leaned my head against the side of the cot, closed my eyes, and listened to Raphael's hushed and ceaseless chanting until I drifted into darkness.

I jerked awake as Raphael lifted me. Before I could protest, he said, "You're running a fever. I'm going to heal you before it gets worse. I've done as much as I can for Malachi right now. And I know him well. He would be very angry with me if he woke up and found you still injured."

Unable to argue, barely able to keep my eyes open, I slumped against him. He carried me to the couch in the living room, then knelt by my hip and closed his eyes, recommencing his rapid muttering. It was rhythmic, like a cadence, and had an eerie, unrecognizable melody. My hip got warm, like he was bathing it in heated water. It felt good. I relaxed and floated, thoughts drifting. The water got hotter and then started to boil. Something was shrieking, maybe a teapot . . . . Nope, that was me.

Through my screams I heard Raphael say, "Sorry, should have put you to sleep first."

Everything went black again.

I awoke in silence. As always, it was still dim and there was little indication of how much time had passed.

I lifted my leg experimentally, surprised and relieved to find that it felt fine. I stood up and examined my hip. A thin, white scar crossed its crest, the only indication I'd even been hurt. I shifted my weight from foot to foot and walked into the bedroom.

Raphael sat on the floor. Like before, his hand rested on Malachi's chest. Malachi's bloody shirt and pants were heaped in the corner, and his body was covered up to his waist with the blanket I'd found last night. I focused my eyes on the floor. "I need to get some clothes. How long have I been sleeping?"

"Not long," said Raphael as he nodded to a dresser. "Try to find something that fits."

I rolled my eyes and laughed. "Absolutely. My last outfit was seriously plus-sized."

I finally found a pair of gray pants near enough to my size that they wouldn't slow me down and a hideous green cotton shirt that was a bit small but reasonably comfortable. I even found a frayed ribbon in the top drawer, which I used to restrain my crazy hair. I turned back to Raphael, who observed me with detached curiosity. Like he was waiting for something.

My eyes flicked back over to the cot. Malachi was so still. "How is he?"

"He is better. Stable."

I took a few steps closer. "Why isn't he waking up?"

Raphael pivoted on his knees, his eyes resting on Malachi's face. "Time will tell. Well," he said briskly, rising to his feet. "I have to be going—patients to see."

"What? How can you leave him alone if he's not awake?"

"He's not alone. You're with him."

"But . . . but . . ." *But I should go.*

"I'll be back later. If you really feel you must leave, please go ahead. No one will stop you." His gray eyes locked onto mine with a crystal clear, entirely unreadable gaze. Then he turned and walked away.

I was still stuttering like an idiot when the front door clicked shut.

I should go. Now.

Malachi might not allow me to leave if I stuck around until he woke up. He might toss me back in a cell. He might force me to go to the Sanctum. He might keep me from my whole purpose for being here. He might condemn Nadia to suffer here forever. Who said anything had changed?

But . . . how could I possibly leave him alone? How could I leave this guy who had risked his life for me even after my stupidity resulted in the death of one of his Guards? How could I leave him alone and helpless? What if he woke up, maybe weak, maybe in pain, and there was nobody here to care for him?

"Oh, you've placed me in a really difficult position, you big jerk. As soon as Raphael comes back, I'm gone."

Until then, I'm here. I'm not leaving you.

Commitment made, at least until reinforcements arrived, I turned around to take my first really good look at him. His olive skin had regained some of its healthy color. His neck, so savaged the night before, was smooth but swirled with red and silver. He would probably bear the scar forever. Or however long people existed around here. My gaze drifted down to his shoulders and chest, his stomach . . . all streaked with blood. A long, thick scar sliced across his left shoulder—a souvenir from his fight with Ibram the sheik—but it didn't hold my attention. Because Malachi had, hands down, the most impressive male physique I'd ever seen up close. Or on television, for that matter. I couldn't stop staring. I guess running around a giant city hunting venomous animal people resulted in some pretty great definition.

"Gah. Look away, Lela. Focus," I coached myself. "Captain, let's get you cleaned up."

A few minutes later, I carried a bowl filled with water and a washcloth into the bedroom. The water in the city smelled extremely strange, sour with a metallic tang. How people managed to keep themselves alive by drinking it—and eating the horrible food—was beyond me. I hadn't eaten since I'd arrived, and . . . wait, that seemed really odd. I'd been in the city for at least two days, and I wasn't hungry at all.

I dipped the washcloth into the bowl, wrung the extra water from it, and got down to business. I hummed to myself as I worked, scrubbing his skin clean, making sure not a smudge remained. I replaced the water in the bowl three times before I was through, wishing there was some decent soap in this place. What was in the bathroom looked gray and gross, and I couldn't bear to inflict it on a defenseless, unconscious person.

I spent a little too much time and attention on his chest and stomach, but I didn't get out of control. I let the blanket draped over his waist serve as my boundary marker. I'd never been able to touch a guy like that, and this seemed like the best way to do it—when he was helpless, unable to rise up and hurt me.

I began to wash his arms, and that's when I saw it. He had been wearing long sleeves every time I'd seen him, usually with those leather cuffs over his forearms. It was so small I almost missed it. A tattoo on his left forearm.

A five-digit number with a small triangle beneath it.

I had paid attention in class. Most of the time. When I saw the tattoo, I had a memory, clear as day, from this video we'd watched in history class earlier in the year. Stick-thin people behind the fences of those concentration camps, hollow eyes beyond pleading. The Nazis tattooed their arms with numbers. Could he have been . . . ?

I traced the tattoo with my fingers. "Where did you come from, Malachi? What's your story?"

I finished washing him, dried him thoroughly, and pulled the blanket up to his shoulders as goose bumps erupted across his skin. I moved up to sit by his head. At rest, Malachi's face didn't have the same ferocity it carried when he was awake. It was softer. He looked younger, like he hadn't been hurt yet. I knew it wasn't true, but still, looking at his relaxed and peaceful expression, I could imagine something different for him.

I ran the palm of my hand over his neck, where the scar was warm and smooth under my fingers, and across the ridge of his collarbone to his chest. I let my hand rest there, over his heart, feeling it beat steadily, unwilling to give up the guilty pleasure of his skin. I did wonder how he'd feel if he knew, if he would push me away, if he would feel it as a violation. I certainly would if our positions had been reversed.

Something in the way he had looked at me made me think he *wanted* me to touch him, though. That didn't make what I was doing right, but this was my chance, as shameful as it was. I wanted to know what it felt like when it was my choice. When *I* was in control.

I brought my face over his, stroking my fingers along his jaw. There were dusky circles beneath his closed eyes. I inhaled the leather scent of his skin. He looked so young up close, so exquisite. I leaned my forehead against his and looked down at his lips.

I was seventeen years old and had never kissed a boy. With everything I'd been through, I hadn't let anyone get that close to me, especially not since Rick . . .

I gritted my teeth and shoved the memories away, not wanting them to spoil this moment. My moment. Unobserved, alone with him, I was so curious to know how it would feel. Was it as great as everyone made it out to be? What would it be like? What would it be like with *Malachi*?

On impulse, I brushed my lips across his mouth. My skin tingled where it touched his. I licked my lips and tried again, lingering for a moment, closing my eyes and pressing in as the boundaries between us dissolved.

Whoa. Stop. I pulled back, heart pounding, completely ashamed of myself.

"What the hell is wrong with me?" Of all people, I knew how it felt not to have a choice, so why was I doing this to him?

"I'm sorry, Malachi," I whispered, settling back from him. "Won't happen again."

I wish I could explain why it happened at all.

I took his hand, tracing the tattoo on his arm, and laid my head against the edge of the cot.

"Wake up, please. Just wake up. I need to thank you, and then I have to go." I called to him, his hand in mine, for minutes, or hours, or days, until exhaustion claimed me once again.

TWELVE

"LELA?" THE SOUND OF his voice, cracked and hoarse, jerked my head up like a high-voltage shock.

His brows were drawn together. "What are you doing here?"

I blinked away tears of relief. "Welcome back. How are you feeling?"

He took a breath and winced. "Like I haven't moved in several days. And like I might not want to for several more."

"Do you need something? Water?"

"No. I don't drink that stuff." He closed his eyes and put a hand to his neck, running his fingers along the swirling scar. "How long have I been out?"

I watched his chest rise as he took another deep breath. "I have no idea how time passes here. It's all shades of dim to me. You were out for a long time." *Too long.*

"Where's Raphael?"

"He healed you and then left . . . a while ago."

Malachi didn't open his eyes, but the subtle tension in his body told me his senses were now on full alert, silently collecting information. I squirmed, wondering if he'd feel me on his skin.

"Did he heal you before he left?" he asked.

"Yes."

His eyes were still closed as he said, very slowly, "And you stayed here. With me."

I said nothing, horrified into muteness as I watched him touch his mouth and draw his tongue slowly along the edges of his lips. I almost blurted out an apology, but that would have meant admitting something I was desperate to hide. Guilt ran hot under my skin. I shut my eyes, unable to look at him anymore.

He sighed. I expected to hear the accusation next. But all he said was "I didn't think I would see you again." I relaxed, my muscles twitching with the release of tension.

That's when I realized I was still clutching one of his hands.

I let go abruptly, as if it had bitten me, and ventured a glance at his face as I gave my prepared explanation. "I wanted to make sure you were okay. I couldn't just leave you alone here. And I wanted to thank you for coming after me, after what I did."

He looked down at his hand, now lying solitary at his side, and then at mine, now curled guiltily in my lap. "You did what you had to. If I'd been thinking, I would have expected you to do exactly what you did. It was a rash decision to put you back in that cell."

I gave him a narrow-eyed look. "You don't seem like the rash type."

He bowed his head to hide a small smile. "I'm not, usually."

"I thought you would kill me for what I'd done."

His expression turned pained. "No. Whatever you think of me, please don't think that. I know it's difficult to believe, but I never meant you harm." He sat up and swung his feet to the floor, pulling the blanket across his lap.

I scooted back a few inches, until my shoulders hit the wall. "I have to go," I muttered. I leaned against the wall as I stood. He started to rise but fell down again quickly, clutching the edge of the cot. A frustrated growl rolled from his throat. I was quite sure he was accustomed to having full control over his body. "Thank you again for getting me away from the Mazikin. But I really need to be going now—"

His hand shot out and closed around mine, but his grasp was gentle. "Tell me one thing before you go. I really want to know. Why would you give up your chance at happiness to come to what you knew was a horrible place? Why would you do that, knowing she *chose* to kill herself? To leave you and everyone else who loved her? Why would you come after her and trap yourself here when she made such a choice?"

Maybe if I could make him understand, he would let me go without a fight. I pulled my hand from his and looked down at my arm. Nadia stared back at me. I closed my eyes and rested my head against the wall.

"I was at a normal school—instead of juvie. I knew from experience I was going to be a total reject. I always had been. And Nadia . . . she was, like, the most popular girl there. The day we met, I helped her out of a bad situation. I didn't think she owed me anything, though. She could have ignored me afterward. That's what anyone else would have done. But instead she walked me to class. Sat next to me. Talked to me. She did it again the next day, and the next day, and the next day. I thought I'd be a freak-of-the-week project for her, but she just kept coming back. She actually seemed to enjoy hanging out with me."

My throat constricted as the memories washed over me. "This one time, one of her other friends, Tegan, was making fun of me, like I was just a loser, clingy, wish-I-was-popular girl. And Nadia didn't say a word. She didn't have to. She just gave Tegan this look that said everything, like if you mess with Lela I will crush your social life under my Jimmy

Choos." I chuckled. "Saved me from getting sent back to the RITS for kicking that girl's ass."

I opened my eyes to find Malachi looking at me like I'd suddenly started speaking a strange, incomprehensible language. Which made sense, actually, because I kind of had. I tried again.

"I'm here because of the way she looked at me, Malachi. She should have looked at me with fear. I did some pretty scary things. Most people would agree I'm a scary person. But that's not how she looked at me. She looked at me as if she saw something else inside of me—something wonderful, something worth knowing—and she was the only person who could make it come out. She taught me things. She gave me things. Amazing things. A vision of myself, different from what I had been. Better, but still me, you know? Dreams of the future, of what I could become. I don't think she really recognized how she was bringing me to life. It came so naturally to her."

I wrapped my arms around my chest. Making the final admission—it hurt to say out loud. "I don't know if I did the same for her. Since we're here right now, my guess would be that I didn't. But it doesn't matter. I never had a friend before Nadia, and I would do anything for her."

He got to his feet, holding the blanket closed at his waist. Even nearly naked and unarmed, he seemed dangerous. And too distracting for me to stay focused. I braced, wondering if he was about to try to stop me. I eyed the door.

"Wait." His voice was quiet, and it sounded more like a request than a command. He swayed unsteadily. I put my hands around his waist to catch him, unwilling to let him fall.

As soon as I touched him, I knew it was a mistake.

His skin burned against mine. My fingers pressed in hungrily, like they had a mind of their own. I watched, amazed, as his skin rippled with goose bumps and he shivered. He steadied himself with a hand on my shoulder, and his fingers brushed the bare skin at my neck. His touch blew a few fuses in my brain. I wanted to rear back and run away. I wanted to put my hand over his and hold it there forever.

I turned to go, completely torn. Nadia was my reason for being here. The only reason. And yet I also wanted to stay. Not in that hellish city, and not to go to the Sanctum, whatever it held for me. I wanted to stay with Malachi. I didn't feel safe with him, and yet I knew he would keep me safe. I had no idea who he was or where he came from, but in some crazy way it seemed like we understood each other. And although I was frightened by the idea of him touching me, I desperately wanted to touch him just one more time.

Out of control. It all felt out of control. With him awake and getting stronger by the minute, there was no more reason to stay and every reason to go. My hand was on the door of the apartment before he spoke again.

"Lela, wait. I'll help you. I'll help you find her." I didn't turn around, but tensed as I felt the heat of his body and realized how close he was. "I know this city better than anyone. I understand its dangers. I could protect you. I'll help you find her. I'll help you get out."

"Why?"

He chuckled. "Because it's obviously the only way to get you out of my beautiful city. Will you let me help you?"

I turned back to him. Usually, I could tell when someone was lying or when they were hiding something. His expression was open and serious and, as far as I could tell, completely sincere. I couldn't help it—I got hopeful. With him on my side, I might actually have a chance.

"Really?"

"Really. But you have to do as I say. If we're together in this, you must follow my instructions or you'll put us both in danger. You'll have to trust me. Can you do that?"

There was always a catch. If only he knew what he was asking. I smiled sadly as I shook my head. "Every time I've trusted someone, it's come back to bite me."

His brows lifted and his jaw tensed. "Lela, who did this to you?" The question seemed to burst from him involuntarily; he took a step back and looked down at the floor, waving the words away. "Never mind. You don't have to promise. Just tell me you'll try."

I could live with that. "I'll try."

THIRTEEN

I HIKED ALONG THE road carrying Malachi's arm and shin guards. He walked next to me, carrying his leather vest and wearing the most ridiculous outfit I'd ever seen. The striped pants he'd found in the apartment sagged on his narrow hips, held up only by his belt, but the pant legs still didn't make it all the way to his ankles. His shirt was too tight on his shoulders but ballooned over his belly. It had been the only one with sleeves long enough to reach to his wrists, and that had seemed important to him.

A shaggy-haired young man walked by, clutching what appeared to be a full key of coke to his chest. His nose was bleeding.

"Holy crap. Is that what I think it is?"

Malachi watched the guy absently wipe his dripping nose with a spotty sleeve and scramble up the steps of an apartment building with his prize. "If you think that is a man who has acquired a kilogram of cocaine for his personal use, then yes."

"Aren't you the cops around here? Shouldn't you bust him?"

"For what? He's not committing a crime. Or, more accurately, he already has, and now he's serving his sentence."

"He's going to kill himself with that stuff."

Malachi gave me a sidelong glance. "It's possible. It won't help him get out of here, though. And I wouldn't worry about him too much, because I suspect those drugs aren't very potent. It won't give him much relief. Nothing will."

I thought of Nadia and those pills she couldn't wait to take. I wondered if there were DRUG stores here, like the FOOD stores, where you could just walk in and take as much as you wanted. "Then how come it's all so available?"

"People can have *whatever* they want here. As much food. As much pornography." He nodded toward the building the young man had just disappeared into. "As many drugs. As many apartments. Whatever they want, whatever they imagine. None of it will help, though. You can't get out until you let all that go. Until you go in search of what you need rather than what you want."

"That's all you have to do?"

He let out a bark of laughter. "It's harder than it sounds. It is impossible to fool the Judge."

"I don't get this place. The only way out is through the Sanctum, but what if you die?"

"If you die, you appear at the Gates of whatever place you belong, and you're ushered in." He raised his eyebrow. "This is the place for the suicides, but there are other places, I have heard. For people with other . . . problems."

I mused for a moment about the kind of horrific place a person like Rick would wind up. It made me feel better to think he'd get what he deserved. "I guess that makes sense. And the Countryside is . . ."

"Just another place. A place where most of us would like to end up." His gaze rose and drifted beyond the distant city wall to the dim outline of snowcapped peaks rising above the beautiful landscape. "When we're judged ready."

"So why don't you just, I don't know, let one of those Mazikin people kill you? Why didn't you let yourself die after Juri bit you? Not that I'd ever root for that guy, but it would have been kind of a heroic death. Wouldn't it have earned you some points?"

He shrugged. "I really don't know, and I don't want to take the chance. If you die before you're ready to get out, you have to start over. At least, that's what I've been told." His face reflected a secret pain. "And I'd like to get out of here as soon as I can."

A warm, unfamiliar feeling filled my chest. He'd known there might be terrible consequences if he died, but he'd been willing to risk it to keep me safe. I glanced up at the swirling scar on his neck, remembering the moments my fingers had been running over the otherwise smooth skin. My face got hot at the memory, and at the knowledge that I'd done it without his permission. And yet the whimsical quirk of his mouth and the searching curiosity in his eyes as he stared down at me told me he might have given me permission if I'd asked.

I quickened my pace, shaking my thoughts back into the right order. "Are you going to let me in on your plan for finding my friend?"

"Sure," he replied, lengthening his strides and hitching up his pants for the fiftieth time. "We're going back to the Station to change into something acceptable. We're going to look at a map. And we're going to get you some gear."

"Can't I just wait outside while you go in?"

He stopped and turned to me, scowling. "What did they do to you when you went to get Raphael?"

"Nothing. Well, nothing that bad. I just . . . I think most of them probably hate me."

His eyebrows shot up. "Did I ask the wrong question? Should I have asked what you did to them?"

"Look," I said defensively, "they weren't listening to me. You were in serious trouble, and they were just standing around. I may have . . . punched Hani in a very sensitive place."

He laughed and shook his head. "You're incredible." He gave me a wry smile when he read the puzzlement in my expression. "I mean that in the most complimentary way, Lela. Thank you for being willing to go back to the Station after everything that happened to you there. If you hadn't, I wouldn't have survived."

"I owed it to you."

"You owed me *nothing*."

I looked away from the intensity of his gaze and started walking again. "I guess we'll have to agree to differ on that one. But if you want to show me how thankful you are, just make them keep their hands to themselves."

"Done."

I was behind him as we entered the Station. Four Guards, Hani included, stepped from the darkest corners of the room and closed in quickly. Their glowing eyes were focused on me. I took a few steps back, preparing to bolt.

"We'll escort her to a cell, Captain," Hani said. His hand was inches from my arm when Malachi's voice, cool, clipped, and precise, froze him in place.

"She's with me."

It was instantly obvious that whatever they thought of him, they were totally afraid to say it to his face—despite the fact that they were all twice his size. They backed off quickly and cautiously. Without another word, Malachi turned to me and gestured down the hall. Then he stepped in behind me, putting himself between me and the Guards. I walked down that hallway slowly, wondering if his eyes were on me, trying to decipher the skipping, unsteady rhythm of my heart.

Malachi's quarters had no windows, no decorations. His room was just like everything else about him—nothing unnecessary, nothing wasted. His narrow cot rested in a corner, right next to something that looked like a hat rack. He walked straight to it and hung his bloody, stained armor over it. A small desk stood across from the rack, but the only things that sat upon it were a fountain pen and a single book, like some kind of journal. Neatly stacked in a corner rose a tower of identical books as tall as I was. *A lot* of journals. Two of the walls were lined with a small arsenal of blades and staffs of varying length, and a giant map covered most of the far wall.

I watched him move silently around his room. Once on his feet, he had recovered quickly from his injuries. He walked over to a trunk at the foot of his cot and started pulling out clothes. I forced my eyes away from him and turned to the map.

It was the city, hand-drawn in painstaking detail, with tiny notations scribbled all over it in some sort of foreign alphabet. I knelt, finding the spot at the southern edge of the map where the Suicide Gates were drawn. My fingers hovered over the worn surface as I tried to trace the path I'd taken, but my eyes quickly got tangled in the labyrinth. Even as a map, this city was impossible. I was so absorbed that when Malachi's hand closed around my elbow, I jerked away reflexively.

"Sorry." He held up his hand to show he meant no harm. Now dressed in fatigue pants and a form-fitting dark shirt that had me staring at his chest a few seconds longer than necessary, Malachi focused his attention on the map. He put his finger on a small, rectangular unit at the level of my waist. "That's the Station." His finger moved down and to the right. "That's where you were when Amid found you." He jabbed his finger at a spot west of the center of the city. "And that's where Sil had you when Ana and I caught up."

"Where were they taking me?"

"Probably to their nest."

"Where's that?"

"I'm not entirely sure. That's something I'm supposed to figure out." His brows pinched together as his gaze dropped to the floor.

I looked at the map, not wanting to pry. "You drew this?"

"Yes. But it changes. It grows. The city is walled, but it expands like a living thing. I try to keep track of it."

"Where are we going to look for Nadia?"

"That's going to be up to you," he said as his eyes wandered over the map. "Can you describe your dreams to me? The ones you had *after* she died, I mean."

"I think I only have to describe one. You've seen her, Malachi. You talked to her."

His eyes widened. He reached out to pull my arm into view but stopped short. He looked at me carefully. "Could you hold your arm up for me?"

I obliged. As he stared at it, I explained. "I saw you through her eyes. You fought a guy named Ibram."

Malachi touched his left shoulder and looked at me in surprise. "You saw me?" He closed his eyes in memory. "That's why you didn't want to tell me why you were here. Why you were so ready to believe I was going to kill you. Why you thought I might go after Nadia. You saw what happened, but you didn't understand it. You thought I was killing innocents, but they were all Mazikin."

I raised an eyebrow. "It's not like you were Mr. Sweet-and-Friendly when we met in person. You did threaten to cut off a sizable chunk of my arm."

His gaze dropped to the floor again. "I never would have done it, but it had to be a good bluff because you were not easily intimidated. I was surprised you believed me so quickly, but I guess it makes sense now."

"Nadia thought you were going to kill her. We both did."

He nodded. "The girl in the alley. I'm sorry I didn't recognize her before. The girl bore a resemblance to the face on your arm . . . but she looked . . . different." He read my expression and shook his head. "Nothing drastic, but she was . . . well, she looked like all the people here do. They don't take very good care of themselves. But when I first saw her, I thought she might be Mazikin, because she was so close to the fight."

"How did you know she wasn't?"

"Mazikin have a particular smell," he explained, returning his attention to my arm.

"Incense. And something rotten." I shuddered, remembering Sil's face so close to my neck.

Malachi nodded as he eyed my spastic fidgeting. "I'm sorry they got close enough for you to discover that." He stepped around me and pointed at a scribbled notation in the upper left quadrant of the map. "It was here. The Harag zone. I'm afraid your friend wandered into a very bad part of town. The Mazikin have been massing there lately. We think their newest nest might be in that area."

When he saw my how wide my eyes had gotten, he said, "If she got into an apartment unit, she would be safe as long as she stayed there."

"I saw her—she did go into an apartment. There was someone stalking her, though. I think it was a Mazikin."

My heart rate kicked up, thinking of that cackling laugh just behind her.

"It probably was. They roam the halls of those buildings sometimes, looking for recruits. But as soon as Nadia crossed the threshold, they couldn't have followed her in."

"And if she leaves?"

The look on his face said everything. It made my chest hurt. "The apartment building had orange walls and pink doors. Could that help us find her?"

He shook his head. "All the buildings in that zone do. That just confirms she was in Harag." He walked to his desk, opened the book, and flipped through it until he found the page he was looking for. His eyes scanned the incomprehensible writing, and then he pointed to one entry. "I fought Ibram only seven days ago," he said. "You must have seen this right before you . . ."

"It happened the night I died." I swallowed the lump in my throat. Had I really been here that long? Those freaky nightmares and visions had been my only real link to Nadia, but I hadn't been inside her head for a whole week. As frustrating and crazy-making as it had been, I would have given a lot to have that connection back. It took me several seconds to blink back the tears and get control of myself. When I succeeded, I looked up to see Malachi watching me with a tenderness that made me swear he wanted to reach out to me, to touch me. I was startled to feel a twinge of disappointment as I glanced down at his hands and saw they were fisted at his sides.

"We'll go soon. We'll find her." His voice was soft but firm. He walked to the door of the room and opened it, calling down the hall. "Rais, please summon Ana. Tell her to come to my quarters."

"You seem certain she made it back."

"She always does," he said. "But I doubt she was able to catch Sil. He's annoyingly fast."

"Is she coming with us?"

Malachi had traversed the room and was buckling a belt around his hips. "Yes, we'll need her for this. But also, she has things that might fit you." He approached and stood next to me by the desk. "Lela, I know you're impatient to leave, and I agree we need to move quickly, but there are some preparations we have to make if we want to be successful. We have a place to look, and that's a great start. More than I expected to have. But that area is the most dangerous part of the city, the worst possible location. If you don't mind, I'd like to give us the best chance of coming back alive. Can you be patient if we don't leave until tomorrow?"

Here it was, a decision point. He was asking me to trust him, but not in so many words. I gazed at his face, translating the messages there, looking for a lie or a trap. Again I saw nothing but determination and sincerity. "Yes," I replied.

He smiled and I kept staring, caught by the way it transformed his stark, fierce face, rendering it whimsical, beautiful.

"Malachi," interrupted a smooth, lethal voice.

Malachi didn't take his eyes off me, but his smile widened. "Ana. Glad to have you back."

"I could say the same. Raphael told me you were in bad shape." Ana strode into his room like she belonged there. For all I knew, she did. And with that thought, an uncomfortable stab of . . . something sliced through my chest. I rubbed away the ache and turned my full attention to her.

Without her bulky coat to conceal the curves, Ana's body was very feminine but emanated an animal strength and confidence that caused my fingers to twitch in readiness for an attack. Her smooth, brown skin glowed with amber undertones, framed by the stark black of her hair, which hung in thick ropes from a ponytail high at the back of her head. Her eyes were tilted up slightly, like a cat's, and their dark depths were fixed on me.

"You must be Lela." She turned to Malachi. "Was she worth it?"

Malachi made a noise in his throat that sounded distinctly like a growl. Ana smiled but didn't look happy.

"I guess so," she murmured.

"Lela needs clothes," he said. "We have a mission, and I'd like you to outfit her. We leave tomorrow morning for the northwest quadrant, Harag zone."

Ana's eyes went wide. "You're taking her to Harag? Didn't we just break our backs to keep her away from there?"

"Ana." There was nothing but warning in his voice.

Her mouth snapped shut, but she looked at Malachi with disgust.

My gaze bounced between the two of them as I tried to figure out what could lie behind his tone and her expression.

Malachi's voice was tight as he issued his instructions. "She'll bunk with you tonight. We will train this evening. Distance weapons only. Please get her settled and properly clothed while I go see Michael."

He turned to me and his face relaxed noticeably, as if he was making a conscious effort not to scare me. "Michael is our weapons supplier. I'll be back after dinner, and we'll have a training session. You were able to handle the small Mazikin on your own, but there are a few things I'd like to show you before we go, in case you have to deal with something more challenging. Will you stay with Ana until I come back?"

He actually seemed to be giving me a choice. Another decision, another request for trust. "I will," I said as I looked at Ana, who crossed her arms over her chest and stared at Malachi with narrowed eyes. *Assuming she doesn't kill me before then.*

But Ana, too, relaxed as her gaze met mine. "Come on, girl, let's get you out of that ugly green shirt."

She marched from the room. As I turned to follow, Malachi winked at me. It took all my concentration not to stumble over my own feet as I headed for the door.

FOURTEEN

ANA'S ROOM SMELLED FAINTLY of cinnamon, welcoming and warm. In spite of myself, I relaxed a little. Compared to Malachi's impersonal, spare quarters, Ana's room was an oasis of color and quirk, the most appealing space I'd come across since arriving in the city. She had a similar arsenal of deadly looking accessories, but her walls were covered in paintings, all done in the same style. Though the colors were muted and dull compared to those on Earth, the strokes were lush and bold, curves and strikes and stabs of paint. They looked like war. Or love. I wasn't sure which, but they made my chest ache.

"Sit down, Lela. Let's work on you. What happened to your hair?"

My hand traveled automatically to my head. I hadn't looked in a mirror since I'd died. "What are you talking about?"

"Oh. It's always that crazy? We need to get it under control before we go. It's asking to be grabbed."

I eyed her spill of ebony hair. "And yours isn't?"

Ana smiled. "Maybe. But those who try lose limbs."

In that instant I decided I liked Ana. I smiled back. "Maybe you could teach me how to do that."

Ana shook her head as she opened the trunk at the foot of her cot, which was carved with intricate markings that looked like Chinese. Or Japanese. Something like that. "Malachi said distance weapons only."

"What does that mean?"

"It means he doesn't want anyone's limbs to get close enough for you to have to slice them off. And he doesn't want you accidentally slicing off your own limbs, either."

I tilted my head, remembering how I'd nearly cut off my leg with Lacey's scimitar. "I guess that's hard to argue with."

"Malachi often is. Here we go!" Ana straightened, brandishing a thick wire brush. She circled me, and I turned in place, not letting her at my back. Ana's eyes narrowed speculatively. "It's just a brush, honey."

I shrugged apologetically. "Habit."

Ana pulled a chair away from the wall. "Sit."

I obeyed and focused on a large painting hanging on the far wall. From a distance, the chaotic strokes of paint came together, and an Asian man's face, deadly and handsome, stared back at me. Ana followed my gaze to the painting.

"Takeshi," she said softly as she picked up a section of my hair and brushed the ends. "He taught us most of what we know."

At the tight, hoarse sound of Ana's voice, my eyes flicked from the painting back to the trunk. "Is that Japanese writing?"

Ana laughed, but it sounded a little sad. "Malachi said you were observant. Yes, it is. And yes, the trunk was Takeshi's."

The sorrow in her voice and her use of the past tense were enough to silence me. I sat quietly while she brushed the tangles out of my hair, reducing it from gravity-defying curls to bobbing waves.

"So," she said, "want to tell me what you did to Malachi?"

I closed my eyes, praying that my cheeks weren't turning red as I thought of all the things I had done to Malachi. I wondered which of them Ana was referring to.

I swallowed. "I have no idea what you're talking about."

Ana kept brushing, her fingers deftly separating my hair into sections, attacking each part systematically. If she noticed a blush, she didn't comment on it.

"He's not acting like himself. Malachi is the most calculating person I know. But he's different with you, like something's not adding up for him."

"Probably because all he wants to do is make sure I leave this city and stop being such a nuisance." Girly hair brushing or no, this was not something I was prepared to discuss.

"Mmm-hmm." Never had a sound dripped with so much skepticism. Mercifully she changed the subject. "Do you have any weapons training?"

I scoffed. "Why do people keep asking me that? I'm a high school student. Or I was. I guess I'm nothing now. But no, no 'weapons training' for me. I'm pretty good at defending myself, though."

"We'll see. That's why Malachi wants you to practice with weapons that keep attackers at a distance. Fists are bad, but Mazikin bites are worse, and if we're going as far as the Harag zone, odds aren't good we'd get back to the Station in time for Raphael to do his thing. So—you'll learn to use the bo staff. Maybe throwing knives. It depends on how good you are because we don't have much time to teach you if he wants to leave tomorrow."

She started to braid my hair. "Keep still. I don't usually get to work on another girl. It makes me feel like a girl. Don't ruin it for me."

I swallowed a chuckle. Not that I had a ton of experience, but this was the freakiest slumber party I'd ever attended. *First we braid each other's hair, then we attack each other with assorted weaponry.* Maybe it wasn't *so* different from your average high school girl get-together.

When Ana finished, she held up a warped mirror. My reflection reminded me of a Picasso painting I'd seen in one of my textbooks. "Um, it's great?"

"Well, it'll keep your hair out of your face. Now. Clothes. I think my stuff will fit you." She dug through her trunk again and came up with a serviceable pair of boots and an outfit that looked almost exactly like the one Malachi had been wearing. I tugged off the icky green shirt and pulled on the navy-blue top, which was soft as it hugged my skin. The pants were a little snug, but also the most comfortable thing I'd had on my body since I'd arrived.

Ana looked me up and down. "You look just like one of the Guard."

She laughed when I shot her a horrified look. No girl wants to be told she resembles a rhinoceros. "One of *us*," she clarified. "You look like one of us."

"Are you and Malachi the only—"

"At present, we are the only human members of the Guard." Ana was suddenly very busy putting things back in her trunk. After a few minutes, she completed her meticulous, and seemingly needless, rearranging. "Since Malachi's not back yet, let's get something to eat, and then we'll go to the training room."

"You know, I'm not really hungry."

Ana looked me straight in the eye. "Ah. I forgot. That's because the food here's not right for you. You're in the wrong place. Malachi knew it immediately. That's probably why he's so crazy to get you out of here."

"The food here's not right for me?" Was that why I wasn't hungry?

"Let me guess—nothing looks good here. Whatever you see here, you can have as much as you like. But none of it tempts you, am I right?"

I winced as the unwelcome image of Malachi's bare chest flashed in my mind. "No, nothing's tempting," I said through clenched teeth.

Ana gave me a quizzical look. "All right, so you're in the wrong place. Most people here are gathering possessions just like they did on Earth, eating, drinking, smoking—some of them even hoard stuff in their apartments, blocking themselves inside. Only people who are ready to be released stop consuming the things that are here."

"What does that mean, though?"

"It means you need to get out of here or eventually you'll starve because you're not getting what you need."

"What? I don't feel hungry!" My hands poked at my stomach like someone else was controlling them.

"It's all right, Lela," Ana reassured, watching my wiggling fingers with amusement. "It takes a while. You have some time. A few weeks, at least."

I hadn't realized I had an expiration date. "And if I eat?"

"It won't nourish you. Don't bother. It's no good, anyway. Be glad you don't have to force it down like the rest of us." Her eyes darted up to mine. "You know, you could go see the Judge and head out into the Countryside . . . maybe fatten yourself up and then come back to look for your friend?"

I clenched my fists just to stop myself from giving her the finger. "Yeah. I'm sure the Gate Guards would have specific instructions to welcome me back with open arms, right? Nice try."

She shrugged.

"Did Malachi put you up to that?" So much for trusting him.

She shook her head. "He probably thought of it, but he's obviously decided he cares what you think about him."

Something in my chest loosened a bit. I felt . . . relieved. I realized I *wanted* to trust Malachi. I tugged absently at my braid as I thought of him—and then I remembered something he'd said. "Malachi told me he doesn't drink the water here."

Ana's expression fell. "Oh yeah. He eats sometimes, but he stopped drinking a few months ago. Lucky him." Envy sucked the life out of her voice. "He won't talk about it with me, but I know what it means. He hasn't started to lose weight yet, but it's only a matter of time. He's on his way out."

"You mean he's going to starve or something?" I wished I'd tried to coax some of the water down his throat while he was unconscious.

"No, I mean *out*, as in out of the city and into the Countryside." Ana's smile was brittle and tense. "I think Malachi's almost done here. I don't know when, exactly, but I guess

I'll know when he stops eating completely." She threw her shoulders back and pulled her ponytail tight with practiced fingers. "Well, I'm starving. Do you want to come with me to the food room?"

My brain was still working over the thousands of questions bouncing around in my skull, but one look at Ana told me the conversation was over. I kept my tongue clamped tightly between my teeth as I followed her purposeful strides out of the room and down the hall.

The "food room" was exactly what it sounded like and very similar to the FOOD store I'd visited. Unappetizing was a generous way to describe it. Ana gathered random items for herself, including a forlorn lump of cheese, a black banana, a hard roll, and some sort of soup that smelled, to me at least, like feet. I didn't mention it to Ana, though.

Other Guards sat at long, wooden tables, piles of food in front of them. Most of their gem-bright eyes were riveted on us as we crossed the cavernous room. It felt a little like Warwick High School, except that all the other kids were more than seven feet tall and heavily armed.

Ana pulled a knife from the sheath at her thigh and scraped at the bits of mold that clung to the face of the cheese. I sat across from her, thoughts racing. If I didn't make it out of the city in a few weeks, I would starve. Malachi hadn't mentioned that, but it explained a lot of his eagerness to get me out. Well, I was just as eager to leave as he was to see me go, as long as I had Nadia with me. Maybe he wouldn't be too far behind. I thought back to the longing in his voice as he talked about what lay beyond the city walls. I was happy that he might be able to get out soon and spent a few moments musing about the smile it might put on his harsh, defiant face.

Ana ate quickly and wordlessly. She seemed subdued after our conversation about eating, and I wondered if she was wishing she had less of an appetite. The room quieted when Ana got up to throw her leftovers away. She acted like she didn't notice. As soon as we stepped into the hall, newly relaxed laughter and teasing filled the room and shook the walls.

I glanced over at Ana. "Is it that you make them nervous or that they think you're hot?"

"Both. There were others before me, but I've been the only woman here for a long time. Long enough for most of these guys to try something and regret it very badly afterward. At first, though, Takeshi and Malachi had to protect me. They never let me go anywhere without them. But it wasn't until I learned to take care of myself that the other Guards really left me alone."

"Had you ever trained before you came here?"

Ana looked me up and down. "You know, I think I was probably like you. I mean, I don't know you, but you have that look. A strong girl. A fierce girl." She gave me a smile that managed to be both sly and sad. "A damaged girl."

I looked away and ground my teeth. Was it that obvious? Like NOT FIT FOR NORMAL SOCIETY was stamped across my forehead.

Only Nadia had made me feel differently. She made me feel like I was good enough, like all I needed to do was read the code and speak the language of that normal world instead of changing myself to fit into it. She once told me that everybody carried their secret savages beneath their skin, and some people just covered them better than others.

I'd wanted to be like Nadia, fitting in but not caring rather than the other way around. But if Nadia had really known what was important and real, why had she bothered to put on that happy face when she was obviously so miserable? Why had she kept herself drugged out on painkillers? And why the hell had she chosen to leave me?

If Malachi and Ana were as good as they seemed, maybe I would have a chance to ask her.

Ana led me down a set of stone steps, the light from the gas lamps flickering in the darkness. The temperature dropped as we descended. Heavy thuds and sharp cracks echoed against the stones. It sounded like there was a fight going on. We reached the door at the base of the stairs.

"He's warming up," Ana said casually as she pushed open the door. The room inside fell silent.

I stepped into a long, rectangular chamber with a high ceiling. Modified gas lamps lined the room, all of them covered with sturdy wire mesh—to keep them from being broken by flying objects, no doubt. Malachi stood at the far side of the room, pulling a shirt on over those amazing abs of his.

"How's Michael?" Ana asked as she approached him.

Malachi rolled his eyes and wiped a sleeve across his sweaty face. "His usual, eloquent self. But he'll have armor for Lela by tomorrow morning."

I looked back and forth between them. Over the last few years, I'd become really proud of my ability to protect myself, my ability to intimidate others into leaving me alone. But right then, gazing at two *actual* warriors, I felt like a stupid high school kid.

The next few hours were brutal. It started out slow enough, with Malachi teaching me to use the staff. He demonstrated the various grips I could use to strike and block basic attacks. He had me practice forward and backward blocks, upward and downward strikes. Over and over again, with increasing speed. By the time he was satisfied that I'd developed a basic comfort with it and was no longer in danger of thwacking myself in the head at inopportune moments, all my muscles were shaking and I was breathing so hard I was certain my lungs were about to explode.

"Time to defend yourself," Ana sang, skipping forward with a scimitar. I panted out a curse and staggered back a few steps.

"Just observe first," said Malachi, taking the scimitar from Ana and handing her a staff. Ana winked at Malachi and spun the staff with dizzying speed. Malachi gave her a stern look. "She just needs the basics. Stop overwhelming her."

Ana stuck out her tongue at him and held the staff still.

I wished I was imagining the graceless, exaggeratedly heavy steps Ana took as she stomped around, but then I noticed that muscle in Malachi's jaw ticking away in annoyance.

Yep, she was making fun of me.

Before I could turn to bolt, Malachi refocused me. "Not all Mazikin are armed, but recently they've been stealing and hoarding Guard weapons. We know of two who are competent with scimitars, and you've met one of them. Oh, and you've seen the other. Sil and Ibram. There were three, but alas, Juri is no longer with us." I heard the grim satisfaction in his voice as he said it and smiled to myself for the same reason. "Anyway, if you see either of them, run. Just run. Get around a corner as quickly as you can and keep going. But with the others, your goal is to disarm if possible and defend yourself if nothing else."

He turned back to Ana and ran straight at her, blade raised. In a blur of movement, Ana met his attack and twisted the weapon from his arms.

"Didn't quite catch that," I said.

"Of course not," he said, stepping back into his starting position. "We'll slow it down for you."

They demonstrated several more times, step by step, how to meet and disarm a relatively inexperienced person wielding a scimitar.

These are the things they don't teach you in high school.

Malachi offered me the staff again. After what felt like hundreds of attempts, I succeeded in completing the series of movements at a normal speed. I even learned a few variations of the same maneuver.

Finally he announced I'd endured enough of the staff. I collapsed to the floor in happiness, ready for a rest and fantasizing about a hot shower. But when I opened my eyes, he was standing over me. He held out his hand tentatively, offering to pull me to my feet, almost as though he was afraid I wouldn't want to take his hand. I reached up and let his long fingers wrap around mine as he tugged me up to stand beside him.

He gave me what I could only interpret as a shy smile. "How do you feel about knives?"

I laughed. "Do you even have to ask? Love them. Love. Them."

He chuckled and handed me one. "These are throwing knives. Notice the double edge? Different from the hunting knife. These will be easier for you to control."

"So next time I can hit something vital?"

He cocked his arm and set his eyes on a cloth mannequin several yards away. "Only as a last resort, Lela, if you have nothing else. But that's the idea." A fraction of a second later, the poor mannequin was dead.

Ana was at least as good as Malachi and seemed to enjoy showing off, spinning around the room while she adorned the mannequin with a necklace of knives. I cracked up when she landed a cluster of knives right in the mannequin's crotch. Malachi's olive skin turned ashen.

"Remind me to be nicer to you," he muttered.

Malachi would not allow me to stop practicing until I got the right form. "You're throwing it like a baseball." He laughed. "Who do you think you are, Lefty Grove?"

He seemed to think he was hilarious, but I just stared. Who the heck was Lefty Grove? Ana sidled up to him and leaned in to whisper, "You're dating yourself, *old man* . . . ."

His face instantly became serious. "Never mind. Back to work."

About a thousand throws later, I was jealous of the knife-riddled mannequin and wishing someone would have as much mercy on me. My right arm burned from shoulder to fingertips. My neck and back were knotted and aching. But I knew how to throw a knife. Yet another practical skill they never bothered to teach in high school.

When Malachi finally relented and started to put away the knives, I sank to the floor, massaging my dead right arm. I looked around the room at their odd assortment of weapons. Scimitar. Staff. Throwing knives. I wasn't exactly an expert—my knowledge came entirely from movies—but they didn't all seem to fit together into a single fighting style.

"Why these weapons? I'm telling you, a rocket launcher and a few AK-47s would do you guys loads of good."

Malachi and Ana looked at each other, and he obviously read something on her face, because he nodded at her.

"I'm done," she said, turning away to pick up a few staffs from the floor and set them in a wall rack. "I need to go get some water and take a shower. And I have to gear up. Lela, you did a good job tonight. I'll see you later."

Ana gave Malachi a playful swat on the ass and bounced from the room. She looked no more tired than when she'd walked in, which made me seriously jealous. That feeling only intensified as I thought about the way she touched Malachi, like she'd earned the right over years. I wiped my sweaty palms on my pants and wished away the foreign ache in my chest.

"To answer your question," said Malachi, slipping several knives into a large cloth pouch, "it's built up over centuries. Some of us bring knowledge of weapons or fighting styles from our lives on Earth and train the others. It gets passed from Guard to Guard, each new person learning from the older ones." He heaved a sigh, like a memory was pressing in on him. "Michael develops new weapons to fit the human Guards' preferences. I imagine it will only be a matter of time before we get a new Guard whose expertise is guns, but I hope I will be gone by then."

He stretched, and it looked like he was pushing his memories back, returning to the present. "I don't know where the scimitar came from. That has been a Guard weapon for a millennium as far as I know, like a tradition. All Guards are trained to use them. The throwing knives—that was an American, actually. He was from the South, during your Civil War, and he left here soon after I became a Guard. Anyway, not everyone carries those because not everyone throws well enough to do anything but give the enemy a weapon. Which is why you should only use yours as a last resort. Oh, and don't bother trying it on Ibram."

"Yeah, I saw."

He nodded. "Now, the staff—that was Takeshi. He could stop anything with it. He was the one who got Michael to modify the batons. It would be hard to tote a full-length staff around the city. The other Guards' batons are just that: they're for crowd control and mostly for threat. But as you've seen, mine and Ana's extend to become staffs. It's better for us because we don't wear the heavy armor. We can fight more opponents at once and keep their teeth away from our lovely, fragile skin."

I busied myself retying the lace on my boot to keep him from seeing my face as I thought about his lovely, fragile skin. "So Takeshi was here before you."

"Yes, he was the one who taught Ana and me."

I handed my knives to Malachi. "She's still grieving for him, isn't she?"

He looked startled. "Yes. It's been years, but I don't think it feels that long to her."

I wanted to ask what had happened, but the look on his face warned me away. Like Ana had when we touched on the topic of Takeshi, Malachi was suddenly deeply absorbed in meticulous, needless activity, positioning and rearranging the knives within that cloth pouch. As he folded it and put it away, I got up and headed to the door, once again dreaming of a hot shower.

"We're not quite done, Lela. If you can't keep attackers at a distance, you'd better be able to fight back when they get close. Hand-to-hand is next."

I froze midstep. "And who was the sadist who brought *that* particular style with him?"

He tilted his head and grinned. "Me."

FIFTEEN

TAKESHI MIGHT HAVE TAUGHT Malachi how to use a staff and throw a knife, but Malachi's merciless efficiency was apparently something he'd learned during his short, brutal life on Earth. As lethal as he was with the scimitar, his body was obviously his weapon of choice. It was something we had in common. The weapons just felt awkward to me, like I might be at more risk for hurting myself than hurting someone else. I was more at home with up-close fighting, and I was pretty good at it. But Malachi made me better.

"When you're fighting, there aren't any rules. You must defend yourself and neutralize your opponent quickly. No fancy moves—you want every encounter to be as brief as possible. Do whatever is necessary to take down your attacker, no matter how cruel it seems. Kind of like what you did to Hani." He gave me a wicked smile. "That was perfect. Except you should have made sure he was down before you ran."

I rolled my eyes. "If I'd done that, six of his buddies would've pinned me to the floor a few seconds later."

He frowned. "Good point. Run faster next time."

"Yes, sir." I grinned and shot him a mock salute.

"Next, use any available object as a weapon. I think you understand this one well. I saw what you were going to do with that beer bottle. It would have been excellent if your attackers weren't wielding swords. If that happens again, just throw it at them and, like I said, run faster."

"Wow, this is helpful. When do I get to hit you?"

He snorted. "You seem so eager. All right then, if it will make you happy."

He beckoned with his hands, inviting me to attack. I stepped forward and aimed a punch at his groin. Hell, it had worked with Hani.

Malachi laughed as he blocked me. "Excellent strategy, Lela, but don't be too predictable."

And then I was on the floor, my arm bent up behind me.

"Stop waiting for the next thing to happen," he instructed. "*Make* the next thing happen. Up."

I jumped to my feet and tried to punch him in the face, but he ducked and yanked my legs out from under me. My breath huffed from my lungs as I hit the floor.

He smiled down at me, his hands curled around my ankles, resting them on the sides of his thighs. "If you had actually hit me, your hand would probably hurt more than my face. Don't forget your elbows. Up."

When I obeyed, he showed me just how useful elbows could be. I was on the floor again within a few seconds, wheezing.

I laid my forehead on the mat and rubbed at the twin aches in my chest, one where he had hit me, one that went deeper. I could tell he was holding back in a major way. He wasn't going easy on me, but he obviously didn't want to hurt me. Every time he knocked me to the floor, his hands lingered a bit longer as he helped me up, and the look in his eyes was warmer. And I liked it. More than I ever expected to.

That didn't mean I didn't want to prove myself. I got up, gritting my teeth, and started to circle him. He watched me as I closed in, his face utterly solemn, like he was actually taking me seriously. I faked to the right and then jerked back and spun, using all my momentum to elbow him in the stomach, which was sort of like elbowing a brick wall. He grunted, but I had no time to celebrate the fact that I'd actually landed a blow, because he immediately planted his foot, took my head in his hands, and brought his other knee up.

"Nice one," I muttered in a nasally voice a second later, my nose pressed flat against his kneecap.

"It's hard to go wrong with a well-placed knee strike." He lowered his knee and lifted my face to his. "Are you all right?"

We were chest-to-chest, and his hands were still on the sides of my face. He'd left himself unguarded. I considered kneeing him in the balls for half a second but was completely distracted when his thumb stroked across my cheek. I sucked in a tight breath, stunned by the heat of his touch and the look in his eyes, my heart skipping unsteadily. After a few seconds of staring at each other, he blinked and his hands fell away.

"Come," he said abruptly. "I'll teach you how to disarm a knife attack."

And so it went. And went. And went. I lost count of how many times I hit the floor, but weirdly, I was enjoying myself and feeling more at ease than I had since arriving in the dark city. I was hopeful and getting excited about heading out to look for Nadia. With Malachi and Ana going with me, how could I not succeed?

Then he attacked me from behind.

It happened quickly. Later, I realized I should have expected it. Maybe it was because adrenaline already ran thick through my veins. Maybe it was because my guard was down, and I wasn't braced against the memories. Maybe it was because he grabbed me around the neck in a frighteningly strong grip, and I couldn't get loose. But when he wrapped his other arm over my chest and I felt his body behind mine, everything went black, and all I could do was scream and claw and kick.

Facedown facedown I can't breathe and he will crush me here and leave me helpless and empty and worthless and bleeding until next time and no one will hear me scream.

When I opened my eyes, I was curled into a corner. My lips tingled, and black spots floated in front of me. My arms were folded over my head, shielding myself from . . . nothing. It was quiet. I lifted my head. Malachi sat a few feet away, and I couldn't read his face. Red furrows tracked across one of his cheeks and the backs of his hands.

"I'm sorry," he whispered.

I wiped the tears from my cheeks with impatient, angry swipes and pushed away the rebellious tendrils of hair that had escaped my braid. "No, I'm sorry. That's embarrassing. I tend to panic when someone gets behind me." I got to my feet shakily, keeping my back to the wall.

He blew out a long breath as he stood. "I knew that. I felt it the night I interrogated you. I saw it in your eyes when Sil grabbed you. But I did it anyway, and I shouldn't have."

"No, you *should* have. Do you think the next Mazikin who gets the drop on me is going to ask for permission to approach from the rear?"

"Why was it so bad this time?" he asked. He looked like he wasn't sure he wanted to hear my answer.

"I don't know. Some times are worse than others."

He winced.

I shook my head, defeated by my own frustration. "I hate feeling out of control," I whispered. "I can't remember what just happened."

"You panicked. I let you go when I realized what was happening, but you didn't stop."

I took a deep breath, eyeing the door. I had regained the feeling in my lips, and my vision had cleared. But I still felt jittery, like I wanted to run. "How long did it last?"

He looked at the floor. "Not long." *Too long,* shouted the slump of his shoulders and the clench of his fists.

"You have to show me what to do," I said firmly.

He didn't answer me and kept his eyes on his boots.

"You have to. You can show me what to do, and maybe I can learn to stay calm. Not freak out. Not black out. If you're so concerned that I'll need to protect myself, then you should do this for me." The silence was deafening. *"Malachi."*

As soon as I said his name, he brought his eyes to mine. They were dark with sorrow. "I don't want to be the one who brings it back for you, Lela. I don't want you to see him, whoever he was, when you look at *me*."

I almost relented because he sounded so sad. But I hated this feeling of losing control, of being helpless. I was frightened of what it might mean if it happened in the arms of an enemy next time. "I'm sorry. That's why you *have* to do this for me."

He turned away. "Fine. Now?"

"Yes."

"Slow first. I approached too quickly last time."

"Okay."

"Go to the center of the room. Close your eyes."

I obeyed, tensing to fight the nausea. But this time, as he came up behind me, he issued nonstop instructions. I clung to his voice and followed it blindly. He showed me how to use my body's instinctive movements, exploit the weakness of the wrist, and pinpoint the attacker's most vulnerable spots in order to shake free. He taught me how to turn and strike once I'd escaped. He made me practice it over and over again. Finally, he approached silently and attacked, and I didn't panic as I evaded him.

It wasn't perfect, or complete, or permanent. But for me it was victory. Malachi didn't look so sure as he wiped the sweat from his face and tidied the room. He kept rubbing the back of his neck, like it was really hurting him. But I was pretty sure he wasn't in any physical pain.

I had gotten exactly what I needed, but I suddenly felt guilty for asking it of him. It seemed like I'd taken something from him, and I didn't know how to give it back, how to make him feel better. I didn't know him at all, I realized. It only felt like I did.

He switched off the lamps as he approached the door and turned to see if I was following. That jittery, uneasy feeling was on me again, but now it was because I had no idea how to fix *this*, whatever had happened over the past hour. And yet I desperately wanted to try.

"Hey, Malachi, I know it's late, and I know we're leaving tomorrow. Before we go . . ." I sucked in a breath and continued quickly. "Before we go, I was wondering . . . if you'd show me what you do for fun around here."

It was the most romantic thing I'd ever said to a boy. But as the words left my mouth, I heard how stupid they sounded. If I'd said that to any guy I'd known before, he'd have snickered and made the worst possible interpretation. It's quite possible the interaction would have ended in violence.

Malachi just stared at me like he was turning my words over in his head, letting them loop around his brain a few times. "Okay," he said. "Come with me." He pulled the door open and ascended the stairs. I followed, swallowing my relief like candy.

He didn't exit the stairway when we reached the main floor. Soon we were climbing up a spiraling staircase into the tower that jutted up from the roof of the Guard Station. My thighs complained bitterly after the grueling workout they'd endured, but I kept quiet as I followed Malachi, who maintained a steady pace as he proceeded upward. I was having a silent argument with myself about whether to break down and ask for a rest when I heard a door open directly above me and looked up to see him climb through it. He held his hand out to me. Wind gusted through my hair and dried my sweat as I took it, letting his strength compensate for the failure of my exhausted legs.

We were at the very top of the tower. It was a small space, only a few feet wide—enough room for only the two of us. The surrounding wall was waist high, an iron railing pressed into the crumbling mortar between the stones.

"I come here," he said softly. All around us, the silent city crouched on its hill, eating the light. I turned in place, thinking Malachi must have used this view to draw parts of his map. It was easier to see and comprehend from here, at least until my eyes hit the solid mass of skyscrapers at the peak of the hill.

He pointed to the wall of buildings. "We'll go to the north, beyond there. That's the oldest part of the city. The buildings . . . I know it sounds strange, but they get taller every year. The oldest ones, in the center, are the tallest. The shorter buildings near the wall are newer. But they get taller, too. You see, if someone in the city wants a house, it grows. If they want a pagoda or a hut or a tower, it grows. All they have to do is want. Wish. Desire. Then the buildings take on a life of their own, fed by the wanting. But what comes of that wanting is never good. Or satisfying. Just . . . big. So the city grows, and the misery within it grows. Like a disease."

"Is there a cure?"

"Sure, but not everyone is willing. I think some people like the disease better. It's more familiar, and they don't want to give it up, even once they know they can be healed of it. The cure itself, of course, can be very difficult to take," he said, sounding regretful.

I thought of Nadia, out there in that vast darkness, alone in her sorrow. But Malachi was saying there was a way out, a way Nadia could be cured of her sadness. She would be made whole again. And I would make sure it happened.

Malachi leaned back against the wall. He pointed to the white building on the far edge of the city, the one that had called to me so clearly just before I'd come through the Gates. It still tugged at me, luring me forward.

"That's the Sanctum," he said.

I took an automatic step back. The building that drew me in like a magnet was the very one I wasn't yet ready to visit.

"Good to know," I muttered.

He closed his eyes as a light gust of wind hit us. It was the closest thing to fresh air I had experienced, and I watched Malachi's chest expand as he breathed it in. I turned back to the east. The buildings were not as tall there, and the wall of the city was easily visible. Beyond that I could see the wild forest. A huge flock of birds burst out of the trees and flew over the canopy. A moon hovered low and fat and bright just above them. At least, I assumed it was bright. The veil that hung over the city dimmed its beauty and rendered its glow weak and gray.

"The darkness is part of the city," Malachi said, seeing me squint. "But if you know how to look, you can tell day from night. You can see the sun. Its light doesn't reach us here, but I've learned to see it."

"How long have you been here?" I was afraid I already knew the answer, give or take. But for his sake, I hoped I was wrong.

He sighed. "The passing of years is more difficult to track than the passing of days. And I try not to think about it. What year is it on Earth now?"

I told him and immediately regretted it.

He looked down at his boots. "Oh, it's been a long time, then. Longer than I thought. I don't want to tell you."

"I'm sorry. I didn't mean to be nosy."

Another sigh. His gaze shifted to me, and he hesitantly said, "I've been in this city for about seventy years." I did some mental arithmetic and nodded. As far as I could remember, it fit. It meant he would have died . . . killed himself . . . in the early 1940s.

He looked wary, like he was trying to figure out my reaction. "You don't look surprised."

I took his hand in mine. As my fingers slipped under the cuff of his sleeve, he flinched, but then he got tangled in my gaze and held still. I pushed the sleeve to his elbow and ran my thumb over his tattoo. "I saw it. When you were unconscious. I didn't know for sure, but I learned something about it in school. About what the Nazis did to the Jews and others who came into the concentration camps."

"Yes. Ana told me they teach it in school now. That people call it the 'Holocaust.' A horrible word, but it fits exactly." He tilted his head, and his eyes locked onto the tattoo. "History. It feels very fresh to me sometimes. At other times it feels like thousands of years ago. And at all times it feels smaller to me than that word. History is big. For me it was just my family, and my neighborhood, and my city, slowly closing in around me. I didn't even notice at first that it was all shrinking and strangling and falling apart. I was too young to understand it. But when I didn't believe it could get worse, it got worse. It kept getting worse."

I squeezed his hand. "I'm sorry." I didn't know what I was sorrier for: what he went through or that I was making him talk about it.

"It's fine," he reassured me, but his voice revealed the lie. He let the moon pull his gaze from his arm, and I watched his expression as it slowly transformed from grief to something softer.

Longing.

He longed to escape. He *was* escaping in that moment. I knew the feeling well, staring at a spot on the wall where the wallpaper peeled away and imagining myself crawling through to the other side, far away from where I actually was, what I was actually going through. How many times had I done that? How many times had I concentrated so hard that I wasn't present in my own body? How many times had it saved me from shattering into a million pieces?

He seemed so distant that I had to ask. "Are you here?"

"No," he whispered.

I didn't know whether to feel happy or sad, because I wanted him to be with *me*, but I wanted him to be free as well. It didn't seem possible to have both. I reached up and touched his face, the swollen ridges where I'd scratched him in my panic, the angular slope of his jaw, the iron-silk feel of his skin.

My hand trailed down to his chest. I spread my fingers to absorb the heat and beat of his heart. I half expected him to push me away. Instead, he spread his arms and gripped the iron railing that surrounded us, leaving himself open, giving me control.

I put my other hand on his waist and leaned forward, resting my forehead against his chest. It was the same position I'd put him in when I made my sorry attempt to seduce him for the nonexistent key. Tonight my heart was beating as fast as it had then, and so was his. Yet there was nothing I wanted from him this time except for him to be right there with me. His knuckles turned white as he grasped the rail, like he was straining. Or *restraining.* But his expression was distant, and it didn't look like he was coming back anytime soon. So I decided to join him.

I took a breath, inhaling the leather and sweat from his skin, and turned around to face the forest. He was behind me. It felt all right because, after tonight, I knew he wouldn't hurt me.

In fact, I knew it hurt him to be the one. The one who played my demon, just to help me exorcise it. Even though it wasn't entirely gone, it was quiet enough for me to take a step back and let the warmth of him race up my spine. I reached out, peeling his hands from their death grip on the railing. I guided his arms around me until I stood, safe, inside the circle of his arms. Apart from the pounding of his heart and the acceleration of his breathing, he didn't give me any hint of how he felt about it. He simply let me pull him around me like a blanket, like a suit of armor.

"Malachi, can I be with you right now, wherever you are?"

He moved very slowly, as if afraid he would wake my memories and fears. But this time I welcomed the tightening of his arms around me and leaned back when his chin came to rest on the top of my head.

"I thought you'd never ask," he said very softly. "Yes."

SIXTEEN

"UP, LELA. TIME TO go," chirped Ana.

I groaned and rolled over. I'd stayed in the tower with Malachi for too long, but it had felt so good that I couldn't be sorry. He'd held me there, wordless, both of us staring at the distant woods, dreaming separately, breathing together, for what might have been hours. Or it might have been only a few minutes.

It wasn't enough.

When the moon had crossed the sky, Malachi had let me go, reminding me that we had to leave in the morning. He'd been quiet, as if only half of him had returned from his journey over the city wall. His cautious avoidance of unnecessary physical contact resumed as soon as we hit the stairs.

I felt the loss, like some barricade had risen up between us, one I'd built to protect myself but now couldn't find a way around.

"Up, up." Ana kicked the leg of the cot. "I can't believe I left you my bed. You barely used it. I thought you'd drowned in the shower." I cracked an eye open in time to see Ana gather the clothes I'd discarded late last night after a brief, cold shower. She wrinkled her nose. "These smell like Malachi."

I turned my head into the pillow. "How far is it to Harag?" I asked, desperate to steer the conversation down a different path.

Ana tossed some clean clothes at me. "We won't get to the edge of it until the end of today, unless Malachi makes us run. But I think he'll let us conserve our energy on this one."

I pulled a shirt over my head. "Hey—will you explain what you said to Malachi yesterday about the two of you breaking your backs to keep me out of Harag?"

"Ooh. I could. But then Malachi would get nasty. That boy has a special gift for creative nastiness."

"Come on, Ana," I whined, "call it girl talk. You don't get much girl talk, right?"

Ana looked suspicious. "You won't tell him I told you?" I shook my head as I pulled on a pair of pants. "Fine. Just remember, I have my own gifts, and most of them involve hitting people's soft spots with pointy things."

She pulled a knife from nowhere and twirled it on her fingers, then put it away just as quickly. "Malachi's number-one mission since the recent Guard murders is to find the Mazikin nest. He's been working on it for weeks. It's gotten him seriously wounded twice. He's been absolutely ruled by it. And you, with your jailbreaking shenanigans, happened to offer him the best chance he's ever had to find it."

"Because Sil was taking me there." Sudden queasiness drew my hand to my stomach. It felt oddly hollow.

"You got it. All Malachi had to do was track you back to the nest, and we would've had them."

"Why didn't he do that?"

Ana shuffled her feet and looked hesitant. "Look, Lela, I kind of like you, so I'm a little bit sorry I disagree with the choice he made. It was the only chance we've had in ages to see where they're taking people."

"Uh huh, got that part. Why didn't Malachi take that chance?"

"Because he couldn't have gotten you out. We don't know how many Mazikin are in the nest, but their population has grown quickly in the last year. Sil and Ibram—and Juri, until a few days ago—have become very strong during that time. They've been recruiting aggressively in recent weeks, like they're getting ready to launch an offensive. We would have been completely outnumbered, especially since we couldn't take a full platoon of Guards with us—Sil would have killed you as soon as he heard them coming. So since it was just the two of us, the only thing we could have done if Sil had gotten you all the way to the nest was watch you go in."

"There wouldn't have been time to send for reinforcements after you found the nest?"

"Remember how far I said Harag was? It would have taken at least a full day."

I remembered the strange way the Mazikin had treated me. They'd actually taken care of me in an ultracreepy kind of way. "They weren't cruel or anything. It's not like they were torturing me. I probably could have handled it for a day or two."

Ana gave me a pitying look. "Malachi didn't tell you what they do, did he? God, he has really lost it. Lela. Honey. *Of course* the Mazikin weren't cruel. They love the ones who look like you. Pretty and strong. They would've taken real good care of you. Right up until the moment they tied you to a table and summoned a Mazikin spirit to possess you. And then, well, it's lights-out. No more Lela. Lela's body's still breathing and moving around, sure, but the real Lela? She's gone." Ana was breathing hard as she turned away and wiped fiercely at her face.

I curled my knees to my chest, now well and truly nauseated. "That's why they look like everyone else. Because they *are* everyone else."

Ana's expression was ice-cold as her eyes locked on mine. "You got it. Once a Mazikin takes possession, there's no going back. The person looks and sounds the same as before. They even have some of the same memories and skills. But the person's soul is gone."

"Like, gone forever? It just gets snuffed out?"

She grimaced. "No. It gets banished to the Mazikin homeland, the place even the Mazikin are desperate to escape. If there's an actual hell, that's probably it."

"So these people end up in hell, not because of anything they did, but because they were unlucky?" I'd gotten the sense there was *some* justice in all of this afterlife stuff, but that definitely didn't sound fair.

"We think there's a way to free them," Ana said quietly. "That's why we kill the Mazikin, even though that has its own consequences. If you kill the possessed body, it banishes the Mazikin spirit back to its homeland, and we think that releases the human soul. But that means the Mazikin can come back and possess someone else. The strongest of them always come back. Malachi has fought Sil in three separate bodies. And Juri—he and Malachi go way back. Malachi must have killed him at least four times, and he's nearly taken Malachi out a time or two as well. In recent years

Juri's even taken to possessing bodies that speak Slovak, just so he can taunt Malachi in one of his native languages."

From what little I knew of Juri, it sounded like something he would do. "And there's no other way to get someone back once they've been possessed? Can't you do an exorcism or something?"

She let out a derisive laugh. "When someone turns Mazikin, killing them is the only option. Otherwise, they keep gathering victims and increasing their numbers. They find easy victims here, but they're not satisfied with that. They're like a virus—they want to escape the city and spread chaos. It's happened before, centuries ago. Human Guards were dispatched to stop them, and they succeeded at the cost of their own lives and countless others. It's our job to make sure that doesn't happen again—and to protect the residents of the city until they're ready to find their way out through the Judge."

"So wasn't Malachi doing his job when he protected me?"

Ana shook her head, and the pitying look returned to her face. "If he was an ordinary Guard, maybe. But Malachi is our leader. It's his job to take the long view, look at the bigger picture, and make hard choices for the greater good. And Malachi is very, *very* good at his job. Yet, for some reason, he wasn't willing to sacrifice you. He knew that either they'd possess you, or you'd get yourself killed in some harebrained escape attempt, or he'd be forced to burn down the nest with you in it. He absolutely refused to take the chance that any of those things would happen."

My stomach did a weird sort of backflip. Nobody had ever thought I was important enough to risk so much for. "But why didn't he want me to know?"

"He doesn't want you to feel guilty."

I stared at Ana as it all clicked into place. "Because he hasn't found the nest yet, others are being sacrificed," I choked out, contemplating the choice Malachi had made. I didn't want that kind of responsibility. I hoped he didn't feel sorry about his decision. As I looked down at my arm and pictured Nadia out there, alone and vulnerable, I wasn't sure he'd chosen right. I got up from the cot and started pacing.

Ana laid a hand on my arm and held on as I flinched, as if she'd known what to expect. "Remember," she warned, looking every inch the predator she was, "you promised not to tell him I told you."

"I won't. But it makes me want to get going."

Ana released my arm. "Right. Your friend. Look—we've got to wait for Malachi. He'll be here soon, and then we'll go." She sat down on her cot. "So, while we wait . . . I gave you some dirt, now you give me some. Is it true, what Malachi told me? You actually left the Countryside to come here, just to find your friend and get her out?"

"Yes."

"You know how stupid that sounds to me, right? It's supposed to be heaven out there. No worries, no danger, no pain, no regret. Everything you need. Why would you risk that?"

I shrugged. "Nadia had all this power and never forgot how to be kind. She was gentle, sweet, and she—"

"So basically, she was a nice person. Got it. And . . . still don't get it."

I threw my hands up. "She gave me a future! Before her I didn't have one. If I got through a day, that was good enough for me. I never imagined it could be different. But she showed me it could be different."

Ana leaned back against the wall and crossed her arms. I couldn't read her expression, but something told me I'd hit a nerve. I ran my hand over my sleeve, over the tattoo.

"When you don't have a future, you act different. You don't plan. You don't try. You just . . . exist. She wouldn't let me do that. She pushed me. Harassed me. Nagged me. It was damn annoying sometimes, but she wouldn't let me slack off. We had fun, too. She took me places I'd never been before. We laughed a lot. I'd never done that with anyone. Life seemed worth living, and a future seemed worth having if it could include stuff like that."

I wiped my face with my sleeve.

When I turned back to Ana, she said very quietly, "I get that. A future would have been nice." She cleared her throat.

"Malachi said you had some dreams and visions about this place before you died, but how much did you really see?"

"I wandered here in my nightmares nearly every night for two years. But I didn't really notice much around me. I was in a fog."

Her eyebrow shot up. "You were a ghost, huh? We can't see them, but Mazikin can. At the core they're spirits, even when they inhabit others' bodies. So I guess they can see the *other* spirits, even those still connected to living human bodies. A few years ago I saw it with my own eyes. Creepiest thing I've ever witnessed. This Mazikin was just talking to the air, stroking at it like there was someone there. It was inviting the ghost to stay, saying it was perfect, that it should come here to live, that it would be taken care of."

I shuddered, remembering Juri's voice whispering all those poisonous words in my ear.

"That Mazikin was so wrapped up in the ghost that it didn't even notice me sneaking up behind it to cut its throat." She paused, caught for a moment in the memory, and then focused on me again. "Wait. If you didn't notice much in those dreams, then how did you know about the Guards' weapons?"

"Once Nadia died, my dreams changed. I saw everything from her perspective, but it was sharper, like I was still myself. I saw the dome of darkness over the city. I saw the Suicide Gates and the Guards. I saw a Mazikin try to take Nadia away—hey, how come some of them run on all fours?"

Ana laughed. "Oh—the old ones, right? There's something about elderly bodies—they don't hold up as well when they're possessed, and they end up running around like animals. I've always wondered if a Mazikin in true form doesn't look more animal than human."

I shuddered. "In one of the visions, I saw Malachi kill two Mazikin and fight off Ibram. Nadia was there, hiding, and she saw the whole thing. Malachi said it happened in Harag, and that's why we're going."

Ana looked at me with amazement. "You saw that? It only happened a week or so ago."

"Why is that surprising?"

"It means you haven't been here for more than a week. When people come through the Gates, they're usually completely disoriented. I know I was. I snapped out of it quicker than most, but at first it was really confusing. . . . But you weren't confused, were you?" Ana blew out a long breath and shook her head, finally believing. "Because you chose to come. That must be it. I mean, I get how important Nadia is to you, but we've never had someone come through the Gates voluntarily, looking for someone else. It's no wonder Malachi's fascinated with you."

For some reason, Ana's comment zinged right through my chest just as painfully as if she'd used one of her knives. "Yeah," I said hoarsely, "no wonder."

There was a sharp knock on the door. Ana gave me a look. "Remember what you promised." She swept to the door and opened it.

I took a breath as Malachi entered the room. He wore a fresh set of clothes, obviously their uniform—the navy-blue fitted shirt and fatigue pants. He had a satchel on his back, the strap slung diagonally across his chest. From the way it clinked as he moved, I assumed it was full of weapons. I bit my lip and fiddled with my bootlaces. He looked really, really good. "We have to stop at Michael's shop to pick up the new armor," he said to Ana. He threw a cautious glance at me. "Are you ready to leave?"

"Absolutely," I said, a little too enthusiastically.

If he noticed my total spasticness, he didn't let on. "Well, ladies, let's get going."

Michael, the weapon master, had a shop at the far west end of the Guard Station, down a long marble corridor lined with ornate gas lamps hanging from decorative sconces. Malachi led the way, his boots squeaking on the smooth, polished floor.

He looked over his shoulder at me. "Take Michael with a grain of salt. He's kind of irritable."

Ana snorted but didn't say anything.

"So, um, Raphael . . . Michael . . . are we going to run into Gabriel somewhere around here?" I asked, wondering if I'd figured something out.

Ana's laughter had a hard edge to it. "No, we don't have a resident Gabriel. And Michael is . . ."

Malachi's lips quirked up. "He's a very special individual. But I believe he is not now, nor has he ever been, in possession of a halo."

At the very end of the hallway, two Guards stood in front of elaborately carved wooden doors.

"Ghazi. Sofian," Malachi greeted as he nodded to each of them. They nodded back and pulled open the doors for us.

"He's in fine form this morning, Captain," grunted Sofian in warning. I could already hear the ranting coming from inside.

"Malachi? Is that you? Get in here, you bloody pillock," a gravelly voice shouted from the far end of the shop.

"What did he just call you?" I whispered as I looked around.

"Roughly translated, an idiot," Malachi whispered back. Ana snorted again.

It was not the tiny, quaint workshop I'd pictured. I'd had some mall version of Santa's workshop in my head. Michael's shop was more like a factory. It reminded me of a giant hardware store, emphasis on the hard. Aisles of metal shelving stretched in front of us, and each contained a different kind of deadly accessory. There were enough scimitars here to equip an army. Knives of all design crowded the shelves: some short, some long, some curved, some serrated, some with terrifying-looking barbs. And armor—stacks and stacks of armor.

"Where does the metal come from?" I asked.

"We don't know," said Ana. "Only Michael knows."

"Malachi! You poxy prat, what kind of nutter abuses a beautiful weapon this way?" Michael shouted above a sharp clanging noise that made me cringe and cover my ears.

Malachi closed his eyes as if praying for patience and led the way toward the back of the shop, down an aisle lined with throwing stars.

I had to ask. "What did he call you that time?"

Malachi gave me a sidelong glance and rolled his eyes. "Again, an idiot. He's really gotten into British slang these days."

"Believe me," said Ana, "it's better than when he was into Chinese profanity. For two years, we were *huàidàn* this and *kuàxiàwù* that. But the worst was—"

"Russian," they said at the same time. We turned the corner.

Michael stood at a forge, wielding a red-hot strip of metal. He was incredibly, impressively, amazingly fat. I marveled for a moment at how someone so huge could move with such ease. And also how he avoided burning the various folds of flab that hung from his limbs, belly, and chin. But as I watched the sweat dripping from his hills and valleys, I began to see his movements as a sort of graceful ballet. The longer I observed, the more beautiful he became. I was reminded of Raphael's indescribable smile, and that's what I was thinking of when Michael noticed me for the first time.

His smile was . . . not so beautiful.

"Well, Gor-don Ben-nett," he said in a slow, appreciative way that made Malachi take half a step in front of me. Michael leaned to get a better view, and I somehow resisted the urge pull Malachi all the way in front of me like a human shield.

"Michael, this is Lela, as I am sure you have realized. Is her armor ready?"

Michael raised his eyebrows, causing folds of flesh to droop over his eyes.

"Bugger. I would've made more of an effort if you'd brought her to see me yesterday. Inspiration, you know."

Malachi started to make that growling noise but caught himself and cleared his throat. "Please, we're in a bit of a hurry this morning." He looked around for Ana, perhaps for support, but she had wandered off to caress a particularly pointy set of knives a few aisles away.

Michael gestured emphatically with the now-black strip of metal. "Keep your hair on, you useless wazzack. I just made your fifth staff and reforged your scimitar for the sixth time this month. And your eighth set of knives—how do you manage to keep bending 'em that way? You throw 'em way too hard. And I just waxed your third set of armor—you ever think of bleeding a little less? Inconsiderate git. So don't rush me, and let me appreciate the scenery. I get tired of looking at your sorry face."

I bit my tongue to keep from cracking up and stepped around Malachi, hoping maybe a feminine touch would speed things along. "Michael, it's nice to meet you. Your skill and productivity—wow. You must never stop."

Michael shot me his gray-toothed smile as he pointed the scimitar-in-progress in my direction. "Finally, someone who appreciates me. You're right, love, I go all day. And all night." He made a rather disturbing movement that may have been meant as a hip thrust but looked more like the swell of ocean waves. It was kind of hypnotic. Probably not in the way he intended, though.

From the corner of my eye, I saw the muscle in Malachi's jaw start to jump. He'd clearly interpreted Michael's movement as it had been intended after all—and seemed rather tense about it. But as long as Michael kept himself, and *all* his tools, at a respectful distance, I figured I could indulge him—provided he gave us what we came for.

"You don't say." I lifted an eyebrow, further experimenting with my skills as a seductress. This guy was kind of an easy target. "Well then, I can't wait to see what you have for me. Want to show it off?"

The muscle in Malachi's jaw had stopped jumping because now his mouth was hanging open. I spared him a glance but had to look away quickly to keep from giggling.

Michael, too, seemed a little off balance. "Uh. Bloody hell. Um, it's over here. Close your mouth, you nancy," he snapped, noticing Malachi's dumbfounded expression. "Miss Lela, step into my office," Michael said, newly charming, as he gestured toward a row of armor racks.

"I asked Michael to modify the frame he uses for Ana," Malachi said quietly.

"And you weren't kidding. *Impressive*," Michael crooned, his eyes skating over my body.

With wide eyes I looked at Malachi, who dropped his head into his hands. If his hair weren't so short, I was sure he would have been ripping it out.

My stomach muscles ached with suppressed laughter. "All right, Michael, shall we see how accurately Malachi described my chest size?"

Malachi made a strangled noise as he followed me and Michael to a set of black armor draped over a rack in the corner. I took a moment to stare at all the leather and metal buckles.

And now I begin my career as a dominatrix.

Michael pulled the breastplate off the rack. "Twelve ounces per square foot of pure feminine beauty," he purred, stroking the front of the thing in a way that made me want to bathe in a vat of bleach. I panicked for a moment when he unbuckled the sides and waddled in my direction. Fortunately, Malachi stepped forward and snatched it from his hands.

Michael muttered something that sounded like "Arsehole" but didn't resist.

"It'll be stiff at first," Malachi explained as he met my eyes and held it up, seeking permission to help me. I lifted my braid from my neck, allowing him to position the leather over my chest and back. Malachi's experienced fingers made quick work of the small buckles that connected front to back along each of my sides. The vest extended down to my hips, where it ended in a delicate flare to give me ease of movement. The whole thing reminded me of a corset, though it wasn't too tight. In fact, it fit perfectly, and that made my cheeks very hot for a few moments.

"I guess you were pretty accurate," I mumbled. "Good job."

"It will deflect most knife and scimitar strikes," he mumbled back. Was I imagining that slight tinge of pink in his cheeks?

Something black flew across the room and hit Malachi in the head. He froze for a moment, eyes wide, looking completely stunned.

"Keep your head in the game, plonker," shouted Michael.

"Whoa," laughed Ana, skipping down the aisle with three new knives swinging from her hands. "Someone got the drop on Malachi. I think it's been a few decades since that happened."

Malachi successfully dodged the next black projectile and caught the two after that. They were my leg and arm protection—greaves and bracers. He ignored the taunts and gave me another questioning look before helping me put them on.

"How do I look?" I posed, flexing my biceps and wiggling my eyebrows. I was glad there was no mirror around, as I was fairly sure I looked like a prat. Or a nutter. Or a git. Yep, one of those.

"You're missing something," Ana replied, holding up a belt. She fastened it around my hips and hooked a baton onto it. "Now you look beautiful. Doesn't she look beautiful, boys?"

Malachi had already turned his attention to his own assorted weapons and did not look up. I didn't know whether to feel disappointed or relieved.

"Ah, there's none so fair as thee, sweet Ana, but she'll do," sang Michael in a rumbling bass, but it took him a few seconds to peel his eyes from me. When he did, he saw Ana's new treasures. "I suppose you want to take those knives with you?"

"Girls like shiny things, Michael," she said, shaking her hips at him. She sheathed the knives with lethal efficiency. Michael actually shivered, shaking the floor like a small earthquake.

"Michael, thank you for your work," Malachi said formally. "As always, it's excellent." He had put on his own armor and looped the satchel over his chest again. He looked . . . Ah, it was just not fair. I swallowed hard. He looked amazing, and I looked like a plonker.

Michael apparently did not share my admiration. "Try not to cock it all up this time, will ya? Bring some of it back in one piece."

"We always do our best," said Malachi, "but we wouldn't want you to get bored. You know what they say about idle hands."

Michael held up his hands and wiggled his fingers at me. He winked. "Don't you worry about my idle hands, boy."

Huh. The few times I'd been to church in my life, I'd never heard anyone describe St. Michael as a morbidly obese guy with a foul mouth and an eye for the ladies. Still, the guy was hilarious. I winked back at him just to be obnoxious.

Malachi grabbed my hand and dragged me down the aisle. "Don't encourage him, please," he muttered.

SEVENTEEN

WE WOULD REACH THE center of the city by midday, or so Malachi informed me. I couldn't tell what time it was. As always, it was dark, just block after block of mismatched buildings and sorrowful faces.

Guards patrolled in pairs, their glowing eyes sweeping the crowds, searching for unusual behavior. Whenever we passed them, they snapped to attention and waited for Malachi to acknowledge them. They all looked the same to me, but he knew each of their names. He would nod or give a few instructions before sending them on their way. One of them leered at me and said to Malachi, "Finally taking one downtown, Captain?"

The expression on Malachi's face made the Guard step back and jerk to attention again. I glanced at Ana for clues, but she was staring at the Guard with the same violent intensity.

When I asked why we couldn't have brought a few Guards with us, Ana answered. "Because this isn't an official mission. Right, Captain?"

Malachi ignored her and kept walking.

I tried to kill both time *and* the tension by asking all the questions that had built up in my brain over the last few days. "So how come you guys don't have phones and stuff?"

"They have not been given to us," Malachi replied. "Guards are outfitted by Michael and supplied with essentials by Raphael. We have not been supplied with a telephone."

I smiled at the thought of him trying to figure out a cell.

"But you said people can grow entire buildings here—so why can't you grow one tiny little phone?" I considered giving it a try, just to see if I could do it.

"Guards don't *grow* anything," Ana said. "It would be considered a dereliction of duty. We have certain privileges, like being able to enter occupied apartments, but we also have rules."

"But haven't you ever been tempted to try?"

Malachi made a strained sound in his throat. "It's an easy decision, if the choice is between a telephone and being released into the Countryside sooner." He stopped and turned to me. "When it's time for you to leave this city, I'd like you to be free to go."

"*Seriously?* I'm not talking about a luxury pimp palace. I'm talking about a phone. Wouldn't it make life easier?"

Ana bumped my shoulder with hers. "If you think anything here is supposed to be easy, girl, maybe you aren't ready to leave after all."

"That's enough, Ana," Malachi said as he pivoted on his heel and resumed the hike. "And Lela, a phone would be completely possible, if a resident of this city ever decided to communicate with another person. But even if they did, who would they call?"

I couldn't really think of a response to that as we trudged past an endless stream of people, all with glazed eyes fixed on the ground. One lady sat on a curb surrounded by piles of shoes. As I watched, a slimy pair of stilettos grew over her previously bare feet. She took them off, added them to a pile, and bent over to stare at her feet again.

I shook my head. "What about cars? Computers? TV?"

"Oh, we have TVs. They're in all the apartments," said Ana. "People gorge on television just like they gorge on food. I myself have been known to indulge at times. Not much else to do. I mean, the BOOK stores in this place suck. The print's too small, and I hate vampires."

Malachi nodded. "As for cars . . . I guess they don't seem important here. People do wander when they first get here, like your friend did, but once they settle in, they tend to stay in one place. Everything they could want is within a block or two, anyway. Some of them never leave their apartments. Besides the Guards, the only creatures who move around this city regularly are the Mazikin, but because they don't actually belong in the city, nothing will grow for them, thank God. And, please forgive me, what is a computer?"

Ana laughed and gave Malachi a playful shove. "They're like these enormous calculators, old man." She gave me an amused look. "Why would anyone want one of those? Oh, I guess maybe an accountant might . . . and I think we have a lot of those here. But no—I think we'd notice if someone's apartment was taken up entirely with circuit boards."

Malachi's smile told me he'd figured something out—and it also made my heart skip a beat or two. "Something tells me times have changed, Ana."

"Yeah," I replied, still staring at his mouth. "I wouldn't be surprised if you run into that kind of thing in the near future. If you think people gorge on TV, wait until you see the Internet."

Ana shrugged. "All right, but whatever that is, it probably wouldn't work that well, anyway. Nothing here does."

As we entered the downtown area, I craned my neck to see where the buildings ended. I could almost feel them breathing, decaying, and yet growing, fueled by the desires and wishes of people who didn't know what they needed. My plan to grow my own iPod just for fun kind of evaporated at that point.

In the downtown section of the city resided those who had absolutely no desire to see beyond what they wanted. Some of them had been here for centuries, the buildings growing and evolving around them, scar tissue over festering wounds. Ana told stories of patrolling these streets, witnessing people lugging massive amounts of garbage into the high-rises. The residents here were willing to defend their precious treasures to the end. They collected junk until they were trapped in their apartments, buried in all their wishes, in all the things they'd collected to fill the emptiness that made them kill themselves in the first place. I wondered what Nadia might have been seeking when she decided to escape her life. What did Nadia think would fill her empty space?

We had been walking in silence for almost an hour, surrounded by high-rises so tall they seemed to join together at the top, closing us in. On the sidewalk, the lamps that provided us with our only light grew weaker and farther apart.

I stumbled a few times in the murk, unable to see the uneven pavement at my feet. "Jeez, can you guys see at all? Aren't you afraid some Mazikin could sneak up on us?"

Ana laughed. "First, thanks for underestimating us like that. And second, no. Mazikin avoid downtown like the plague. It's too much, even for them. Especially for them."

I squinted and tried to see what lay ahead of us, but it was completely black. "They don't seem like the types to be afraid of the dark."

Malachi held his arm out to keep me from walking farther. "It's not the dark, Lela. It's this. Right in front of us. The dark tower. Put your arm out."

I obeyed and then yanked my hand back immediately. I couldn't really say why it felt so bad, but touching that building felt profoundly, overwhelmingly, instinctually *wrong*. I looked up at Malachi for an explanation, and even in the darkness I could read the regret on his face.

"We have to go through it," he explained. "It's not something we can go around. We've tried. The other Guards have no problem going through it, but for us, for humans, it's . . . harder."

I stared at him blankly. I didn't understand what he was talking about—we couldn't go around it? We'd been walking around buildings all day.

"But . . ." I pointed to the corner where the building seemed to end. Malachi nodded for me to try it. I did, walking along the edge of the building, but it somehow expanded and contorted to prevent me from going around it.

I returned to his side. "How come it does this?"

Malachi sighed. "This tower is right at the center of the city. It's probably been here since this place was created. It stands in the middle of all of this misery, all these lost people. And if buildings can grow out of people's wishes and desires, why can't one grow out of their fears? It's some sort of vortex for feelings and memories—"

"Malachi, say it plain and simple," snapped Ana. "Walking through here will make you feel bad, Lela. Really bad. But you just keep walking, and *do not stop*, all right? No matter what you're feeling, or what you remember, don't stop walking. It's not that far. Keep your mind on your feet."

My eyes bounced back and forth between Ana and Malachi. I should have noticed this change stealing over the two of them during the last hour. Ana looked mad, almost grimly determined. And Malachi looked sick. He was already sweating.

I wanted to take his hand and reassure him. I felt stupid even thinking about it as I watched him square his shoulders and lift his chin, setting his eyes on the low, square entryway, the only way to get to the other side. Yeah, I wanted to reassure him, but I also wanted him to pick me up and carry me through this awful place.

He turned to me. "We could go back and circumvent all of downtown, but it would take two extra days to get to Harag. It's why we came this way. But we could go back if you want. We don't have to go through. I should have told you. I just didn't—"

"I didn't want to frighten you," mocked Ana, mimicking his accent with devastating accuracy. Malachi snapped his mouth shut and gave her a withering look, but she didn't back down. "Malachi, you have got to get your eye on the ball here. She is not a little girl. She is—"

"Standing right here," I interrupted angrily, "and will see you guys on the other side." I marched into the dark tower, wanting to get it over with before the dread could bubble up and suffocate me.

The last thing I heard as the door of the building slammed shut behind me was Malachi calling my name.

EIGHTEEN

I HAD THOUGHT THE city was silent, but I didn't understand silence until that moment. As I took my first few steps into the soaring lobby, I imagined this was what it felt like to be completely deaf. My boots faltered noiselessly, and I knelt quickly to brace myself.

And immediately had to suppress the urge to barf.

When my fingers hit the floor, I realized why it was so difficult to keep my balance: it was soft and slick, a living thing. I stood up quickly, fighting my gag reflex as I wiped my hand against my pants.

Remembering Ana's advice, I took careful steps deeper into the cavernous mouth of the building. I thought about turning back to wait for Malachi and Ana, but as I looked toward the door, all I saw was a smooth wall.

It was pulsing, thrumming gently.

Just a thousand more miles of weird. Keep moving forward. Don't stop, and don't freak out.

The air was saturated, wet and warm. It settled into my skin and onto my tongue, sour and rank.

Then I recognized the smell.

I bowed my head and wrapped my arms around myself, trying to keep it together as my heart rate accelerated painfully. The air was full of Rick. His breath: beer and cigarettes. His scent: stale sweat and gasoline.

Keep moving forward, Lela, it's not real. My fingernails bit deeply into my palms as I stumbled onward, no longer trying to fight the helpless retching that doubled me over every few steps.

When I felt his hands on me, I spun around, lost my balance, and ended up on my back. And when I looked down, my armor and boots were gone. I was wearing that too-tight, too-short nightgown Rick always made me put on before I went to bed. He was here. He would hurt me again. I screamed with noiseless terror.

No no no, I argued silently with myself. *This is* not *real.*

I spent a moment trying to calm down, squinting up at the strange carvings on the ceiling of the dimly lit lobby.

They squirmed—undulating shadows. What if they were coming to get me?

My feet slid as they tried to gain traction on the slimy floor.

Breathe and get up. Get up.

I stopped flailing, forcing myself into more deliberate movements. I slowly rolled to my stomach and got to my hands and knees. I was covered in blood and slime. I sat back, frantically wiping my hands, desperate to scrape it off. But the memories hung from me in sticky ropes. They webbed my hands, caught between my fingers. I couldn't get away from the smell.

Then his weight was at my back, pressing me into pink sheets, buckling my arms and trying to force my face into my own pillow.

It's not real, I chanted as I pushed back and got up unsteadily, limbs shaking, teeth chattering in the warm, humid air. *Keep walking.* I barely lifted my feet as I slid along the squishy organ of the floor, gelatinous ooze squishing between my toes. *This will not beat me. Memories cannot kill me. I am stronger than that.* I clenched my teeth. *I am stronger than that, and that is why I am here.*

I walked, back stiff against the assault of his hands, his body. Ah, Holy Mother, I wanted to lash out, just as I had the night I'd finally fought back. I wanted to smash his face, to kick, to tear, to destroy him. My muscles cramped with the desire to attack. But he wasn't really there, and if I gave in to that instinct, I'd lose my balance and end up on my back in the slime again. *Keep walking. You've already defeated this ghost.*

The sound of Rick's voice dropped me to my knees. "This is your fault for flaunting it in front of me. Keep quiet, you little slut."

Rick's voice droned on, telling me all the reasons I deserved it. All the reasons I wouldn't tell anyone. All the reasons it was my fault. All the reasons I'd asked for it. And no one would care because I was just a throwaway, a disposable girl.

My fingers curled over the veined floor. It bled.

Rick's voice got louder. It was coming from inside my skull. He was in there with me.

I clutched at my head, hair tearing loose under my fingers.

I had to dig him out.

Look around; find the way out, a different voice said.

Malachi's voice.

I froze, searching the gloom. Had he followed me in? Was he coming for me?

No, I was alone, but I clung to his voice desperately. Something about it eased the pain in my head a little, enough for me to get to my feet, holding my arms out for balance.

Find the way out. Keep walking. This isn't real.

It got worse, every touch sinking in, every shove and pinch and push and grab and twist and I fell to my knees again a few steps later, surprised my head wasn't splitting open. *I can't,* I thought. *I can't take this.*

Yes, you can, whispered Malachi, his voice sliding beneath the nauseating rhythm pulsing inside my skull. *It's not real. You are strong enough. Get on your feet. You're almost there.*

I screamed again, this time in anger—a battle cry. I stomped against the slick skin of the building, driving my heels into its flesh.

With every lift of my foot, I chanted, *I am strong enough.*

With every breath, I repeated, *This is not real.*

Up. Down. In. Out.

When my voice failed me, Malachi's filled in, completing the sentences, adding the missing words.

But with every step, more of the building's tissue stuck to my feet. It got harder to lift them. The floor was sucking me down, breathing me in, swallowing and digesting me. I wanted to give up. I suddenly knew that if I stopped struggling, everything else would stop, too. If I didn't fight anymore, I could just lie there forever, entombed in silence.

This evil building was offering me a choice: all the horror would end if I lay still and let it have me. It was tempting. I was so tired. And the assault, more than memory now, seemed like it would never end. I didn't know how much more I could take without breaking completely. It would be nice to rest. To sleep.

To be done with everything.

With that wish, it was like my eyes were opened for the first time. I looked at the walls, the ceiling, the floor . . . and I *saw.* Thousands of people, interwoven, eyes closed, at rest. Backs and fronts and arms and legs and hands and hair. They were the squishy surface beneath my feet, all melded together and smoothed over by a sticky membrane. They were the undulating shadows on the ceiling and walls. They were the reason the building was so immense. They were its conquests, its sustenance, its backbone. Sleeping for eternity, no more pain, no more . . . anything.

And instead of being horrified, I was drawn in. A wave of sleepiness rolled over me and I fell to one knee and welcomed it. My heart beat sluggishly, ready to fall silent forever.

Don't give up, pleaded Malachi's voice, cracking with desperation. *Please don't give up. I'm right on the other side of the door. I want to see you again. I need to see you again. Please.*

Somehow, it was enough to draw me to my feet one more time. Just the idea he might need me to make it through. I could see him again if only I kept moving. . . . My face smacked against a hard surface.

A door.

I ripped it open and fell through it, nerveless and panting.

Malachi caught me in his arms and carried me away from the mouth of the building. He sat down on the curb, holding me against his chest. He wasn't wearing his armor anymore. His smell, leather and clean, warm skin, filled my nose, replacing the choking stench of Rick. I sucked in deep lungfuls of it, unable to get enough.

His hands ran over me, and as they did, I noticed I wasn't wearing that terrible too-tight, too-short nightgown after all. I was wearing the Guard uniform. My clothes and armor were clean and intact. I'd thought I was covered in the building's saliva, but I was completely dry.

Malachi gasped, and his fingers closed around mine. Silently, he pulled away several long, curling strands of hair tangled around my fingers. He touched my palms gently, running his fingertips over the bloody divots left by my fingernails. He put his hand on my cheek and tilted my face up to his.

I stared at him shamelessly, sinking deep into the black-brown depths of his eyes. They were filled with concern. For me. I can't describe how that felt to me. I almost burst into tears but managed to cling to my cool with white-tipped fingers.

Malachi searched my face, as if he wasn't sure I was all there. "Can you hear me? Are you all right?"

"That really sucked," I mumbled hoarsely.

"Yes, I think that just about captures the experience." He squeezed me tighter. It felt incredibly good.

My brain came back online, and I started to process what I was seeing. He was very pale. "Are *you* all right?"

He nodded. "Yes. I've been through there hundreds of times, so it's not as bad as it once was. I get through pretty quickly. But I almost didn't make it out the first few times."

"How did you get past me? I went in first."

"I probably walked right by you without either of us knowing. You are always alone in there, left to fight your own worst memories. It's why the Mazikin are so terrified of this place. They can't handle both their own memories and those of their human hosts. They never make it through."

I looked up at the menacing black silhouette of the tower, imagining what Malachi might have seen as he walked through the building. For me, the Holocaust was history. For him, it was *memory*.

I wrapped my arms around him and pressed my face against his neck, wishing I could chase away his memories and keep him safe. His pulse raced against my cheek, and his breath rushed out in a huff.

He froze for a moment, but then put his hand on the back of my head. He held me there, comforting me, maybe comforting himself.

"I was getting worried," he said. "I went in after you. I tried to call you back and explain more about it, but you were already gone. I'm so sorry I didn't explain it earlier. I should have tackled you when you bolted for the door." He drew in a shaky breath. "It took you a long time to get through."

"I almost gave up. And I saw . . ." I didn't want to describe what I'd seen.

He stroked my hair for a moment, then seemed to catch himself and pulled his hand away. "I know what you saw. Some cannot bear to re-experience the worst parts of their lives. They lie down and give up. The building, it . . ."

"Eats them?"

"Well, yes." He looked down at me. "I don't think it hurts."

"No, it looked like . . . nothing. Like not existing. It was really tempting for a few seconds there. I wanted all of it to stop. But then I heard you talking to me." His eyebrows shot up, and I paused. "You weren't talking to me?"

He shook his head. "You heard *my* voice? You're sure it was mine?"

"Yes. It's what got me through. You told me to keep walking. And you . . ." I trailed off, not sure I wanted to tell him the rest, as it appeared to be a figment of my imagination.

He shivered against me. "Never mind," I said quickly. "Are you sure you're okay?"

"I'm better than I was, now that you're through. I guess I should be honored that you came up with my voice to help you do it."

I ducked my head, totally embarrassed. "Sure, anytime." I looked around. "Where's Ana?"

"She always runs through and then needs some extra time to clear her head. She'll be back soon."

I was becoming increasingly aware of how close we were to each other, of how his arms were tight around me, of how little effort it would take to close the distance completely. Heat pooled in my cheeks.

"I think I'm all right now," I said quietly. He raised an eyebrow in question, as if the intimacy of our position hadn't occurred to him. Then his gaze fell to my cheeks, and he noticed my blush.

"Sorry," he mumbled as he set me down on the curb and got to his feet, like he suddenly needed the distance. He walked over to a pile of gear heaped on the sidewalk and put his armor on again, all smooth, efficient movement. His body had a grace all its own; every motion had its purpose. I sighed and wiped my mouth, wondering if the drool was visible from a distance.

"Ah, Lela made it through. Good girl," Ana called out as she approached. Her face looked a little raw, like she'd been scrubbing at it. What had she seen as she went through the tower? She saw me looking and swiped a hand across her cheek, like she thought there might be a stubborn tear still clinging there. She gave me a tense smile. "Glad to see you're not fatally damaged."

I winced at her description. For some reason, I wished Malachi hadn't heard it. He pretended he hadn't and appeared entirely focused on getting ready to resume our trek through the city.

Ana held out her hand, offering to pull me from the curb. "It's always hardest the first time. Now you know what to expect. And you know you're stronger than it is." I accepted the help and rose to my feet. Ana looked me over. "We'll have to rebraid your hair tonight, girl. You did a number on yourself in there."

I put my hand to my hair, abruptly understanding that I probably looked like a total freak show. I hadn't thought about it while Malachi held me. The way he looked at me made me feel . . . beautiful. Now I felt anything but.

Almost frantically, I pulled the rubber band from the bottom of the braid and ran my fingers through my hair. I bent over and shook it out, letting it fall heavily around me. It bounced happily around my face, delighted to be released.

When I raised my head, Malachi was watching me. The look on his face took my breath away and brought the heat back to my cheeks . . . and everywhere else.

He turned away quickly. "Ladies, let's go. We've got to make good time if we're going to get to Harag tonight." He shouldered his pack and walked up the street.

NINETEEN

WITH ANA'S HELP, I removed the armor I'd worn all day. It had become more flexible as I walked and turned out to be pretty comfortable. By the time we got to Harag zone, I'd almost forgotten I was wearing it. But once it was off, I felt the difference. Newly freed, I slumped onto the couch with a sigh.

Ana laughed at my boneless sprawl. "Toughen up, girl. Today was easy."

"Piece of cake," I agreed, looking around our temporary home. We were in an apartment building a few blocks into the zone. Apparently, Malachi spent so much time in Harag lately that he'd claimed this apartment for himself. Although there were a dozen far-flung Guard outposts within the sprawling city, he and Ana also had several apartments, places where they could stash extra equipment and supplies, nurse wounds that didn't require immediate attention, and rest safely after long patrols.

This apartment looked no different from the one near the Station, where I'd spent those few days with Malachi. It had one bedroom, which contained a narrow cot and a chest of drawers. The small living room held a couch, a coffee table, and, sitting atop a squat table against the wall, a television.

I went up to the heavy, square TV and peeked behind it to see how it was plugged in. I hadn't actually seen any electronic or mechanical devices in the city yet. The streets and all the buildings were lit with gas lamps, and I hadn't seen any light switches or outlets. When I saw the back of the TV, I shuddered and nearly fell backward. It was attached to the wall by a cord, all right.

An umbilical cord. At least, that's what it looked like to me.

I warily backtracked to the couch, really, *really* glad I hadn't had anything to eat recently. I spent the next few minutes trying to fool myself into believing I was *not* sitting in the sparsely furnished stomach of a living, breathing creature.

Ana sat down next to me on the couch and followed my gaze to the television.

"Reruns," she said. "*The Brady Bunch*. And lots of commercials for hair products."

"Seriously?"

"Yes. At least, that's what it's been in recent years."

Malachi walked in from the bedroom, armor still on. He looked too big for the apartment when he was wearing it. He saw us staring at the television and laughed.

"I was completely puzzled when they first appeared in these apartments and replaced the radios. I never turn them on, but Ana is a *Brady Bunch* addict."

I eyed Ana with suspicion. "I thought you might have better taste."

Ana sniffed. "It's sweet. I used to watch telenovelas only, but I decided to branch out as my English got better. I don't even want to know what you would see when you turn it on."

"What, you mean it's different for different people?"

"Sure," said Malachi. "It's whatever you want to see. But the reception's not that good."

"And they never show my favorite episodes," Ana complained, tossing a throw pillow at Malachi.

I rolled my eyes. Of course. Whatever you wanted to see, but you couldn't see it very well, there were lots of commercials, and it never quite hit the spot. Television in hell.

Malachi snapped his baton to his belt and looked at me. "I'm going to do a quick patrol to the east to see what kind of Mazikin activity we're going to have to deal with. We'll use this as our base and start searching the zone tomorrow, all right? We'll go door-to-door if we need to."

"Thank you," I said quietly, touched by his consideration.

He smiled at me, nodded at Ana, and walked out the door.

Ana got up and went into the kitchen. She opened a bread box on the counter and, with a shudder, closed it quickly. She rummaged through the pantry, removing a can of vegetables and some tinned meat. After a few futile seconds spent searching for a can opener, she whipped out a knife and tore into the cans. The sickening plops of food chunks hitting the bottom of a bowl made me turn away. I didn't want to make Ana feel worse about having to eat that stuff, so I took my churning stomach into the living room.

I parted the curtains in time to see Malachi walking down the street, headed deeper into the zone, his strides smooth and assured. I set my forehead against the filmy glass, clinging to the sight of him for as long as I could.

"He won't be gone long. Don't worry about him," Ana said blandly. I turned to see her, spoon in hand, digging into the brown mush in her bowl. "He knows how to keep out of sight."

"They all seem to know who he is. They call him by name," I said. It seemed like that would make him a target, and he was out alone with no one at his back.

"Of course they do. He's like the Mazikin bogeyman. He's been their worst nightmare for decades and succeeded in keeping their population pretty small until recently."

"But what about you? How come they don't seem to know you as well? They wanted to recruit you, so obviously they had no idea you're a Guard."

Ana paused in the midst of her methodical scooping and chewing. "Malachi made sure of it. No one who's seen me has survived. He does all the interrogations himself. He goes into all the worst places by himself. It's better that way because I can serve as bait. It's all ruined now, of course, because Sil got away."

I closed my eyes to shut out the guilt. "I'm sorry, Ana."

"It couldn't last forever. Mazikin have a weirdly collective memory. I'm surprised it worked as long as it did. Anyway, there's a flip side to the Mazikin knowing Malachi by sight. It makes them cautious. Even if they spot him, which is unlikely, they wouldn't attack unless they had him very outnumbered."

My stomach did an uncomfortable jackknife, and I threw her a sour look. "Oh, good. Thanks for that image."

"Lela, that boy can take care of himself. Why is it your job to worry about him?"

Because I care about him much more than I should. "It's not—but shouldn't it be yours?"

Ana shook her head stiffly. "No. Way. We're colleagues. If he gets himself killed, it's because he was stupid."

"Now I know you're lying."

Ana poked her spoon at me. "Girl, you have no idea what we've been through, so I suggest you keep your mouth shut."

I didn't risk more words. Instead I rolled my eyes and turned back to the window. Malachi had disappeared. I stared at the place he'd been.

Ana sighed. "Look, I'm sorry. I can't really afford to feel anything for Malachi. I've known him for nearly four decades, and we've bled together, laughed together, and fought together that entire time. He's like my brother. But I can't care about him like one. If I did, I might not survive it. Can you understand that? He's going to leave or he's going to get killed. Either way, he's gone."

Ana's voice was shaking, and in it I heard the tears she would not shed. I decided to risk getting gutted with the spoon. "You're not talking about Malachi anymore."

The bowl clattered into the sink.

"Fine. You want to hear about it? About me and Takeshi? Let this be your lesson, because don't think I can't see what's happening between you and Malachi." She saw me open my mouth to protest. "Shut up and listen.

"First you need to understand: I came from a rough place. El Salvador is not like America. After my papa died, my mama worked the fields morning to night, and so did I.

I wasn't even eighteen and my back and hands ached so bad I didn't want to move sometimes. I looked at my mama, all worn out and hunched over, and I knew that was my future. But I also knew how big the world was—my parents let me go to the missionary school when I was a little girl. They probably regretted it after—I was so desperate for a way out of Rancho Viejo.

"The men from the People's Revolutionary Army had a base in the hills outside the village. My mama had warned me about them, but they were kind to me when I passed by to fetch water. They talked to me about a better life, and it was the escape I'd been looking for. I started sneaking out at night to visit them."

She gave me a sad smile. "They taught me how to fight a little. I never thought I'd need it, but it made me feel like I had some control over my life. Over myself. I didn't give them much in return. Just some tortillas and beans. My mama would have been so upset if she'd known. And you know what? She would have been right. Because a few months later, the death squad came. They accused us of helping the guerrillas. Nobody knew what they were talking about. Nobody except me. But I kept quiet, too stupid and selfish to speak up."

Ana covered her face with her hands. Her voice was so flat and quiet, like each word was dragging her further back in time. "I tried to get away when they started going door-to-door, but they caught me and dragged me back to my mama. I fought them, but they said they would hurt her, so I gave up. She screamed at them to let me go, that I was a good girl, that I would never help the guerrillas. They laughed at her. And then they held us down and hurt us from the inside out. I thought it would kill me, and when they used their machetes to make my mama's blood splash on my face, I wished it had."

I shivered and wrapped my arms around my middle as she continued to speak. "They left me there, lying in her blood. Broken after all. My mama died believing in me. Protecting me. And I was too much of a coward to do the same for her. I might as well have killed her myself. So I used a rope and a tree to finish the job that the death squad had started. When I got here and figured out where I was, I wasn't even surprised. I was just . . . all I wanted to do was fight and kick and claw at anything that crossed my path. But Takeshi . . ."

The springs on the couch creaked as she sat down. "He put me back together after I came here. I didn't want his kindness at first. It was too much. I didn't deserve it. But no matter how many times I lashed out, he was right there, ready for more. So strong. Like he could take the worst of me and not even flinch. It took years, but he was able to reach me. And once he did, there was no room in my heart for anything but him. I loved him so much my chest hurt every time I looked at him. I wanted him so badly it was a taste in my mouth. He made the mistake of loving me, too. Looked at me like I was the most amazing thing he'd ever seen, like I wasn't just worth *something*; I was worth *everything*."

She got up and walked slowly toward me, looking deadly once again. "He loved me so much that he hid the fact that he'd stopped eating and drinking, that it was time for him to go. For *months*.

"I knew he was losing some weight, but he brushed it off and made a big show of being hungry and eating in front of us. I guess he decided he would rather stay in this hell instead of going out into all that beautiful heaven without me. And you know what happened? He got so weak he was taken by Mazikin while out on patrol."

"Oh my God, Ana, I'm so sorry." I looked away. I didn't want to see the expression on her face as she told me about her lost love.

"Yeah. When he died, most of me died. So if you think I'm going to let the rest of me die when Malachi goes, you're crazy. He understands, you know. He loved Takeshi, too. I think both of us decided it was too dangerous to care for people here."

I laid my hand against the grime that coated the window, letting the sweat from my palm and fingers streak clarity along the glass. I thought about Ana and Takeshi, in love in the middle of a war zone, unable to protect each other, knowing eventually they would be separated, probably violently.

Had Takeshi made a mistake, choosing to stay with his love? Should he have chosen heaven over her? Had Ana made a mistake by falling in love in the first place? Was it so different from life on Earth? And could Malachi, after everything he must have been through in both places, afford to care for anyone beyond his duty to them as a Guard?

It seemed like he *did* feel more for me than that. Every time he looked at me, whenever I put that whimsical smile on his face, the few times he'd touched me, almost from the moment we met. Whatever was between us covered me like armor, made me feel safe and scared at the same time. I wasn't sure how deep it went for him. I could have been reading it all wrong. But if I was really honest, it was going to be pretty difficult for me to say good-bye when the time came.

I comforted myself with the memory of what Ana said about Malachi's time in the city drawing to an end. Maybe he would join Nadia and me out in the Countryside. I wondered what he'd be like when he didn't have to carry the promise of death with him wherever he went. I wanted to find out.

I turned away from the window, rubbing the grit from my palms, and saw Ana watching me. "You've got to be careful, Lela. This place is made to tear you down. That's what it is. It tears you down so that when you go before the Judge, you'll accept the verdict—no matter what it is. It makes falling in love very dangerous."

"Falling in . . ." I forced out a laugh, which sounded really loud and high-pitched. Maybe I had a little crush. But love? I couldn't even fathom what that might feel like. Especially here. Especially with Nadia still out there somewhere.

Especially because it felt really, *really* out of control.

"Ana, I think you're getting carried away. I haven't even been here for two weeks, and I'm going to get out of here as soon as I find Nadia. That's what I need to do, nothing else."

I crossed the living room and headed for the bathroom. I desperately needed a shower, almost as much as I needed to escape Ana's knowing stare, her sad smile, her tragic story, and all the lessons I didn't want to learn.

"Yeah, I know why you're here. Just make sure you don't confuse what you want and what you need," Ana said just before I put a closed door between us.

TWENTY

DON'T CONFUSE WHAT YOU want and what you need. The words echoed in my mind a few hours later. What did *that* mean?

The sound of a door closing jerked me from fitful sleep and dreams of Malachi battling a thousand Mazikin who all wore Nadia's face. I leaped up and then forced myself to take slow steps toward the bedroom door, ashamed of how badly I wanted to see him again. I pulled the door open to find him standing right in front of it, arm raised to knock.

He took a step back, opened his fist, and ran his fingers through his hair, looking sheepish. "Ana went out to patrol the west side of the zone. She'll be back in a few hours."

He walked into the living room and sat on the couch, propping his long legs on the coffee table. It looked like he'd just taken a shower; his glistening hair was sticking up in messy spikes on the top of his head. I held onto the doorframe to keep from walking forward to touch it.

He gestured toward the kitchen. "I assume you don't need anything to eat or drink?"

"No, I guess not." I gave in to temptation and sank down next to him.

He laid his arm along the top of the couch and gave me a once-over. "How are you feeling?"

I shrugged. "I'm excited to look for Nadia, but I'm scared she won't be here. What if she didn't stay in that apartment?"

"We'll comb every corner of this zone if we have to," he reassured me. "If she's here, we'll find her. If she's not, we'll search the surrounding area. But I chose this apartment for us because the alley where she was hiding is just a few blocks from here."

I thought back to that night, the first time I'd seen him. "I knew you were dangerous, you know. Nadia thought they were going to kill you. They had you surrounded, and you were wounded. But I could tell."

He leaned his head back and closed his eyes. "How could you tell? I thought they were going to kill me that night, too."

"I could tell by the way you moved," I admitted.

"That's funny, I thought the same thing about you."

I chuckled. "Did I look all scary when I was unconscious and bloody in your arms? Were you intimidated?"

He flashed a killer smile, and it made me want to kiss him. I caught myself leaning in and drew back just as quickly.

"I could tell because you didn't give up, because you never stopped fighting," he said. "As soon as you regained consciousness, you were on full alert, crouched on the floor in that sheet." He laughed quietly. "It's why I gave you those enormous clothes. It's why I wouldn't give you a belt. And it's why I didn't have the key with me in the room. I had a feeling you were capable of almost anything."

My eyes flew wide. "*You* picked out those tent clothes for me?"

He cracked open an eye and threw me a sidelong glance. "Of course. I wanted to give you every disadvantage I could. Plus it was kind of funny watching you hold your pants up like that."

I slapped him on the arm. "Well. That was just . . . mean. And I can't believe you bothered."

"You can't? Lela, if I'd had the key, you probably could have gotten it off me." He shifted uncomfortably, sinking farther into the couch and crossing his arms over his chest. "Do you want to watch television or something?"

Or something. I gave myself a hard mental slap. "Sure, what will be on?"

He looked up at me, brown eyes speculative. "I'd like to find out." He got up in a single, smooth movement and pressed a button on the front of the television, then returned to the couch. The opening sequence of *Buffy the Vampire Slayer* flashed in front of us, cloudy with static. It barely mattered—it brought an instant, huge smile to my face. I almost clapped with delight. Just like a two-year-old.

Malachi stared at it blankly. "What on earth is this?"

"It's *Buffy*! It's an old show, but I think I've seen every episode online."

We watched in silence for a few moments. Predictably, it was one of my least favorite episodes—it involved hyenas. I hate hyenas. They're the supercreeps of the animal world.

"I think I see why you like this show so much," Malachi said softly. "She's very strong."

"I always liked the idea of a tough girl who could jam a stake through the bad guy's heart."

"And those vampires turn to dust right after. That would be nice. I wish Mazikin did that." He sounded kind of wistful.

"I wish foster dads did that, too."

Malachi kept his eyes on the television, but his hands curled over the edge of the couch cushions in a white-knuckled grip. "Foster dad," he said slowly. "Not that it makes it better, but please tell me that means it was not your actual father."

I let out a breath. "Yes, that's what it means. Foster parents take care of kids whose parents can't or won't take care of them. My mother couldn't. She was very mentally ill. I don't know who my father was. She never told anyone."

"So this 'foster dad' took you into his home?"

I felt very sorry for those couch cushions. "He was near the end of a long line of foster homes. I don't remember much before I was almost ten years old, but I know I had a few. After that, I guess I had a pretty bad run. Nothing worked out. One of them hit me, which isn't allowed. The social worker found out when someone at school got suspicious about the bruises. As for the rest, one of them got evicted, one moved out of state, one got divorced, one had another kid with so many problems she couldn't take care of me, too, and one just decided not to be a foster parent anymore. I kept getting moved, and then I ended up at Rick and Debbie's."

I stared at the television to keep from thinking about it too much. It was such a pathetic story, but I was able to tell *this* part of it pretty matter-of-factly.

Malachi turned to me, and his hard expression softened. I could tell he was trying to see if I was all right. I braced, expecting him to ask me what had happened. That's what everyone else had done, including Nadia and Diane. My stomach churned as I watched him considering his words. He inclined his head toward mine.

"You don't have to say anything else," he said. "I'm sorry he hurt you, that he took things from you."

I stared at him for a second, waiting for him to lean away, to look uncomfortable and change the subject. But he was utterly still, looking back at me, waiting to see if I had anything more to say. And to my surprise, I found that I did.

I pulled my knees to my chest. "You know the worst part? I spent almost a year of my life in a juvenile detention center because I refused any sort of medical exam and wouldn't tell anyone what he did. I guess I didn't want to admit it had really happened."

He sat up straight like he'd been shot through with electricity. "They put you in a *detention* center? For what?" I was pretty sure he was picturing something much worse than the RITS.

"It wasn't that bad, Malachi. I mean, it was gross, and I had to watch my back. But I'm tough, and after a few months people figured that out and left me alone."

His hands shook as he pressed them flat across his thighs, like he was doing his best to keep them there. "I don't understand. Why were you the one imprisoned if he was the one who . . . who . . ."

"It happened the night I tried to kill myself. It felt like there was no other way out. He found me before it was too late and brought me back. But I was still in the same situation, and I couldn't take it anymore. I just sort of . . . snapped. I beat the shit out of him. I broke his nose and jaw. I gave him a concussion. I wanted to kill him. I could have killed him. But I stopped myself. And Debbie, my foster mom, called the police. They probably would have given me a lot less time if I'd told them what he'd been doing, but I couldn't bear it to talk about it. I . . . I actually can't believe I'm talking about it now, to you."

I pressed my forehead to my knees and covered my head with my arms. Should I have kept my mouth shut? Would he look at me differently now that all he'd suspected had been confirmed?

Damaged: that was what Ana called me. But I didn't want to be damaged. I wanted Malachi to see me as whole. Not broken. Not used.

Very gently, he peeled my arms away and nudged my chin up with his fingers. He took my hand and cradled it in his. "Please don't hide your face from me, Lela." He wore this shy, adorable expression that made my heart skip a beat.

I tucked my hair behind my ear and looked at our hands. Mine looked small and safe, held between both of his. I wanted to curl up in those hands, warm and protected, and rest there for minutes, or hours, or days. I wanted to hide, with him, and I didn't want to think about it anymore. I wanted to act on it. I scooted closer, burrowing up under his arm until it was around my shoulders.

"I'm sorry," I whispered. "I need this. Do you mind?"

He sighed and leaned back, guiding my head to rest on his chest. "No, I don't mind."

We sat in silence, letting a few staticky episodes of *Buffy* pull us away from our worries. He absently stroked my hair, winding it around his fingers, smoothing it against my back. I relaxed into him, and he laid his cheek on top of my head. It felt good. Better than good. Normal. Safe. Clean and right and whole . . . and not at all what I expected when I decided to come to hell.

"Lela, can I ask you something?"

"Mmmm?" I was half asleep, drunk with the feeling of being held in his arms.

"What did my voice say to you in the tower? What did you hear?"

"You said you needed to see me again. It's okay, I know it was just my imagination."

"Maybe. I always hear my brother's voice when I go through. Right when I need it, when I want to give up, I hear it. But this time the voice I heard was yours."

"Really? What did I say?" I murmured.

"You said you needed to see me again, too."

"Did it help?"

"More than you'll ever know."

I tightened my arm around his waist, wanting nothing more from the moment than what it was. I realized how unusual that was, considering the city and all its misery, considering you could have anything you wanted, but it would never be satisfying.

That simple moment, touching him, feeling him breathe, his hand stroking my hair—it was all I could have hoped for, all I could have wanted. I was filled up with it, this warm, buzzing feeling in my chest, and it was *completely* satisfying.

I wondered if it might be what I needed after all.

TWENTY-ONE

I AWOKE IN SILENCE. I'd been dreaming of comforting Malachi as he wept over the body of a Mazikin who looked a lot like me. In the dream, I'd realized that the dead Mazikin was my mother.

I kept my eyes closed, letting my awakening brain reconnect with my body. Malachi wasn't with me; I was alone on the couch. I must have fallen asleep there, leaning against him, taking what I needed from him.

A musty, coarse blanket had been spread over me. Its worn edges tickled my cheek. I wondered if he'd covered me, if he'd thought I might get cold. Just the possibility made me feel warmer than the blanket ever could have.

I mulled over the past few days and the changes they had brought. In all my life, I couldn't remember letting people make physical contact in any but the most necessary ways. I always braced whenever I thought someone might touch me, shied away when they tried, and lashed out, intentionally or not, when that touch hurt or reminded me of things I wanted to forget. It protected me, but it also kept me from getting close to other people, physically *and* emotionally.

I guess this was the damage Ana referred to.

Even people who cared about me, like Diane. Like Nadia. How many times had I flinched when they patted my back? How many hugs had I shrugged away? I hadn't been able to stop myself, even when I saw the hurt looks on their faces.

I had thought I'd lost the ability to enjoy being touched. I thought maybe I'd never had it in the first place. I had believed that was the way it would be for the rest of my life.

With Malachi, something was different. All my instincts were still in place; they buzzed with alarm when he caught me off guard. But they were silent since my escape from the dark tower and my humiliating admission of what had happened to me. In fact, I had *wanted* Malachi to touch me. I had been sure it was the only thing that might help. It felt good. Amazingly good. Like the shape of him, the scent of him, his texture, his movement, his rhythm had been made for me.

Whatever I felt for him had hit me quickly and grown fast and uncontrollable over a matter of days. With every moment I spent with him, every quiet, considerate action he'd shown, every cautious and gentle touch, I sank deeper into it. I had no idea how I was going to climb out.

It's dangerous to fall in love in hell. But was that what was happening? I didn't know what it was supposed to feel like. I loved Nadia, but that was a different thing, and it certainly didn't feel like this. My feelings for Nadia were powerful. They made me determined and strong. My feelings for Malachi were fragile and hopeful, vulnerable and easily crushed. I wanted to be near him, to lean on him. I wanted him to put his arms around me. I wanted to comfort him, hold his hand. And last night I'd been sure I wanted to kiss him, although that felt a little frightening—too out of control. It all felt out of control.

I rubbed my face with my hands, knocking away the sleep.

Ana was right. This was not the place or the time to fall in love, or develop a mad crush, or whatever this was. Those feelings could only get in the way of what I really needed to do: find Nadia and get her out of here.

Malachi chose that moment to enter the apartment, looking gorgeous and strong . . . and bloody. I sat up and threw off the blanket. We were so far from the Station, from Raphael.

"What happened? Are you all right? Where's Ana?"

Malachi looked amused at my rapid-fire questions and glanced at his arm, where his shirt was torn and edged with blood. "Take a breath, Lela. Ana is patrolling to the north. I went west and had to jam myself into some rafters in an old warehouse to keep a small group of Mazikin from spotting me. I wanted to see where they were going, but I lost them. This," he said, waving his elbow at me, "is nothing. Now—are you okay? You look a little pale."

I rubbed my hands over my face again. "I'm fine. I was afraid you'd been bitten," I muttered sheepishly.

"Well, thank you for your concern." He sounded sincere enough for me to venture a glance at his face from between my fingers. "Hi," he said when he saw me peeking at him. "Did you sleep well? Did you dream of Buffy?"

I shook my head and stretched. "No Buffy dreams. But I did sleep well. What's our plan for today?"

He'd gone into the kitchen and was running water over the scratch on his arm. He pressed a towel to it as he came back into the living room. "Ana's going to be a while, I think, so I was wondering if you wanted to train a bit. We'll start our search when she gets back. This area is crawling with Mazikin, so I'd like you to be ready. You haven't practiced fighting in your armor yet."

"Ah, joy. Well, color me medieval. Give me a few minutes."

I ran to the bathroom, groaning as I caught sight of my hair in the mirror. It looked like a hyena had draped itself over my head. I would have to ask Ana to rebraid it, but for now a ponytail would have to do. By the time I emerged, Malachi had laid out my armor and weapons. I eyed the buckles on the sides and sighed. In hell, Velcro was too much to ask.

Malachi clearly understood my expression. "Do you want some help?"

"If I thought you needed the comic relief, I'd say no. But if you want to actually be able to train before Ana returns, I think the answer is yes."

He picked up the breastplate and helped me lower it over my head. He quickly fastened the buckles along my sides, then stuck his fingers under the shoulder openings and shook it a little. His eyes skimmed over my chest and slid up to my face. "Is that too tight? Can you take a deep breath without feeling restricted?"

I forced the words over my clumsy tongue, too distracted by the curve of his mouth, by the warmth in his gaze. "It's . . . um . . . great." His cheeks turned ruddy when he heard the breathless sound of my voice. He only gave me a moment to look, though, and then he was kneeling before me, fastening the greaves onto my shins. I looked down at the back of his neck, partially shielded by his collar, vulnerable and smooth skin edged by pure black hair. I was sure that skin would be deliciously warm if I touched it. My fingers twitched, and I clenched my fists.

Malachi reached over and grabbed my bracers. He got to his feet and fastened them to my arms. While he was absorbed in his task, I watched his face, the fringe of his lashes, the light shadow of stubble along his jaw, the soft upward curve of his lips. Oh, man. Dangerously beautiful.

Malachi looked at me and raised an eyebrow. "I assume you can manage the belt by yourself?"

I rolled my eyes at him. "Nope, that's too complicated for me."

I bent to retrieve it, but he was faster. With a mischievous smile, he knelt again, pulling the belt around my hips until it was snug, notching it securely and tucking the end into the belt loop. His fingers brushed against my belly and the feeling just about made me fall to the floor. I grabbed his hands and stepped back, pushing away from him.

His face changed instantly from playful to horror stricken. He stood up and backed away quickly. "I'm sorry, Lela. I didn't mean to overstep—"

"No . . . no, you're fine." My mind raced as I tried to find a way to explain my reaction in a way that didn't sound completely pathetic. *I just realized exactly how much I'd like to stand here and let you do that all day.* He needed some explanation, because he clearly believed he'd awakened some terrible memory for me.

"Malachi," I soothed, reaching out to take his hand, willing to do anything to wipe that expression from his face. "You just startled me . . . . I don't mind when you touch me." *Please touch me again.*

He gave me a searching look, and then his thumb stroked over the back of my hand. "Okay," he said, a slow, painfully sexy smile spreading across his face and making my heart race. But then something flickered in his eyes—indecision, maybe. He let go of my hand and started to take off his own armor.

"I don't get it," I said. "Aren't we going to train?"

"Yes," he said, eyes on the buckles at his shoulders, "but Mazikin don't wear armor, so I won't when I train you." In less than a minute he was finished. "Come on, let's go to the roof. We'll have more room there and won't risk destroying the fine china and antique furniture."

I snorted and followed him, praying I wasn't about to make a fool of myself yet again.

"This one's not very well lit," he said as he looked around, "but you've got to get used to fighting in the dark anyway. Excuse me for a moment." He walked over to an elderly guy who was sitting in the middle of the gravel-covered roof clutching two nearly empty bottles of what appeared to be gin. I sniffed the air for any hint of rot or incense, but all I smelled was alcohol. Malachi leaned over so his face was in the man's line of sight. "You will be more comfortable in your own apartment," he said kindly.

"I am in my own apartment," mumbled the guy. His eyes glinted as the bottles refilled themselves with scummy, cloudy liquid. He lifted a bottle to his lips, gulping desperately. He barely seemed to notice as Malachi picked him up from the ground, carried him to the stairwell, and deposited him gently on the top step.

As soon as the door closed behind him, Malachi was back to business, like he did that kind of thing all the time. "With Mazikin, your biggest concern is keeping their teeth away from you. It's one of the reasons we wear the armor on our forearms and shins—it's pretty effective if you want to block a bite. But don't forget their fingernails—they're nasty. Not venomous like their teeth, but if you get scratched, it will get infected, and it will be bad."

I rubbed at the back of my hand where Sil had dug his fingernails in, grateful that Raphael had been around to heal me so quickly—especially when Malachi turned and lifted the back of his shirt. Four thick, jagged lines tracked diagonally from his ribs to the small of his back. I cringed. He looked over his shoulder and smiled grimly.

"Juri," he said. "The one time he caught me without my vest on. He and I met many times before that night in the alley."

"Same here." I crossed my arms over my chest and squeezed.

Something fierce sparked in Malachi's eyes. "He spoke to you. He said you—"

I held up my hands to silence him, not wanting to hear those words again. "Yeah. I guess he'd seen me when I was here before. As a ghost. He recognized me. And he seemed really glad to see me."

In the flesh, Juri had whispered.

I shuddered and turned away from Malachi. This was no way to be strong. I needed to pull myself together.

Malachi's voice was tender as he said, "You saved me that night, you know. Thank you for depriving him of his final victory."

I slowly turned around. "Ana said he likes to taunt you in your native language, that he steals the bodies of people who speak Slovak just so he can."

Malachi shuffled backward, examining the surface of the roof, the footing and traction it offered. "Slovak's not my native tongue, not really. It was the language spoken in the city where I lived."

"Wait—how many languages do you speak?"

He bit his lip and looked off at an angle. I could tell he was trying to count them all. "I speak seven languages. And I know many, many obscene words in about twelve more, thanks to Michael."

Suddenly, I felt very young and undereducated, but I pressed on, wanting to know more about him. "What's your native tongue?"

"I have two, actually. Yiddish, from my father, and Romani, from my mother." He laughed, and I could almost taste its bitterness. "You can only imagine what *that* was like, to be a Gypsy Jew when the Nazis came to Bratislava. Not that it was easy before that, but it only got harder."

"What was Bratislava like when you were growing up?" I didn't want to admit I didn't even know what country it was in.

He tilted his head and looked at me with narrowed eyes. "Are you stalling, Lela?"

I took a step back at his expression. "No way. Just interested. Are you asking me to start kicking your ass now? You only had to say so."

He crouched low, and I tensed to keep from backtracking again. My flinch drew that whimsical smile onto his face. "Stay relaxed. Just do what your instincts tell you."

Then I'd be kissing you instead of fighting you.

My civilized, grown-up brain gate-crashed the hormonal party and told me to control myself. This kicked off a loud mental argument that distracted me from his approach. He was on me in the next second, reaching out with clawed hands to mimic the attack of a Mazikin. Fortunately, I managed to duck under his arm, turn, and deliver a sharp kidney punch.

"Whoa," he said, sounding pleased, rubbing his back. "That was lovely. Try that again."

The next hour or so was tremendously fun. Exhausting, but fun. He gave me fewer instructions this time, sticking to some basic principles rather than telling me exactly what to do. He was merciless in the creativity of his attacks but gentle in their execution. He didn't want to hurt me, but he did want me to fight back and make it dirty.

"You wait too long to finish me off," he complained. "You always stand around to see how I'll react. You did the same thing with those two female Mazikin. Don't do that if you get attacked again. Keep fighting until they don't move when you hit them. Only then do you stop."

I lunged for him again, but as always, he was too freaking fast and dodged to the side. He made a grab for my leg, and I spun out of the way, slipping in the gravel but managing to stay upright. Only problem: my awkward flailing allowed him the moment he needed, and he was behind me in an instant. His arm snaked around my neck, but this time, and much to my own surprise, it barely fazed me.

I broke his hold and actually succeeded in pulling him off balance. In my giddiness and triumph, I jumped onto his back as he stumbled, wrapping my arms around his neck and hanging on for dear life. He laughed and staggered, grasping my knees and swinging me around playfully. I leaned forward and bit him lightly on the shoulder, completely astonished at myself. He gasped and fell to one knee, then started chuckling again.

"Bite them back. I hadn't thought of that."

I was laughing too, mostly out of relief that he hadn't been totally offended by my crazy behavior.

"Probably because a real Mazikin tastes gross," I said, *whereas you taste quite nice*. "But anyway, you're paralyzed by my venom. So tell me about Bratislava."

"All right. I give up. I'm at your mercy. So, be merciful. Get off my back, and I'll tell you about Bratislava."

I squeezed him a little tighter because it just felt so freaking good. "You mean I shouldn't keep biting you until you stop moving? Ah, well, your loss." I slid my hands up over his chest and shoulders, slowly letting him go, half wondering where the real Lela had gone, half enjoying that this flirty creature had temporarily taken her place.

He turned and gave me a solemn look. "In all respects, you are one of the dirtiest fighters I have ever met." He sat down on the gravel, dusting his hands on his thighs. "And that's a compliment. So. Bratislava is a beautiful city. It's right on the banks of a river, the Danube. It is an ancient city with a long history, and there is an enormous ruined castle that sits right in the middle of it, just on a hill. I don't know if it survived the war. I imagine it looks quite different these days. I'm not even sure what country it belongs to at this point. It was Czechoslovakia, but it changed during the war."

I sat down next to him. "Malachi," I said gently, "I want to hear about *your* city, not *the* city."

He shot me a rueful smile, knowing I'd caught him trying to give me the cheap tourist guide version. "My city was a neighborhood with narrow cobbled streets. My father owned a shoe shop, and we lived just above it. But I was hardly ever there. I was always running after my brother, Heshel, and his friends, trying to keep up with them."

"And were they good boys or bad boys?"

"Well, they were good boys who became bad boys." Malachi wrapped his arms loosely around his knees and looked up at the indigo-black sky. "I was sixteen when the laws were changed and they said we couldn't go to school anymore. I was seventeen when they said my father couldn't own his shop, when they made us move to the Jewish Quarter. I was eighteen when they made us sew the star onto our clothes. One at a time these big changes came, but every day there were smaller ones. The circles under my father's eyes became darker and deeper. My mother got thinner. She lost her laughter. And my brother and I lost our belief that the world was safe. There were gangs on the streets. No one would stop them from attacking and hurting us. So my brother and his friends, especially one of them, Imi, started fighting back. Imi was a wrestler, an athlete, and he taught us to defend ourselves. And we did, for a while."

"That's where you learned to fight like you do?"

"Yes, I learned how to fight on the street, and it's come in very handy over the past several years."

Several years. Malachi had been fighting for several decades, and apparently it started before his short life even ended. After he died, there had been no rest. What had he done to deserve this fate? Had he just been unlucky?

"Do you ever get to take a break here? I mean—I guess there's no vacation time . . . ."

He laughed. "Do I get to go on holiday—is that what you're asking? Where do you think we are?" His face turned serious and sad. "When I am released from the city, then I will rest."

"Ana said you've stopped drinking the water and you're not eating often. She told me it means you might be ready to leave soon."

His long fingers curled over a handful of gravel. "Ah. She noticed. Well, it's just a sign, not a guarantee. The only way to get out of this city is to go before the Judge. He decides when someone is ready to leave, and his word is the law. I will only go when I am relatively certain of a positive verdict. It's coming soon, though—I can feel it." He lifted his eyes to mine and smiled. "But I still have things to do here, right?"

"Thank you for what you're doing for me. And for Nadia." I reached out and touched his face. He closed his eyes and sighed as I ran my fingers along the ridge of his cheekbone.

"You're going to have to get out soon, too, you know," he said quietly. "Nothing here will nourish you because you don't belong here. You'll be fine for a while, but you can't stay here forever looking for her. You'll starve."

My hand fell into my lap. "Ana told me. So I guess it's important to find Nadia as soon as possible, for both of us."

He opened his eyes, and I sank into his gaze, totally lost in those dark brown depths.

"For both of us," he repeated, as if he was trying out the sound of it.

In that moment I could picture it: journeying outside the city with him, Nadia beside us, exploring that beautiful Countryside. Together.

TWENTY-TWO

I SANK DOWN ON the steps outside the apartment building, exhausted and discouraged. We'd been looking all day. Seventeen high-rises. Nothing.

At every door, Malachi or Ana pounded and entered. Every apartment contained a single resident. All were unresponsive to inquiries about Nadia and unable to look at my arm for more than a moment. They were too busy staring at the television. Sitting motionless at a table. Crying in the living room. Gorging in the kitchen. Shooting up in the bathroom.

One chunky middle-aged dude was in the bedroom, writhing on top of what appeared to be a headless body. Judging from the telltale stringy slime that hung over the edge of the cot and jiggled with each of his movements, he had grown the body himself. I had to wait in the hallway, gagging at the sight and at my own memories. After that, Malachi said we'd be more efficient if we stopped questioning people—so now, once we saw that the person inside an apartment wasn't Nadia, we immediately moved on.

Although I'd been aware that it would be a long, painful process, I hadn't really been prepared for it emotionally. A crest of anticipation carried me past each threshold, followed a few seconds later by a crash of disappointment. It sucked the hope right out of me.

Malachi touched my shoulder. "Are you ready to go? I was hoping to get through another five buildings today."

Ana came out of the apartment building shaking her head. "We have to keep moving, guys, or this is going to take years."

I got to my feet slowly. "Lead the way."

Malachi's brows drew together. "We might be at this for days. You understand that, right?"

"I do. I just . . . I didn't know how it would feel."

"Lela, I thought you were some kind of tough girl, but now I'm starting to wonder," Ana barked. "This was always a long shot. You've got to prepare yourself—we might not find her."

"That's not helpful," warned Malachi.

She put her hands on her hips and took a step toward him. "What do you want me to say? I'm not willing to soften the truth for her like you are. I'm starting to wonder why I need to be here. I mean—you and I should be patrolling, searching for the nest. Instead, we're here, looking for one person in a city of millions."

"Go then," he replied in a flat voice. "If that's what you—" His attention was suddenly drawn to something above us. I tilted my head up to follow the line of his gaze, but then my face collided with the front of his breastplate as he grabbed me and staggered back. A few feet behind us, Ana cursed fluently.

"What—" I slapped my palms against his chest in protest. Despite my attempts to shove away, he wouldn't let me go. Then I heard it: an awful, splattering crunch. I froze in Malachi's arms. He was breathing hard, hugging me tight. His hand came to rest on the back of my head, pressing my cheek to the engraved surface of his armor.

"I never get used to that." Ana sounded like she was about to be sick.

Malachi laid his hand on the side of my face, lifting my chin so I could meet his eyes. They were dark with sadness. "We're going to turn around and head down a different block, all right?"

"Malachi," I said, pushing against him, "let me go. What just happened?"

He didn't release me, either unwilling or unable to let go. "A suicide."

My eyes went wide and I stopped fighting him. I swallowed hard. "Are you telling me someone just jumped from one of these buildings and landed right next to us?" My voice sounded very small.

Malachi nodded slowly, not taking his eyes off mine.

"Malachi, Lela, get a move on."

He looked over his shoulder and nodded before turning back to me. "I'm going to let you go." It was more like he was asking me than telling.

"I'm fine. You don't have to protect me like this." I hoped he wouldn't notice the clamminess creeping across my exposed skin.

He smiled, but it looked a little painful. "I'm sorry. It was reflex. I'll try to keep my hands to myself next time." He let his arms fall to his sides.

"That's not what I meant," I mumbled.

Disoriented, I turned in exactly the wrong direction. The wreckage of a human body lay scattered in front of me. After that first second I could barely see it because all I could picture was my own body plunging from the cliff, hitting something hard. I'd hit something hard.

No sound made it past the roaring in my ears, no words made it past my screams, no thoughts made it past the memory that had finally caught up with me: my last memory of my life on Earth.

I awoke on a cot.

Narrowing my eyes in the dim light, I saw our supplies organized against the wall. I was in the bedroom of the high-rise apartment where we'd stayed the night before. I lay still for a few moments, trying to recall what had happened after Malachi's arms fell away from me, but was distracted by the voices coming from beyond the closed door of the bedroom.

"—doing your job. I swear, what has gotten into you? Just over a week ago, finding it was all you cared about, and that made sense to me. And now?"

"Now I have an additional objective." I had to strain to hear Malachi's considerably lower, considerably calmer voice. I sat up slowly, trying not to make a sound.

"That's a pretty convenient way of describing her. Lets you off the hook, doesn't it? Malachi, have you counted your mistakes in the last few days? The number of times you sacrificed duty and practicality to protect her? More than you've made in the last seven decades, I bet."

I winced at Ana's words. She was probably right, and I felt guiltier by the second for pulling Malachi away from his responsibilities.

"Helping her is the right thing to do. And she is strong, she—"

"Strong? Did you not witness her fall apart after that guy hit the pavement? Did you not just carry her unconscious body for several blocks? Did you not—"

"Tell me what your first week in the city was like," he snapped. "Or shall I tell you about mine? Here is what I know: neither you nor I were as put together as she is. You are comparing her to us as we are now."

"That's who she needs to be if she's going to accomplish the ridiculous task she's set for herself," Ana countered.

"She is special—you can see that. It's why you agreed to help me in the first place. She had visions of her friend—she either had this ability within her or she was *chosen* to have it. Either way, that makes her exceptional. And then, on top of all that—she *knew* what this place was like. She wandered here in her dreams. She *suffered* here, Ana. She was terrified of having to return. But she came anyway. She was willing to give up her own eternal comfort, happiness, and safety in order to try to find her friend."

"And that's the only reason you're helping her?"

My ears strained in the silence that followed. I was dying to know the answer to that question myself. He must have made some response, because Ana continued speaking a moment later. "You aren't fooling me. You of all people should know better than to play with fire like this. And regardless of how *special* she is, the two of you cannot continue on like this forever. She will fade away soon. What are you going to do if she's not willing to give up? Are you going to hog-tie her and drag her to the Sanctum? How far will you go to save her? How much will you sacrifice before this is over?"

I wrapped my fingers around the edges of the cot to keep myself in place while I fought the urge to press my ear against the door.

"Whatever," said Ana after several seconds. "I have to get out of here. I'm going to patrol to the northwest, so at least one of us is doing the job we're pledged to do."

The door slammed. I lay back on the cot and turned to the wall, heart hammering. I pulled my knees to my chest and squeezed my eyes shut.

Ana had not made any secret of her impatience with Malachi, but I hadn't known the extent of her frustration. She obviously thought he was making a huge mistake by helping me find Nadia.

The bedroom door squeaked open. Soft footsteps approached. Malachi's movements were almost silent as he knelt beside my cot. I held my breath as he sat there, wondering if he would touch me. *Wanting* him to touch me. And then he sighed, like he had lost some battle inside his own head. His hand brushed my back and his fingers found the tip of my braid where the loose ends looped and coiled. He stroked my hair gently. I allowed myself a tiny breath as I stayed perfectly still, face to the wall, smiling and fighting tears at the same time. When I finally lifted my hand to wipe my eyes, he withdrew abruptly. I turned over and looked at him.

"How are you feeling?" he asked warily.

"Embarrassed. I'm so sorry I freaked out like that." I put my hands to my eyes to block out the flash of memory that jolted my brain.

Through my fingers, I watched Malachi's hands rise from his knees and drop again, fists clenched. He seemed afraid to touch me without express invitation.

I reached out shakily and took his hand. I uncurled his fingers and laid his palm against mine. The contact was real and warm. It slowed my heartbeat to a manageable pace. I wanted more. I wanted to crawl inside him and hide.

"I fell off a cliff," I whispered, then looked into his eyes. "I landed on the rocks. I remembered it when I saw that guy, how he . . ."

I leaned forward, breathing hard, burying my forehead against his knees and our hands. He put his arm around me, gathering me to him, then shifted and snaked his other arm under my knees. He carried me into the living room, holding me curled against his chest.

He sat down on the couch with me in his lap. I pressed my face against his neck, slowing my breathing by pacing it with his and focusing on the warmth of his hand as he laced his fingers with mine.

As the panic cleared, I laid my head on his shoulder and memorized the stark angles of his face, the high bridge of his nose, the ridge of his brow, the cut of his jaw. Without thinking too much about it, I skimmed my fingers over them. As soon as my skin made contact with his, he closed his eyes and leaned into my hand.

"Malachi, what happened to the guy who jumped? You said you never know where you'll end up if you die . . . ."

He tilted his head and let my fingers slide through his hair. "I have no doubt he appeared back at the Suicide Gates. Suicide is never the escape it seems. If you kill yourself, you will appear at the entrance to the city and be led right back in. There are a few citizens who are chronically recycled, who are so absorbed in their issues that they don't notice they never end up anyplace new; the Gate Guards recognize them as they shuffle through. They have to start all over again."

"Ana told me the Mazikin get a chance to start over, too, when you kill them. There's no way to get rid of them permanently?"

Malachi took my other hand and placed it on his neck, over the scar from his last battle with Juri. "I don't think it will happen on my watch. The only way to keep them all away permanently is to make sure not a single one of them is left in the city. As long as one remains, they can bring others in. We have set fire to dozens of Mazikin nests in the last several decades, but at least one of the Mazikin always seems to escape." His quiet laugh was saturated with sadness. "Maybe they've figured out all my tricks."

I wrapped my arm over his chest and squeezed. He'd fought so hard for so many years. And after all that, he felt like he had failed. Like he was leaving the job unfinished. But that wasn't fair. Obviously Mazikin had been in the city for a very long time, possessing the bodies of suicides. Easy victims, Ana had called them. But then a thought occurred to me. "Hey, you said Mazikin never make it through the dark tower. How come you don't just dump them in there?"

He pressed my hand to his side, like he needed me closer. "That's exactly what the Guards did for years. Until, many years ago, I was interrogating a Mazikin, and she admitted to me that killing the possessed body frees the human soul from the Mazikin realm. So what if trapping the Mazikin forever in the dark tower also traps the human soul in the Mazikin realm? Damned to slavery and suffering for eternity? I couldn't imagine allowing that when there was a way to stop it. Not everyone agreed, though. I argued about it with Takeshi for years, but he would not stop the practice. But after he . . . died . . . I was in charge. I forbade the Guards to send Mazikin to the tower."

He gave me a wry look. "They still do, of course. I punish them if I catch them, but I cannot be everywhere at once. But that's why I never leave a Mazikin alive. What if I can release that human soul to go wherever it needs to go next?"

"Wouldn't that mean the soul just comes back here?"

He shook his head. "Not always. It depends on the person, on the progress they've made wherever they are." He paused, and when he spoke again, it was in a dry, strangled voice. "Lela, if you don't go before the Judge soon, *you* will die. Do you understand that?"

"Where will I go then?"

"You might end up back at the Suicide Gates if you let yourself die, but you wouldn't be the same as you are now. You would belong to the city—you would be one of the suicides. I suppose you could end up in the Countryside. Or you could go somewhere else. There is no way of knowing."

I don't want to go somewhere else. I want to stay with you.

The thought was so startling in its strength and truth that I jerked in surprise.

"What is it?" He looked like he thought he had crossed another line and widened the span of his arms, releasing me.

"Don't." I pulled his arms back around me. His eyes asked question after question, begging for answers. I didn't have any. I only had questions of my own. "Will you force me out of the city?"

He shook his head firmly. "I will never force you to do anything, I promise. I won't make that mistake again. But short of that, I will do whatever I can to get you out safely. Whatever is necessary."

"Ana thinks you're neglecting your other duties."

His expression hardened. “Ana and I work together very well, and I respect her immensely, but we do not always agree.”

“I don’t feel good about pulling you away from whatever you should be doing.”

He grazed my cheek with the backs of his fingers. “Then don’t worry. This is what I should be doing.”

I shivered at his touch and laughed. “*This* is what you should be doing? Right now?”

Uncertainty drew his hand back, but then he read my playful look. “Yes. And maybe this.” He skimmed a finger from my temple to the base of my neck. He smiled as I shivered again, and his eyes lit on my mouth.

Control be damned. I wanted to kiss him. I wanted to drown in him, forget about everything, and never resurface.

Malachi looked into my eyes, checking in with me. He took a breath and moved closer, until his lips were just over mine. “And also, thi—”

The apartment door burst open, and both of us jumped to our feet. Malachi instinctively dove for a weapon. I crouched low, startled out of my mind, nerves jangling. We didn’t have time to relax when we saw it was Ana, because she immediately started barking at us.

“Malachi, you are not going to believe this. I’m pretty damn sure I just found the Mazikin nest, and it’s only six blocks to the northwest.”

Malachi jammed his half-drawn scimitar back into its sheath. "How can you be certain?"

Ana cocked her head at him. "Boy, I *have* been around for a while. How many of these things have we cleared out? The building looks abandoned, but there's activity in the basement. I hid in a *Dumpster*," she said, narrowing her eyes at Malachi, "so Michael's going to have to make me some new armor because that smell never comes out. You *will* back me up on that one. Anyway, I watched the building. This is it, baby. I saw a whole group go in—one of them had a Guard scimitar at his belt. And there was an old one with them."

I shuddered at the memory of Doris and her creepy four-legged lope.

Malachi stepped forward, totally focused on Ana. "Did you see Ibram or Sil?"

"No. And they weren't inside, either. I could see in through one of the windows."

"Do you know how many are in there?"

"A few dozen, but—" Ana gave me a very strange look. "Lela, would you excuse us?"

"What? Oh. Sure." I headed for the bedroom, still completely short-circuited by Malachi's almost-kiss.

He held out his hand to stop me. "Hold on. Ana, you can say whatever you have to say in front of Lela. This is her mission, too."

Ana clenched her teeth as she glared at Malachi. "Fine. But you're going to be sorry you said that." She turned to me and pointed to my tattoo. "I think I found your girl."

My jaw dropped. Hope and overwhelming fear swamped all my thought processes.

"Where?" I could barely get the word out.

Ana looked back at Malachi. "I'm pretty sure she was in the group of recruits I saw enter the building."

"You mean she's been possessed?" Tears welled in my eyes. This could not be happening. Not after all my hard work to reach her.

"No, not yet. She was crying. Mazikin are usually freakishly cheerful unless they're under attack, so she's obviously still herself."

Malachi and Ana stared at each other. "Options," said Malachi.

"Full frontal assault," Ana replied. "We'll draw a platoon of Guards from the nearest outpost and go in hard."

Malachi shook his head sharply. "Two problems with that. First, the nearest outpost is thirty blocks to the north. We don't have time to go there, summon them, wait for them to gear up, and bring them back. That would take all night. And second: direct assault is too dangerous for Nadia. If she's killed, she'll probably come back through the Suicide Gates, but we wouldn't have time to get word to the

Gate Guards—they're at least two days away. She'd get lost in the city and we'd never find her again. Other options."

"None." Ana massaged a knot in her shoulder. "If we try to sneak in, they'd recognize you in an instant, and probably me as well. And the building's tight. I checked the first floor. They've sealed all but one street-level entrance to the basement. Ducts, too."

I let out the breath I'd been holding. "I'm going in."

Malachi whirled around, eyes wide. "No, you're not."

I took a step back at the fierce expression on his face. "I have to. If I don't, they'll take her, possess her. Didn't you *just* tell me the souls they possess go to a place more hellish than here? I need to go in there and get her out."

He shook his head again. "No. We'll handle this. You will not. How can you even suggest—"

"Are you serious?" I snarled. "You know that's the only reason I'm here, right?" Malachi's gaze dropped to his feet. "Besides, based on your 'options,' it sounds like I'm the *only* one who can go in. I can let them recruit me. And Ana, you said they like ones like me, so I can—"

"Lela." His voice was rock hard, daring me to argue. "If you go in there, the odds are good you will *not* come out. There are dozens of Mazikin in that basement. We won't be able to stop them if they try to hurt you. If they try to possess you. There has to be another way."

I met his eyes defiantly. "I'm not helpless. And if you back me up, I could get her out."

I turned and walked into the bedroom, unable to look at him anymore. I began rifling through the chest of drawers. Ana came in and started to rummage through the closet, tossing various weapons and boxes onto the cot. Malachi followed but stopped at the doorway.

"What are you doing?" he asked.

"I'm finding civilian clothes." My hands shook as I dug through the musty garments.

"I won't let you do this," he said flatly.

I walked toward him, one hand on my hip, one finger up and waving. "Excuse me? Were you here a minute ago when you promised not to force me to do anything? Did I miss the fine print that said you were *lying*?"

"You're not even supposed to be here!" he yelled as he closed the distance between us. "I promised to help you find her, not to help you get killed!"

"I'm going to get her out of there! I will *not* turn my back on her again!" *And I will not let you go on a suicide mission.*

His palms shot out and hit the chest of drawers on either side of me, trapping me in the cage of his arms. He leaned over me, right in my face. "This is insane! What makes you so sure you're the solution to this problem?"

"Because this is the best of all your suck-ass options!"

His voice shook me all the way to my bones. "Why are you so willing to throw yourself away? Are you worth *nothing*? How can you—"

I clapped my hand over his mouth. I needed him to shut up. But the warmth of his skin—it made me want to cry. I ducked under his arm and backed off, hands in the air. I had to disconnect before I exploded. I couldn't stand the look on his face. It enraged me and tore my heart out all at the same time.

"I'm not going to argue with you, Malachi. This is a done deal."

"I can't. I can't help you do this." He shook his head, eyes casting around the room, looking everywhere but at my face.

"This is the best and safest plan to get her out."

"Not for you." His face twisted into an agonized grimace as he raked his fingers through his hair. "I can't do this."

He turned on his heel and stalked out of the apartment.

TWENTY-THREE

I STARED AT THE door he'd just slammed. I hadn't expected him to be thrilled with my plan, but I hadn't expected him to freak out, either.

My mouth opened and closed a few times as I turned to Ana, who shook her head. "I had a feeling this would happen. You're asking a lot from Malachi."

"I'm just asking him to go with a less risky plan. I can't let you guys go in there to get killed when there's a possibility I could get her out."

"Less risky? That's not how he sees it. Malachi will risk his own life in a second. He does that every day, and today he has more reason than ever. But risk you? That's almost impossible for him. He's let himself care for you, Lela, and he's having trouble dealing with it. You and your plan just hit every button he has."

"I don't understand. You *know* this is better, Ana. You know I have the best chance to get her out, right?"

She sighed. "I do."

"Malachi's not stupid. He understands that, too. I know he does."

Ana walked over to her pile of gear. "Of course he does. But remember—things aren't adding up for him like they did before. It's not all cold calculation, not when you're involved. In fact, I can guarantee you he's only thinking about one thing right now. He thinks you're about to make his worst fear come true. Again."

"What are you talking about?"

"Remember I told you Takeshi was taken by the Mazikin?"

Ana began to arrange her weapons on the floor, preparing to systematically arm herself for whatever might happen. I watched her, a chill riding over my skin. She paused, head bent, fingers running over the insignia on her breastplate, over her heart.

"Malachi and I went looking for him when he didn't return from his patrol. We found him west of downtown, walking back to the Station. I was so relieved. Takeshi had never been late before, so I had been worried out of my mind. I ran to him. Malachi was right behind me. But just as we got close, Malachi shoved me to the side and drew his scimitar."

She closed her eyes and sank to the floor. "It was the smell. That's how he knew. I smelled it, too, but I didn't care. I wasn't thinking. It almost got me killed. If Malachi hadn't pushed me out of the way, one of Takeshi's knives would have been buried in my chest. It ended up buried in Malachi's shoulder instead.

"I couldn't believe it at first. I tried to get between them because I just couldn't accept that Takeshi had been taken, that he was gone. Malachi had to fight both of us at first." Her mouth twisted bitterly as she straightened and pulled one half of her breastplate aside, lifting her shirt to reveal a long scar across her ribs. "That's what took me out of the fight and knocked some sense into me. But Takeshi's body had gotten so weak that the Mazikin inside him was no match for Malachi. I will never forget the look on Malachi's face as he cut Takeshi's throat. It's the same look he gave you right before he walked out that door."

My stomach felt hollowed out. "He's afraid they'll turn me into one of them, and he won't be able to stop it. He's afraid he'll have to kill me."

"Now you get it. The other Guards like to send Mazikin into the tower. Easy. Just shove them through those doors and job done. But Malachi always kills them, because he believes he's liberating the possessed soul. After Takeshi died, I wanted to believe it, too. I *do* believe it. I don't feel bad about killing them at all. Malachi is different, though. I can tell he feels something every time he kills. And it would be even worse than it was with Takeshi if you got turned—because of how he feels about you." Ana was strapping knives to her legs and looked intent on her task, but I saw the liquid tracks shining on her face.

"How can it be worse? Takeshi was his mentor. They'd been working together for years. You said Malachi loved him. Malachi . . . Malachi barely knows me," I mumbled, trailing off at the end.

Ana shot me a disgusted look as she continued to lash weapons to every conceivable part of her body. "That boy's on his knees for you. And I know you feel it, too. Sure, you've got other priorities, but I can see it in your face when you look at him."

Ana pulled a knife and stabbed it at the door, staring me down with her fierce cat's eyes. "He's dying inside right now because he's going to have to send you into that nest. Remember how determined he was to prevent that from happening? He knows letting you go in is the safest thing for Nadia, so he'll do it. He'll do it for you because he respects you and wants to please you. Because he made you a promise. But all he really wants to do is get you out of here, to carry you far away and never let any of them touch you."

I took a deep breath and set my shoulders. I wanted the same thing, for him to carry me away, but I had to go through with this. It was why I had come here. "I have to get Nadia out of there. I can't let them take her."

Ana nodded. "Well, we're going to do our best to get this done. But be realistic. Now that she's in there, the odds aren't great. The only thing we have going for us right now is that Ibram and Sil aren't there. Many others are, though, and we're going to have to go in blind, with no backup. We have no time to do surveillance, to get a sense of what we're dealing with. I know this is the least risky plan, but there's still a possibility none of us will get out."

She opened one of the boxes she'd pulled from the bedroom closet and carefully removed its contents—several black spheres the size of golf balls. She loaded them into a satchel. When she saw me watching, she held one up.

"Michael's handy new innovation. The only explosives in the city. You go in and grab Nadia, and we'll be right outside, creating the mother of all distractions and waiting to cover you as you get her out."

It felt like a semitruck had just parked on my chest. I could tell myself that Malachi and Ana would be safer if I went in, but they would lay themselves on the line for me and Nadia no matter what plan we used. I was scared out of my mind, for all of us. And the memory of my time with the Mazikin—the smell of incense and rot, the clutch of fingernails on my skin, the sight of that animal movement—made me want to curl into a ball and never move again. Only one thing could make me feel better. Only one thing had comforted me since I'd arrived in the city, offered me solace in this hellish place, made me feel stronger and more able to face all of it . . . but he had just stormed out.

"He'll be on the roof. He always goes up when he needs to clear his head," Ana said quietly. "But hurry. We can't afford to wait much longer. I'm going to go watch. If anything changes, I'll come get you."

I didn't need any more encouragement than that. I was out the door and in the stairwell a few seconds later. I was panting by the time I reached the final flight of stairs. The metal door leading to the roof creaked as I opened it, but Malachi didn't turn around.

He stood at the edge, leaning against the half wall that ringed the roof, looking out over the city. I walked toward him slowly, giving him a chance to turn to me, but he didn't. I was about to ask him if he had escaped over the walls again when he broke the silence.

"Why are you here? I thought you'd be getting ready."

"I am ready."

He spun around too quickly for me to step back. He reached behind me and yanked the rubber band from the bottom of the braid Ana had so meticulously woven this morning before our search.

"What are you doing?" Before I could protest further, he briskly threaded his fingers through my hair and unraveled it. "Hey! Stop it!" I tried to push his hands away, but he ignored me. "What is your problem?"

His hands fell to his sides, and he took a few steps back. "You'll look more attractive to them this way," he said in a dead, flat voice.

I tucked a stray bit of hair behind my ear. "Listen, Ana told me what you had to do to Takeshi." The muscle in his jaw began to tick. "I wanted you to know I understand the risk. I understand what you might have to do."

His fists clenched. "You understand nothing. You think giving me *permission* to cut your throat makes this better?"

"I thought it might. I don't want some Mazikin wearing my skin. I'd want you to end it if it came to that."

He scoffed. "Well, that's very generous of you, Lela, since *you* would be long gone. But think about this as you so casually give me your blessing: The Mazikin who takes you will look at me with your eyes when I corner her. Her skin will be as soft as yours when I touch it. When I cut her, she will scream with your voice. And when I stand over her body, watching blood soak the beautiful hair that looks and feels *exactly* like yours, do you think I won't feel like I've killed you?" His voice broke and he turned away.

I swallowed the lump in my throat and splayed my hands against his back, certain the contact would comfort us both.

I was wrong.

"Don't touch me."

I let my hands drop. "I'm sorry. I—"

He turned around and leaned forward. "What, Lela? What did you think touching me would accomplish? Do you know it gets worse for me every time you do?"

He might as well have slapped me. I looked down at my feet, wishing someone else *were* wearing my skin. "If you don't want me to touch you, then why haven't you ever stopped me?"

He advanced on me, raising his arms in shaky frustration. "I never said I didn't want you to touch me! That is exactly the problem. Every time you put your hands on me, I don't want you to let go.

"And if you touch me now, I *won't* let you go," he said more softly. "I won't let you go after her. I won't be able to. Please don't put me in that position. Don't make me break my promise to you. Don't make this harder . . . ." He wrapped his arms around his body. It made him look helpless.

I wanted to respect his request to keep the distance between us. But my fear made me selfish and his admission that he wanted me made me bold.

"I have to go after Nadia. You know I have to. You know it's the only way she'll have a chance, and you know it's the best way for Ana as well. Even if you don't care about your own safety, I know you care about Ana's. But I'm about to chicken out because I'm so terrified. And I won't be able to do this if I *don't* touch you. It's the only thing that makes me feel safe."

I took the chance he might push me away and reached out.

"Lela," he moaned as he took a step back and found himself up against the half wall. "Don't ask this of me."

I laid my hands on his waist and skimmed them around his back. He shivered at my touch. I pressed my cheek to his chest, absorbing the warmth of his skin through his shirt, inhaling deeply to draw his scent into my lungs and embed it there forever. "Let me do this, just for a few minutes before I go."

Like that night in the Guard tower, he spread his arms, allowing me to touch him, to have control. His fingers curled over the bricks, which looked like they might crumble beneath his grip. He looked up at the veil of darkness that hung over us.

I touched his face, running shaking fingertips across the ridge of his cheekbone. His eyelids fluttered shut. I inched closer, until his breaths shook my rib cage, until his heart beat furiously against mine, until touching him was not enough—I needed *him* to touch *me*. I put all my needs and desires and hopes and fears into one word, the most powerful one I could think of.

"Malachi."

He made a ragged sound as his arms encircled me, crushing me against him. One of his hands slid up my back to the nape of my neck. I raised my head and found his gaze hard on mine.

"Don't do this to me," he whispered.

Then he kissed me.

It was nothing like the kiss I'd stolen from him when he'd been unconscious. That kiss was an echo, sweet but hollow. This kiss was a living thing. A wild and dangerous thing. It spread its wings and carried us out over the city, over the walls. Malachi tasted like the forest, like the sun, like every dream I'd ever had about what this moment should be.

I wrapped my arms around his neck, drawing him closer. Oh God, it was so out of control, but in this really sweet, beautiful way. I never thought I'd be allowed to have that feeling. I thought it had been completely beaten out of me, but here it was, untouchable and clean.

Malachi moved with me, let me in, held me tight. He made this noise, this vulnerable and sexy moan, and I would have fallen if he hadn't been holding me up. I pushed my fingers through his hair as he lifted me from the ground, never taking his mouth from mine.

The sound of the metal door clanging open wrenched me painfully back into the city. I could still taste the forest on my tongue as I pulled away from him. He leaned his forehead against mine, breathing hard.

"Don't do this to me," he kept repeating softly, barely audible over the crashing beats of my heart.

"Lela, Malachi, we're losing time. Sil has arrived at the nest. We can't afford to wait until Ibram gets there, too." Ana's deadly serious voice yanked me all the way back into reality, reminding me what was at stake tonight.

Malachi lowered me to the ground but did not let me go. His arms tightened around me as his lips moved silently. His eyes were squeezed shut, like he was in pain, or praying, or both.

"We have to go," I murmured, pushing against him gently, wondering if he would keep his vow to not let me go, wondering if I would find enough strength to protest if he did. But he allowed me to back away. He spread his arms again, letting his hands find their places along the wall. I turned and walked quickly to the door, avoiding Ana's eyes.

As I entered the building, I looked back to see Malachi standing against the wall, head bowed, chest heaving, fingers curled around the bricks, crushing them to dust.

TWENTY-FOUR

I WANDERED ALONG THE street, absorbed in my thoughts, trying to look like the rest of the residents of the city. Easy pickings. It wasn't as hard as I'd expected. In fact, I was so deep in the ocean of my confusion about Malachi that I could barely pay attention to my surroundings. I licked my lips, still able to taste him there. I almost called his name, almost begged him to come out from wherever he was hiding and carry me away. I was certain he was close and certain he would come. All I had to do was say his name. I resisted the urge, knowing one false move could end our hard work and our mission.

Footsteps echoed up a nearby alley, and my heart lurched into my throat as an old Mazikin burst into the open and came to an abrupt halt in front of me. It was the racist old man I'd met just before Amid nabbed me.

"Ah, I thought those Guards got you," he cackled as he rose to his feet, wiping his dirt-covered hands on his pants. "You need a place to stay, my girl." He reached for me, and I tensed to keep from slamming my fist into his toothless face by sheer reflex.

"I . . . I guess I do need a place."

"You're in luck. We've got shelter a block from here. Lots of friends for you. Lots of young ones." He turned, but kept his grip on me. "I've got one!" he called.

Another Mazikin stepped from the alley. The sandy-haired young man approached us with a smile on his face. I swallowed back my nausea as their stale, rotten smell grew more intense.

"Good job, Clarence," said the man as he reached out and touched my hair. "She's got such color in her cheeks. Not pale like the others. She's perfect. Let's get her back. Sil's doing a batch tonight—he'll be starting soon."

My heart raced. *A batch*. What if I was too late? What if Nadia had already been possessed by the time I arrived? Those thoughts steadied my steps as I allowed the Mazikin to escort me down the block. It took all I had not to look around to see if I could catch a glimpse of Malachi, my lifeline, my . . . yeah. He was so much more than a lifeline, and I might never get to tell him.

Within a few minutes, we arrived at a huge building that looked like an old warehouse. The windows on the upper floors were dark, but the casement windows, sunk below the surface of the sidewalk, glowed with cold, greenish-yellow light.

Clarence and Sandy-Hair led me down a short flight of steps and opened the door for me. Clarence kept his gnarled hand around my upper arm as we descended another flight of steps and rounded a corner.

It was a huge, open basement. Support columns jutted up every several feet. The high casement windows lined the far wall. In the center of the room sat what looked like a conference table, but there were no chairs around it. Instead, it was surrounded by squat ceramic bowls giving off thick clouds of smoke that hazed the ceiling. Now I knew where that sickening smell of incense came from. A section of rope was tied to each leg of the table, and the ends lay tangled across its surface.

I had a feeling I knew what it was and wanted to stay as far from it as possible.

The room was filled with Mazikin of all shapes and colors and sizes. They talked and laughed together, teeth flashing, hands running up and down each other's arms, fingers twining through each other's hair. Men and women, old and young, they seemed unable to converse without touching. Some of them tussled playfully, scrambling like animals across the floor, knocking their cheerful companions over in their scuffles. At least two loud and enthusiastic couples were up against the wall right next to me doing considerably more than scuffling.

Oh, that's just . . . I turned my head away.

And saw Nadia.

Her eyes were glazed, and tears streaked down her face. Her features were puffy and gray, and her hair hung lank and greasy across her face. I had known she'd look different from the last time I saw her: still and perfect in her coffin. Even so, it didn't stop my heart from breaking, just a bit. It made me all the more desperate to get to her.

She was sitting on the floor with a group of people who stared at the jolly chaos around them but didn't seem to be noticing any of it. They weren't talking to each other. They weren't examining the room or the bizarre people in it with any sort of curiosity or fear. They weren't trying to escape. They simply sat, gazing down at their laps or off into space, absorbed in their own misery.

Clarence guided me toward them. "You'll just sit here with some of our newcomers. Don't worry—you'll be partying with the rest of us before you know it." He gave me a wink and squeezed my arm painfully.

"Um, thanks." I pulled away and dragged my feet to the edge of the group. "I'll stay here."

I nudged a few hapless souls out of my way in an effort to get to Nadia. She was so close. I could almost touch her. This was it. She would probably be upset and startled when she realized I was here in the city with her, knowing I was dead, too. She would be mad at me for putting myself in this situation, but when she understood that I had come for her, it would change everything. She'd lose that glazed look and come back to herself. I reached out to touch her arm.

"Where did you get that one?" Sil's voice sliced through my concentration and froze me in place, reminding me that I shouldn't have lost awareness of my surroundings. I turned my face to the wall but knew it would do no good. I knew Sil was, at this very moment, pointing right at me.

"Found her on the street not two blocks from here. She's quite something, isn't she?" explained Clarence, who shuffled over to stand next to Sil. "Girl with the hair. Come here," he cooed, clearly proud of his prize. He gripped my arm and tugged me over a few bodies to stand in front of Sil.

I raised my head and met Sil's inquisitive stare but was careful to keep my face blank. "Oh. Hi. Do I know you?"

Sil smiled and rolled his eyes. "Lela, yes? I will never forget the girl who helped me escape certain death, and I doubt you've forgotten me. The last time I saw you, you were trying to hit my darling Lacey with Malachi's staff. He came to get you and brought his feisty friend. It looked like you were on their side."

"No. I don't know why he came to get me. But he . . . he was wounded in the fight with Juri, and I escaped from him when he tried to take me back to the Station."

Sil giggled, a high-pitched noise that made me cringe. "*You* escaped from Malachi? I'm sorry, girl, that's a little hard to believe."

"Right, well, maybe under normal circumstances, but as far as I know, Malachi might be dead. When I left him, he was unconscious and couldn't move—your friend Juri bit him pretty bad."

Sil caught several locks of my hair with his fingers. He jerked me forward as he brought them to his nose. "Hmm. I think I can smell him on you." His hand shot out and wrapped around the base of my neck. In a fraction of a second, his nose was pressed to the side of my face.

"Yesss," he whispered as he inhaled. "His nasty smell is *all* over you. When was the last time you saw him?"

I took a deep breath, cursing inwardly. Of course Malachi's scent was all over me—I'd been in his arms only an hour or so ago. I would have given anything to be back there at that moment. I gulped and stood very still, trying not to gag as Sil's rancid breath huffed across my face.

"I saw him a few days ago, lying on a cot in an empty apartment south of downtown. I got away as quickly as I could." I took another shallow breath through my mouth. "I hope the bastard's dead. And you guys were so nice to me, I guess I thought maybe I could find you again."

Sil rolled our faces together until we were nose-to-nose and his teeth were an inch from my chin. His fingers tightened around my neck as his giggly face turned vicious and hard.

"I don't believe a word you're saying. You obviously don't belong in this city. You can pretend all you want, but I knew it from the moment I saw you. That's why I went to the trouble of taking you with me instead of killing you that night at the Guard Station. You are so much stronger than the others. You will be an excellent host for one of our family. But now you are ruining a very special evening for us. For the first time in five *hundred* years, we are so close to getting out . . . . I'm tempted to tear your throat out right now."

We are so close to getting out . . . ? What if the Mazikin did find a way out into the Countryside? What would that mean?

I didn't have more than a moment to think about it, though, because Sil pulled back and eyed me speculatively.

"I'm surprised he would use you as bait after the way he looked at you. But if this is a trap, I'd better take care of you now. We'll see how he looks at you when you're wearing *our* scent." His high-pitched giggle returned and almost pierced my eardrums. "I wonder if he'll hesitate when it comes time to kill you. Maybe it will be enough for one of us to sneak up and chop off his head! Clarence, watch this one. She's second up, and it won't be long. If she moves, bite her. I won't be angry."

Clarence's face crumpled. "This one is perfect," he whined. "You want me to damage her?"

"You won't ruin her. She's strong enough to survive until she receives one of our sisters and becomes immune to the venom. So if she causes trouble, dig in."

Sil shoved me backward, where I landed in a sprawl atop the dazed suicides. With no change of expression, they leaned out of the way to accommodate. I settled between them, watching Sil carefully. He walked jerkily over to one of the pairs of lovers and slapped them away from each other. Although I couldn't hear his words, the urgency of his body language told me all I needed to know. He was sending them outside to guard. Or to fetch the still-missing Ibram.

Either way, not good.

I was tempted to run for it, to try to get out and warn Malachi and Ana that the Mazikin were on to them. But then I turned back to look at Nadia. With a quick glance at Clarence, who was watching me with newfound wariness, I once again inched toward my friend.

"Hey—what do you think you're doing? Didn't you hear what Sil just said? Do you really want me to bite you?"

I couldn't stop myself before I snapped, "Dude. Do you even have teeth?"

I instantly regretted being such a smart-ass when he dropped into a crouch and smiled wide, revealing that he had precisely four.

Four very sharp canine teeth. They had been filed.

"I have all I need to stop you in your tracks, girl, so stay where you are. I don't want to damage you."

I stared at Nadia, who was still too far away to reach. I looked back at Clarence, who glared at me with unwavering focus. Damn. I was stuck, and I had no idea when Malachi and Ana would strike, or if the Mazikin's suspicion would delay them.

Sil skittered around the room with an agitated stride. He gathered several Mazikin around the conference table, where they conversed in low tones and repeatedly glanced in my direction.

A female Mazikin turned and pointed, and Sil nodded. They approached our group and stopped in front of a swarthy, well-built guy who looked like he was in his late twenties.

The female, an older Asian woman, squatted in front of the guy. "Come with me, brother. We'll take care of you." She took his hand and pulled him to his feet.

"Wait," said Sil, placing his hand on the guy's shoulder. "He's got to be a certain type. Juri prefers eastern European."

Juri? I closed my eyes, silently begging Malachi and Ana to accelerate their timetable. I opened them in time to see Sil lean close to the swarthy guy and speak a few words in a language I didn't understand. Swarthy's face was impassive. Sil tried again, this time in a more guttural language. Swarthy stood there, staring. Sil tried a third time, and I could have sworn it was the same language Juri had spoken to Malachi in the alley. Swarthy's face twitched, his eyes sparking with dim recognition.

"Oh, excellent," Sil crowed. "He's Slavic. Absolutely perfect. Juri is going to love this body." He took the man's other hand and led him to the conference table.

I kept my eyes on them, and so did Clarence. I used that as an opportunity to scoot closer to Nadia. She was just a few bodies away now. Sil and his companion stripped Swarthy of his shirt and helped him up onto the table. He didn't resist, just did as they instructed. The look of self-absorbed torment never left his face, nor did he show any awareness of his predicament. The other Mazikin swiftly tied each of the man's limbs to the table. In unison, they stirred the incense in the bowls, causing a thick cloud of sickly sweet smoke to hover near the ceiling. The Mazikin encircled the table, hands joined, heads bowed.

I watched with a growing realization of just how bad this was. They were bringing Juri back. Right. Now. My heart stopped.

The Mazikin around the table chanted louder, catching the attention of even their most entangled friends. Soon, every Mazikin was entirely focused on the center of the room. I took advantage of their distraction and pushed my way toward Nadia, reaching her just as the chants reached a fever pitch.

I grabbed her shoulders. "Nadia!" She looked up at me blankly, but I saw the shadow of recognition in her eyes. Not what I'd hoped for, but it was a start. "Nadia? Can you hear me?"

Nadia's brows rose in question. "Lela?" she choked out hoarsely.

Oh, man. I almost drowned in my relief. "Yes, I'm here. It's going to be okay." I wrenched her into a hug, the first time I'd ever hugged her, and realized she was kind of floppy. "I was so worried about you. I know what you're going through, but you're going to be fine now. You'll be fine."

I turned in time to see the incense cloud coalesce over the table, taking the shape of some sort of four-legged, barrel-chested creature. I gripped Nadia tighter.

"I just want it to end," whimpered Nadia. "They told me they could make it end."

I gritted my teeth. "They lied. But now you're going to be all right. Just stick close to me. I have some friends who are going to help us get out." *If they get here in time.*

"Juri!" shouted Sil, jerking my attention back to the table. He raised his arms toward the cloudy silhouette and spoke in a language that included a lot of hissing and grunting and coughing.

The smoky beast hovered for a few moments and then contorted in the air. I watched in horror as it dove into the man on the table. He screamed and arched violently. Everything but his shoulders and heels rose from the table, muscles seizing. He fell back, writhing and jerking. His agonized shrieks continued for long seconds before falling silent. The Mazikin around the table began to clap, and the rest of the room joined them, cheering and whooping loudly.

Swarthy craned his neck and waited patiently as his new family untied his feet and hands. His eyes glinted with cunning and cruelty. The resurrected Juri reached over and gave Sil a hug. Sil whispered something in his ear.

Juri's eyes narrowed and he turned. He smiled when he saw me.

"Mine."

TWENTY-FIVE

JUST ONE WORD, BUT I heard it easily, even over the violent cursing playing like a loop track in my head.

My eyes skimmed over the room, doing something I should have done several minutes ago—assessing available weapons. Malachi would be disappointed to know how badly I'd messed this up. I could only hope I'd have a chance to explain, but it seemed unlikely at this point.

A man next to me wore a belt with a heavy buckle. I wondered how long it would take me to remove it from his waist. There was a crumbled brick and a rusty tin can in the corner. I mentally calculated the distance. I turned my attention to the ropes on the table, eyeing the knots that held them in place. Even as I did, I knew it was too late. Juri and Sil were approaching fast. I let go of Nadia and scooted a few feet away from her, then rose to my feet to meet the threat.

"We are very lucky tonight, my friend," chuckled Sil. "Not only is she the one you wanted—I'm almost sure she's Malachi's girl. She carries his scent."

"She is *not* his!" the new Juri shouted as his eyes flashed bright with hatred.

Sil stopped chuckling.

Juri snaked an arm around my waist before I could shrink back. He clutched me to him and buried his face against my neck, drawing his nose from my shoulder to my jaw as I struggled to get away. He was incredibly strong.

"Ah, Sil, you are right," he said in guttural English. "Malachi has been here. It will take hard work to erase the stink of him from her skin." His breath shuddered from deep in his chest, like the idea excited him. "Let's get her to the table."

No freaking way. I took advantage as he loosened his grip and rammed my knee into his balls. He huffed and doubled over, releasing me. I shoved him aside and took two steps toward Nadia before he caught hold of one of my legs. I hit the floor between two passive suicides. They didn't even turn their heads to me.

"Sil! Clarence! Kenzi!" Juri growled. "Take her to the table!"

The three Mazikin ran forward and grabbed me, one of them on each side, one holding my arms twisted behind my back. They hustled me to the table, the toes of my boots scraping the ground. I twisted and fought, wishing desperately that Malachi would get on with his distraction, seeing as our worst nightmare was about to come true. What the hell was taking him so long?

Juri loomed in front of me again, pinning me back against the table. He groped for the neck of my shirt and began to tear it off me, but as his friends released my arms, I clapped my hands sharply over his ears. He howled and punched me in the stomach, sending me to the floor. In a haze of pain, I tried to scramble under the table. One of them grabbed my ankle and dragged me back—but not quickly enough to keep me from hooking my fingers over the edge of an incense bowl and bringing it along with me.

I took a breath as they lifted me off the floor and scooped my hand into the blazing bowl. Screaming with pain, I came up with a huge handful of smoldering embers and flung them into the faces of the four Mazikin trying to wrestle me onto the table. They let me go and stumbled back, yelling, fingers scraping at their eyes.

I ignored the agony of my ruined hand and threw myself over the table, trying to get back to Nadia. Someone caught my legs again and I fell face-first onto the table. I kicked out, bashing Sandy-Hair in the face. He brought his elbow down on the back of one of my thighs, sending a numbing throb through my leg. Juri and Sil appeared in front of me, faces gray with ash, teeth bared. Their hands closed over my wrists and flipped me over. Two other Mazikin pinned my feet.

A massive explosion shook the building and everything shattered. I closed my eyes and turned my head against the hail of debris and dust. This was my only chance. Malachi and Ana were right outside, putting their plan into action. I only had a few minutes if I wanted to get Nadia out. I wrenched my arms free from Sil and Juri, who were gaping at the sizable hole that now graced the far wall. The Mazikin at my feet released me when a second explosion collapsed one of the support columns near the exterior wall and sent smoke and fire shooting into the room. Everyone scattered, screaming and running in all directions. Only the suicides in the corner remained stationary.

I rolled to the side and got my good hand on the hilt of Sil's scimitar, sliding it free before he could do anything about it. I leaped from the table and sprinted toward Nadia, ready to meet anyone who pursued me with deadly force. Or my best effort at it, at least.

Sil took me up on the challenge and proved to be as fast as I'd feared. He jumped to the side as I swung the blade and tackled me when I left myself unguarded. I brought the hilt of the scimitar down hard on the top of his head, and he yowled and reared back, straddling me. I jerked my knee up, hitting him in the back. He fell forward, right into my waiting elbow strike. He rolled off me, but just as I turned to get to my feet, he did his worst. His jagged fingernails carved stinging, fiery trails across my belly. I screamed and kicked him in the face, sending him into unconsciousness.

Kill him now, whispered Malachi's voice in my head.

But I hesitated. I'd never killed someone in cold blood, and I had no time to stand around thinking about whether I could deal with the pain Malachi felt when he killed someone—even a Mazikin. I turned back to Nadia and dropped the scimitar. I had only one hand, and I would need it to help her.

A third explosion caused the front of the building to collapse, closing the hole and leaving the narrow front entrance as the only means of escape. Crap. Well, at least the Mazikin were still distracted. I dashed to Nadia and took her hand. "Come on. We have to get out of here."

"Is it going to end soon?" she asked, eyes glazed again, making me wonder if she'd found—or maybe created—more of those pills somewhere along the way.

"I can help you," I promised, "but you have to help yourself first. Get up and come with me."

Nadia allowed me to yank her to her feet and tow her toward the door. Then I heard it: the most wonderful sound in the world. Over the screaming, and the crying, and the crunching of feet scrambling over debris, it filled my ears. Malachi's voice. He was calling my name.

Roaring it, more accurately, loud enough to carry over the din. He was so near, just outside. All I had to do was climb the stairs.

I pushed Nadia through the entryway and onto the staircase. I didn't make it more than two steps before Juri's hand latched onto my ankle.

I hooked my arm around the railing and tried to shake him loose, but it was impossible.

"Nadia," I yelled. "Keep going. Go up. Go out. They'll recognize you. Go!"

Nadia turned and gazed at me with this detached, dazed look. But she did as I asked. I didn't have time to feel relieved. Juri, eyes blazing, face blistered and bleeding, expression contorted with rage, grabbed my shoulders and wrenched me around.

"This new body's obviously not going to last long," he hissed from between clenched teeth, "so I might as well enjoy its final moments."

He dragged me by the hair back into the massive room. The chamber was littered with bodies and debris. Sil lay limp against the wall at the far side. With the exception of about five suicides sitting in the corner, the basement was now almost empty. From outside, shrieks and yells and smaller explosions cut through the muffled silence in the room. Malachi was still shouting my name.

Juri threw me to the ground and was on top of me in an instant. "I can hear the esteemed Captain of the Guard outside. He is calling for you. Be a nice girl and answer him."

I pressed my lips shut, unwilling to give him the satisfaction. His hand closed over my burned fingers and I screamed.

He smiled down at me, excited by my pain. "Very good."

I brought my knee up, but he was ready this time and shifted out of the way. He punched me in the side, knocking the breath out of me. "My, you're as nasty as he is. How do you think he'd like to find your body, Lela? It looks like I won't be able to turn you tonight, so I guess the only thing left is to leave my mark on you for him to find." He reached between us and wrenched at my sweatpants, ripping them down the front.

"Help!" I shrieked, turning my face to the suicides. "Don't let him do this!"

They didn't look at me. They wouldn't help me. They couldn't even help themselves. They would die here tonight. Maybe they'd end up back at the Gates, recycled, marching in to complete the unfinished work they'd been sent here to do. If I hadn't gotten Nadia out, she'd probably be among them, waiting for death to claim her again.

Juri's fingernails scraped against my skin, right over the gouges Sil had left, making me arch and scream as he pulled my pants down just below my hips. I writhed beneath him, hands scrabbling around for something, anything with which to fight back. No way was this happening. I caught my breath again as screeching, echoing memories rose in my mind, threatening to choke me, to take me from right now and strand me in that stale bed with pink sheets.

"Lela!"

I pushed the memories away. Malachi was calling my name, bringing me back to the present. I threw my hip up right as Juri succeeded in unbuttoning his pants. It unbalanced him, and I twisted to hit him in the neck with my elbow. I reached far enough with my functional hand to snag a nearby hunk of cement and slammed it into his face.

He howled with pain as his fist rocketed forward, glancing off my chin. I brought the cement down again, and this time it crunched into his nose. But he kept coming, punching at me, trying to bite me, trying to tear my pants off.

My vision spotted with black as I hit him with the hunk of cement again.

And again.

And again.

Hands closed around my shoulders. "Lela, stop." Someone removed the cement from my numb hand as I continued to scream. When had I started screaming?

"Stop," said Malachi. "You can stop. He's not moving anymore. Open your eyes."

His fierce face was right in front of mine. It was the most beautiful thing I'd ever seen. He held my face in his hands, blocking out the sight of everything but him. "We have to get out of here. This building is going to collapse. Can you walk?"

I blinked a few times, trying to remember what had happened. "Of course," I said hoarsely. "No problem."

"Come on." He reached for my hand but drew back as I whimpered. He squinted in the darkness. "What's wrong with your hand?"

"Burned."

He cursed and reached for my other hand. "Let's go," he said in a tight voice as he tugged me toward the door.

"Where's Nadia?"

"She's with Ana. We have to hurry."

He led me up the stairwell, arms around me, gently supporting me. It seemed like he was afraid to put too much pressure on my skin, like he was worried he would hurt me. But it didn't matter. Every part of me had been broken already. My body ached from all the punches it had taken. My belly was on fire where Sil had sliced me with his jagged fingernails. My burned hand throbbed dully. My ripped pants hung from my hips. I wanted to tie the torn edges together, but that would have taken two hands. We made it to the top of the steps. Malachi moved in front of me so he was the first out the door.

Just as I raised my foot to step over the threshold, Malachi shoved me back. I lost my balance and fell against the doorjamb. I looked up in time to see him draw his baton and extend it. We were surrounded by at least eight Mazikin who had clearly been waiting for him to come out of the building. I wouldn't have thought they'd be so organized without Sil to lead them . . . which meant someone else was leading them.

"Lela, please stay there," Malachi said calmly as he moved forward into the circle of enemies, drawing them away from the door, away from me.

More alert now, adrenaline shooting through my veins, I scanned the area, searching for the one person who could have set this trap. Ibram had obviously arrived.

There he was, engaged in a wicked scimitar battle with Ana. I whipped my head back to Malachi, who had already downed three of the Mazikin. He remained in the center of the battle, spinning and jabbing so quickly I couldn't track all his movements. I stepped out of the doorway and craned my neck, looking for Nadia. She was huddled against a pile of rubble, arms folded over her head, right behind Ana and Ibram, who were doing their best to slice each other to ribbons.

Two Mazikin came out from behind a nearby Dumpster, eyes fixed on me. I looked around for something to defend myself with, but with only one working hand and some possible internal injuries, I doubted I'd be that effective. Malachi spotted them as well. He didn't say anything, but the tempo of his movements became more urgent. Three more Mazikin down. Only two remained, plus the two who were closing on me fast, teeth bared.

Ana screamed, drawing everyone's attention. She was suddenly surrounded by a group of Mazikin who had emerged from an alley on the other side of the warehouse.

There were dozens of them.

Ambush.

"Ana!" Malachi shouted, ruthlessly finishing off his remaining opponents. He leaped over the heap of fallen Mazikin, drawing his throwing knives in midair. The two Mazikin who'd been loping toward me turned and ran on all fours in Ana's direction as she screamed again. They didn't make it far, falling simultaneously with knives deep in their backs. But it didn't make any difference for Ana. Ibram stood and watched, a cruel smile on his face. Even from dozens of yards away, I could see why. The Mazikin had overwhelmed her, taking her to the ground. They bit and tore at her in a sort of feeding frenzy.

"Throw, Malachi, throw!" shrieked Ana. "Do it!"

Malachi ignored her and ran toward them. Ibram made a quick motion with his hand, and the Mazikin lifted the struggling Ana to her feet. They hustled her down the street.

"Throw, Malachi, now! Don't let them take me," she screamed, the pain and panic evident in her voice.

I stumbled forward in horror, unable to do anything. They were too far away. They were going to escape. With Ana.

"Throw!" she screamed again.

Malachi stopped dead and roared in frustration. There were too many Mazikin. At least twenty of them. The mob carried Ana up the street, Ibram leading the way, blade flashing. Malachi turned to me, his face helpless and tortured. I knew he didn't care about the odds; he wanted to go after Ana. I also knew he didn't want to leave me wounded and defenseless. I didn't have time to help him make his decision. What would I say anyway?

Go, rescue Ana, and die in the process.

Stay safe, leave her to die, and come to me.

I stared at him, paralyzed. Ana screamed again. Malachi's expression became diamond-hard with certainty. He reached for one of the black spheres strapped to his chest. In a single, smooth motion, he hurled it up in the air. It landed right behind the mob and exploded with enough force to shatter the windows in the buildings on both sides of the street.

The blast knocked me off my feet. I raised my head, ears ringing and popping, in time to see Malachi get to his feet and run straight toward the fiery carnage.

Oh, God.

I ignored both my vicious pain and my numb disbelief as I staggered forward. I limped past Nadia, who was shaking and crying, her hands pressed over her ears. But she was unharmed, and she wasn't going anywhere.

The clash of metal on metal echoed up the street. I almost howled with frustration. Somehow Ibram had survived and was able to fight. I started to run. I passed the first body lying in a heap on the sidewalk, dozens of feet from the origin of the blast.

I reached the crater at ground zero and ran past, scanning each broken, blackened face. Malachi was several yards ahead, slamming his scimitar against Ibram's. He was so obviously enraged I was afraid he would make a stupid mistake and get himself killed.

A crumpled figure about ten feet away stirred and moaned in a ravaged yet familiar voice.

"Ana!" I ran to her and bit back my cry. Her beautiful face was utterly savaged. Ragged bite wounds covered her neck. Her eyes were swollen shut. Blood seeped from her nose, her mouth, her ears. I sank to my knees beside her, searching for some way to help.

"Did we get him?" Ana whispered.

"Malachi is fighting him now. It looks like Ibram's the only one who survived," I assured, wanting to stroke her, to offer comfort, but no part of her was undamaged. There was nowhere to touch.

Ana read my mind easily and chuckled, a wet, gurgling sound. "It's all right, Lela. I can't feel a thing."

I'd have known she was lying even if I hadn't been able to read the agony on her face. As much as I wanted it to be true, there was no way the venom worked that quickly. I wasn't going to waste time arguing with her, though.

"I don't know how to thank you," I choked out. "Nadia's all right. I'm all right."

"No you're not," she rasped. "I can hear it in your voice."

I carefully took her hand. It was the least ruined part of her. It was a small hand, deceptively small to be so deadly. "I'm going to be fine. I kicked some ass, Ana. You would have been proud."

"Good girl. Now listen to me. Where's Malachi?" A tear rolled from one of her eyes.

Grunts and shouts and metallic shrieks rang through the street, echoing off the buildings above as Malachi and Ibram fought. "He'll come as soon as he can."

Ana sighed and coughed. More blood trickled from her mouth. "You have to tell him. Tell him I loved him. I always have. Tell him he was my true brother. Tell him thank you a thousand times for saving me, for keeping me myself. He was the only one who understood."

I could barely see Ana's ruined beauty through the haze of my tears. "I'll tell him."

"Thank you. And—I need you to do something else for me."

"Anything."

"Make sure he gets out of the city. He deserves to get out of here. He needs it. Please, no matter what it takes, make sure."

"I will," I promised. "I'll do whatever it takes."

Ana's hand twitched in mine as Malachi's roar split the night. Ibram shrieked and fell to the ground. The impact of metal on bone was audible even from a distance.

Ana smiled, and then her face relaxed for the last time.

TWENTY-SIX

I WRAPPED MY BURNED hand in a towel. I didn't want to look at it. I didn't want Malachi to see it either. As I ran the bathwater and the room filled with its strange smell, I tried to ignore the stabbing pains across my belly. All of me ached. That part of me screamed.

When the tepid water was deep, I turned it off. I was tired and filthy enough that it even looked inviting. But it wasn't for me.

"All right, Nadia, this is going to feel good. Come on."

With my good hand, I guided Nadia, silent and passive, into the tub. I sat on the edge and poured some water over her head. It didn't look like she'd bathed since arriving in the city. She barely lifted her arms, barely blinked an eye, barely seemed to care about the thick layer of grime peeling off her like a second skin. By the time I helped her out of the water, it was gray and cloudy.

"Maybe we'll work our way up to a shower."

Nadia nodded compliantly.

I helped her get dressed and brushed her long, blonde hair. "There. Now you look like you used to," I soothed.

Nadia closed her eyes and began to cry. I had never felt more helpless, and that was really saying something. After everything—the work, the pain, the death and sacrifice—I still didn't know how to help my best friend. I took a deep breath.

It's going to get better. It just hasn't hit her yet that she's safe, that she can relax.

Then I hugged her, just like I had at the nest, trying to make up for a year of brush-offs. I'd never hugged her when she was alive. She'd always been a touchy-feely person, and I don't think she ever understood why it was so hard for me. I always felt like I was letting her down. But Malachi had changed me, and it was a little easier now. I wrapped my arms around her and tried to let that hug speak for me. *I'm so sorry I walked away. I promise you I'll make this better. I won't fail you again.*

If that hug spoke for me, though, her reaction spoke for her. She didn't push me away, but she didn't hug me back, either.

I squeezed her a little harder, like I could jump-start her somehow. She stayed limp and quiet. Then I realized maybe I was just being selfish, like I was pushing her too hard because it would make *me* feel better. And what *she* really needed was a little time, a little rest. So I made myself let her go. She stood back from me like it had never happened, glassy-eyed, looking as hollowed out as I felt.

More exhausted than ever, I took her hand and led her to the bedroom. I helped her sit on the cot. "I'm going to get you something to eat."

I went into the kitchen, noting with an ache in my chest that Malachi had not yet returned. He had stayed behind to make sure none of the Mazikin survived, including Sil. I'd told him what Sil said about being close to getting out, and Malachi responded with predictably grim determination. He was going to cut the throats of every single Mazikin who had survived the battle. He was going to blow the entire building and let it collapse on what remained of the nest.

And then, I suspected, he would spend some time with Ana's body, to say his final good-byes to his companion of the last forty years. I'd told him what Ana had said, about her gratitude, her love. He had nodded silently and walked away from me.

I wondered if he would ever forgive me for creating the situation that led to Ana's death. For being the barrier that prevented him from going after her when she needed him most. For costing him time. For costing him his strategic advantage. For costing him so much.

All I'd ever done was take from him, use him to get what I needed. I'd been merciless, even when he asked me for mercy, when he asked me to spare him from the closeness he'd known would make things harder for him. Had I listened to him? No. I'd expected him to endure it all, just because he was the strongest person I'd ever met.

I closed my eyes against the tears as I dug through the pantry, wondering how I was going to open a can with one hand. Finally I found a can of fruit cocktail with a peel-off top and grabbed it eagerly. With a spoon tucked between two of my fingers, I carried the bounty back to Nadia.

"You need to eat something," I said softly. She shook her head. "I'm sorry, but you need to. I'll feed you. All you need to do is open your mouth."

It took me ages to get the can of fruit into Nadia. When the last gray-green grape disappeared into her mouth, I put the can aside and nudged her back onto the cot. "You can sleep now, and I'll make sure you're safe."

I did my best to disguise my panic over her near-catatonic state. This was not quite what I had expected. I'd thought she might snap out of it when she saw me, but it didn't seem to have any effect on her at all.

I covered her with a blanket. "I'll be just outside."

When I emerged from the room, Malachi was sitting on the couch, his head in his hands. I knew he was aware of me, but he didn't move or look up. He was probably furious. He probably hated me. But I couldn't help it—I wanted to be near him. I took a few steps toward him, waiting. Finally, he spoke.

"Everything is done. But . . . I couldn't find Sil's body. I think he escaped."

"Oh no," I whispered, swaying in place. I'd had the chance to kill him and hadn't taken it. My fault. Again. What consequences would this latest mistake bring? "Are you going to hunt for him?"

"Yes. But not tonight." He raised his head and looked at me for the first time. His eyes were shining with pain, and mine welled up at the sight.

"I'm so sorry, Malachi, for everything." I could barely get the words past the lump in my throat. I wanted him to hold me, to comfort me, but couldn't ask it of him. I couldn't ask it of him ever again.

"You don't have to be sorry. Ana and I made our choices. I can live with those choices." His voice was flat. Dead.

"Where is she now?"

"I don't know. If she comes back through the Gates, she'll be spotted and retrieved by the Guards, but she will . . . not be the same. I'll find out if she's been seen when we get back to the Station." He hung his head again.

I wanted to offer him an ounce of what he offered me. Just a tiny bit of comfort. But I was afraid to try because he might see my efforts as selfish, given my past behavior. I clenched the fist of my good hand.

He stood up, looking way too big for the room. I stared at the floor, unwilling to meet his eyes. It was too painful, all this wanting, all this wishing, all this knowing that I was not what he needed. That I wasn't good for him.

He unbuckled his breastplate and stripped it off, then did the same with the rest of his armor. He set everything next to the couch. I kept my eyes on his boots as they moved toward me. His fingers nudged my chin, lifting my face to his.

"Hey, how are you?"

Miserable. Hurting. Needing you. "I'm fine."

"No you're not. Let me see your hand."

"It's fine." I stared at the front of his shirt. It was easier than looking at his face.

"Don't lie to me," he said quietly.

I took a few steps back. His warmth was too much. Too much to be close to and not lean into.

He sighed. "Lela, I'm trying here. Please don't do this."

"Do what? I'm going to go take a shower," I mumbled. I fled back to the bathroom as quickly as my bruised legs would carry me. I didn't try to stop my tears. He was being too nice.

I peeled off my ruined clothes and cringed when I caught sight of the slashes across my belly. There were three of them, each several inches long, all oozing blood. The skin around the wounds was an angry red, swollen and tender. My left hand bulged and seeped with blisters, surrounded by charred skin. Those spots were numb, though, so at least they weren't painful. I wasn't a doctor but knew enough to realize I was in bad shape.

I turned on the faucets. Maybe just cleaning the wounds, along with the rest of my pathetic carcass, would make things better for the moment.

But my wounds were so painful that I repeatedly had to lean against the wall and take several breaths to keep from passing out. And then the helpless tears kept coming, so I sat on the floor of the shower, curled into a ball, thinking about Ana and Malachi and what I had done. By the time I finally stepped from the tub, I was shivering and weak, and did not feel much better. I put on some old, baggy flannel pajamas I'd dug out of one of the drawers. It took several minutes to fasten the buttons.

When I opened the bathroom door, Malachi was sitting on the floor just outside. I almost stumbled over him. He was on his feet in front of me with amazing speed.

"I'm sorry I took so long," I said, feeling selfish again. "You must have needed a shower at least as badly as I did."

"I went to another apartment and took a shower."

I stared at the tight navy-blue T-shirt that covered the expanse of his chest. He was close enough for me to collapse into him. Ah, God, it was so tempting. His voice snapped me out of my trance. "You don't look good. Are you going to let me take a look at your hand?"

"No."

His response came from between clenched teeth. "Why?"

"Because I'll be fine until we get back to the Station with Nadia. Did you get hurt?"

"Nothing serious. Just a few scrapes. But I'm worried about you."

I shook my head. "You don't have to worry about me. I got what I came here for, and we'll be out of your hair as soon as we can get to the Judge. You don't have to worry about it anymore."

He took my face in his hands. "Please. You know I can't stop worrying about you. And I don't know how to give you what you need unless you tell me."

"You don't have to give me anything. You've given me enough. Too much." I tried to pull away, but his hands tightened, preventing me from escaping.

"Then I'll tell you what I need. Will you listen to that? Are you at all interested?"

I met his eyes, embarrassed that I hadn't bothered to ask. "Yes, tell me what you need."

His forehead touched mine. "I need you. I need you safe and well and whole. I need you to be okay, because that's the *only* thing that will keep me from going crazy right now. And I need you to let me look at your hand."

Without another word, he picked me up and carried me to the couch. I didn't fight him. How could I argue when he put it that way? I didn't really believe this was what he needed, but at that exact moment, I didn't have the strength to tell him so. He set me down gently, and his hand closed over my left wrist.

Very carefully, he opened my curled fingers. I was paying close enough attention to hear his breath hitch. He got up and returned with a small satchel, from which he removed bandages, scissors, and various other supplies. I turned my head away as he went to work.

"How did this happen?" he inquired casually, with the tiniest tremble in his voice.

"There were these big bowls of incense near the table they used as their altar or whatever you call it. They were trying to get me on the table, and I threw the embers at them. It was the only thing I could think of at the time. Kind of regretting it now, though."

He rubbed a sharp-smelling ointment onto my palm with the lightest of touches. I took a few deep breaths to keep from passing out from the pain.

"You amaze me."

"You admire my capacity to injure myself or to take a beating and keep going?" I turned my head to try to read his expression, but his head was bowed.

"Both. Things must have been desperate if you had to do this to yourself. They got very close, didn't they?"

"Yeah. I'd be in the Mazikin homeland right now if you hadn't set those explosions off when you did."

Malachi began to wind gauze around my hand. "Several Mazikin came out of the warehouse shortly after you went in. They spotted us setting the charges, so we had to silence them. One of them must have slipped past us and found Ibram—and I guess he had a small army with him. All hell broke loose after that. I'm sorry it took me so long to get to you. I thought there might be more time."

"It's all right. I thought there would be, too. But it took Sil only a few seconds to spot me and only a few more to figure out I'd just been with you."

Malachi froze in the middle of taping the bandage closed over the back of my hand. "What?"

"They said they could smell you all over me."

"I . . . I didn't think of that. I'm sorry." He ran a hand through his hair and stared at the ceiling.

"Why should you be sorry? I was the one who insisted you touch me, right? I'm *not* sorry about it. I can't be, even if I try." *I want your scent on me every day from now on.* I shook my head to clear it. "It kind of got them agitated. Especially Sil and Juri."

Malachi looked down at me, over my body and all the damage that had been done, and his expression filled with a new horror. "Juri?"

"I think Sil moved up the timetable for resurrecting him when he saw I was there. When Juri saw me . . . you know. He seemed to think I was his property. But he also seemed pretty eager to get back at you." I shuddered and stared at Malachi's face, letting it block out the memory of Juri's.

Malachi's eyes were dark with something I couldn't quite read. "That was Juri in a new body, wasn't it? He ripped your pants. He was trying to—"

I couldn't bear to hear the word come off his tongue, so I interrupted. "Yes." I looked down at my hand, still throbbing but now neatly bandaged. I swallowed. "Did I kill him?"

He laid a hand on my cheek and then buried his fingers in my wet hair. He looked at me with this sad sympathy. "Yes."

I took in a sharp breath. I had killed a man. I smashed his face with a hunk of cement. I made his heart stop beating. And I . . . I didn't feel anything. I didn't feel triumphant. I didn't feel sorry.

Malachi's fingers tightened in my hair. "Did he . . . before you . . ."

"No, he didn't . . . ."

His shoulders sagged as some of the tension drained from them. "Good."

I looked at him cautiously. "And if he had?"

He pinned me with an intense stare. "It wouldn't change how I look at you at all. But if I ever meet him again, I will make him suffer for what he tried to do."

He smoothed a hand over my hair. "Lela . . ." He sighed and shook his head. He was silent for a full minute before he said, "I was afraid I'd never see you again. When Nadia came out and you weren't behind her, I panicked."

I chuckled hoarsely. "The great Malachi is capable of panic?"

He leaned over and kissed my cheek. His jaw scraped against my skin as he whispered in my ear, "Where you are concerned, it appears I am capable of just about anything."

Chills raced up my spine, along with total confusion. I couldn't understand why he was being kind after I had screwed everything up so badly. He drew back to look in my eyes, and his expression was crystal clear. He was seeking permission, begging me to invite him in.

Guilt and sorrow and love and need and regret all tumbled through my mind. I didn't want to think anymore, especially as his breath skimmed over my skin, but I didn't want to make yet another mistake. So many things were my fault. Sil escaping. Ana dying. And Malachi seemed to be paying for all of it.

"I made so many mistakes tonight. I am so sorry—"

I said those final words against his lips and swallowed the rest as he kissed me. My mind went blissfully blank as his mouth moved with mine. No pain, no more fear. Just him. Just him and me and an open Countryside, heaven, and all the time in the world.

"I don't need apologies," he breathed against my mouth. "I need this."

I wrapped my arm around his neck and pulled him closer. His hand stroked across my ribs and slid down to my belly.

I gasped with pain as it all came crashing back.

He jerked up, panting. His eyes widened as his gaze settled on my belly. I looked down and winced. Three narrow trails of blood stained the front of my pajama top.

Malachi's face took on that diamond-hard expression again. He unbuttoned my top, briskly knocking away my feeble attempts to stop him. He sucked in a breath through his teeth when he saw the wounds. His hand flexed over my hip, firmly holding me in place as I tried to turn away. "Is this what I think it is?"

I cringed at his tone and the deadly look in his eyes. I nodded. His eyes flashed with rage. "You should have told me about this immediately."

"It could wait. I had to get Nadia settled, and you had more important things to do."

He cursed as he dug through the satchel and pulled out another tin of ointment. He opened it and proceeded to smear its contents all over my bare stomach, scratches and all. He was less gentle this time, and whatever he was spreading on my skin stung like a mother and made me hiss from the pain.

He glared at me, but I didn't miss the glint of worry in his eyes. "Why do you do this to yourself? Don't you remember what I told you about Mazikin scratches? We have to go. Now." He stood up.

I grabbed his hand. "No. Nadia's sleeping. She needs to rest."

"And you need Raphael as soon as possible." He tore his hand loose and stalked around the room, gathering our belongings.

The idea of trekking through the city right now was overwhelming, and I knew Nadia needed to sleep. She had looked so tired. "Look, I need to rest. Please." He continued walking, strapping on armor with every step. "Just a few hours. I got pretty beaten up today. *Malachi.*"

He froze in his tracks and turned to me. "You have two hours. Then we're going."

"You aren't staying?"

He fastened the remaining buckles with a wrenching tug and was fully armed within a few moments. He went to the door and yanked it open, not bothering to turn and look at me.

"No. I need to go kill something."

TWENTY-SEVEN

A FEW HOURS LATER we were trudging south along the cobblestone road. When Malachi had returned to the apartment and woke me up, the look on his face confirmed that he was still furious with me. Now I was doing my best to pretend like I wasn't in horrible pain, because something about it put him in a homicidal mood. As a result, my teeth ached from swallowing back the whimpers and groans that tried to escape with every step.

I held Nadia's hand. She was unlikely to keep walking without being led. Malachi strode silently by my side but had not looked at me since we left the apartment. We reached a major intersection, and he turned left. I followed his path with my eyes and looked up to see the dark tower looming in the distance.

I froze. "No."

Malachi looked over his shoulder at me. "This is the quickest way. We'll be back at the Station by nightfall."

I shook my head as my hand tightened over Nadia's. "She can't go through the tower. She won't make it."

"You must see Raphael soon." Malachi closed the distance between us in less than a second and laid a hand across my forehead. "You're already starting to run a fever. This infection is serious, and it *will* kill you."

I took a step back and shook him off. "There's no choice. Just get us there as quickly as possible without going through downtown."

He grasped my shoulders. "It will take almost two days to go around. You may not have that much time."

"What are the odds I'll get to the Station alive if we go around downtown?"

"Less than twenty percent."

I rolled my eyes. "Oh ye of little faith. I thought I amazed you, but obviously you don't give me much credit." His grip on me turned steely, letting me know I was sorely testing his patience. "Fine. Twenty percent. Now, look at Nadia. Look at her."

He did his own eye roll but complied. Nadia stared straight ahead, not paying attention to our conversation. Her pupils were pinpoints once again. Tears stained her face. Malachi looked back at me, but his rigid expression gave nothing away.

"Tell me the odds she'll make it through the tower. Look me in the eye and tell me that freaking monster building won't eat my friend," I said harshly, though all I wanted was to fall into him, to comfort both of us in the face of this hopeless situation.

He shook his head stiffly. "I've already lost Ana," he said hoarsely. His hands slid from my shoulders to my neck, resting there lightly, his thumbs brushing my skin. He lowered his forehead to mine and closed his eyes. "If I lose you . . ." He abruptly released me and turned his back. He marched straight ahead, taking the route that would allow us to avoid downtown—and the dark tower. I followed with heavy feet, weighed down by my tainted victory.

To pass the time, I spoke to Nadia, urging her to recall the times we'd had together. I babbled on and on—about the first time she took me to Newport and made me eat a quahog, about the time she'd tried to teach me one of her cheers and I'd fallen on my ass, about the time we should have been studying for a history exam but spent the evening trying to build a model of the Eiffel Tower out of Twizzlers. I kept looking for a sign, any glint of growing awareness, any hint she was coming back to herself. But she remained unreachable. Tears seeped constantly from her eyes, and the only time she spoke was to ask when it would end. My chest throbbed with anger and fear every time those words left her mouth. This was *not* how it was supposed to go.

Malachi set the pace, and it was brutal. He didn't ask us to run, but he didn't allow us to take breaks either. He allowed me to stop briefly to force some water down Nadia's throat, but that was it. His expression was cold and his voice was icy. He did not make eye contact.

I wondered if it was better for him that way, if it was what he should have done ages ago. I wondered if it would protect him from what I was feeling now. From the ache in my chest every time his eyes slid past me without looking. From the lance of pain through my heart every time he brushed past me without stopping. From the sting of tears in my eyes as I thought about how badly I wanted to lean on him, to feel his hands on me, to taste his mouth on mine.

I supposed I should have been glad. This was good for him, right? I had taken so much from him, and now he wasn't going to let me take any more.

As time passed, I lost count of the rounds of fever and chills, each one leaving me weaker. I kept my eyes glued to Malachi's purposeful strides as he led us through the city. As long as he was in front of me, I stumbled forward, towing Nadia along. It felt like I was running after him but couldn't quite keep up. My heart raced. I couldn't catch my breath. My feet grew farther and farther away as my head stretched from my neck like a helium balloon on an endless string.

And then I was amazed to find myself on the ground. I had no idea how I got there.

I wasn't there long. Malachi lifted me from the street, and then I was in his arms. He didn't say a word.

"Make sure Nadia keeps walking," I mumbled.

He nodded.

My head bobbed against his shoulder. I stared at the side of his face. "I'm sorry I'm hurting you."

He continued walking, his face hard, refusing to look at me.

I wanted to touch him, to stroke my fingers down his cheek, but I couldn't lift my arms. I sighed. "You're so freaking beautiful, Malachi. I could look at you for a million years and never get tired of it."

The muscle in his jaw began to twitch. I squinted to bring it into focus. Everything was blurry. I giggled, finding my sudden inability to see terrifically funny. But some rational part of me knew it was a very bad sign. It might be the last time I ever got to look at him. I found myself desperately wishing I had my camera.

"In case I don't get to tell you later, thank you for everything."

"Shut up." He clutched me against his chest. "I don't want to hear this right now."

"You're the only person I've ever wanted to touch . . . me," I wheezed. I tried to take a deep breath, but the air was too thick. It was drowning me.

"Lela, you're delirious. Save your breath." His voice was harsh, but I heard its shakiness.

"Whatever you say."

He snorted. "'Whatever you say'? Now I know you're delirious." But he lifted me higher and held me closer, tucking my head into the crook of his neck. "We'll be back at the Station in a few hours," he said softly. "Stay with me."

I smiled against his skin. "I'm not going anywhere."

TWENTY-EIGHT

I'M NOT GOING ANYWHERE. That's the last thing I remember saying before the world bled black and the walls caved in, suffocating and burying me. Flashes of memory interrupted the long, slow slide into the abyss. Most were of Malachi. The part of my brain that remained functional mused over that irony, considering how briefly I'd known him. It was hard to care, to call anything else to mind. Only his face mattered. It was the only thing that came to me without effort, like reflex, like breathing. Wherever I was going, part of him would go with me. Willingly given or not, it was mine to cradle, to carry, to sustain.

Voices cut through the fog from time to time, but the only one I recognized was his. I couldn't understand what he was saying, but I knew he was there with me, wherever I was. Nothing hurt except the nagging regret that, despite all he'd given me, I'd given him so little. I wanted the chance to give him something, to give him the best of me, as pathetic as it was, damaged and broken, warped at the edges, hardly worth having. I decided that if I had the chance, if he asked, if he needed, it was his.

People touched me, and there was nothing I could do to stop them. I was dimly aware of being moved, shifted, carried, turned. I couldn't open my mouth to ask what was happening, couldn't let them know I was still aware, still there. I wanted to ask where Nadia was, to make sure she was all right. I wanted to talk to Ana, but then remembered she was dead. I wanted to talk to Diane, but then remembered she was living.

But most of all, I wanted Malachi.

Malachi.

"He's not here, Lela." A gentle voice. A beautiful voice. But it wasn't his. I drifted again.

Malachi?

"Lela, stay with me. Can you open your eyes?" The beautiful-voice-that-was-not-Malachi's spoke again. Someone stroked my face.

"Malachi?" My voice was barely mine. It was a thread of a voice, not a voice at all.

"No, Lela, it's Raphael. Can you look at me?"

My eyelids fluttered. They each weighed a ton. "Lela, come back from wherever you are. You've got unfinished business here."

"What?" I opened my eyes. Unfamiliar room. Unfamiliar cot. A lamp sat next to the cot. A man sat next to the lamp. Raphael.

He smiled his amazing smile. "Welcome back."

"Did I make it to the Station?" The details were pretty fuzzy. I remembered a lot of walking.

He shook his head. "You continued breathing, but that's about all I can say for you. Malachi carried you after you collapsed."

"Nadia?" I croaked.

"She's here. Malachi is with her. He's been with her for days. He only leaves her when he goes on patrol, or when he comes to see you."

I lifted my hands to touch my face, noting the faint scars that lined my otherwise-healed left hand. Everything felt so disconnected, as if parts of me had floated away. "Days?"

Raphael nodded. "You were in very bad shape when you arrived. The infection was advanced. There was a lot of organ damage to mend, not to mention your hand. And you are weak because the city does not nourish you. I wasn't sure I'd be able to get you back."

"Ana? Was she seen? Has she been found?"

Something sparked in his eyes. "No. She did not reenter the city. Malachi spoke to each of the Gate Guards personally."

I watched him carefully. "Malachi's been busy."

"Very. He's needed it."

I bit my lip. "Is he angry with me?"

"You can ask him yourself. I summoned him when you started to wake. He should be here soon."

Joy and fear jolted through me. It must have shown on my face because Raphael squeezed my hand and asked, "Do you want me to stay with you?"

A knock at the door interrupted my frantic thoughts. Raphael gave my hand another squeeze and stood up. "Come," he called.

Malachi stepped through the door, and I stopped breathing for a few seconds. There weren't really words for how he looked to me. Well, maybe one. He looked uncertain. His eyes darted to Raphael, who said, "She's going to be fine. She's lucid." Raphael patted Malachi's arm affectionately as he headed out the door.

Malachi wasn't wearing his armor, but I could tell he'd just come in from patrol. He smelled of the streets, of sweat and leather. I closed my eyes and inhaled.

"Lela?"

I opened my eyes. "Malachi?"

He sat down in the chair next to the cot, looking completely unsure of what to do with himself. I slid my hand along the sheet and flipped my palm upward, an invitation. He gazed down at it for several seconds. Hesitantly, as if afraid I might break, he placed his hand over mine.

As he stared at our entangled fingers, something inside him seemed to shatter. He closed his eyes tightly and grimaced, gritting his teeth. He lowered his head and laid it against my side. I ran my fingers through the thick, black hair on the back of his head. He wrapped his arm around my waist, pulling me closer. His shoulders began to shake, and he took a deep, shuddering breath. He was crying.

I bowed my head over his and folded my arms over his back. "Malachi, I'm sorry. For everything."

"Don't."

I held him until his quiet sobs slowed and the tremors finally subsided. "Do you know how long you've been unconscious?" he asked, his voice muffled. "Did Raphael tell you?"

"Um, a few days?"

"Twelve days. It's been twelve days."

My breath caught. "I'm sorry."

He raised his head and quickly wiped the tears from his face. He stared at me with narrowed eyes. "Why do you keep apologizing?"

"Because you keep being upset at me. And I don't know how to fix it."

He gave a sniffling, raspy laugh and shook his head. "It's easy, really, or it should be. Be alive. Be well. Can you manage that?"

"I'll try." I brushed my fingers across his cheek, catching a final tear with my thumb. "Did you miss me?"

He rolled his eyes. "Are you actually going to make me answer that?"

"I missed you." I felt totally shy and stupid. I'd never done this sort of thing before. I sat up shakily, supporting myself with arms that felt like overcooked noodles.

He reached out and threaded a few locks of my wild hair between his fingers. "I was under the impression you weren't aware enough to miss anything."

"That was true for the most part. But not completely." I took his hand and laid it against my face. "You were definitely on my mind."

He got up and sat next to me on the cot. "Did I miss you?" He took my face in his hands and kissed me gently, but it was enough to send my heart rate straight off the charts. He trailed kisses from the corner of my mouth down to the base of my neck. "I'm glad I was on your mind, because I almost lost mine."

"I'm sorry—"

"Lela, shut up."

And then his lips, his mouth. I wrapped my arms around his neck and let him pull me onto his lap, my legs draping over his.

My senses came back online—smell, taste, touch—flaring to life within my brain. Then everything short-circuited in sparks and flashes the moment he fisted a hand in my hair and folded his arm across my hips, holding me hard against him. It all seemed uncomplicated at that moment. Just him. Just his lips, his hands. Just the way he made me feel, like the most beautiful creature in the world, like someone pure and whole.

Raphael cleared his throat. We froze, eyes popping open at the same time. Malachi kissed me once more, a light brush over my lips, before turning a blank, hard face toward the intruder.

"Malachi, I need to speak with you."

Malachi's arms tightened around me. He didn't seem to care that Raphael had discovered us in this position. The only thing that appeared to bother him was the interruption. "I hope this is an emergency."

"I wouldn't disrupt your reunion for any other reason. There's been a report of a breach at the eastern wall."

I scrambled off Malachi's lap as he rose to his feet. He didn't let go of my hand.

"Confirmed or suspected?"

"Suspected. But another Guard has been killed. Emir."

Malachi cursed. "I will go. Please tell Rais to gather a unit and meet me in the assembly area."

Raphael nodded and left. Malachi turned to me with an apology on his face. "This is the third reported breach this week. Something is happening. I have to go."

"I know," I said quietly, but I couldn't release my grip on his hand.

"Listen—we didn't get to talk about it, but you should go see Nadia." He sat down next to me on the cot again.

"How is she?" I was almost afraid to hear the answer.

He gave me a guarded look. "I've spent a lot of time with her. I think she's a little better. She's in Ana's quarters."

I put my hand to the side of his face, smoothing my fingers along his cheekbone. "Thank you for taking care of her."

"It was the only thing I could do." He closed his eyes and leaned against my hand.

"I don't want you to go." I scooted forward until my forehead touched his. "I'm sorry. I know that's selfish."

He smiled. "You can be selfish. It makes me feel wanted. And I . . ." He chuckled softly. "I want you to want me."

I drew back and looked at him, eyebrows raised, but he didn't let me get far, tangling his fingers through my hair and bringing me close. His lips brushed mine, once, twice, suffusing my entire body with heat. "I love the way you taste," he whispered.

I kissed him. I wanted him all over me. I wanted to wrap him around me like a cloak. I wanted everyone to know. I knew I'd gone crazy, but I couldn't bring myself to care about that when my tongue slid against his. His groan blew every fuse in my body.

"Lela," he said breathlessly, "I'll be back soon. I won't be gone more than half a day."

"But you have to go."

"Yes."

I reluctantly unwound my arms from his neck and watched him shift uncomfortably before getting up. He looked down at the floor for a few moments, then took my hand. "When I get back, we should talk. Will you be up for that?"

"Yes." I looked at him cautiously, trying not to let my brain spin out of control as it came up with a thousand possibilities for what he might want to talk to me about. But his expression gave nothing away, and he didn't say more. He simply gave me a too-brief kiss before striding out the door.

I walked down the hallway toward Ana's quarters, stopping every few yards to lean against the wall and catch my breath. So weak. I wondered how much longer I had until I faded away completely. Until I starved. Based on how I was feeling now, it seemed like a matter of days rather than weeks.

I had run out of time.

I would have to get Nadia out soon or risk leaving her alone and helpless in the city. Maybe I could just wait for Malachi outside the city walls. Maybe I could camp there with Nadia until he was released from his service. Maybe that's what he wanted to talk about. Maybe he was thinking the same thing.

I turned the corner of the dead-end hallway that housed Ana's quarters. One of the massive Guards stood outside the door, arms folded. I recognized him immediately.

Amid.

What the hell? How could they post a nut like Amid outside Nadia's door? What was she, some type of criminal?

"What are you doing here?" My question came out harsh and hoarse. His head jerked up immediately. Sea-green eyes regarded me with contempt.

"Preventing your little friend from escaping."

"She hasn't done anything wrong," I snapped as I approached, letting the wall hold me up, putting all my energy into the ferocity of my voice.

"I'm not the Judge, Mazikin-lover. I'm just the Guard," he sneered.

"Go. Get out of here. I'll take care of her." I pointed down the hall, dismissing him.

He shook his head. "You don't give me my orders."

I closed my eyes and took a deep breath, sincerely wishing I could punch that freaking rhinoceros right where it hurt most. "Look. She's my friend, and she'll be really scared if she comes out and has to deal with you. How about you just take a break and go to the food room? I'm not giving you orders. I'm just telling you that you won't get in trouble if you take a break."

He grunted at me, took a few steps, and peeked around the corner. Then he walked away, grumbling what I was sure were horrible insults.

I leaned against the door and pushed it open, unprepared as the scent of leather mixed with cinnamon greeted me. Ana. I wiped a tear from my face. Where had Ana gone when she died? Had she found Takeshi? Were they out there in the Countryside, together at last? I really hoped they were. I didn't want to contemplate the alternatives.

Nadia was hunched over Ana's desk, writing.

"Hey," I called. "Feeling better?"

She whirled around, and her eyes went wide when she saw me. Just as Malachi had said, she looked better. Her hair was clean and brushed, and her clothes were neat, though ill fitting.

"Lela? Malachi said you were still sleeping."

I shuffled forward, blinking back tears. Her face, her voice . . . Nadia looked and sounded like herself, like I remembered her. "I woke up," I managed to whisper. "What have you been up to?"

Nadia flipped over the page on which she'd been scrawling and smiled. It didn't quite reach her eyes, but I was used to that. "I've been getting better," she said. "Malachi's been great."

"Have you been eating?"

She nodded. "He said that was the first thing you'd ask. He brings me food and apologizes every time that it's gross. He's incredibly sweet for being so hot. Usually the hot ones are jerks."

My beautiful friend thought my beautiful boy was hot. Huh.

"Malachi's one of a kind," I said cheerfully. And loudly.

Nadia tilted her head and gave me the I-can-see-straight-through-you look I had thought I'd never see again. I almost started crying. I had missed her so much.

"Lela, he is stone-cold crazy about you. Stop being insecure. It makes your voice sound weird."

I did start to cry. My Nadia. Here she was.

She rose from her chair and put her arms out but waited for me to come to her. She looked a little uncertain, but she was still willing to try, and there was no way I was going to let her down. I walked straight to her and hugged her fiercely. "I'm so glad we found you."

"You didn't hurt yourself to get here, did you?" she asked.

"Oh, no, I just . . . had an accident. But when I woke up here, I decided to try to find you. I knew all about this place—I'm so sorry I didn't warn you before. Believe me, I know exactly what you're going through now. But that's all going to change when we go out into the Countryside. Wait until you see it—"

I had to stop talking because she was squeezing me so tightly I could barely breathe. I leaned back to try to read her expression, but her face was blurry.

"Are you okay?" she asked as I swayed. "You look kind of pale."

Unable to stand any longer, I let her guide me to Ana's cot and sank onto it. Black spots floated in front of my eyes. "I'm a little fuzzy. I think I spent all my energy sending Amid away." I rubbed my eyes, trying to stop the spinning.

"Amid? Was that the Guard?" Nadia went to the door and peered out. I could just see her figure bobbing among the spots.

"Yes," I breathed.

Nadia leaned over. Her face swam in front of mine. "Maybe you should lie down." She pushed my shoulder, and I flopped back on the cot.

She stroked my cheek. Her brows were drawn together in concern. "I'm going to go get that doctor for you. What was his name?"

That had to be a good sign—Nadia was able to worry about someone other than herself. She was so much better. It was going to be all right.

"Raphael." I covered my face with my hands, wishing I'd given myself a few more hours of rest before traipsing around the Station. But it had been worth it just to see she was okay. "I'm sorry. I think I kind of overdid it."

She squeezed my hand, her grasp lingering for a few seconds before letting me go. "It's okay. I'll get Raphael. Wait here."

I heard Nadia pull open the door and then shut it again. I lay still, focusing on breathing slowly and riding out the sloshing waves of nausea. Apart from my physical state, the rest of me was giddy with happiness. Nadia had come back to herself.

After a few minutes, my head cleared, and I was able to sit up. Raphael would be here any minute, and I would get to tell him I was fine. No help needed. Testing my strength, I got to my feet and took a few steps. A bit shaky, but no problem.

The single piece of paper on the desk caught my attention. What had Nadia been working on? I took a few steps closer, knowing I shouldn't pry but unable to stop myself. I had so few hints at what had been going on with her. I'd buried my head in the sand when she needed the most help, so maybe being a nosy friend wasn't the worst thing in the world. I flipped over the paper.

Dear Lela,

Thank you for trying so hard to save me. You are a true friend. You always were, even when I didn't really deserve it. You made the last year of my life worth sticking around for. But in the end, it was too painful to stay. I was just a fake, and everybody would have figured it out sooner or later. Including you. There was nothing inside me, just a pretty, empty shell. I've always been empty, and I couldn't stand it anymore. Now I'm here, but it's no better. I need it to end. If you're reading this, I'm gone. Please don't come after me.

I barely took the time to read past the word *gone* before I was limping down the hall, screaming Nadia's name, screaming for Raphael, for Malachi, for anyone and everyone. I made it halfway down the corridor before collapsing to the floor, and then kept crawling on all fours, shrieking hoarsely.

I'd fallen for it.

I hadn't even considered that Nadia was capable of planning something like this. It hadn't seemed possible. I had wanted to believe she was all right so badly that I'd ignored every sign . . . *again*.

"I'm an idiot," I cried, bonking my head against the stone floor, tears mixing with the dirt beneath my fingers and turning it to mud.

Something crashed into the hallway with explosive force. I looked up to see Malachi sprinting toward me. He hadn't left with his unit yet. I reached for him, and he pulled me to my feet and held me against him.

"She's gone," I blurted before he had a chance to say anything. "She said she was going to get Raphael for me, but she left a note. She's gone." I couldn't control my sobs.

Malachi put a hand to my cheek and made sure I was looking at him. "There was a Guard at the door. How did she get away?"

"I sent him away," I whispered, suddenly realizing why Amid had been posted there in the first place. He hadn't been kidding when he said he was preventing her from escaping. I was a first-class moron. He'd been there because it wasn't the first time Nadia had tried something like that. And I hadn't even considered that possibility.

"I'm so sorry. I didn't think."

"Raphael!" Malachi called. He looked around and spotted one of the other Guards. "Rais, get Raphael. Hurry please." He turned back to me and gently wiped the tears from my face. "I'm going to go get her. She can't have gotten far. Please, don't worry."

Raphael turned the corner, looking serene but moving quickly. "Lela, how about you come with me?" He seemed to know exactly what was happening. "Malachi, I've got her. Go."

Malachi gave Raphael an unreadable look, kissed my forehead, and spun on his heel. He was out of sight in just a few seconds.

I sagged and Raphael caught me.

"Damn it." I clenched my teeth and struggled to hold myself upright. I hated having to watch Malachi walk away, strong and independent, and being left behind, stupid and useless. Once again it was all my fault.

"Lela, you're going to have to learn that you're not the solution to all problems," Raphael murmured quietly, though he may as well have punched me in the gut. The solution to all problems? I was the freaking *cause* of all problems.

He put an arm around my shoulders. I was too tired and too ashamed to wrench myself away. He led me to my room and helped me onto the cot. "Malachi will have no trouble finding her. You know he's quite adept at tracking people. This is the fourth time Nadia has attempted to escape, so he'll have an idea of where she's going."

"Why? Why would she do this? She's safe here. She was so scared when she was out in the city by herself."

Raphael sighed and pulled the covers over me. "But out there she didn't have to accept that other people care about her."

"What?"

"Your friend is convinced she is unlovable, unreachable. Depression can do that to a person. She thinks no one can understand her. She ignores all evidence to the contrary, and it has led her to make some very tragic decisions." Raphael took my hand. His was warm, almost hot.

"I came here to get her. I gave up everything for her. I can get her back if I just have a little more time." I wasn't willing to accept any other possibility. Once we were out of the city, bathed in that piercing sunlight, Nadia would feel better. How could anyone feel good in a city smothered in constant darkness?

Raphael patted my hand. "Lela, *everyone* has lessons to learn." He smiled that smile, dazzling me with its nondescript beauty. "Do you want to sleep?"

I turned my face to the pillow. My head pounded with dread and frustration. I couldn't stand the thoughts looping around my brain. "Yes."

Without another word, Raphael put his hand to my forehead, and everything went black.

TWENTY-NINE

WHEN I AWOKE, MALACHI was sitting on the chair next to my cot, his head resting beside mine. It looked incredibly uncomfortable, but he was asleep.

I took a moment to watch him, remembering when he'd been unconscious and how badly I'd wanted him to wake up. Now I wanted him to sleep. Shadows lay beneath his eyes, bordered by the dark fringe of his lashes. He probably hadn't had a decent night of sleep since I'd come into his life. His cheekbones looked sharper somehow, and even though his cheeks were suffused with healthy color, they were hollower than when I'd first met him. I wondered if he'd started losing weight. If his body was telling him it was time for him to get out of the city. If he'd already started to weaken. He'd always seemed indestructible, but looking at him sleeping there, I could see the truth. He was human, just like me.

I ran my fingers through his stark black hair and kissed the tip of his nose.

Malachi's eyes snapped open. "You're awake," he whispered.

"Did you find her?"

He nodded. "I got her in time."

My heart stopped. "What do you mean, 'in time'?"

He sat up and looked at me with that guarded expression, and now I understood what it meant. "I found her on the roof of a high-rise a few blocks from here. It was a near thing."

I sat up stiffly. "Are you telling me she was going to try again? Is that what you're saying?"

He hesitated a moment, then nodded.

My friend killed herself. I went to hell to rescue her. I killed someone, nearly got killed myself. A very good person died helping me save her. Then, after all that, my friend tried to kill herself *again*.

I waved my arms in the air like an idiot. "I can't believe this! What the fuck is wrong with her? I don't understand how she could do this. I came for her. I did all of this for her, and she fucking ran away from me.

"And you," I shrieked as I pointed at Malachi, who'd been sitting very still as I lost my mind, "you told me she was better. Why did you say that?"

He sat up a little straighter. "Because she *is* better. Just not recovered. That would take a lot longer."

"How on earth can being actively suicidal be *better*?"

"Because depressed people sometimes do stupid things when they have more energy. She was getting better and had more energy."

"That doesn't make any sense."

"Yes, it does."

"How can you defend her?" I yelled.

He stood up suddenly and his chair crashed to the floor, which shut me up for a moment. "Because I *was* her! I understand her! You *don't* understand," he growled as he stepped away from me. "You've forgotten. You're so much stronger now, too far past it. But *remember*, Lela, what made you try to take your life that night. Some people *can't* keep fighting. Some people want to escape. Some people are not ready—are not able—to find a way to deal with what's in front of them. Sometimes there's no one to help them. Sometimes they don't know how to ask for help. Sometimes it feels like there's no choice but to end it. No other way out. And sometimes it's impossible to see past that."

His expression changed from frustration to fear—like he knew I was going to look at him differently after this conversation. He stared at the floor for a moment, took a deep breath, and raised his head. "Nadia is not ready to go before the Judge. She will never be allowed out of the city in her condition."

No. No. Stop saying everything I already know.

"She can stay here," he said. "We'll have someone watch over her until she's ready—"

"You're wrong," I sobbed. "You saw her, how much she was hurting. She can't stay here. She deserves mercy. She deserves to get out."

His eyes widened and he shook his head. He approached the cot and sat next to me. "You talk about mercy like Nadia has a right to it. Like she's earned it with her suffering. But that's not the way it works."

I pushed his hand away as he reached for me. "If anyone deserves mercy, it's her. She's a good person, Malachi, the best. She's kind. She's gentle. She never did anything wrong!"

He leaned until his face was inches from mine. The look in his eyes was deadly. "Tell me then," he said slowly, annunciating every word in his clipped, precise accent, "when in your life did you ever receive mercy? Don't you *deserve* it as much as Nadia does? Did that foster dad show you mercy? Did the people in the detention center? And what about me? What about my family? What about my people? Didn't we *deserve* mercy?"

He laughed bitterly. "Mercy is not a right. Mercy is a gift from one to another. It can't be earned. You can't claim Nadia has a right to it any more than the millions of other souls who reside here."

He looked away from me, focusing on the gas lamp at my bedside. "When I came here, I think I was like her. I don't know how long I was here before I started to snap out of it; my memory of that time is quite hazy. But when I became more aware, I was angry. So angry. After all I had been through, after what I had suffered, how could I be in this hellish place? My only crime was escaping."

The look on his face, that sad, helpless expression, killed my anger in a second. I laid a hand on his arm.

He sighed and kept his eyes on the lamp.

"How old were you?"

"I was almost nineteen."

"Where were you?"

"Auschwitz," he whispered.

"How did you do it?"

He took a breath. "Electric fence. They surrounded the camp, keeping us in, helping some of us escape in the only way that was possible."

Oh my God. I scooted forward and put my arms around him, and as always, he leaned into me. It hurt to think of him doing that to himself, but I still wanted to understand. "Why?"

"I hadn't been there very long. I was sick. We were all sick. The train ride to the camp killed my father. He was already so weak. And my mother, she . . . they took her away as soon as we got to the camp, with all the older ones and the very young. But I had Heshel. We were together, and he was strong. He said we could survive. We would work, and eat whatever they gave us, and adapt, and live, and when we got out we would escape to Palestine. It was a dream—one we could have realized if we'd gotten out of Bratislava in time. Imi, my brother's friend—he got out. But my family stayed while the noose closed around us."

Malachi wiped a sleeve across his face and closed his eyes. "Heshel was such a believer. Every moment, he encouraged me, encouraged others. He would have been a great leader. That's what he was meant for."

My heart began to beat faster as the tension built in Malachi's body, drawing his muscles tight.

"We were at roll call one morning, and the guards were angry because someone stole something. I can't remember what. They decided to teach us a lesson. They started randomly shooting people from the line, just to create terror and show they were in charge. I was swaying, sick and weak, and I knew they would choose me. Heshel did too, so he, he . . ."

Malachi stopped and seemed to be trying to catch his breath. I closed my eyes and breathed with him. "He made a commotion, coughing and heaving, and he distracted them, drew their attention. And they . . ."

In the moments before he spoke again, I held onto him. His eyes were dry, but his expression echoed the pain of his memories.

"Afterward, I could not imagine going on. My death seemed inevitable anyway. I knew all of us were going to die. I was angry. It was not where I was supposed to end up. I was strong. My brother was strong. We were educated. We had money. We were good boys. But there we were, being slaughtered like cattle. I could not see a way out, and without my brother, I had no strength to continue. I threw myself onto the fence two days after Heshel was killed." He laughed sadly. "I thought I would see him again. I thought he would be waiting for me in Olam Ha-Ba, the afterlife."

He rose abruptly and walked across the room, leaving my arms to fall to my sides. "When I became aware of myself here, I was shocked. Obviously, this was not Olam Ha-Ba. So where was I? Sheol? Gehenna? A place for the wicked? But I had never done anything wrong! How could I be anywhere but in a good place? I was furious that my naive expectations had been violated. There I was, awake, aware, just like Nadia is now. I had more energy, but I had not recovered. The only difference between us is that she is suicidal, and I was homicidal. So here's the stupid thing *I* did: I stormed the Sanctum."

My jaw dropped. "You . . . what?"

"The Sanctum is hard to miss. I asked one of the Guards what it was. He told me about the Judge. I decided I would go before the Judge and demand my right to get out and see my brother. To go where I deserved after all I had suffered." He bent over and picked up the overturned chair. He set it down next to the cot and gripped the back of it tightly. "When I attempted to go in, one of the Guards got in my way. I dropped him and kept going. I took out three Guards before they could stop me, and by then I was in the Judge's chambers, running up the aisle."

"Did you see the Judge?"

He grimaced. "Yes, the Judge was waiting for me. He congratulated me for getting past the Guards. Then he asked me if I was ready to receive his decision. Of course I was—I expected to be freed! Who could hear my story and not have mercy?"

I gave him a sad smile. "I'm guessing the Judge?"

Malachi nodded. "He sentenced me to serve. He sentenced me to this." He gestured at the walls, at his own body.

"For how long?"

"Until I am ready to leave. Ana was the same way. Takeshi as well. All of us, sentenced to lead the Guards of this city for decades, maybe centuries, maybe until another death, because we were powerful enough to fight our way into the Judge's chambers and stupid enough to expect that we would be handed a free ticket out once we got there."

The thoughts I'd been pushing back since Nadia ran away bubbled to the surface. Malachi watched me carefully. "Lela, don't take this lightly. There could be dire consequences for Nadia if you send her before the Judge in her current state of mind."

Those thoughts exploded into my consciousness like a volcanic eruption.

He was right. He was completely right.

This was what I'd already realized but hadn't wanted to admit. There was no other way around it. I was certain Nadia needed to get out of the city, that it was the only thing that would make her better. But if I wanted to get her out, I couldn't just send her before the Judge and hope for the best. I would have to do better than that. And I would have to do it soon, because I wouldn't be around much longer.

Malachi sat down on the cot and took my hand. This time I didn't resist; I was too numb with disbelief and sorrow. Then he looked at me with this incredibly hopeful, vulnerable expression, and I almost moaned aloud as my heart tore right down the middle.

"I'm going to go before the Judge again soon," he said quietly. "I think I'm ready. And . . . and I thought maybe . . . I wondered if—"

I leaned forward and kissed him, unable to hear the words come out of his mouth. I'd never be able to say no if he actually asked. He was going to leave the city. He wanted me to go with him. He wanted to be with me. He wanted us to explore whatever was out there together. But I had to take Nadia before the Judge. I was going to offer myself in her place. I was going to beg for mercy and give myself as payment. It was the only way to get her out.

I pushed him onto his back, desperate to feel his body against mine, eager to let him distract me from my grief, from my torn heart. Ana was right, as always—I had gotten needing and wanting completely mixed up. What I *wanted* was to fix Nadia, to be her knight in shining armor, or whatever the girly equivalent of that was.

What I *needed* was to be with Malachi, to let him protect me and know me, and to do the same for him.

But it was too late. I had already committed to my plan. I'd made my decision before I'd ever met him. I would not fail the only friend I'd ever had a second time. Which meant I would have to fail Malachi.

I nearly started crying again, but instead I parted my lips and tasted him, and let that sensation carry me away. He tangled his hands in my hair and groaned. "I don't think I've ever told you how much I love your hair," he breathed.

I started to laugh. "Are you serious? It's an out-of-control mess."

"It's wild, like you. It fights back, like you do." He chuckled. "Like you, it cannot be stopped."

We spent a few moments giggling, chest-to-chest, as he pulled my hair around our faces like a curtain. It was like having a little clubhouse. Members only.

"Does being in here make you want to tell me secrets?" I asked playfully, blinking back tears.

"You know what?" he said as he peered up at me with that killer smile. "Sure. Here's one: if I hadn't locked you up in that cell the night we met, I would have kissed you then. I wouldn't have stopped kissing you. If you'd asked, I'd probably have handed you the keys and let you club me over the head. I'd have thought it worth it just for the chance to kiss you."

"So why did you stop me?"

"Because I could tell you didn't really want it. I saw how scared you were. It made me realize how much I wanted you to feel differently about me."

You have no idea how differently I feel. And how miserable I am to feel this way right now.

I nipped at the underside of his jaw, and he gasped and pressed me closer. I ran my tongue along his neck, and he moaned. He was mine. He would not refuse. "Malachi. Stay with me tonight."

He froze. He stayed quiet long enough for me to get nervous. But then he said, "Are you sure? I thought—"

"This is what I want. Please, stay with me." *Because tomorrow when you go out on patrol, I am going to the Sanctum. I will be trapped here for years just when you are about to get out.*

Malachi slid his hands down my sides and held me tight as I kissed him breathlessly, relentlessly. It all felt out of control, and I wasn't really ready to do any more than this. I needed more time to get used to the idea of letting another person touch me like that. But time was something I did not have.

His heartbeat pounded against my chest. He looked like he was bracing himself for something. "Lela . . . you are the most beautiful, stubborn, amazing, frustrating, powerful girl I've ever met." He took a deep breath. "I—"

I pressed my lips to his. I thought I knew what he was going to say, and again, I couldn't let him. I couldn't let him say it and then discover I was gone.

Instead, I would have this last memory with him, because this was all we had left.

THIRTY

AS SOON AS MALACHI left to "attend to some last-minute business," I was up and pacing. I decided to go check on Nadia to keep myself from going crazy while I waited for him to return to me for the last time. To start our final hours together. He would think it was a beginning. I knew it was the end.

I tiptoed down the halls, weaving my way through the labyrinth of the Station toward Ana's quarters. As I neared the chamber that housed the holding cells, I heard Malachi's voice raised in argument. My feet stuttered to a halt. I wondered if I should walk by, if he'd be upset that I was out and about. Then I caught what he was saying and pressed myself against the wall to listen.

"All I'm asking for is a few hours. I don't think that's unreasonable."

Raphael's cool voice was calm but firm. "You are asking for a great deal more than that. I cannot support you."

"You don't understand. She will not allow this. She would never consent."

"Have you actually talked to her about it?"

Malachi's bitter laugh echoed off the walls. "You obviously don't know Lela. She would gut anyone who tried to come between her and Nadia, including me. At this moment, I can promise you that she is planning to sacrifice herself for Nadia. I saw it in her face. I can tell by the way she's acting. I can tell by what she's not letting me say." He sighed and then continued, voice hardened. "I won't let her do this."

"Maybe you should take some time to think about this, Malachi. Once it's done, you can't undo it."

"I had hoped Nadia would get better fast enough. That she wouldn't hold Lela back. But after today I know it's not going to happen. Nadia is far from ready, and Lela is starving to death. I felt each of her ribs as I touched her just now. She's pale as a ghost. She's unsteady on her feet. She's so strong, but she has run. Out. Of. Time. And she won't leave without Nadia. Raphael, I warned her. I told her I'd do whatever was necessary."

"You are so sure about your course of action?"

His voice was ice. "Completely. If you make Lela sleep for a few hours, I can take care of Nadia. Then Lela will be free to go, like she should have been all along."

What the . . . *Take care of Nadia?*

"Malachi, be reasonable, you—"

"When Lela wakes up, take her straight to the Sanctum. I won't be around. She won't have to see me. She won't have to know exactly what I've done. Can—"

"You mean you don't want to face her. Cowardice is not your style, Captain."

I jumped at the sound of metal slamming on wood. "Can you get her *out*?" shouted Malachi.

I clamped my hand over my mouth to hold back my scream. I didn't really have words in my head, only this wall of white noise, a roar that blocked out any intelligent thoughts. He was going to hurt Nadia. He was going to kill her—send her back to the Gates to start over, making it impossible for me to find her. Once again I'd missed all the signs. I'd thought he would help me. I'd thought I could trust him.

"I think you're doing this wrong." Raphael still sounded perfectly calm.

"I know what you think, but that's not what I asked. I asked if you could get her out."

"Of course I can," said Raphael dismissively.

Malachi sighed again as his voice gave way to sadness. "Will you make Lela sleep? Just give me a few hours—"

I didn't wait to hear more. I slipped past the nearly closed door of the holding cell chamber and sprinted down the hall. I kept my hand pressed over my mouth against the shriek of misery trying to wriggle itself free. I didn't see anyone until I rounded the corner to Ana's quarters. Rais stood outside, arms folded.

"Another breach," I panted. "Malachi needs you. He's gathering a unit. He sent me to watch Nadia so you can go."

Rais unfolded his arms and squinted down at me. "Run," I ordered. "He needs every Guard he can get. Wake the others. All are needed. He asked for you specifically."

Rais puffed out his chest and smiled. "Thank you. Your friend has been quiet and will give no trouble." He turned and set off at a jog that shook the floor beneath my feet.

I leaned against the wall, trying to catch my breath, preparing myself for what was next. I wrenched open the door. Nadia was curled in a tight ball on Ana's cot, but she looked up when I barged in.

I ripped the covers off her. "Haul ass, Nadia, it's time for it all to end. I'm going to give you your wish."

Nadia blinked at me. "You are?"

"You got it. I understand now. But you have to help me. Can you get up and come with me? I know the place to go."

Nadia sat up swiftly with a grim look on her face. "Yes."

I went straight to Ana's cabinet and shuffled through her equipment. I spotted my own armor propped against the wall. It took a few frantic minutes, but I managed to get the vest on. I pulled one of Ana's shirts on over it, not wanting any of the Guards to see it as we left the Station. I put on a belt and clipped a small knife to it, just in case. I tugged on a pair of Ana's boots. It all smelled like her, so I had to wipe more tears away. I wondered what she would do if she were here. Would she help me? Would she help Malachi kill Nadia? I honestly didn't know. I didn't want to know.

Nadia watched me intently. "Where are we going?"

"We're going to a place where you can get what you want. An end. Don't you want it to end?"

She narrowed her eyes. "Why are you helping me?"

I shrugged. "Because I love you."

She tilted her head like she was actually trying to process that. I realized I hadn't ever told her. *Ah, how am I an idiot? Let me count the ways.*

I held Nadia's hand as we ran along the halls. I was completely sure Malachi would be waiting around every corner we turned. He had read me *so* freaking easily. At any moment he would discover I was gone, and he would come after us.

I hated not having him on my side. And I was terrified of having him as an enemy. I knew he didn't want to hurt me. He thought he was helping me. But obviously he didn't understand me at all if killing my best friend was how he wanted to do it.

I would not have another chance to get Nadia out if he caught us. I could only hope Rais was capable of quickly spreading the rumor of another breach. I hoped it would distract Malachi long enough. I ran along the final hallway, heart hammering, and skidded to a stop a few yards from the front entrance, putting my arm up to slow Nadia. "We're going to stroll out of here, like we're going for a walk, all right?"

Nadia nodded.

Predictably, Hani emerged from a dark corner just as I got my hand on the front door. "Do you have Malachi's permission to be taking her out? He dragged her back in a few hours ago."

I gave him my sweetest smile. "We've reached an understanding with Nadia, haven't we?"

I looked at Nadia, who nodded compliantly. Then I looked back at Hani with a serious face. "Why would you think I'd do anything without Malachi's permission? We all know what he does when his orders are not obeyed."

Hani shivered. "Go ahead."

"Thanks, Hani, enjoy your day," I said cheerfully as I hustled Nadia out the door and into the street.

"Where are we going?" she asked, obviously doubting my sincerity.

"Just follow me." I closed my eyes and pictured the view of the city from the top of the tower.

"This way." I took Nadia's hand and started running in the direction I'd seen the Sanctum. Even if Malachi hadn't shown me where it was, I swear I could sense it, like a string tied around my heart, tugging me toward it. Hopefully, that would keep me from getting lost. Maybe, over the next few decades, I'd get to know the city as well as Malachi did. Maybe I'd become as good a Guard as he'd been.

And maybe, just maybe, they'd allow me to have his quarters once he'd been freed. Maybe they'd let me live in that space, dwelling in my memories of him. I wondered how long his scent would linger there. I knew it was stupid to think like that in light of what he had planned to do, but I couldn't help it.

We'd run at least two dozen blocks when I took a quick left turn between two dilapidated, multistoried town houses. Our feet splashed into what appeared to be wet cement, and I stopped dead as a violent rumbling shook the ground. The giant puddle of thick, gray ooze clutched at my boots and then slithered away, piling upon itself, doubling in size. I backtracked rapidly as an embryonic house grew in front of us. It was no taller than a man, but it was expanding rapidly, blocking our path. Clutching Nadia's hand, I turned to go back, and ran right into a frizzy-haired woman who was all elbows and cheekbones. She fell over and lay still, never taking her eyes off the pulsing, oozing house.

"I want one of my own," she chanted to no one in particular.

"Time to reroute, Nadia," I said, tugging her along a side street. We'd just managed to detour around the proud homeowner and her slimy newborn town house when a Mazikin charged out of the alley to crouch before us, baring his four fangs and hissing.

"You," Clarence snarled. "I could smell you coming. You killed my family, girl."

Nadia whimpered and got behind me. Apparently, although she wanted it all to end, death-by-Clarence was not the method of her choosing. I could actually understand that. It didn't sound good to me, either. I pushed her behind a Dumpster and stepped away from her, wishing I felt a little stronger. And less dizzy. "I didn't kill your family. Well, maybe one, but he *really* asked for it." I widened my stance and scanned the mouth of the alley. "So, are you on your own now?" I might be able to handle one stinky old man, but not if he brought friends.

Clarence growled at me and tensed, preparing to spring. "Sil and the others have already gotten out, stupid girl. We have finally spread beyond these accursed walls. Now the fun begins. I'm on my way to join them. Sil will be happy to hear how badly I damaged you before I left."

I smiled grimly but groaned inwardly. This was going to be my problem to deal with if I became a Guard. Sil had succeeded. The Mazikin were going to multiply and keep causing trouble—on both sides of the wall. This was only the beginning of the battles I would have to fight. I hoped that once the Judge sentenced me and I belonged in the city, I'd be strong enough to do it.

It looked like I'd have to fight my first battle before then, though. I was tired, woozy, and raging with grief over Malachi's betrayal—but I hadn't forgotten what he'd taught me. I rolled my neck on my shoulders. "Come on then, Clarence. Show me those funky teeth up close."

Clarence obliged and Nadia screamed. He barreled into me, chomping down on my ribs and driving me backward until we slammed into the Dumpster. He came up with nothing but a mouthful of leather. *Thank you, Michael.*

I raised my elbow and nailed Clarence between the shoulder blades. He threw me to the ground and scuttled out of the way before I could grab him. He ran for Nadia, but I jumped up and kicked his ass—literally. He howled and hit the pavement but got up quickly and ran at me again. This time I stepped sharply to the side, grabbed Clarence's shoulders, and delivered a knee strike to the face. Clarence was a toothless wonder after the first blow. With the second, he was unconscious.

I stood over him, fingers curled over the knife. I did not want to do this. But I'd made so many mistakes, and I didn't want to make another. I figured I'd better get used to it. I knelt and did what was necessary. Nadia screamed again. And I felt nothing. Again.

I held out my bloody, shaking hand. "Come on, Nadia. Let's go."

We were close. The streets were brighter, and there were more people on the sidewalks. More Guards, too. They watched me with suspicion as I dragged Nadia past, but I knew it was because there were two of us together, not because they recognized me. There was no way Malachi could have notified them of my escape this quickly. For the first time, I was really glad there was so little modern technology in hell.

The dazzling white building was just ahead. I increased my pace. "Nadia, we're almost there," I breathed. "It'll be over soon."

I hit the steps with wild eagerness and did not see Raphael before I crashed into him. He caught my shoulders in his incredibly warm grasp and held me before him.

"You made it."

I struggled to pull free. I had made it too far to fail now. "Don't," I pleaded. "I know what you were planning, and you can't. Please. I need to get her in there."

"I'm not here to stop you," he said as he released me.

I looked around, expecting Malachi to emerge from some shadow, knives drawn. I wouldn't let him take Nadia from me. I wouldn't let him hurt her.

"He's not here, Lela. Not yet. But you should hurry. I have no doubt he's on his way."

I tilted my head and looked at Raphael. Something about him just did not add up. "How did *you* get here so fast?"

He gave me his brilliant smile. "Come. Your case is being expedited." He took my arm and steered me up the steps, allowing me to tow Nadia along. A line of people snaked out of the building and down the street. They looked different from the other residents of the city. Alert and aware. Their faces were bright, their skin almost glowing. These people were talking to each other, some deep in conversation, some laughing and shaking hands. They looked excited. They looked hopeful.

I followed Raphael past the crowd. He led me through the enormous, carved wooden doors and into a lobby with high, arched stained-glass windows. Oceans, mountains, angels, and . . . were those hyenas?

The sun shone through the intricate designs, making a mosaic of the white-marble floor. The sun. It couldn't be found anywhere else in the city, but here it was vivid and piercing.

Before us was another massive door, this one stretching from the floor to the top of the cathedral ceiling, several dozen feet up. "I know what you're thinking, and you're wrong," said Raphael as we came to a stop at the head of the line.

"Um, I'm wrong and you *are* just a doctor?" I asked absently, distracted by the magnificence, and general scariness, of these new surroundings. Malachi had been right. This wasn't like any courthouse I'd ever been in before.

Nadia didn't seem to notice. She didn't even look around. She was just waiting. Like a lemming, maybe. Waiting for her turn to jump off the cliff. She looked nothing like the people waiting in line to see the Judge. My heart sank. Even if I could get her released, would she be all right on her own?

"No," Raphael corrected. "You're wrong about Malachi."

I stared at the floor and nodded pathetically. "I know. I *was* wrong about Malachi. But I understand now."

"Are you so sure?"

"I heard you. I heard what he was planning to do."

Raphael chuckled softly. "Yes, men in love do crazy things."

My jaw dropped. "*Crazy* isn't quite the right word. *Homicidal* might be more appropriate, don't you think?" The enormous chamber entrance began to open. I watched its progress with dread.

"No. *Misguided* was the word that came to my mind. But also *noble. Selfless. Sacrificial.*"

"You people have a really strange set of values," I snapped as the courtroom doors swung wide.

Raphael laughed again. I turned to look at him and took an immediate step back. His face was blazing, lit up by the stained glass and the sun, completely transformed, now fearsome and beautiful and completely inhuman.

Holy crap.

"Listen to me, little girl." His voice echoed off the marble, reverberating back at me, shaking my insides. "Malachi would never harm Nadia."

Raphael had never been anything but gentle, but I realized I had no idea what he might be capable of. At that moment he looked like he could bring down the building just by raising his eyebrows. Maybe this was *the* Raphael. Maybe I had just pissed off a freaking archangel.

"Why didn't you help him, then?" I squeaked.

He changed instantly, back to his average, freckled appearance, so quickly I wondered if I had imagined his momentary . . . whatever that had been. I squinted at him.

"Because Malachi is meant for something else, Lela," he said, like it should have been obvious to me. He inclined his head toward Nadia and shrugged. "He wasn't meant to sacrifice himself for *her*."

He might as well have smacked me in the head.

"Sacrifice *himself*?" I whispered as the world tilted on its axis. He wasn't going to hurt Nadia. He was going to offer himself so Nadia could be freed. For *me*. So I wouldn't have to. "Oh my—"

"You've got that right," Raphael said conversationally as he shoved me and Nadia into the Judge's chambers.

THIRTY-ONE

I PULLED NADIA UP the aisle, unable to see what lay at the front of the room. It appeared to stretch on forever, all pristine white, making the walls and floor and ceiling hard to tell apart. Guards stood at attention every few yards. Not even their eyes shifted as we walked by.

"Is this the place?" Nadia asked.

"Yes, this is the place," I replied. I shielded my eyes with my hand and peered into the brightness. When we passed the final Guard, I saw a figure in the distance sitting at a small white desk. "We're going to talk to this . . . this . . ."

I couldn't figure out what to call the person I was looking at. As we drew closer, I could see it was female, which surprised me. Malachi had referred to the Judge as male.

But this person was definitely a woman. In fact, she looked a lot like Diane. Surrounded by the stark white walls, her skin and robes were darkness, deep and soothing. Her hair was silver. Her smile was friendly. For some reason, that made her scarier.

"Lela and Nadia. You came a little sooner than I'd expected, but you're welcome here anyway." Her voice was soft and thick, like caramel. "Let's get this hearing started," she continued, and her voice rose and sharpened, ringing in my head. "Here's how this works. You make your plea, and I'll hand down my verdict. Who wants to start?"

She grinned and looked at Nadia. Nadia stared at the floor.

The Judge looked at me and let out a boom of laughter. "Baby, why are you looking at me like that?"

"I was sort of under the impression you were a . . ." I had this horrible thought, like, what if this really *was* a man, just a totally feminine one, or one who enjoyed cross-dressing? What if I insulted her . . . or him?

She clutched her side with laughter that echoed through the chamber. "Lela, you are so funny. I *am* a woman. I thought that might be better for you. Plus, I felt like wearing heels."

I stared at her, wondering why I had the sudden urge to fall to my knees and hide my face. Her laughter died. She tilted her head and examined me. *Bug, meet bug zapper.*

"Make your case," she commanded.

"Your Honor," I began shakily, "I'm here to ask you to, er, consider . . . lettingNadialeavethecity." It all came out in a rush, and I swayed in place.

The Judge shook her head and smiled without showing her teeth. "Baby, I don't think Nadia's quite ready for that."

My heart sank again, but . . . well, my mouth didn't sink with it. "But she needs—"

The Judge's laughter was harsher this time, razor edged. It hurt my ears. Next to me, Nadia fell to the floor and folded her arms over her head. I wanted to help her. But I was having trouble getting my arms and legs to obey me. The Judge silently glided closer to me. It seemed like her feet weren't really touching the floor—nothing moved that smoothly or quietly—but her flowing robes concealed whatever lay beneath.

"You think you know what she needs? Baby, you don't even know what *you* need. You come here thinking you can deal with me. You think you can convince me to let your friend out for free. You obviously have no idea who you're messing with."

I shook my head. "I don't expect you to let her out for free."

I caught the predatory spark in her eyes as I spoke. She looked like she might eat me for breakfast. Or maybe just a snack.

She snorted. "I'm not going to eat you, baby."

She was this weird combination of sharp and soft, like I wanted her to hug me, but I also wanted to run like hell.

"Lela, do you want me to let you out? I will, you know. You don't belong in this city. You may have needed it once, but not anymore. You're beyond that now." The Judge raised her arm and pointed. The Countryside unfurled before us. It was breathtaking: golden and soft, lush with life. It made my chest ache, but in a good way.

"Do you want to go out there?" she asked gently.

"I do." I took a breath, getting ready to make my offer, to do what I had come here to do. I took a few seconds to think of Malachi. I was still reeling from Raphael's words and the fact that I'd left Malachi without saying good-bye, without thanking him, without telling him how much I felt for him, without apologizing for all the pain I'd caused him, without begging his forgiveness for misjudging him. And now I had to make a commitment that was going to keep me from him for a very long time, if not forever. For a crazy moment I wondered if he might wait for me outside the wall. I dismissed that pathetic thought quickly—that was just me being selfish again. Why should he sacrifice more for me than he already had? No. This was for the best. I would remain here, and he would go. He would be free to move on without me to hold him back, to hurt him—

"Honey, shut that brain of yours up for just a minute and think about where you are. Focus, baby. Say what you came here to say."

"I want you to release Nadia. And keep me." I sounded braver than I felt, but I knew I didn't fool her.

Her eyes flashed with a carnivorous amusement that made my knees knock together. "*Hmmm.* You think you're the solution to this problem. You want to be in control, to fix it. That's what brought you to this place."

"I might have dreamed about this place before, but after she died, everything changed. I was inside her head. That's what brought me to this place: visions of Nadia," I managed to squeak. "Any chance you, ah, had something to do with that?"

Her lips curled slightly, like she was trying not to laugh. "Are you under the impression that you were forced to come here?" Her voice dripped with both humor and some serious back-the-eff-up danger.

My heart stuttered in my chest. "No," I whispered.

She scoffed. "You were the one who made the decision—the visions didn't do that for you. You could have chosen to stay safe in your bed. You knew how bad this place was, but you came anyway. You could have chosen the Countryside. But you didn't. What brought you here was your belief that you could fix Nadia, that you were the magic pill she needed to take."

I wanted to argue with her. But then I thought about it. All my sacrifices *were* based on the assumption that I was the solution. And with everything that had happened since I'd found Nadia, it looked like the Judge was right. I had thought I would rescue Nadia. But nothing I'd done had changed things for her. I couldn't fix my broken friend. Not even here, not even now.

"But I can, honey. And I'm going to let you help me. You've been through so much, and you've been brave. You're going to turn out all right, I can tell. So I'm going to give you this gift."

The Judge glided over to Nadia, who looked completely boneless, and put her hands on my friend's shoulders. "Nadia, look at me." She obeyed, and the Judge patted her head as if she were a small child. "Now, get up and walk over here."

Nadia let the Judge help her to her feet and took a few steps toward me. Her gaze was downcast, and she looked like she was about to faint. The Judge put her arm around Nadia's shoulders. "Lela's got some questions for you." She nodded at me. "Go ahead, baby."

I took a deep breath and let it all come out. "Why did you do it? Was it me? Was it because I was so mean that night? Was it because I walked away?"

Nadia stared at me, this sad, slow, glazed look. I almost turned away. I almost begged her not to answer me. I wasn't sure I wanted to hear anything she had to say.

The Judge sighed and kissed Nadia on the cheek. Nadia's eyes widened. She stood up straight and met my gaze. "Of course it wasn't you. You were the only reason I stuck around as long as I did. I told you—I wanted to know your secret. Do you know how many times I looked at you and tried to pretend I was looking in a mirror? I wanted to be that strong, too. And I borrowed your strength for a long time, and it kept me going. But I just couldn't do it anymore, Lela. I was really tired, and it wasn't fair to you, either. You have to understand that it was all fake. My life was fake. I was a fake. You were friends with somebody who didn't exist. You thought I was this nice, happy person, but I wasn't. You thought I had answers, but I didn't. You thought I could go with you, that I could keep up, but I couldn't. I knew if you ever met the real me, you'd probably just walk away. Everyone would. I couldn't fool them for much longer, and it hurt to keep pretending."

Nadia blinked. She looked mildly surprised that she'd been able to string together so many words at once.

It didn't matter how many words she'd said. They didn't make any sense to me. How could she really believe that? "But you didn't have to fool anyone. We all loved you—"

"No, you loved the *illusion* of me."

I did love Nadia, but I wanted to punch her. Like I was too stupid to tell the difference between someone who was fake and someone who was real. I could tell. I only wished I'd shown her that when she was still alive. But I hadn't. I'd pretended that she just needed some cheering up and then she'd be fine. Like everyone else, I'd pretended not to see the real her because it scared me too much. Maybe it reminded me of how desperate and sad I'd once been. Maybe I couldn't stand to think of her like that. And in the end, the thing I feared the most—that she would leave me—was exactly what had happened.

The Judge interrupted my mental meltdown. "Show her," she instructed.

"Show her what?"

"Your arm."

I waved my arm in front of Nadia, suddenly embarrassed that beneath my sleeve was a tattoo of her face. It was way too little, way too late. Pathetic.

The Judge laughed out loud. "Baby, you're like a television show I can't stop watching. It's not too late, but it will be if you don't mind me. Get over yourself and show your friend the tattoo before I get irritated."

She stopped smiling and stared at me with this unblinking, soul-penetrating gaze. Yipes. I rolled up my sleeve and held out my arm.

"Now, tell Nadia why *you're* here, Lela."

I didn't say anything, still mad. At her. At myself.

"Baby, this is your *chance*," she said. "Trust me. Don't waste the opportunity I'm giving you."

I heard the warning in her voice and swallowed hard. Nadia stared at my arm. All right, this was it. Maybe I could make up for the times I'd failed her. "I may have wanted to live, but I wasn't really living. You saved me when I didn't even think I needed it. You showed me a future I never thought I could have. That was real."

Nadia winced, but then she looked up at me, so I continued. "I wouldn't be with you in this crazy place if you hadn't done those things for me. I came here because of what you mean to me. I came here because I love you—and I never thought you were perfect. You see your face on my arm. I finally recognized the real you, and guess what? That's who I love. The real you is who I came here for. Look—I'm sorry I shut you out and was afraid to really see what was happening. I'm sorry I ran away. Maybe we wouldn't be here if I'd listened to you, if I'd challenged you. I'm so sorry I screwed that up—but I do love you. And I desperately wish I'd said that to you when you were alive."

Nadia kept staring. There was a glimmer in her eyes, like maybe something I'd said hit home. But it was just a glimmer. No big revelation, no shining moment.

I looked at the Judge, helpless. "I don't know what else to say."

"It may not seem like it now, but that was enough. It's a start." The Judge turned to Nadia and put her hand, tipped with very long, very purple fingernails, on the side of Nadia's face. "Nadia. You are in so much pain. Look at me. Do you want to feel better?"

Say yes. Say yes. But Nadia actually seemed uncertain. It was freaking unbelievable.

And then, all of a sudden, it hit me.

Malachi had said some people found the sickness easier than the cure. For Nadia, accepting that she was good enough to be loved really *was* harder than being miserable and alone.

I felt so sorry for her. I wanted to cry. And I realized that the Judge had done this for me, not for Nadia. I couldn't fix Nadia—I was nowhere near enough. Nadia had things to work out, and I couldn't do it for her. I could only make sure she knew how I felt about her, how much she meant to me. The Judge had simply given me the chance to hear Nadia out and to be honest about my own feelings. That was the gift: helping me understand my friend and forgive her for leaving me.

The Judge gently took Nadia's shoulders and turned her toward the shimmering Countryside. "Can you see what's in front of you, baby?"

"I don't know," whispered Nadia, narrowing her eyes.

"Look," instructed the Judge. "See what's in front of you."

Nadia gasped and started to cry.

The Judge looked over her shoulder at me and smiled. "All right, Lela. I'm going to accept your offer. Nadia will be released. Think of it as parole. And you—"

The door to the chamber crashed open, filling the room with an ocean of noise.

"Wait!"

I swung my gaze to the back of the room in time to see Malachi, staff whirling, take out the four Guards nearest the entrance. He moved with deadly precision, and his expression was one of absolute desperation and determination. I had to clap my hand over my mouth to keep from calling his name. I had to tense every muscle to keep from running straight to him.

"Malachi," the Judge whispered harshly, putting her hands on her hips. I guess she was not so impressed with him.

"Malachi, Malachi," mumbled the Guards, looking around in alarm. Those nearest the door stepped back in unison, and those nearer to us followed suit, moving away from the devastating arc of his staff.

When he saw no one was trying to stop him, Malachi threw down his staff but kept running, his eyes fixed on the Judge. "Stop! Please! I request to be heard," he shouted as he ran. He skidded to a stop a few yards from me and fell to his knees, hands up and weaponless.

The Judge laughed as she stared down at him. "You've changed since the first time I saw you, but you still have a flare for the dramatic entrance."

Breathing hard, Malachi lowered his head and put his hands on his thighs. "I'm sorry. Please hear me."

"You haven't changed in this respect, either. Still arrogant. Boy, you have just disrupted a hearing. *Again.*" The Judge's voice echoed painfully off every surface in the room, like there were a thousand of her, all talking at the same time. I clamped my hands to my ears for a few moments.

Malachi flinched and kept his head down. "I apologize for my arrogance. Please, I have something to say."

The Judge waved her hand. "You can wait until after I've rendered my verdict on these two." But her smile held something else.

Expectation.

Oh no. He's going to—

"I offer myself."

The Judge's smile grew wide with satisfaction. Her teeth gleamed white as the walls. "I will listen."

Malachi raised his head to look at her. "I offer my service in exchange for this girl's freedom." He pointed to Nadia.

"That girl is paid for, my boy."

Malachi's eyes went round. "No. *No.*" He turned to me for the first time. "Lela, please, no. You don't know what you're doing. You don't know what it's like, trying to keep up with the Guard. It's dangerous. It's grueling. It's *lonely*." His face twisted into an agonized expression. "Please, don't do this."

I shook my head and smiled at him sadly. "I have to."

Malachi turned back to the Judge, his face hard with determination. "Mazikin have breached the wall. You need me to take care of this, especially since Ana is gone. Lela won't be able to. She's too new. She'll need training—"

"Oh, I don't know," drawled the Judge as she glided over to me and laid a hand on my head. "Lela has many talents. You aren't giving her enough credit."

Malachi closed his eyes and nodded. "I know what she is capable of. But you could have me instead. I have served well for almost seventy years. This is a crucial time."

"Oh, you have no idea," she crooned, stroking my hair absently. "Tell me, Malachi, what could make you storm my chambers for a *second* time? No one in history has had enough nerve. What made you come here?"

"You know why."

The Judge paused midstroke and closed her hand around a section of my hair. She didn't pull, but I didn't dare move, either. "Of course I do. But I want to hear you say it, dear boy. Cheer up! This is your chance to say what's on your mind without her interrupting you!"

Malachi sighed as he gazed at me. Even from that distance, the heat of his expression blew several circuits in my mind. "Because of the way she looked at me. She should have looked at me with fear. I did some pretty scary things. Most people would agree I am a scary person."

I stared at him, amazed as he echoed my own words so flawlessly.

"But that's not how she looked at me. She looked at me as if she saw something else inside me—something wonderful, something worth knowing—and she was the only person who could make it come out. She taught me things. She gave me things. Amazing things. A vision of myself—different from what I had been, better, but still me. I don't think she really recognized how she was bringing me to life. It came so naturally to her."

He wrapped his arms around his body, holding himself together. I knew what was coming next. I almost rushed forward but was frozen in place, the Judge's hand tangled in my hair.

"I don't know if I did the same for her," he said quietly. "Since we're here right now, my guess would be that I didn't. But it doesn't matter. It doesn't change how I feel. I love her, and I would do anything for her."

No one in my life had ever said that to me. *No one* had ever told me they loved me. And now this boy, this strange, dangerous, amazing boy, had done it.

The Judge released my hair and clapped a few times. "Malachi, how sweet. This time you interrupted my proceedings and beat on my Guards for a *selfless* reason. This is definite progress."

Malachi's eyebrows rose, and I recognized the hope in his eyes.

It dimmed with her next words.

"But it's not up to you. Lela, this decision will be yours." She turned her midnight gaze on me. I shrank back. "You will decide his fate and your own. Allow Malachi to remain in my service indefinitely, and you and Nadia can leave the city together. Otherwise, you are mine for as long as I need you. Nadia can go, but you will stay and serve."

I looked at Nadia, who would be healed and happy and golden in the sunlight of the Countryside. I could go with her and avoid all the pain and horror of being a Guard. I wouldn't have to fight anymore. Peaceful happiness lay just a few short steps away, something I'd never experienced in all my life.

Except . . . except those few moments with Malachi when everything had fallen into place. Those moments had given me a taste of happiness, of love, of perfect contentment. I looked at him now, his eyes pleading, begging me to give him up, to toss him away and forget about him, to go with Nadia and be happy. How could I let him do this? He had given me so much and taken so little. As it turned out, this was the one thing I could give him. Ana's final words echoed in my head.

Make sure he gets out of the city. Whatever it takes.

"I will," I whispered.

"What?" inquired the Judge. "Speak up, baby." Her deep black eyes shone with anticipation.

I stared at Malachi, memorizing his starkly beautiful face. "I would have loved to go with you. I wanted that. I will hold it in my heart always, that dream of you in the sunlight. Thank you for everything, for sacrificing so much for someone like me."

He stood up, hopeful again. "Lela, do you accept this? Will you let me—"

"Take care of yourself, Malachi," I blurted. I turned quickly to the Judge, unable to look at him as I said, "Release him. Take me."

Many things happened at once. Malachi shouted "No!" and lunged toward us. The Judge flicked her wrist and sent him flying. He landed on several Guards who had gathered at the back of the room.

The Judge blocked my view of him in the next moment, her smile wide and glistening. She backed me against her desk, suddenly towering over me. "You'll be leading my new unit," she said cheerfully. "I hope you like traveling."

I peered up at her. "What? You mean around the city?"

"You heard Malachi. There's been a breach. Mazikin have escaped. Ever heard the phrase 'all hell broke loose'? That was coined the last time they got out. You're going to lead my field unit, charged with tracking them down before they're able to establish their operations outside the wall."

My mouth dropped open. "I'm going to the Countryside?"

The Judge's laughter rang over the din, over Malachi's hoarse shouts as the Guards tried to hold him back. But at least that meant he was okay. He was alive.

"No, baby. It's so much worse than that. They're tearing at the boundaries between life and death. Listen to me. It's going to be hard. Remember this, no matter what happens: you won't face anything you can't handle. And you won't be alone."

She put her hands on my face, and the sight of her blinded me to everything else. She was gentle, but the contact of her skin on mine gave me the oddest feeling—like I was about to be struck by lightning. "You're leaving now. Welcome to the Guard. Good luck."

Everything flashed and then disappeared.

THIRTY-TWO

I LAY FLAT ON my back, staring at the purple-and-orange sky. Waves slapped at the rocks below me. I could barely breathe. My brain scrambled desperately to make sense of where I was and how I got there. I sat up and looked around. I was on the rocky trail, right where I'd started. I touched my face, my hair. I looked down at the flip-flops on my feet.

I didn't die. It wasn't real.

I closed my eyes.

It was all in my head. He was all in my head. He wasn't real.

"And that means I'm officially crazy," I said aloud, stunned. Malachi had felt so real.

That's when I noticed there was someone sitting next to me.

I reared back and saw . . . the most average-looking man I'd ever seen.

"You can't sit here much longer," he said. "The morning hikers are on their way. And you're not crazy. At least, not officially. Let's go." He stood up.

"Raphael?"

He raised his eyebrows and looked me over. "Did you hit your head or something?"

"No. But I don't understand what's going on." In a total daze, I got up and started to lean over the rocky precipice. I remembered falling so clearly.

Raphael's fingers encircled my wrist. "You don't want to do that, trust me."

"Did you glue me back together or something?"

"No. You left quite a mess for me to clean up." He gave me a somber look. "Just like when somebody commits suicide in the dark city—when one body is destroyed, another appears outside the Gates to be led back in. This is an unusual situation, but the same principle applies."

My heart fluttered in my chest. "So. I actually died."

"I suggest you take my word for it." He gestured for me to step away from the cliff's edge, then turned and headed up the trail.

I staggered after him.

"This is your new assignment," he said. "Your unit will be based here. Your mission is to find and eliminate the Mazikin threat."

He stepped onto the street and strolled toward my car.

I looked up and down the road. "This is Rhode Island, right? I mean, this isn't some crazy hell dimension that just looks like Rhode Island?"

Raphael handed me my keys. "We believe Sil popped up near here, but we're not exactly sure where. It seemed like a good place to start."

"Wait a minute," I said. "Isn't this a little too convenient? Sil comes through a breach that just happens to be in Rhode Island, and I happen to come from here?"

His face became completely blank. "I have absolutely no idea what you're talking about."

I slumped against the side of my car, my head spinning off its axis.

I was back. I was alive.

But I was dead.

And now I was going to battle Mazikin in freaking Rhode Island. This was going to be interesting—and that was good, because it would get my mind off a few things.

Or at least one big thing.

"Um, so . . . what do I do now?"

"You'll go back to your old life. We'll contact you when we've gotten some things settled. The Judge thought it best for you to finish high school. She's very pro-education. But your missions will start very soon."

I rolled my eyes. I couldn't even count how many kinds of weird were packed into what he'd just said. Raphael looked at me expectantly. He gestured toward my car. "Well, off you go. Go be a normal American teenager."

I put my hand on the door handle but couldn't bring myself to open it. I wanted to stay with Raphael for just a few more moments. If he was real, it meant Malachi was real.

He patted my arm. "Just ask me, Lela."

"How is he? Did she release him into the Countryside?" I wanted to think of him in the sunlight. Even though I'd never be able to see it, I could picture him, that killer smile on his face. It made me happy and incredibly sad all at once.

"No."

It felt like I'd just been clotheslined. "What? She said if I agreed to serve she would release him!"

"That's not *exactly* what she said. And there are consequences for storming into the Judge's chambers and interrupting a hearing. She doesn't take that sort of thing lightly." He squeezed my arm. "She stripped him of his rank and sentenced him to another term of service."

My face crumpled in grief as the tears fell. All I could think about was that night in the Guard tower, that look of pure longing on Malachi's face as he gazed out over the wall of the city.

"Oh no," I choked. "This was my fault."

Raphael smiled sympathetically. "There you go again. Listen—Malachi made his choice. He knew the likely consequence the moment he entered the chambers. He was not surprised at her decision."

I hid my face and cried. It was too much. I had taken everything from him: his chance for freedom, his chance to rest and be free. His chance to be happy. He had given it up for nothing. Raphael gently patted my back but remained silent. It didn't matter. Nothing he said could make it better.

"Is he all right?" I asked quietly.

"Malachi knows his job. He does his duty."

I clenched my teeth to hold back my scream of frustration. "That's not what I asked."

"He's fine, Lela, and he's still Malachi. He accepted a very dangerous mission as soon as you left."

I waved desperately, cutting him off. I put my hand to my mouth, holding in more sobs. I didn't want to know more. I already felt guilty enough. I opened the car door.

"I'll wait for you to contact me," I managed to say, then got into my car, slammed the door shut, and drove away.

I was awakened by sunlight glaring through my window, my dream of Nadia fresh in my mind. I was in her head, seeing what she saw, feeling what she felt. She sat by the sea, looking out on crystal blue waves. For a crazy second, I thought she might be considering drowning herself, but then I noticed her thoughts were completely calm. Someone was sitting next to her. She didn't turn enough for me to see who it was, but the person was holding her hand. She was happy. She was loved, and she knew it. She didn't want to be different than she was. She didn't want anything more than what she had.

"Thank you," I whispered, rubbing my fingers over the tattoo. Whatever was coming would be bearable now that I knew she was in the Countryside.

I rubbed my eyes. The sun. It seemed so foreign now. I had grown quite accustomed to darkness. There was a knock at my door. "Yeah," I groaned. I'd been asleep for less than an hour.

Diane popped her head in, smiling brightly. It reminded me of the Judge's face just before she'd sent me back. I shuddered.

"Baby, it's after eight. You're gonna be late for school if you don't get your butt out of that bed. You know the rules of this house."

I sat up. She grimaced. "Are you okay?"

"Yeah," I lied. "I'm fine."

"Well, you've got a doctor's appointment this afternoon at two. I'll pick you up from school." Which meant she didn't trust me to go there myself.

I nodded. I would cooperate with her . . . to a point. She was going to be pissed when I exercised my right to refuse a physical exam, but I was in no mood to explain my shiny new scars. Hopefully, I could convince the doctor I was sane without stripping down.

I got myself ready and drove to school, music blaring, trying not to think of Malachi, of his face as I offered up myself for his freedom, which he would never get. I tried not to think about what might be happening to him at that very moment. Half of me was trying to devise some way to get back to the city, but I knew I'd never be allowed to be with him if I did anything to hurt myself. At this point, I knew it didn't work like that.

I pulled into the student lot and spent several minutes sitting in my car. Tegan parked her silver BMW a few spots away. She slid from the car, all sharp, stylish angles and carefully coordinated accessories, and skipped over to a few of Nadia's other friends, accepting their hugs and sad smiles.

Then she turned around, like she'd forgotten something in her car. We locked eyes and she beckoned to me. As the new queen bee, I guess she'd decided to be generous and take up Nadia's charity case.

It was suddenly all too much. With what I hoped was a friendly smile, I waved at Tegan, grabbed my pack, and headed for the back of the school.

I might have quit a year ago, but now I really needed a cigarette.

There were plenty of kids along the rear fence, sneaking in a preclass smoke. I flashed a menacing look at Dirty Jeans. He smirked and turned away, muttering in low tones to his friends. It was extremely tempting to pick a fight with him, just to work out some of my sorrow and anger. I watched him carefully as I bummed a cigarette from the girl next to me, assessing his weak spots.

"Could someone help me find the library?" a voice asked in a clipped, precise accent. I whirled around.

He looked different in the sunlight.

Everything about him was intensified. The angles of his face, the shine of his black hair, the depth of his eyes. But it was him. It. Was. Him.

I took two running steps and jumped on him, sending him crashing backward into the chain-link fence. I wrapped my arms around his neck and my legs around his waist, clinging tightly, terrified he was a figment of my imagination and might disappear at any moment. He threw his arms out and grabbed the fence to stop us both from sliding to the ground.

"I'm sorry," he said in a strangled voice. "I am not familiar with this American greeting."

I pulled back and looked at him. That wasn't exactly the response I'd been expecting. His brows lifted in confusion. So did mine.

"Malachi?"

"Yes, I'm Malachi. I'm a foreign exchange student?" He looked completely baffled.

All the blood in my body flowed to my feet.

"Don't you know me?" I whispered. This was the cruelest of cosmic jokes.

He held his expression for a moment more, and then his face transformed, his killer smile sending my blood rushing back to all the right places. "Surprise."

I slapped him on the arm. "You jerk," I snarled through pathetic, girly tears. But I held him tighter, pressed myself closer.

He put an arm around me and tangled one of his hands in my hair. "You're even more beautiful in the sunlight, Lela."

His kiss was sweet and fierce at the same time. It earned him a round of sarcastic applause from the smokers gathered along the fence. I didn't care. He tasted just like before, only better.

Somebody walked by and bumped roughly into my shoulder. "Dude, I suggest you tie that bitch up before you f—"

Malachi's hand shot out and caught Dirty Jeans around the throat. He pulled away from my mouth but held the rest of me firmly against him.

"Forgive me," Malachi said calmly as he watched Dirty Jeans struggling to breathe. "English is not my first language, so I'm sure I misunderstood what you just said." After a few more seconds, he released his grip and smiled in an amiable, I-could-kill-you-with-one-hand sort of way. "Would you like to repeat it?"

Dirty Jeans stumbled back, rubbing his neck and looking around for his friends, who had cringed against the fence and were busy watching the empty, cloudless sky. He eyed Malachi up and down and then spared a glance at me. I grinned brightly at him, still wrapped like an octopus around my beautiful boy. Dirty Jeans shook his head and walked away.

Malachi stroked my cheek with his fingers. "You see?" he said proudly. "I am excellent at this type of operation. I'm very good at making friends."

"Raphael told me you were sentenced to more service. I'm so sorry, Malachi—"

He shook his head and leaned his forehead against mine. "*Shh.* I got exactly what I needed. I don't want to be anywhere else."

I took a breath, afraid he would disappear at any second. "Are you really here?"

He kissed me gently. "Lieutenant Malachi Sokol, reporting for duty, Captain."

"What?"

"I've been assigned to your field unit," he whispered as he nuzzled my neck. Oh, man. Heaven. Help. Me. "I'm afraid I'm already being shockingly insubordinate."

"Fine, then," I laughed breathlessly, "I order you to kiss me again."

He raised an eyebrow and said his next words against my lips, sending chills rocketing through my body. "Yes, ma'am."

ACKNOWLEDGMENTS

I would like to thank Kathleen Ortiz, my incredible agent, for guiding me through this process, cheering me on, calming me down, and for being real (and realistic), hilarious, patient, and relentlessly *T. rex*-ish when necessary. Becky Yeager, for pulling my manuscript from the slush and honoring it with the term "nightmare fuel." Nancy Coffey, for a pep talk I'll never forget, and Joanna Volpe, for support and strategery. Courtney Miller, for giving Lela a chance, and for being this story's fearless advocate. Jayne Carapezzi, for making it better. And to The Black Rabbit, who brought me to tears by capturing the entire story in a single, powerful image.

I could not have survived without my writing friends. My beloved beta readers: JD, Jaime Lawrence, Jenn Walkup, and Stina Lindenblatt—thank you for tough love and constant encouragement. My favorite teen critic: Leah Block, please continue to set me straight. Online buddies who have become close friends: Lydia Kang, who is grace in electronic form, and Brigid Kemmerer, the ace of the talk-down, who sends me the literary equivalent of eye candy whenever I need it. You have all made this writing thing more rewarding than I ever anticipated.

And finally, thank you to the people who hold me together in "real" life. Paul Block, for being a better mentor than I deserve (and also for having an endless supply of M&M's in your office), and Liz Cantor, for simply being cool. My beautiful sisters, Cathryn and Robin, for delighting me by being who you are (and for being willing to claim me as your big sis). My mother, Julie, for being the best listener in the world, and my father, Jerry, for your wisdom, and for the thousands of hours you spent reading to your little girls. Joey, for tolerating me when I transformed from sane person to crazy writer almost overnight . . . and never changed back. And to Asher and Alma, who taught me how fierce love can be. Without all of you, I couldn't have done this.

SNEAK PEEK: BOOK TWO

CHAPTER ONE

My captor paced the entryway with heavy footsteps while I sat in a wooden chair backed against the wall. My heart beat hard against my ribs, keeping time with my primitive, animal thoughts: escape escape escape.

My rational side, dwarfed by all my instincts, somehow managed to get a few words in edgewise:

It's not like this is a life-threatening situation.

I'll get out of it alive.

I hope.

I leaned forward and planted my feet on the floor, eyeing the door, estimating the number of seconds it might take me to bolt from this chair and make it through, wondering if I was fast enough to get away.

The fierce gaze of my jailer told me she was thinking the same thing. She halted in front of the door and crossed her arms over her chest. "Don't even think about it, Baby. I'm responsible for you. This is a big deal."

I leaned my head back and banged it softly against the wall. "Only because you made it one."

Diane made her all-purpose *mm-mm-mm* sound of disapproval. "You've just gone through something big, and now—"

I was saved from a lecture by a knock at the door, but the knowledge of who it was sent my heart rate skyrocketing. I stood up on shaky legs as Diane turned the knob and swung the door open wide.

I was still getting used to seeing him in regular clothes rather than armor and fatigues. It was only yesterday that he showed up at my school, looking like an ordinary high school student instead of a deadly Guard. Well, "ordinary" probably wasn't the right word. He couldn't look ordinary if he tried. And he was trying. Tonight he wore jeans and a grey, zipped-up hoodie. His face, angular and stark, olive skin and ink-black hair, eyes so dark they looked like solid ebony circles, was arranged in an expression I'd seen once before.

He was doing his best to look harmless, but he wasn't good at it. He still looked like he could kill someone without breaking a sweat.

Probably because he could.

"Ms. Jeffries?" Even though he spoke perfect English, every consonant was harder, every vowel deeper, resulting in this clipped, precise accent that perfectly matched his appearance. He held out his hand. "Malachi Sokol. So nice to meet you."

I drew up alongside Diane in time to see her eyebrows nearly hit her hairline. She'd spent her entire career working as a guard and administrator down at the medium-security prison, so she had a pretty keen sense of danger, and Malachi had obviously triggered her alarms. She shook his hand and stepped back to allow him into the entryway. "Nice to meet you, too. Lela said you just arrived here in the States?"

"Yes, it's a brief exchange program. An opportunity to experience American culture before I graduate," he replied, but his focus had already shifted from Diane.

To me.

His smile stole my breath, a devastating curl of his lips as his eyes hit mine. From behind his back, he produced a small bouquet of flowers, a few yellow and white blooms and several green-white buds, wrapped in thin plastic cellophane. "These are for you."

It took me a few seconds, but I managed to get my hands and fingers to work together to take the flowers from his hand. "Thanks," I said, but it came out as a choked whisper.

Malachi's brows lowered and concern flashed in his eyes before he turned back to Diane. "I'd like to introduce my host father." He gestured toward the front steps.

The most average-looking man in the world stepped into the entryway and held out his hand. "Ms. Jeffries. I'm John Raphael. Thank you so much for inviting us to dinner. I was so pleased to hear Malachi had already made a friend."

And then he smiled. It made him look like what I suspected he actually was, transforming his face from forgettable to indelible, from ordinary to angelic. Whenever he smiled I wished I had my camera.

The tension melted from Diane's body as she shook Raphael's hand. Her face relaxed into a warm smile. "I was happy to," she said, which nearly made me laugh, because we'd had a raging argument this afternoon about whether I could go out with Malachi tonight. It was the first time I'd ever asked to go out with a boy, the first time I'd ever mentioned one, actually, and judging by the way she'd clutched at her chest when I did, it really caught her by surprise. Especially because things had been so miserable since Nadia killed herself. Diane couldn't understand how I'd just "snapped out of" my grief.

She didn't know I'd followed Nadia into death. That I'd seen my best friend again. That I not only suspected Nadia was in a better place—I knew it at a bone-deep level. I'd made sure of it, in fact.

I'd sold my own freedom to make it happen.

While Diane and Raphael chatted about the joys of parenting teenagers, I went to the kitchen with the flowers, staring at those thinly veined buds while my throat got tight. I opened a cabinet to pull out a plastic vase, and when I closed it, Malachi was right there.

"You don't like them?" he asked.

I shook my head. "I love them. It's just . . . no one's ever given me flowers before." I turned my back, rolling the delicate stems between my fingers. It was one of those cheap grocery-store bouquets. Tegan, who had ascended to the status of resident Queen Bee of Warwick High school since Nadia's death, would have scoffed at the already-wilting necks, the scraggly little petals. But to me . . .

Malachi's fingers skimmed along my shoulder. "I've never given a girl flowers before." He laughed quietly. "I hadn't actually seen a flower up close in a long time."

He'd spent the last several decades in a walled city of cement and steel and slime, where the only things that grew were the festering wishes of the dead, sorrowful people trapped there. Nothing green or lush or *real* could grow because it was always dark, always dusk or midnight, never day. Well, that wasn't exactly true. Something had grown between *us*.

I turned back to him and reached for his hand. I wasn't used to this yet, this permission to touch. His skin was so warm. Real. *Here.*

"Unbelievable," I whispered.

He grinned and pulled me toward him, but at that exact moment Diane entered the kitchen, and Malachi let me go and stepped back with an awkward throat-clearing noise.

"I hope you like pasta," she said to Malachi. It sounded friendly enough, but her expression was all warning.

"I suspect I will love anything you cook," he replied. I had no doubt that was true. He probably hadn't had a decent meal since he'd actually been alive. Back in the 1930s.

Malachi and I set the table while Raphael poured us each a glass of lemonade. Diane had insisted she meet both Malachi and his "people" before she allowed me to go out with him. She kept giving him these narrow-eyed looks, like she was wondering if he'd come armed. I was wondering the same thing. And also, it was hard to tear my gaze from him. I'd seen Malachi do amazing and deadly things, but I'd never seen him do anything as basic as setting forks on a table. By the way he watched his own hands carefully put each piece of cutlery into place, it was obvious he was thinking about it as well. It made me want to hug him, to ask him what was going on inside his head, to know him better. Maybe there would be time to do that now that we were here, on Earth, and not trapped in hell.

"Where exactly are you from?" Diane asked him as we sat down to eat.

"Bratislava," he said. "Slovakia."

"What do your parents do?"

My throat got tight again as I watched him give Diane a small smile that was huge with sadness. "My father owns a shoe store," he said slowly. "My mother, she stays at home. She's a very good cook." He bowed his head for a second and then looked back at Diane. "I miss her cooking."

The sharp edges of Diane's expression and voice immediately rounded and softened. "You're homesick, poor baby."

Malachi swallowed and took a breath. "Always. But I'm happy to be here. And happy to have met Lela."

"Thank you for agreeing to let Lela drive," said Raphael, passing the garlic bread to Diane. With gratitude, I realized he was drawing attention away from Malachi to allow him a chance to recover from the mention of his parents, who had died horribly at the hands of the Nazis so many years ago.

"Actually, I think it's good for Lela to do the driving," said Diane. She'd told me she wanted me to be able to dump Malachi and drive away if he got "handsy."

Raphael was a charming dinner companion and had no trouble getting Diane talking about herself, her family, her pride that I was college-bound. As he kept her going, I watched Malachi eat. Another thing I'd never gotten to witness. It was pretty hypnotic. Every bite looked like an act of worship, like he was forcing himself not to shove it all in his mouth at once. He told Diane how delicious it was at least ten times. She probably thought he was kissing her ass, but I knew it for what it was—the absolute truth. The food in the dark city sucked.

"We need to leave soon if we're going to make that movie," I said as we finished up. Now that I had drunk deeply of the well of awkwardness that was this dinner, I was ready to make a break for it.

"Which theater are you going to?" asked Diane. "Not Providence Place, all right?"

Here we go. "No, but it's really not a big—"

She gripped her fork like a weapon and glared at me. "You're not going anywhere near that city until they catch those crazies."

Raphael wiped his mouth with his napkin. "I saw the news report. The footage was quite grainy. It's possible it was a dog."

Diane looked at Raphael like he'd betrayed her. "A dog wearing jeans and sneakers?" She took a bite of pasta, her jaw working harder than necessary. When she swallowed, she said, "I'm not saying it's a werewolf or whatever. I'm not crazy. But a guy running around on all fours? Probably a meth head.Those people do crazy things. Either way, these two are staying away."

"The theater is in Warwick, Ms. Jeffries," Malachi offered, earning him a nod from Diane. We'd rehearsed this part after school, and he looked relieved that he'd gotten it right.

"What are you seeing?" she asked, finally relaxing.

"Night Huntress," he recited. "It's gotten great reviews."

"I heard it was a gore fest," she grumbled as she began to clear the table.

I held in my half-hysterical giggles as I helped get the dishes into the sink. "Thanks for dinner. And for being cool."

She shrugged and hmphed. "You've earned my trust, Baby. Just keep it up, all right?"

"No problem," I said. "You don't have to wait up."

"Nice try. It's a *school* night. You're lucky I'm letting you out at all. Be back by ten." Diane leaned out of the kitchen and fixed Malachi with a suspicious gaze. "You'd better take care of this girl, young man."

Malachi closed the distance between us and took my hand. He gave Diane a deadly serious look. "Ms. Jeffries, I swear to you, I will protect her with my life."

Diane let out a brief bark of laughter. She had no idea he'd already done exactly that at least a dozen times.

She let us go with a minimum of fuss, even though she wouldn't let Raphael escape without a hug, which he seemed happy enough to give her. No matter what she thought of

Malachi, it was obvious she thought Raphael was all right, which would help a lot. As soon as she closed the front door, Raphael turned to us. "Mission accomplished. Have fun tonight, you two. I'm needed back at the house. Summon me if you require my assistance."

"We won't," said Malachi, squeezing my hand. "But thank you."

"Actually," I said, "can you help me out with Diane? This curfew . . . "

Raphael nodded. "When she's not on the night shift, which should suit your patrol schedule very well, Ms. Jeffries will be sleeping very soundly."

I bit my lip. I hated to do this to Diane. "Thanks."

As soon as Raphael pulled his very generic-looking grey sedan away from the curb, Malachi and I got into my beaten-up old Corolla. I sat there for a second, my heart skipping, unable to believe I was sitting in a car with Malachi, overwhelmed by the complete ordinariness of the moment, no matter how bizarre the circumstances. I glanced over to gauge his reaction, only to find his black-brown gaze hard on mine.

"Please let me kiss you now," he said in a low voice that raised the temperature inside the car by about a thousand degrees.

"We shouldn't . . . maybe Diane is—"

He leaned forward slowly, giving me a chance to stop him, and then his fingertips were on my cheek as his nose traced along my jawline, breathing me in, melting me down.

"Just for a second," I whispered.

I didn't have time to say anything else before his lips met mine, setting me on fire, making me feel like the earth was falling out from under me. He took my face in his hands, his long fingers stroking at my temples. My hand slid up to his neck, to the smooth, silver-swirled scar that was a souvenir from Juri, a deadly enemy and the first person—no, *thing*—I'd ever killed.

Malachi's tongue traced mine as our kiss deepened and my thoughts scattered, leaving me with only the taste of him, the halting rhythm of our breaths, and a bone-melting hunger that made me feel like I was inching toward the edge of a very high cliff.

His fingers tangled in my unruly curls as he scooted closer. I put my hand on his chest to feel the thunder of his heart against my palm. But when my fingers drifted to his stomach, they did not find the hard ridges of muscle I'd expected.

Malachi felt the tremble of laughter run through me and pulled back from my mouth. "I had to put them somewhere." He sounded like he'd run a mile, and it made me glad that I wasn't the only one.

I looked toward the front of the house, wondering if Diane was peeking at us through the curtains. The sun had already dipped below the horizon, so I figured it was dark enough. I leaned back and pulled his hoodie up, revealing the six throwing knives holstered against his torso.

"I knew you'd come prepared," I said.

"I brought you some as well," he said, pulling a pack from the backseat. "Michael dropped these off for us this afternoon and Raphael tucked them in here when we arrived this evening."

I unzipped the pack a few inches and peeked inside, taking in the knives, two batons, and *good God*. "He gave us *grenades*?"

Malachi shrugged as he left a trail of heated kisses along my jaw, scattering my thoughts again. "It will be up to you whether we use them or not, *Captain*," he mumbled against my neck.

As much as the feel of him made me shiver, that word was enough to make my insides shrivel. Malachi must have felt me tense, because he moved back to his side of the car and watched me take a few shaky breaths. "You're going to be fine, Lela. I'm here to help you."

I gripped the steering wheel for a moment, then pulled the keys from my pocket and jammed them into the ignition. "My first real patrol as a Guard," I said quietly, wishing saying it out loud made it sound real instead of crazy.

Wishing it made me feel brave instead of scared enough to pee my pants. Wishing it made me feel proud instead of angry as hell at the Judge, the seemingly all powerful-being I was pretty sure had coldly manipulated both Malachi and me into this situation.

"Your first patrol as a Guard," Malachi repeated in a voice that told me nothing about what he was thinking. He pulled the pack from my lap and set it at his feet, then leaned back and smiled at me, all relaxed. Like we really were just going to the movies. "Let's go hunting."